REVENGE
WEARS
PRADA

Lauren Weisberger is the bestselling author of *The Devil Wears Prada*, which was published in forty languages and made into a hugely successful film starring Meryl Streep and Anne Hathaway. Weisberger's three other novels, *Everyone Worth Knowing*, *Last Night at Chateau Marmont*, and *Chasing Harry Winston* were all bestsellers. A graduate of Cornell University, she lives in New York City with her husband and two children.

www.LaurenWeisberger.com

LAUREN WEISBERGER

REVENGE
WEARS
PRADA

The Devil Returns

HARPER

Harper
An imprint of HarperCollins*Publishers*
77–85 Fulham Palace Road,
Hammersmith, London W6 8JB

www.harpercollins.co.uk

Special overseas edition 2013
2

First published in Great Britain by
HarperCollins*Publishers* 2013

ISBN: 978-0-00-749806-2

Set in Meridien by
Palimpsest Book Production Limited, Falkirk, Stirlingshire

Printed and bound in Great Britain by
Clays Ltd, St Ives plc

MIX
Paper from
responsible sources
FSC **FSC™ C007454**
www.fsc.org

For R and S,
with love

1

as long as she lived

The rain fell in sideways sheets, cold and relentless, the winds whipping it in every direction, making an umbrella, slicker, and rain boots nearly useless. Not that Andy had any of those things. Her two-hundred-dollar Burberry umbrella had refused to open and finally snapped when she tried to force it; the cropped rabbit jacket with the oversize collar and no hood cinched fabulously around her waist but did nothing to stop the bone-chilling cold; and the brand-new stacked suede Prada pumps cheered her with their poppy fuchsia color but left the better part of her foot exposed. Even her skinny leggings left her legs feeling naked, the wind making the leather feel as protective as a pair of silk stockings. Already the fifteen inches that had blanketed New York were beginning to melt into a slushy gray mess, and Andy wished for the thousandth time that she lived anywhere but here.

As if to punctuate her thought, a taxi barreled through a yellow light and blared its horn at Andy, who had committed the grievous crime of trying to cross the street. She restrained herself from offering him the finger – everyone was armed these days – and instead gritted her teeth and hurled mental curses his way. Considering the size of her heels, she made decent progress for the next two or three blocks. Fifty-Second, Fifty-Third, Fifty-Fourth . . . it wasn't too far now, and at least she'd have a moment or two to warm up before beginning the race back to the office. She was consoling herself with the promise of a hot coffee and maybe, just maybe, a chocolate chip cookie, when suddenly, somewhere, she heard *that* ring.

Where was it coming from? Andy glanced around, but her fellow pedestrians didn't seem to notice the sound, which was growing louder every second. *Br-rrring! Br-rrring!* That ringtone. She would recognize it anywhere for as long as she lived, although Andy was surprised they were still making phones with it. She simply hadn't heard it in so long and yet . . . it all came rushing back. She knew before she pulled her phone from her bag what she would find, but she was still shocked to see those two words on her caller ID screen: MIRANDA PRIESTLY.

She would not answer. Could not. Andy took a deep breath, hit 'ignore,' and tossed the phone back into her bag. It started ringing again almost immediately. Andy could feel her heart begin to beat faster, and it got more and more difficult to fill her lungs. *Inhale, exhale,* she instructed herself, tucking her chin to protect her face from what was now pounding sleet, and *just keep walking*. She was less than two blocks from the restaurant – she could see it lit up ahead like a warm, shimmering promise – when a particularly nasty gust propelled her forward, causing her to lose her balance and step directly into one of the worst parts of a Manhattan winter: the black, slushy puddle of dirt and water and salt and trash and god knows what else so filthy and freezing and shockingly deep that one could do nothing but surrender to it.

Which is exactly what Andy did, right there in the pool of hell that had accumulated between the street and the curb. She stood, flamingo-like, perched gracefully on one submerged foot, holding the other one rather impressively above the watery mess for a good thirty or forty seconds, weighing her options. Around her, people gave her and the slushy little lake wide berth, only those with knee-high rubber boots daring to tromp directly through the middle. But no one offered her a hand and, realizing that the puddle had a large enough perimeter that she couldn't jump to escape in any one direction, she steeled herself for another shock of cold and placed her left foot beside her right. The icy water rushed up her legs and came to a stop on her lower calf, subsuming both fuchsia shoes and a good five inches of leather pant, and it was all Andy could do not to cry.

Her shoes and leggings were ruined; her feet felt like she might lose them to frostbite; she had no option for extricating herself from the mess except continuing to slog through it; and all Andy could think was, *That's exactly what you get for screening Miranda Priestly.*

There wasn't time to dwell on her misery, though, because as soon as she made it to the curb and stopped to evaluate the damage, her phone rang again. It had been ballsy – hell, downright reckless – to ignore the first call. She simply couldn't do it again. Dripping, shivering, and near tears, Andy tapped the screen and said hello.

'Ahn-dre-ah? Is that you? You've already been gone for

an eternity. I'll ask you only one time. Where. Is. My. Lunch? I simply won't be kept waiting like this.'

Of course it's me, Andy thought. *You dialed my number. Who else would be answering?*

'I'm so sorry, Miranda. It's really horrid out right now, and I'm trying my best to—'

'I'll expect you back here *immediately*. That's all.' And before Andy could say another word, the line was disconnected.

No matter that the icy water trapped in her shoes was squishing around her toes in the most disgustingly imaginable way, or that it had been hard enough to walk in those heels when they were dry, or that the sidewalks were growing slicker by the second as the rain started to freeze: Andy began to run. She sprinted as best she could down one block and had only one more to go when she heard someone calling her name.

Andy! Andy, stop! It's me! Stop running!

She would recognize that voice anywhere. But what was Max doing there? He was away that weekend, upstate somewhere, for a reason she couldn't quite remember. Wasn't he? She stopped and turned, searching for him.

Over here, Andy!

And then she spotted him. Her fiancé, with his thick dark hair and piercing green eyes and rugged good looks, was sitting astride an enormous white horse. Andy didn't particularly like horses ever since she'd fallen from one in second grade and shattered her right wrist, but this horse looked friendly enough. Never mind that Max was riding a white horse in midtown Manhattan in the middle of a blizzard – Andy was so ecstatic to see him, she didn't even think to question it.

He dismounted with the ease of a practiced rider, and Andy tried to remember if he'd ever mentioned playing polo.

In three long strides he was at her side, enveloping her in the warmest, most delicious embrace imaginable, and she felt her whole body relax as she collapsed into him.

'My poor baby,' he murmured, paying neither the horse nor the staring pedestrians any mind. 'You must be freezing out here.'

The sound of a phone – that phone – rang out between them, and Andy scrambled to answer it.

'Ahn-dre-ah! I don't know what part of "immediately" you don't understand, but—'

Andy's whole body was shaking as Miranda's shrill voice drilled into her ear, but before she could move a single muscle, Max plucked the phone from her fingertips, tapped 'end' on the screen, and tossed it with perfect aim directly into the puddle that had previously claimed Andy's feet. 'You're done with her, Andy,' he said, wrapping a large down comforter around her shoulders.

'Ohmigod, Max, how could you do that? I'm so late! I haven't even made it to the restaurant yet, and she's going to kill me if I'm not back there with her lunch in—'

'Shhh,' he said, touching two fingers to Andy's lips. 'You're safe now. You're with me.'

'But it's already ten after one, and if she doesn't—'

Max reached both hands under Andy's arms and lifted her effortlessly into the air before gently depositing her sidesaddle on top of the white horse, whose name, according to Max, was Bandit.

She sat in shocked silence as Max removed both her soaking wet shoes and tossed them to the curb. From his duffel bag – the one he carried everywhere – Max pulled out Andy's favorite fleece-lined bootie-style slippers and slid them onto her raw, red feet. He settled the down comforter over her lap, tied his own cashmere scarf over her head and around her neck, and handed her a steel thermos of what he announced was specially sourced dark hot chocolate. Her favorite. Then in one impressively fluid motion, he mounted the horse and picked up the reins. Before she could say another word, they began to trot down Seventh Avenue at a good clip, the police escort in front of them clearing the way of traffic and pedestrians.

It was such a relief to be warm and loved, but Andy couldn't get rid of the panic she felt at not completing a Miranda-assigned task. She'd be fired, that much was sure, but what if it was worse than that? What if Miranda was so livid that she used her limitless influence to make sure Andy never got another job? What if she decided to teach her assistant a lesson and show her exactly what happened when one simply walked out – not once but *twice* – on Miranda Priestly?

'I have to go back!' Andy shouted into the wind as their trot became a run. 'Max, turn around and take me back! I can't . . .'

'Andy! Can you hear me, sweetheart? Andy!'

Her eyes flew open. The only thing she felt was the pounding of her own heart as it raced in her chest.

'You're okay, baby. You're safe now. It was just a dream. And from the looks of it, a really horrible one,' Max crooned, cupping her cheek with his cool palm.

She pushed herself up and saw the early morning sun streaming in from the room's window. There was no snow, no sleet, no horse. Her feet were bare but warm under the buttery soft sheets, and Max's body felt strong and safe pressed against her own. She inhaled deeply, and the scent of Max – his breath, his skin, his hair – filled her nostrils.

It was only a dream.

She glanced around the bedroom. She still felt half asleep,

fuzzy from being awakened at the wrong time. Where were they? What was happening? It took a glance at the door, from which hung a freshly steamed and utterly gorgeous Monique Lhuillier gown, before she remembered that the unfamiliar room was actually a bridal suite – *her* bridal suite – and she was the bride. Bride! A rush of adrenaline caused her to sit straight up in bed so quickly that Max exclaimed in surprise. 'What were you dreaming about, baby? I hope it didn't have anything to do with today.'

'Not at all. Just old ghosts.' She leaned over to kiss him as Stanley, their Maltese, wedged himself between them. 'What time is it? Wait – what are you doing here?'

Max gave her that devilish grin she loved and climbed out of bed. As always, Andy couldn't help but admire his broad shoulders and tight stomach. He had the body of a twenty-five-year-old, only better – not too hard and muscled, but perfectly tight and fit.

'It's six. I came in a couple hours ago,' he said as he pulled on a pair of flannel pajama pants. 'I got lonely.'

'Well, you better get out of here before someone sees you. Your mother had some whole big thing about us not seeing each other before the wedding.'

Max pulled Andy out of bed and wrapped his arms around her. 'Then don't tell her. But I wasn't going to go all day before seeing you.'

Andy feigned irritation, but she was secretly glad he'd sneaked in for a quick cuddle, especially in light of her nightmare. 'Fine,' she sighed dramatically. 'But get back to your room without being seen! I'm taking Stanley out for a walk before the masses descend.'

Max pushed his pelvis against hers. 'It's still early. I bet if we're fast we can—'

Andy laughed. 'Go!'

He kissed her again, tenderly this time, and let himself out of the suite.

Andy gathered Stanley in her arms, kissed him squarely on his wet nose, and said, 'This is it, Stan!' He excitedly woofed and tried to escape, and she had to let him go so he wouldn't scratch her arms to shreds. For a few lovely seconds she managed to forget the dream, but it quickly reappeared again in all its detailed realness. Andy took a deep breath and her pragmatism kicked in: wedding-day jitters. A classic anxiety dream. Nothing more. Nothing less.

She ordered breakfast from room service and fed Stanley bits of scrambled eggs and toast while fielding excited phone calls from her mother, sister, Lily, and Emily – all of whom were champing at the bit for her to begin preparations – and leashed Stanley up for a quick walk in the brisk October air before the day got too frantic. It was slightly embarrassing to wear the terry-cloth sweatpants with a hot-pink BRIDE emblazoned across the butt that she'd received at her bridal shower, but she was secretly proud, too. She jammed her hair into a baseball cap, laced up her sneakers, zipped up a Patagonia fleece, and miraculously made it out to the sprawling grounds of the Astor Courts Estate without seeing another living soul. Stanley bounded as happily as his little legs would allow, pulling her toward the tree line at the edge of the property, where the leaves had already changed into their fiery fall colors. They walked for almost thirty minutes, certainly long enough for everyone to wonder where she'd gone, and although the air was fresh and the rolling fields of the farm were beautiful and Andy felt the excited giddiness of her wedding day, she couldn't get the image of Miranda out of her mind.

How could this woman still haunt her? It had been nearly *ten years* since she bolted from Paris and her soul-destroying stint as Miranda's assistant at *Runway*. She had grown so much since that dreaded year, hadn't she? Everything had changed, and for the better: the early post-*Runway* years of freelancing, which she'd proudly parlayed into a steady gig as a contributing editor writing for a wedding blog, *Happily Ever After*. A few years and tens of thousands of words later, she was able to launch her very own magazine, *The Plunge*, a beautiful glossy high-end book that was three years into the endeavor and, despite all predictions to the contrary, was actually making money. *The Plunge* was getting nominated for awards, and advertisers were clamoring. And now, in the midst of all her professional success, she was getting married! To Max Harrison, son of the late Robert Harrison and grandson of the legendary Arthur Harrison, who'd founded Harrison Publishing Holdings in the years right after the Great Depression and had built it into Harrison Media Holdings, one of the most prestigious and profitable companies in the United States. Max Harrison, long on the circuit of most eligible bachelors, a guy who'd dated the Tinsley Mortimers and Amanda Hearsts of New York City, and probably a fair number of their sisters, cousins, and friends, was her betrothed. There would be mayors and moguls in attendance that afternoon, just waiting to cheer on the young scion and his new bride. But the best part of all? She loved Max. He was her best friend. He doted on her and made her laugh and appreciated her work. Wasn't it always true that men in New York weren't ready until they were ready? Max had started talking marriage within months of their meeting. Three years later, here they were, on their wedding day. Andy reprimanded herself for wasting another second thinking about such a ridiculous dream and led Stanley back to her suite, where a small army of women had gathered in a nervous, twittering panic, apparently wondering if she'd fled the scene. There was a collective audible sigh of relief the moment she walked in; immediately Nina, her wedding planner, began issuing directives.

The next few hours passed in a blur: a shower, a blowout, hot rollers, mascara, enough spackle foundation to smooth the complexion of a hormonal teenager. Someone tended to her toes while another fetched her undergarments and a third debated her lip color. Before she could even realize what was happening, her sister, Jill, was holding open Andy's ivory gown, and a second later her mother was cinching the delicate fabric in the back and zipping Andy into it. Andy's grandmother clucked delightedly. Lily cried. Emily sneaked a cigarette in the bridal suite bathroom, thinking no one would notice. Andy tried to soak it all in. And then she was alone. For just a few minutes before she was expected in the grand ballroom, everyone left her to get themselves ready, and Andy sat perched awkwardly on a tufted antique chair, trying not to wrinkle or ruin any inch of herself. In less than one hour she would be a married woman, committed for the rest of her life to Max, and he to her. It was almost too much to fathom.

The suite's phone rang. Max's mother was on the other end.

'Good morning, Barbara,' Andy said as warmly as she could. Barbara Anne Williams Harrison, Daughter of the American Revolution, descendant of not one but two signers of the Constitution, perennial fixture on every charitable board that socially mattered in Manhattan. From her Oscar-Blandi-coiffed hair to her Chanel ballet flats, Barbara was always perfectly polite to Andy. Perfectly polite to *everyone*. But effusive she was not. Andy tried not to take it personally, and Max assured her it was all in her head. Perhaps in the early days Barbara had thought Andy was another of her son's passing phases? Then Andy convinced herself Barbara's acquaintance with Miranda had poisoned any hope of bonding with her mother-in-law. Eventually Andy realized it was just Barbara's way – she was coolly polite to everyone, even her own daughter. She couldn't imagine ever calling that woman 'Mom.' Not that she'd been invited to . . .

'Hello, Andrea. I just realized I never actually gave you the necklace. I was racing so frantically this morning trying to get everything organized that I ended up late for hair and makeup! I'm calling to let you know that it's in a velvet box in Max's room, tucked into the side pocket of that vile duffel bag of his. I didn't want the staff to see it lying about. Perhaps you'll be more successful in persuading him to carry something more dignified? Lord knows I've tried a thousand times, but he simply won't—'

'Thanks, Barbara. I'll go get it right now.'

'You'll do no such thing!' the woman trilled sharply. 'You simply cannot see each other before the ceremony – it's bad luck. Send your mother or Nina. Anyone else. All right?'

'Of course,' Andy said. She hung up the phone and headed into the hallway. She'd learned early on that it was easier to agree with Barbara and then go on to do what she pleased; arguing got her nowhere. Which is exactly why she was wearing a Harrison family heirloom as her 'something old' instead of something from her own relatives: Barbara had insisted. Six generations of Harrisons had included that necklace in their weddings, and Andy and Max would, too.

Max's suite door was slightly ajar, and she could hear the shower running in the bathroom when she stepped inside. *Classic*, she thought. *I've been getting ready for the last five hours and he's just now getting in the shower.*

'Max? It's me. Don't come out!'

11

'Andy? What are you doing here?' Max's voice called through the bathroom door.

'I'm just getting your mom's necklace. Don't come out, okay? I don't want you to see me in my dress.'

Andy rummaged around in the bag's front pocket. She didn't feel a velvet box but her hands closed around a folded paper.

It was a piece of cream-colored stationery, heavyweight and engraved with Barbara's initials, BHW, in a navy script monogram. Andy knew Barbara helped keep Dempsey & Carroll in business with the amount of stationery she bought; she had been using the same design for birthday greetings, thank-you notes, dinner invitations, and condolence wishes for four decades. She was old-fashioned and formal and would rather have died than send someone a gauche e-mail or – horror! – a text message. It made perfect sense that she would send her son a traditional handwritten letter on his wedding day. Andy was just about to refold it and return it when her own name caught her eye. Before she could even consider what she was doing, Andy began to read.

Dear Maxwell,

While you know I do my best to allow you your privacy, I can no longer hold my tongue on matters of such importance. I have mentioned my concerns to you before, and you have always pledged to consider them. Now, however, due to the imminence of your upcoming wedding, I feel I can wait no longer to speak my mind plainly and forthrightly:

I beseech you, Maxwell. Please do not marry Andrea.

Do not misunderstand me. Andrea is pleasant, and she will undoubtedly make someone an agreeable wife one day. But you, my darling, deserve so much more! You must be with a girl from the right family, not a broken family where all she knows is heartache and divorce. A girl who understands our traditions, our way of life. Someone who will help shepherd the Harrison name into the next generation. Most important, a partner who wants to put you and your children ahead of her own selfish career aspirations. You must think carefully about this: do you want your wife editing magazines and taking business trips, or do you desire someone who puts others first and embraces the philanthropic interests of the Harrison line? Don't you desire a partner who cares more about supporting your family than furthering her own ambitions?

I told you I thought your unexpected get-together with Katherine in Bermuda was a sign. Oh, how delighted you sounded to see her again! Please, do not discount those feelings. Nothing is decided yet – it is not too late. It is clear you've always adored Katherine, and it is even more clear she would make a wonderful life partner.

You always make me so proud, and I know your father is looking down on us and rooting for you to do the right thing.

All my love,
Mother

She heard the water turn off and, startled, dropped the note to the floor. When she scrambled to pick it up, she noticed her hands were shaking.

'Andy? You still here?' he called from behind the door.

'Yes, I'm . . . wait, I'm just going,' she managed to say.

'Did you find it?'

She paused, unsure of the right answer. It felt like all the oxygen had been sucked from the room. 'Yes.'

There was more shuffling, and then the sink turned on

and off. 'Are you gone yet? I need to come out and get dressed.'

Please do not marry Andrea. Blood pounded in Andy's ears. *Oh, how delighted you sounded to see her again!* Should she fly into the bathroom or run out the door? The next time she saw him, they'd be exchanging rings in front of three hundred people, including his mother.

Someone knocked on the suite's front door before opening it. 'Andy? What are you doing here?' Nina, her wedding planner, asked. 'Good god, you're going to ruin that dress! And I thought you agreed you wouldn't see each other before the ceremony. If that's not the case, why didn't we do pictures beforehand?' Her constant, unrelenting talking drove Andy crazy. 'Max, stay in that bathroom! Your bride is standing here like a deer caught in headlights. Wait, oh, just hold on a second!' She scurried over as Andy tried to stand and fix her dress at the same time and extended her hand.

'There,' she said, pulling Andy to her feet and smoothing her hand over the dress's mermaid skirt. 'Now, come with me. No more disappearing-bride antics, you hear? What's this?' She plucked the note from Andy's sweaty palm and held it aloft.

Andy could actually hear the pounding in her chest; she briefly wondered if she was having a heart attack. She opened her mouth to say something, but instead a wave of nausea came over her. 'Oh, I think I'm going to—'

Magically, or maybe just from lots of practice, Nina produced a trash can at exactly the right moment and held it so tightly to Andy's face that she could feel the plastic-lined rim pressing into the soft underside of her chin. 'There, there,' Nina nasal-whined, oddly comforting nonetheless. 'You're not my first jittery bride and you won't be my last. Let's just thank our lucky stars you didn't have any splash-back.' She dabbed at Andy's mouth with one of Max's T-shirts, and his smell, a heady mixture of soap and the basil-mint shampoo he used – a scent she usually loved – made her retch all over again.

There was another knock at the door. The famous photographer St Germain and his pretty young assistant walked in. 'We're supposed to be shooting Max's preparations,' he announced in an affected but indeterminate accent. Thankfully, neither he nor the assistant so much as glanced at Andy.

'What's going on out there?' Max called, still banished to the bathroom.

'Max, stay put!' Nina yelled, her voice all authority. She turned to Andy, who wasn't sure she could walk the couple hundred feet back to the bridal suite. 'We've got to get your skin touched up and . . . Christ, your hair . . .'

'I need the necklace,' Andy whispered.

'The what?'

'Barbara's diamond necklace. Wait.' *Think, think, think. What did it mean? What should she do?* Andy forced herself to return to that hideous bag, but thankfully Nina stepped in front of her and pulled the duffel onto the bed. She rooted quickly through its contents and pulled out a black velvet box with *Cartier* etched on the side.

'This what you're looking for? Come, let's go.'

Andy allowed herself to be pulled into the hallway. Nina instructed the photographers to free Max from the bathroom and firmly shut the door behind them.

Andy couldn't believe Barbara hated her so much that she didn't want her son to marry her. And not only that, but she had his wife chosen for him. Katherine: more *appropriate*, less *selfish*. The one, at least according to Barbara, who got away. Andy knew all about Katherine. She was the heiress to the von Herzog fortune and, from what Andy could remember from her early rounds of incessant Googling, she was some sort of minor Austrian princess whose parents had sent her to board at Max's elite Connecticut prep school. Katherine had gone on to major in European history at Amherst, where she was admitted after her grandfather – an Austrian noble with Nazi allegiances during World War II – donated enough money to name a residence hall in his late wife's honor. Max claimed Katherine was too prim, too proper, and all-around too polite. She was boring, he claimed. Too conventional and concerned with appearances. Why he dated her on and off for five years Max couldn't explain quite as well, but Andy had always suspected there was more to the story. She clearly hadn't been wrong.

The last time Max had mentioned Katherine, he was planning to call and inform her of their engagement; a few weeks later a beautiful cut-crystal bowl from Bergdorf's arrived with a note wishing them a lifetime of happiness. Emily, who knew Katherine through her own husband, Miles, swore Andy had nothing to worry about, that she was boring and uptight and while she did, admittedly, have 'a great rack,' Andy was superior in every other way. Andy hadn't thought much more about it since then. They all had pasts. Was she proud of Christian Collinsworth? Did she feel the need to tell Max every single detail about her relationship with Alex? Of course not. But it was a different story entirely reading a letter from your future mother-in-law, on the day of your wedding, imploring your fiancé to marry his ex-girlfriend instead. An ex-girlfriend he had apparently been *delighted* to see in Bermuda during his bachelor party and whom he had conveniently forgotten to mention.

Andy rubbed her forehead and forced herself to think. When had Barbara written that poisonous note? Why had

Max saved it? And what did it mean that he'd seen Katherine a mere six weeks earlier and hadn't breathed a word about it to Andy, despite giving her every last detail of his and his friends' golf games, steak dinners, and sunbathing? There had to be an explanation, there simply had to be. But what was it?

2

learning to love
the hamptons: 2009

It had long been a point of pride for Andy that she almost never went to the Hamptons. The traffic, the crowds, the pressure to get dressed up and look great and be at the right place . . . none of it felt particularly relaxing. Certainly not much of an escape from the city. Better to stay in the city alone, wander the summer street fairs and lay out in Sheep Meadow and ride her bike along the Hudson. She could walk into any restaurant without a reservation and explore new, uncrowded neighborhoods. She loved summer weekends spent reading and sipping iced coffees in the city and never felt the least bit left out, a fact that Emily simply refused to accept. One weekend a season Emily dragged Andy out to her husband's parents' place and insisted Andy experience the fabulousness of white parties and polo matches and enough Tory-Burch-clad women to outfit half of Long Island. Every year Andy swore to herself she'd never go back, and every summer she dutifully packed her bag and braved the Jitney and tried to act like she was having a great time mingling with the same people she saw at industry events in the city. This weekend was different, though. This particular weekend would potentially determine her professional future.

There was a brief knock at the door before Emily barged in. Judging from her expression, she was displeased to find Andy flopped on the luxurious duvet, one towel wrapped around her hair and another under her arms, staring helplessly at a suitcase exploding with clothes.

'Why aren't you dressed yet? People are going to be here any minute!'

'I have nothing to wear!' Andy cried. 'I don't understand the Hamptons. I'm not *of* them. Everything I brought is wrong.'

'Andy . . .' Emily's hip jutted out in her magenta silk dress, just under where the billowy fabric was cinched tight by a triple-wrapped gold chain belt that wouldn't have fit around most women's thighs. Her coltish legs were tanned and accessorized with gold gladiator sandals and a glossy pedicure in the same shade of pink as her dress.

Andy studied her friend's perfectly blown-out hair, glimmering cheekbones, and pale pink lip gloss. 'I hope that's some sort of sparkle powder and not just your natural exuberance,' she said uncharitably, motioning toward Emily's face. 'No one deserves to look that good.'

'Andy, you know how important tonight is! Miles called in a trillion favors to get everyone over here, and I've spent the past month dealing with florists and caterers and my fucking mother-in-law. Do you know how hard it was to convince them to let us host this dinner here? You'd think we were seventeen and planning a kegger the way that woman went over all the rules with me. All *you* had to do was show up, look decent, and be charming, and look at you!'

'I'm here, aren't I? And I'll do my best to be charming. Can we agree on two out of three?'

Emily sighed and Andy couldn't help but smile.

'Help me! Help your poor, style-challenged friend put together something remotely appropriate to wear so that maybe she'll look good while begging a bunch of strangers for money!' Andy said this to appease Emily, but she knew she'd made some strides in the style department over the past seven years. Could she ever hope to look as good as Emily? Of course not. But she wasn't a total train wreck, either.

Emily grabbed a pile of the clothes from the middle of the bed and scrunched her nose at all of them. 'What, exactly, were you planning to wear?'

Andy reached into the mess and extracted a navy linen shirtdress with a rope belt and coordinating platform espadrilles. It was simple, elegant, timeless. Perhaps a touch wrinkled. But certainly appropriate.

Emily blanched. 'You're lying.'

'Look at these gorgeous buttons. This dress wasn't inexpensive.'

'I don't give a shit about the buttons!' Emily shrieked, tossing it clear across the room.

'It's Michael Kors! Isn't that worth something?'

'It's Michael Kors *beachwear*, Andy. It's what he has models throw on over bathing suits. What, did you order it online from Nordstrom?'

When Andy didn't say anything, Emily threw up her hands in frustration.

Andy sighed. 'Can you just help me, please? I'm at a reasonably high risk of getting back under these covers right now . . .'

With that, Emily flew into high gear, muttering about how hopeless Andy was despite Emily's constant efforts to tutor her in cut, fit, fabric, and style . . . not to mention shoes. The shoes were *everything*. Andy watched as Emily ferreted through the tangle of clothing and held a few things aloft, immediately scowling at each one and unceremoniously discarding it. After five frustrating minutes of this, she disappeared down the hallway without a word and reappeared a few moments later holding a beautiful pale blue jersey maxi-dress with the most exquisite turquoise and silver chandelier earrings. 'Here. You have silver sandals, right? Because you'll never fit into mine.'

'I'll never fit into that,' Andy said, eyeing the beautiful dress warily.

'Sure you will. I bought it in a size bigger than I normally wear for when I'm bloated, and there's all this draping around the midsection. You should be able to get into it.'

Andy laughed. She and Emily had been friends for so many years now that she barely even noticed those kinds of comments.

'What?' Emily asked, looking confused.

'Nothing. It's perfect. Thank you.'

'Okay, so *get dressed*.' As if to punctuate her command, the girls heard a doorbell ring downstairs. 'First guest! I'm running down. Be adorable and ask all about the men's work and the women's charities. Don't explicitly talk about the magazine unless someone asks, since this isn't really a work dinner.'

'Not really a work dinner? Aren't we going to be hitting everyone up for money?'

Emily sighed exasperatedly. 'Yes, but not until later. Before then we pretend we're all just socializing and having fun. It's most important now that they see we're smart, responsible women with a great idea. The majority are Miles's friends from Princeton. Tons of hedge fund guys who just love investing in media projects. I'm telling you, Andy, smile a lot, show interest in them, be your usual adorable self – wear that dress – and we'll be set.'

'Smile, show interest, be adorable. Got it.' Andy pulled the towel off her head and began to comb out her hair.

'Remember, I've seated you between Farooq Hamid, whose fund was recently ranked among the fifty most lucrative investments this year, and Max Harrison of Harrison Media Holdings, who's now acting as their CEO.'

'Didn't his father just die? Like, in the last few months?' Andy could remember the televised funeral and the two days' worth of newspaper articles, eulogies, and tributes paid to the man who had built one of the greatest media empires ever before making a series of terrible investment decisions right before the 2008 recession – Madoff, oil fields in politically unstable countries – and sending the company into a financial tailspin. No one knew how deep the damage ran.

'Yes. Now Max is in charge and, by all accounts, doing a very good job so far. And the only thing Max likes more than investing in start-up media projects is investing in start-up media projects that are run by attractive women.'

'Oh, Em, are you calling me attractive? Seriously, I'm blushing.'

Emily snorted. 'I was actually talking about me . . . Look, can you be downstairs in five minutes? I need you!' Emily said as she walked out the door.

'I love you too!' Andy called after her, already digging out her strapless bra.

The dinner was surprisingly relaxed, far more so than Emily's hysteria beforehand had indicated. The tent set up in the Everetts' backyard overlooked the water, its open sides letting in the salty sea breeze, and a trillion miniature votive lanterns gave the whole night a feeling of understated elegance. The menu was a clambake, and it was spectacular: two-and-a-half-pound pre-cracked lobsters; clams in lemon butter; mussels steamed in white wine; garlic rosemary bliss potatoes; corn on the cob sprinkled with *cotija* cheese; baskets of warm, buttery rolls; and a seemingly endless supply of ice-cold beer with limes, glasses of crisp Pinot Grigio, and the saltiest, most delicious margaritas Andy had ever tasted.

After everyone had stuffed themselves with homemade apple pie and ice cream, they shuffled toward the bonfire one of the servers had set up at the edge of the lawn, complete with a s'mores spread, mugs of marshmallowy hot chocolate, and summer-weight blankets knit from a heavenly soft bamboo-cashmere hybrid. The drinking and laughing continued; soon, a few joints began circulating around the group. Andy noticed that only she and Max Harrison refused, each passing it along when one came to them. When he excused himself and headed toward the house, Andy couldn't help but follow him.

'Oh, hey,' she said, suddenly feeling shy when she ran into him on the sprawling deck off the living room. 'I was, uh, just looking for the ladies' room,' she lied.

'Andrea, right?' he asked, even though they'd just sat next to each other for three hours during dinner. Max had been involved in a conversation with the woman to his left, someone's Russian-model wife who didn't appear to understand English per se, but who had giggled and batted her eyes enough to keep Max engaged. Andy had chatted with – or rather listened to – Farooq as he bragged about everything from the yacht he'd commissioned in Greece earlier that year to his most recent profile in *The Wall Street Journal*.

'Please, call me Andy.'

'Andy, then.' Max reached into his pocket, pulled out a pack of Marlboro Lights, and held them toward Andy, and even though she hadn't had a cigarette in years, she plucked one without a second thought.

He lit them both wordlessly, first hers and then his, and when they'd both exhaled long streams of smoke, he said, 'This is quite a party. You girls did a tremendous job.'

Andy couldn't help but smile. 'Thanks,' she said. 'But it was mostly Emily.'

'How come you don't smoke? The good stuff, I mean?'

Andy peered at him.

'I noticed you and I were the only ones who weren't . . . partaking.'

Granted, they were only talking about smoking a joint, but Andy was flattered he'd noticed anything at all about her. Andy knew about Max – as one of Miles's best friends from boarding school, and as a name in the society pages and media blogs. But just to be sure, Emily had briefed Andy on Max's playboy past, his penchant for pretty, dumb girls by the dozen, and his inability to commit to someone 'real' despite being a whip-smart, good guy who was ceaselessly devoted to his friends and family. Emily and Miles predicted Max would be single until his forties, at which point his overbearing mother would place enough pressure on him to produce a grandchild, and he would marry a knockout twenty-three-year-old who would gaze at him worshipfully and never question anything he said or did. Andy knew all of this – she had listened carefully and done some research of her own that seemed to confirm everything

Emily said – but for a reason she couldn't quite pinpoint, the assessment felt off.

'No story, really. I smoked in college with everyone else, but I never really liked it. I would sort of slink off to my room and stare at myself in the mirror and take a running inventory of all the poor decisions I'd made and all the ways I was deficient as a person.'

Max smiled. 'Sounds like a blast.'

'I just sort of figured, life is hard enough, you know? I don't need my supposed recreational drug use making me unhappy.'

'Very fair point.' He took a drag off his cigarette.

'And you?'

Max appeared to think about this for a minute, almost as though he were debating which version of the story to tell her. Andy watched his strong Harrison jaw clench, his dark brows knit. He looked so much like the newspaper pictures of his father. When his eyes met hers, he smiled again, only this time it was tinged with sadness. 'My father died recently. The public explanation was liver cancer, but it was really cirrhosis. He was a lifelong alcoholic. Extraordinarily functional for a large part of it – if you can call being drunk every night of your life functional – but then the last few years, with the financial crisis and some tough business fallout, not as much. I drank pretty heavily myself starting in college. Five years out it was getting out of control. So I went cold turkey. No drinking, no drugs, nothing but these cancer sticks, which I just can't seem to kick . . .'

Now that he mentioned it, Andy had noticed that Max only drank sparkling water during dinner. She hadn't thought much about it, but now that she knew the story, part of her wanted to reach out and hug him.

She must have gotten lost in her own thoughts because

Max said, 'As you can imagine, I'm a really great time at parties lately.'

Andy laughed. 'I've been known to disappear without saying good-bye just so I can go home and watch movies in my sweatpants. Drinking or not, you're probably a better time than I.'

They chatted easily for another few minutes while they finished their cigarettes, and after Max led her back to the group, she found herself trying to catch his attention and convince herself that he was nothing more than a player. He was remarkably good-looking; Andy couldn't deny that. Usually she was allergic to the bad boys, but tonight she thought she saw something vulnerable and honest. He hadn't needed to confide in her about his father or admit to his drinking problem. He had been surprisingly forthright and totally down-to-earth, which were two qualities Andy found immensely appealing. *But even Emily thinks he's bad news,* Andy reminded herself, and considering her friend was married to one of the biggest party boys in Manhattan, that was saying something. When Max said good-bye a little after midnight with a chaste cheek kiss and a perfunctory 'Nice to meet you,' Andy told herself it was for the best. There were plenty of great guys out there, and there was no need to get stuck on a jerk. Even if he was adorable and seemed perfectly sweet and genuine.

Emily appeared in Andy's room the next morning at nine, already looking gorgeous in miniature white shorts, a batik-print blouse, and sky-high platform sandals. 'Can you do me a favor?' she asked.

Andy draped an arm across her face. 'Does it involve getting out of bed? Because those margaritas crushed me last night.'

'Do you remember talking to Max Harrison?'

Andy opened an eye. 'Sure.'

'He just called. He wants you, me, and Miles to go to his parents' place for an early lunch, to talk numbers for *The Plunge*. I think he's serious about investing.'

'That's fantastic!' Andy said, not sure if she meant it more for the invitation or the news about the funding.

'Only Miles and I are having brunch with his parents at the club. They just got back this morning and they're raring to go. We've got to leave in fifteen minutes and there's no getting out of it – trust me, I tried. Can you handle Max on your own?'

Andy pretended to consider this. 'Yeah, I guess so. If you want me to.'

'Great, it's decided then. He'll pick you up in an hour. He said to bring a bathing suit.'

'A bathing suit? I'm sure I'll also need to—'

Emily handed her an oversize DVF straw tote. 'Bikini – high waisted for you, of course – the cutest little Milly cover-up, floppy sun hat, and SPF 30, oil-free. For afterward, bring those belted white shorts you wore yesterday and pair them with this linen tunic and those cute white Toms. Any questions?'

Andy laughed and waved good-bye to Emily before dumping the contents of the tote on her bed. She grabbed the hat and the sunblock and tossed them back into the bag, adding her own bikini, jean shorts, and tank top. There was only so far she was willing to go with Emily's dictatorial costuming, and besides, if Max didn't like her look, that was his problem.

The afternoon was perfection. Together Andy and Max went tooling around in Max's little speedboat, jumping in the water to cool off and feasting on a picnic lunch of cold fried chicken, sliced watermelon, peanut butter cookies, and lemonade. They walked on the beach for nearly two hours, barely noticing the midday sun, and fell asleep on the cushy lounge chairs beside the Harrisons' glistening, deserted pool. When she finally opened her eyes what felt like hours later, Max was watching her. 'You like steamers?' he asked, a funny little smile on his face.

'Who doesn't like steamers?'

They each threw one of Max's sweatshirts over their bathing suits and jumped in his Jeep Wrangler, where the wind whipped Andy's hair into a wonderful, salty mess and she felt freer than she had in ages. When they finally pulled up to the beach shack in Amagansett, Andy was converted: the Hamptons were the best place on earth, so long as she was with Max and there was always a bucket of steamers with cups of melted butter beside her. Screw city weekends. This was heaven.

'Pretty good, aren't they?' Max asked as he shucked a clam and tossed the shell in a plastic discard bucket.

'They're so fresh some of them are still sandy,' Andy said through a full mouth. She munched her corn on the cob unself-consciously despite a dribble of butter running down her chin.

'I want to invest in your new magazine, Andy,' Max said, looking her straight in the eyes.

'Really? That's great. I mean, that's more than great, it's fantastic. Emily said you might be interested, but I didn't want—'

'I'm really impressed with everything you've done.'

Andy could feel herself blush. 'Well, to be honest, Emily has done almost everything. It's incredible how organized that girl is. Not to mention connected. I mean, I don't even know how to put together a business plan, never mind a—'

'Yeah, she's great, but I mean everything *you've* done.

28

When Emily approached me a few weeks ago, I went back and read almost everything you've written.'

Andy could only stare at him.

'The wedding blog you write for? *Happily Ever After*? I have to tell you, I don't read much about weddings, but I think your interviews are excellent. That feature you did on Chelsea Clinton, right around the time she got married? Really well done.'

'Thank you.' Her voice was a whisper.

'I read that investigative piece you did for *New York* magazine, the one on the restaurant letter-grading system? That was so interesting. And the travel piece you did on that yoga retreat? Where was that? Brazil?'

Andy nodded.

'It made me want to go. And I assure you, yoga is not my thing.'

'Thanks. It, um . . .' Andy coughed, trying hard to suppress a smile. 'It means a lot to hear you say that.'

'I'm not saying it to make you feel good, Andy. I'm saying it because it's all true. And Emily has given me an initial sketch of your ideas for *The Plunge*, which I think sound terrific, too.'

This time Andy allowed herself a wide grin. 'You know, I have to admit I was skeptical when Emily approached me with her idea for *The Plunge*. The world didn't seem to need another wedding magazine. There just didn't seem to be any place in the market for it. But as she and I talked it through, we realized there was a serious lack of a *Runway*-esque wedding magazine – super high-end, glossy, with gorgeous photography and zero cheese factor. Something that featured celebrities and socialites and weddings that were financially out of reach for most readers but that still played to their daydreams and plans. A book that offered the sophisticated, savvy, style-conscious woman page after page of inspiration on which she could model her own wedding. Right now there's a whole lot of baby's breath and dyeable shoes and tiaras, but there isn't anything showing a more sophisticated bride her options. I think *The Plunge* will fill a real niche.'

Max stared at her, a bottle of root beer clutched in his right hand.

'Sorry, I didn't mean to give you the full pitch. I just get excited talking about it.' Andy took a sip of her Corona and wondered if it was insensitive of her to drink in front of Max.

'I was ready to invest because the idea is solid, Emily's very convincing, and you're extremely attractive. I didn't realize you can be every bit as convincing as Emily.'

'I went overboard, didn't I?' Andy buried her forehead in her hands. 'Sorry.' She said the words, but she could think of nothing other than Max calling her extremely attractive.

'You're not just a good writer, Andy. We can all get together in the city and discuss the details next week, but I can tell you right now that Harrison Media Holdings would like to be a principal investor in *The Plunge*.'

'I know I speak for Emily and myself when I say we would love that,' Andy said, immediately regretting her formality.

'We're going to make a lot of money together,' Max said, holding his bottle up.

Andy clinked it. 'Cheers. To being business partners.'

Max looked at her weirdly but clinked her bottle again and took a sip.

Andy felt momentarily awkward but quickly reassured herself she'd said the right thing. After all, Max *was* a player. Linked to models and society stick figures. This was business, and *business partners* sounded good and smart.

The mood had changed, that much was clear, so Andy

wasn't surprised when Max dropped her back at Emily's in-laws' right after their late-afternoon steamer expedition. He kissed her on the cheek and thanked her for a great day and made no mention whatsoever of getting together again, save for a meeting in his company conference room with Emily and a full legal and accounting team.

And why would he? Andy wondered. Just because he'd flirted a little and called her attractive? Because together they'd spent a single perfect day? None of it meant a damn thing more than due diligence on Max's part: he was scoping out his investment, being his usual charming and adorable self and having a little flirtatious fun on the side. Which was, according to Emily and everything she could find online, exactly what Max did, and did well and often. Clearly, none of it meant he was the least bit interested in *her*.

Emily was ecstatic to hear how successful the day had been, and the meeting in the city the following Thursday was even better. Max committed Harrison Media Holdings to a staggering six-figure number to get *The Plunge* up and running, more than either of them had even dreamed of, and, almost even better, Emily wasn't able to join them for the spontaneous celebratory lunch Max proposed the three of them share.

'If you had any idea how hard it was to get this appointment, neither of you would even suggest I skip it,' Emily said, rushing off to some celebrity dermatologist she'd been waiting nearly five months to see. 'She's harder to get an audience with than the Dalai Lama, and my forehead wrinkles are getting deeper by the second.'

So once again Max and Andy went alone, and once again, two hours turned into five, until finally the maître d' of the midtown steakhouse politely asked them to leave so he could set their table for a dinner reservation. Max held her hand as he walked her home, thirty blocks out of his way, and Andy loved the way it felt to walk alongside him. She knew they made a cute couple, and their attraction to each other elicited smiles from strangers. When they reached her building, Max gave her the most incredible kiss. It was only a few seconds, but it was soft and perfect, and she was alternately pleased and panicked that he didn't push for more. He didn't mention anything about their seeing each other again, and although Max most certainly went around kissing girls wherever and whenever he felt like it, something intangible told Andy she would be hearing from him again soon.

Which she did, the very next morning. They saw each other again that evening. Five days later Andy and Max had separated only grudgingly to go to work, taking turns sleeping over at each other's apartments and choosing fun activities. Max took her to a favorite family-style mob-esque Italian place deep in Queens, where everyone knew his name. When she raised her eyebrows at him, he assured her it was only because his family had gone there at least twice a month when he was growing up. Andy took him to her favorite West Village comedy club, where they laughed so hard at the midnight show that they spit their drinks across the table; afterward, they roamed half of downtown Manhattan, enjoying the summer night, not finding their way back to Andy's place until nearly sunrise. They rented bikes and took the Roosevelt Island Tram and tracked down no fewer than half a dozen gourmet trucks, sampling everything from arti-sanal ice cream to gourmet tacos to fresh lobster rolls. They had mind-blowing sex. Often. By the time Sunday rolled around, they were exhausted and satiated and, at least in Andy's mind, very much in love. They slept until eleven and then ordered in a huge bagel spread and picnicked on Max's living room carpet, alternating between a real estate make-over show on HGTV and the U.S. Open.

'I think it's time to tell Emily,' Max said, handing her a latte he'd made with his professional espresso machine. 'Just promise me you're not going to believe a word she says.'

'What, that you're a huge player with commitment issues and a tendency to go for ever-younger girls? Why would I listen to that?'

Max swatted her hair. 'All grossly exaggerated.'

'Uh-huh. I'm sure.' Andy kept her tone light, but his reputation did bother her. This felt different, granted – what playboy lies around watching HGTV? – but didn't all the girls probably think that?

'You're four years younger. Doesn't that count?'

Andy laughed. 'I guess so. It helps knowing I'm barely thirty – a baby, for all intents and purposes – and you're way older than that. Yes, that part's nice.'

'You want me to say something to Miles? I'm happy to.'

'No, definitely not. Em's coming over to my place tonight to order sushi and watch *House* reruns. I'll tell her then.'

Andy was so caught up in wondering how Emily would react – betrayed that Andy hadn't told her sooner? Irritated that her business partner had gone and gotten herself involved with their financier? Uncomfortable because Max and Miles were such good friends? – that she'd entirely overlooked the likelihood that Emily had suspected something all along.

'Really? You knew?' Andy said, stretching a sock-clad foot out on her secondhand couch.

Emily dipped a piece of salmon sashimi in soy sauce and popped it into her mouth. 'You think I'm a fucking idiot? Or rather, a blind fucking idiot? Of course I knew.'

'When did you . . . how?'

'Oh, I don't know. Maybe when you showed up at Miles's parents' place after your day together looking like you'd just had the best sex of your life. Or maybe it was after our meeting at his office, when the two of you couldn't stop staring at each other – why do you think I didn't come to lunch? Or the fact that you've completely vanished this past week and didn't return phone calls or texts and have been shadier about where you've been hiding out than a high school kid trying to duck her parents? I mean seriously, Andy.'

'For the record, we definitely did not sleep together that day in the Hamptons. We didn't even—'

Emily held her hand up. 'Spare me the details, please. Besides, you don't owe me any explanations. I'm happy for you both – Max is a great guy.'

Andy looked at her warily. 'You've told me a hundred times what a womanizer he is.'

'Well, he is. But maybe that's in his past. People change, you know. Not my husband, that's for sure – did I tell you I found text messages with some chick named Rae? Nothing solid, but definitely requiring further investigation. Anyway, just because Miles has a roving eye doesn't mean Max can't settle down. You might be just what he's looking for.'

'Or I may be his flavor of the week . . .'

'No way to tell but time. And I say that from experience.'

'Fair enough,' Andy said, mostly because she didn't know what else to say. Miles had the exact same reputation as Max, but without any of the soft side. He was affable enough, certainly social, and he and Emily seemed to have a lot in common, like a mutual love of parties, luxury vacations, and expensive clothes. For all the years they'd been together, though, Andy still felt like she didn't really know her best friend's husband. Emily made frequent, casual comments about Miles and his 'roving eye,' as she called it, but she shut down whenever Andy tried to delve deeper. As far as Andy knew there had never been any concrete proof of infidelity – at least nothing public, that much was certain – but that didn't mean much. Miles was savvy and discreet, and his job as a television producer took him away from New York often enough that anything was possible. It was likely he cheated. It was likely Emily knew he cheated. But did she care? Did it drive her crazy with worry and jealousy, or was she one of those women who looked the other way so long as she was never publicly embarrassed? Andy always wondered, but it was the single subject they had come to some unspoken agreement never to discuss.

Emily shook her head. 'I still can't really believe it. You and Max Harrison. In a million years, I never would've thought of setting you guys up, and now look . . . it's wild.'

'We're not getting married, Em. We're just hanging out,' Andy said, although she'd already fantasized about what it would be like to marry Max Harrison. A crazy thought to be sure – they'd known each other under two weeks – but already things felt different than they had with everyone she'd ever dated, with the possible exception of Alex all those years earlier. It had been so long since she was this excited about someone. He was sexy, smart, charming, and, okay, pedigreed. Andy had never imagined herself marrying someone like Max, but nothing about it sounded terrible.

'Look, I get it. Enjoy. Have fun. Keep me in the loop, okay? And if you do get married, I want full credit.'

Emily was Andy's first call when, a week later, Max asked her to be his date to a book party Max's company was throwing in honor of one of its magazine editors, Gloria,

lauren weisberger

who'd just published a memoir about growing up as the daughter of two famous musicians.

'What do I wear?' Andy asked in a panic.

'Well, you're officially cohosting, so it better be something fabulous. That eliminates pretty much your entire "classic" wardrobe. You want to borrow something of mine or go shopping?'

'Cohosting?' Andy all but whispered the word.

'Well if Max is the host and you're his date . . .'

'Oh, god. I can't handle this. He said there are going to be a ton of people there because it's Fashion Week. I'm not prepared for that.'

'You'll just have to channel the old *Runway* days. *She'll* probably be there too, you know. Miranda and Gloria definitely know each other.'

'I can't do this . . .'

The night of the party, Andy showed up to the Carlyle Hotel an hour early to help Max oversee the setup, and his expression alone when she stepped into the room, wearing one of Emily's Céline dresses accessorized with chunky gold jewelry and gorgeous high heels, made it all worthwhile. She knew she looked great, and she was proud of herself.

Max had taken her into his arms and whispered how stunning she looked in her ear. That night, as he introduced her to everyone – his colleagues and employees, various editors and writers and photographers and advertisers and PR execs – as his girlfriend, Andy swelled with happiness. She chatted easily with all his work people and tried her best to charm them, and, she had to admit, had a wonderful time doing it. It wasn't until Max's mother showed up and homed in on Andy like a shark circling its prey that Andy felt herself get nervous.

'I simply had to meet the girl Max can't stop talking

about,' Mrs Harrison said in some kind of crusty, not-quite-British, probably-just-too-many-years-on-Park-Avenue accent. 'You must be Andrea.'

Andy glanced quickly around for Max, who hadn't even hinted his mother might be in attendance, before turning her full attention back to the toweringly tall woman in the tweed Chanel skirt suit. 'Mrs Harrison? What a pleasure to meet you,' she said, willing her voice to stay calm.

There was no 'Please, call me Barbara' or 'Don't you look lovely, dear,' or even 'It's so nice to meet you.' Max's mother brazenly appraised Andy and pronounced, 'You're thinner than I thought you'd be.'

Pardon? According to Max's description? Or her own reconnaissance? Andy wondered.

Andy coughed. She wanted to run and hide, but Barbara rattled on. 'My, my, I remember being your age, when the weight would just fall off. I wish it was like that for my Elizabeth – have you met Max's sister yet? She should be here soon – but the girl has her father's body type. Bearish. Athletic. Not overweight, I suppose, but perhaps not quite feminine.'

Was that really how this woman talked about her own daughter? Andy instantly felt sorry for Max's sister, wherever she was. She looked Barbara Harrison in the eye. 'I haven't met her yet, but I've seen a picture of Elizabeth and she's just beautiful!'

'Mmm,' Barbara murmured, looking unconvinced. Her dry, slightly leathery hand wrapped around Andy's bare wrist a bit more tightly than was comfortable and pulled – hard. 'Come, let's sit and get to know each other a bit.'

Andy tried her best to impress Max's mother, convince Barbara that she was worthy of her son. Granted, Mrs Harrison had wrinkled her nose when Andy described her work at *The Plunge*, and she'd made some vaguely disparaging comment about Andy's hometown not being anywhere near Litchfield County, where the Harrisons kept an old horse farm, but Andy didn't leave the conversation thinking it was a disaster. She'd asked interested, appropriate questions of Barbara, told a funny anecdote about Max, and explained how they'd met in the Hamptons, a detail Barbara seemed to like. Finally, out of desperation, she mentioned her stint at *Runway*, working under Miranda Priestly. Mrs Harrison sat up a little straighter and leaned in for further questioning. Did Andy enjoy her time at *Runway*? Was working for Ms Priestly simply the best learning experience she could have imagined? Barbara made a point of mentioning that all the girls Max grew up with would have killed to work there, that they'd all idolized Miranda and dreamed of one day being featured in her pages. If Andy's little 'start-up project' didn't work, might her future plans include a return to *Runway*? Barbara had become downright animated, and Andy did her best to smile and nod as enthusiastically as she could manage.

'I'm sure she loved you, Andy,' Max said as they sat in a twenty-four-hour diner on the Upper East Side, still both amped up from the party.

'I don't know. I wouldn't say it felt like love,' Andy said as she sipped her chocolate shake.

'*Everyone* loved you, Andy. My CFO made a point of telling me how funny you were. I guess you told him some story about Hanover, New Hampshire?'

'It's my go-to anecdote for Dartmouth people.'

'And the assistants were tittering all over the place about how pretty and sweet you were to them. I guess a lot of people don't take the time to talk to them at parties like these. Thanks for doing that.' Max offered Andy a ketchupy fry and when she refused, popped it into his own mouth.

'They were all so genuinely nice. I loved hanging out with them,' she said, thinking how she really had enjoyed meeting everyone, Max's icy mother being the only exception. Plus she was thankful: Miranda hadn't shown up. It was a blessing, but given her new romance and the Harrison family circles, Andy knew the time would come.

She reached across the table and took Max's hand. 'I had a great time tonight. Thanks for inviting me.'

'Thank *you*, Ms Sachs,' Max responded, kissing her hand and giving her a look that caused her stomach to drop in that telltale way. 'Should we head back to my place? I think this night is just getting started.'

3

you're walking, sister

'Don't worry, sweetheart, everyone's nervous on her wedding day. But I'm sure you know that. You must have seen it all by now, am I right? You and me, girl, we could write a book!'

Nina guided Andy into the bridal suite with a hand planted firmly in the small of her back. The spectacular reds and oranges and yellows of the changing leaves stretched out for miles through the large picture window that spanned the length of the suite. Fall foliage in Rhinebeck had to be the best in the world. Mere minutes before the view had filled her with happy memories of growing up in Connecticut: crisp fall days that heralded football games, and apple picking, and later, a return to campus to start a new semester. Now the colors looked muted, the sky almost ominous. She grabbed the antique writing desk for support.

'Can I get some water?' Andy asked, the acidic taste in her mouth threatening to make her sick once again.

'Of course, dear. Just be careful.' Nina unscrewed the cap and handed it to her.

The water tasted metallic.

'Lydia and her team are almost done with your bridesmaids and mother, and then she'll be back to touch you up.'

Andy nodded.

'Oh, sweetheart, everything's going to be just fine! A little case of the butterflies is perfectly normal. But those doors will open and you'll see your handsome groom waiting at the end of the aisle for you . . . you won't be able to think of anything in the world but walking into his arms.'

Andy shuddered. Her soon-to-be-husband's mother hated her. Or at least didn't approve of the wedding. She knew most brides and their mothers-in-law had issues, but this went beyond. It was a bad omen at best, a potential nightmare at worst. Surely she could work on the relationship with Barbara. She'd make a point of it. But she'd never be Katherine. And what about Katherine in Bermuda? Why had Max *failed to mention the whole interaction*? If there was nothing to hide, why was he hiding it? Regardless of what had unfolded, she needed an explanation.

'Which reminds me – did I ever tell you about my bride who was marrying the Qatari oil czar? Real feisty girl with a quick mouth on her? They had just under a thousand people, rented out Necker Island in the British Virgin Islands and flew in all their guests. Anyway, they'd been fighting all week, arguing about everything from the seating assignments to which of their mothers would get the first dance. Normal stuff. But then on the morning of the wedding, the bride makes a comment to her cousin about her career as a television anchor, something like "So and so said he thinks

I only have another six months, maybe a year doing local before I get an offer from one of the networks," and the Qatari just flipped. Asked her in this real low, angry voice what she was talking about – hadn't they agreed she would no longer work after the wedding? And I'm like, whoa! This is a pretty big issue to have not worked out beforehand.'

Andy couldn't focus on anything but the knot of tension in her forehead. A dull ache. She desperately wanted Nina to stop talking.

'Nina, I really—'

'Wait, this is the best part. So, I leave them alone to hash it out, and when I come back a half hour later, they seem okay. Problem solved, right? So boom, boom, boom, the groom walks, the bridesmaids walk, the cute little flower girls walk, and then it's just the bride, her father, and myself. Everything is going according to schedule. Her song begins, the entire ballroom turns to look at her, and with this huge beautiful smile on her face, she leans in close to whisper in my ear. You know what she says?'

Andy shook her head.

'She says, "Thank you for making everything so perfect, Nina. This is exactly what I wanted, and I'm definitely going to use you for my next wedding." And then she took her father's arm, held her head high, and walked! Do you believe it? *She walked!*'

Despite feeling uncomfortably warm, almost feverish, Andy got goose bumps. 'Did you ever hear from her again?' she asked.

'Sure did. She divorced him two months later, and she was engaged again a year after that. Second wedding was a little smaller but just as pretty. I get it, though. It's one thing to call off an engagement or even a wedding once the invitations are out – it's hard, but it happens. But on the actual day? You're walking, sister. Get yourself down that aisle and do whatever you have to do afterward, you know?' Nina laughed and took a swill from her own water bottle. Her ponytail bobbed cheerily.

Andy nodded meekly. She and Emily talked about that all the time. In the almost three years since they'd launched *The Plunge*, they'd seen a handful of weddings called off in the final weeks before the big day. But on the actual day itself? Not one.

'Come, let's get you in the chair with the cape on so you'll be ready for Lydia. She knows to tone down the makeup once they're finished shooting the portraits. Oh, I'm just so excited to see this on the page! It's going to sell a trillion copies.'

Nina was tactful enough not to say what they were both thinking: this wedding would sell a trillion copies not because Andy was a cofounder of the magazine she would be appearing in, or because Monique Lhuillier had personally designed Andy's one-of-a-kind wedding gown, or because Barbara Harrison had expertly sourced the finest wedding planner, florists, and caterers money could buy, but because Max was the third-generation president and CEO of one of the most successful media companies in America. No matter that the economic downturn combined with some poor investment decisions meant Max had to sell off the family's real estate piece by piece. That Max worried constantly about the financial viability of the company mattered very little to the general public: the Harrison family name, combined with good looks, impeccable manners, and impressive educations, helped maintain the illusion that Max, his sister, and his mother were worth far more than they were in reality. It had been years since they'd been named to *Forbes*'s richest-Americans list, but the perception remained.

'It sure is,' she heard a voice behind her sing. 'This wedding is going to sell us right off the newsstands,' Emily said with a twirl and a curtsy. 'Do you realize this may be the first nonhideous bridesmaid dress in the history of wedding attendants? If you insist on bridesmaids – which I personally think are tacky to begin with – then at least these dresses aren't terrible.'

Andy swiveled in her chair for a better look. With her hair swept up and her long, graceful neck on display, Emily looked like a gorgeous, delicate china doll. The plummy shade of the silk brought out the rosiness in her cheeks and accentuated her blue eyes; the fabric draped languidly across her chest and hips and flowed down to her ankles. Leave it to Emily to show her up on her own wedding day, and in a bridesmaid dress no less.

'You look great, Em. I'm so glad you like the dress,' Andy said, relieved for the momentary distraction.

'Let's not get carried away. "Like" is a little strong, but I don't despise it. Wait, turn around, let me get a look at you . . . wow!' She leaned in so close that Andy could catch a whiff of cigarettes layered with breath mints. Another wave of nausea instantly followed but it passed quickly. 'You look fucking gorgeous. How on earth did you get your boobs to look like that? Did you get implants and not tell me? Are you kidding me, withholding information like that?'

'It's amazing what a good seamstress can do with a pair of chicken cutlets,' Andy said.

Nina was shouting, 'Don't touch her!' from across the room, but Emily was too fast. 'Mmm, very nice. I especially like this fullness right here,' she said, pressing Andy's décolletage. 'And this ridiculous rock you're wearing against those killer boobs? Yummy. Max will like.'

'Where's the bride?' Andy heard her mother call out from

the suite's living room. 'Andy? Sweetheart? Jill and I are here with Grams and we all want to see you!'

Nina ushered in her mother, sister, and grandmother and administered various admonitions for everyone to give Andy enough space, saying that she was feeling a bit light-headed and please only stay for a moment, before she finally left to oversee some other last-minute detail.

'What does she think this is, hospital visiting hours?' Andy's grandmother said. 'What is it, dear, are you feeling a little nervous for your wedding night? That's only natural. Remember, no one says you have to like it, but you do have to—'

'Mom, can you stop her?' Andy muttered, fingers to temples.

Mrs Sachs turned to her own mother. 'Mother, please.'

'What? All the kids think they're experts today because they jump into the sack with anyone who glances in their direction?'

Emily clapped her hands in delight. Andy looked at her sister pleadingly.

'Grams, doesn't Andy look beautiful?' Jill offered. 'And how special that she's wearing earrings similar to the ones you wore at your wedding? That teardrop shape never goes out of style.'

'Nineteen years old, an innocent virgin when your grandfather married me, and I got pregnant on the honeymoon, just like everyone else. None of this freezing-your-eggs nonsense you girls have to resort to. Did you do that yet, Andrea? I read somewhere that all girls your age should freeze their eggs, man or not.'

Andy sighed. 'I'm thirty-three, Grams. And Max is thirty-seven. Hopefully we'll have children at some point, but I can tell you we're not planning on starting tonight.'

'Andy? Where is everyone?'

'Lily? We're back here! Come in,' Andy called.

Her oldest friend swept into the room, looking lovely in the halter-style dress she'd chosen using the same plum silk as the other bridesmaid dresses. Next to her, in yet another style of the same fabric, stood Max's younger sister, Elizabeth, who was in her late twenties. She and Max had the same general build, strong legs and wide shoulders, perhaps a touch too wide for a girl. But the crinkles around Eliza's eyes when she laughed and her perfect smattering of freckles softened her look, feminized it. And the all-natural blond mane that cascaded down her back in thick, shiny waves was spectacular. Elizabeth had just started dating Holden 'Tipper' White, an old classmate from Colgate. They'd met at an annual charity tennis tournament in honor of his father, who'd flown his plane into a mountain in Chile when Tipper was twelve. Andy had a startling thought: Did Elizabeth think Andy wasn't good enough for Max, too? Did she and her mother talk about it, sit around pining for Katherine, with her impressive golf handicap and lilting, aristocratic accent?

Her thoughts were interrupted by Nina.

'Ladies? May I have your attention, please?' Nina stood at the doorway, looking anxious. 'It's time to start assembling outside the great hall. The ceremony will begin in approximately ten minutes. My team members have your bouquets and will meet you downstairs to show you your places. Jill, your sons are ready?'

Andy forced a smile. Her mother, grandmother, and friends said good-bye, wished her luck, squeezed her hand. Too late now to say something to Jill or Lily, let them tell her she was overreacting.

The sun was close to setting, the October days growing

shorter, and the dozen tall silver candelabras added exactly the drama Nina had promised. Andy knew that the seats were beginning to fill, and she imagined they were all enjoying the passed flutes of champagne and the soft harpsichord music that had been arranged for these exact preceremony moments by one of the myriad thoughtful planners.

'Andy, sweetheart? I have something for you,' Nina said, closing the distance between the door and Andy's chair in three strides. She held out a piece of folded paper.

Andy took it and looked at her questioningly.

'From before? When you got sick? I guess I stuck it in my pocket.'

Andy must have looked stricken, because Nina rushed to reassure her. 'Don't worry, I didn't read it. It's terrible luck for anyone but the bride or groom to read a love letter on the day of a wedding, did you know that?'

Andy felt a familiar roil in her stomach. 'Will you give me a moment, please?'

'Of course, dear. But just a moment! I'll be back to escort you downstairs in—' Andy closed the door on the rest of the sentence.

Andy unfolded the letter and moved her eyes once again over the words, although they had already been seared forever in her memory. Without thinking, she moved as quickly as she could in her dress toward the bathroom, where she neatly tore up the paper and tossed the pieces into the toilet.

'Andy? Sweetheart, are you in there? Do you need any help? Please don't try to use the bathroom yourself, not at this stage,' Nina called through the door.

Andy stepped out of the bathroom. 'Nina, I—'

'Sorry, honey, it's just that time, you know? Everything

we've been planning for the last ten months, all perfectly executed for this very moment. Did I tell you I saw your groom? My goodness, he looks spectacular in that tuxedo. He's already down the aisle, Andy! He's right there waiting for you.'

Already down the aisle.

Andy felt like she couldn't control her own legs as Nina guided her around the corner. There, beside the double doors, stood her beaming father.

He walked toward her and, taking her hand in his, kissed her cheek and told her how beautiful she looked. 'Max is a very lucky guy,' he said, holding out his left arm so she could link her arm through it.

The simple words almost unleashed a tsunami, but Andy managed to choke back the lump in her throat. Was Max 'lucky'? Or was he, as his mother suggested, making a colossal mistake? Just one word to her father and he would make it all go away. How desperately she wanted to lean in and whisper, 'Daddy, I don't want to do this just yet,' the way she did when she was five and he'd encouraged her to dive off the board into the deep end of the community pool. But as the music filled the space around her, she realized in an almost out-of-body way that the ushers had opened the double doors and the entire room had stood to greet her. Three hundred faces turned to look at her, smile at her, cheer her on.

'You ready?' her father whispered in her ear, his voice jarring her back to reality.

She took a deep breath. *Max loves me,* she thought. *And I love him.* They'd waited three years to marry at *Andy's* insistence. So her mother-in-law didn't like her. So her husband's ex cast a long shadow. These things didn't define their relationship, right?

Andy looked at her friends and family, colleagues and acquaintances, and, suppressing all doubts, focusing on Max's smiling eyes as he stood so proudly down the aisle, she told herself everything was fine. She took a deep breath in through her nose, thrust her shoulders back, and once again told herself she was doing exactly the right thing. Then she began to walk.

4

---

and it's official!

The sound of the phone ringing woke her in the morning. She sat up with a start, once again unsure of where she was for just a moment, until it came to her in a jumbled rush. The faces beaming at her as she moved one leg in front of the other, slowly making her way down the aisle. The look of tenderness and adoration Max gave her as he reached to take her hand. The conflicted feeling of love and fear when his lips touched her own, sealing their union in front of everyone they knew. Posing for photos on the terrace while their guests enjoyed cocktail hour. The band announcing them as Mr and Mrs Maxwell Harrison. Their first dance to Van Morrison. Her mother's tearful, heartfelt toast. Max's fraternity buddies singing a bawdy yet charming rendition of their college fight song. Cutting the cake together. Slow-dancing with her father. Her nephews break-dancing to 'Thriller' while everyone cheered them on.

The evening had been picture-perfect from the outside, of that she was sure. No one, least of all her new husband, seemed to have any idea what Andy was going through: the thoughts of sorrow and anger; the confusion Andy felt when Barbara gritted her teeth through the least-personal let's-wish-the-happy-couple-congratulations toast she'd ever heard spoken by the mother of a groom; the constant wondering if Miles and Max's other friends knew something about Katherine and Bermuda that she didn't. *What now?* she wondered. *Do I bring it up?* Jill, her parents, Emily, Lily, all her friends and family, all Max's friends and family, had warmly congratulated her throughout the night, hugged her, admired her dress, told her she was a beautiful bride. Glowing. Lucky. Perfect. Even Max, the person who was supposed to understand her best in the world, seemed oblivious, giving her knowing looks all night, glances that said, *I know, me too, isn't this fun and perhaps a bit silly but let's enjoy it because it'll only happen once.*

Finally, at one in the morning, the band stopped playing and the last of the guests picked up his elegant linen gift bag stuffed with local wine, honey, and nectarines. Andy followed Max to the bridal suite. He must have heard her retching in the bathroom, because he was doting and solicitous when she came out.

'Poor baby,' he crooned, stroking her flushed cheek, wonderful as always whenever she didn't feel well. 'Someone had too much champagne on her wedding night.'

She didn't correct him. Instead, feeling feverish and nauseated, she allowed him to help her out of her dress and into the massive four-poster bed, where she sank her head gratefully into the mountain of cool pillows. He returned with a cool washcloth and draped it across her forehead, all the while chattering about the band's song selections, Miles's clever toast, Agatha's scandalous dress, the bar running out of his favorite whiskey at midnight. She heard the sink in the bathroom, the toilet flush, the bedroom door close. He climbed in next to her and pressed his bare chest against hers.

'Max, I can't,' she said, the sharpness in her voice apparent.

'Of course not,' he said quietly. 'I know you feel awful.'

Andy closed her eyes.

'You're my wife, Andy. My *wife*. We're going to make such a great team, sweetheart.' He stroked her hair and she could have cried from the tenderness of it. 'We're going to build the most beautiful life together, and I promise I'll take care of you, always. No matter what.' He kissed her on the cheek and flicked off the bedside lamp. 'Sleep now and feel better. Good night, my love.'

Andy murmured good night and tried, for the thousandth time that day, to forget about the note. Somehow, sleep came within moments.

The strips of sunlight beamed through the slats in the sliding wooden balcony doors, indicating it was now morning. The hotel phone had briefly stopped ringing but it started again. Beside her Max let out a small groan and rolled over. It had to be Nina calling to announce that it was warm enough for the brunch to be held outside; it was the last remaining decision to make about the weekend. She darted from the bed, wearing only her underwear from the night before, and sprinted into the living room, eager to answer the phone before it could wake Max. She simply couldn't fathom facing him yet.

'Nina?' she said breathlessly into the phone.

'Andy? Sorry about that, sounds like I interrupted some-thing . . . I'll call back, go have fun now.' Emily's smile was apparent through the phone.

'Emily? What time is it?' Andy asked, scanning the room for a clock.

'Sorry, love. It's seven thirty. I just wanted to be the first one to congratulate you. The *Times* write-up is fantastic! You're on the first page of Weddings and the picture is gorge! Was that one from your engagement session? I love that dress you're wearing. Why haven't I seen it before?'

The *Times* write-up. She'd almost forgotten. They had presented all their information so many months earlier, and even once the fact-checker had called to substantiate everything, she'd convinced herself there was no guarantee of inclusion. Ridiculous, of course. With Max's family back-ground the only question was whether they'd be the featured couple or a regular announcement, but she'd somehow pushed it to the edge of her mind. She had submitted the information at Barbara's appeal, although she could see now that it was a mandate, not a request: Harrison family weddings were announced in the *Times*, period. Andy had told herself it would be something fun to show their children one day.

'They hung a paper outside your door. Get it and call me back,' Emily said and hung up.

Andy shrugged on the hotel robe, turned on the room's coffee maker, and grabbed the purple velvet bag hanging off the room's door, then dumped the huge Sunday *Times* on the desk. The front page of the Sunday Styles section featured a profile on a pair of young nightclub owners and, below that, a write-up on the emergence of root vegetables in trendy restaurant dishes. Then, just as Emily promised, their little section of glory: the very first wedding listed.

Andrea Jane Sachs and Maxwell William Harrison were married Saturday by the Honorable Vivienne Whitney, a first-circuit court of appeals judge, at the Astor Courts Estate in Rhinebeck, New York.

Ms Sachs, 33, will continue to use her name professionally. She is cofounder and editor in chief of the wedding magazine The Plunge. *She graduated with distinction from Brown.*

She is a daughter of Roberta Sachs and Dr Richard Sachs, both of Avon, Connecticut. The bride's mother is a real estate broker in Hartford County. Her father is a psychiatrist with a private practice in Avon.

Mr Harrison, 37, is president and CEO at Harrison Media Holdings, his family-owned media company. He graduated from Duke and received an MBA from Harvard.

He is the son of Barbara and the late Robert Harrison of New York. The bridegroom's mother is a trustee of the Whitney Museum and sits on the board of the Susan G. Komen for the Cure charity. Until his passing his father was president and CEO of Harrison Media Holdings. His autobiography, titled Print Man, *was a national and international bestseller.*

Andy took a sip of coffee and pictured the signed copy of *Print Man* Max had been keeping in his bedside table since the day they'd met. He'd shown it to her after they'd been dating six, maybe eight months, and although he'd never said as much, she knew it was his most prized possession. On the inside cover Mr Harrison had merely written 'Dear Max, see attached. Love, Dad,' and paper-clipped to the jacket itself was a letter, written on a plain yellow legal pad, four pages in total and folded in the classic over-under style. The letter was actually a chapter of the book Max's dad had written but never included for fear it was too personal, that it might embarrass Max one day or reveal too much of their lives. In it he began with the night Max was born (during a heat wave in the summer of '75) and detailed how, over the next thirty years, Max had grown into the finest young man he could hope to know. Although Max did not cry when he showed it to her, Andy noticed his jaw clenching and his voice getting husky. And now the family fortune was all but devastated due to a number of terrible business decisions Mr Harrison had made in the final years of his life. And Max felt personally responsible for restoring his father's good name and making sure his mother and sister were always cared for. It was one of the things she loved most about him, this dedication to his family. And she firmly believed Max's father's death had been a turning point for Max. They'd met so soon afterward, and she always felt lucky she'd been the next girl he dated. 'The last girl I'll date,' he liked to say.

She picked up the paper again and continued to read.

> The couple met in 2009 through a pair of mutual friends who introduced them without warning. 'I showed up for what I thought was a business dinner party,' Mr Harrison said. 'By the time we got to dessert, all I could think of was when I'd see her again.'
>
> 'I remember Max and I sneaking away from the rest of the group to chat alone. Or actually, maybe I got up and followed him. Stalked him, I guess you could say,' Ms Sachs said with a laugh.
>
> They began to date immediately in addition to developing a professional relationship: Mr Harrison is the largest financier of Ms Sachs's magazine. When they became engaged and moved in together in 2012, each pledged to support the other's career endeavors.
>
> They will divide their time between Manhattan and the groom's family estate in Washington, Connecticut.

Divide their time? she thought to herself. *Not exactly.* When the family's dire financial situation came to light after Max's father passed away, Max had made a series of tough decisions on behalf of his mother, who was too distraught to function and, in her own words, didn't 'have a head for business like the men do.' Andy hadn't been privy to most of those conversations since it was in the very early days of their dating, but she remembered his anguish when the Hamptons house sold a mere sixty days after the perfect summer day they'd spent there, and she recalled some sleepless nights when Max realized he had to sell his childhood home, a sprawling Madison Avenue town house. Barbara had resided in a perfectly lovely two-bedroom apartment in an ancient, respectable co-op on Eighty-Fourth and West End for the last two years, still surrounded by a number of beautiful carpets and paintings and the finest linens, but she'd never recovered from losing her two grand homes, and she still harped on about what she referred to as her 'banishment' to the West Side. The oceanfront penthouse in Florida had been sold to the DuPont family, friends of the Harrisons who played along with the charade that Barbara no longer 'had the time or energy' for Palm Beach; a twenty-three-year-old Internet millionaire scooped up the Jackson Hole ski chalet for pennies on the dollar. The only property that remained was the country house in Connecticut. It was on fourteen acres of splendid rolling farmland, complete with a four-horse stable and a pond big enough for rowboats, but the house itself hadn't been renovated since the seventies and the animals were long gone due to their expensive upkeep. The family would have to invest too much money to update the property, so instead they rented it out as often as they could, weekly or monthly or sometimes even by the weekend, always through a trusted, discreet broker so no one would know they were renting from the fabled family.

Andy finished her coffee and glanced again at the announcement. How many years had she been reading those pages, devouring the photos of the happy brides and handsome grooms, evaluating their schools and jobs, their future prospects and their backgrounds? How many times had she wondered if she would be included among them one day, what information they would list about her, whether or not they would include a picture? A dozen times? More? And now, how strange to think of other young women, curled on couches in their studio apartments, sporting messy ponytails and torn sweats, reading about Andy's marriage, thinking to themselves, *A perfect couple! They both went to good schools and have good jobs and they're smiling in that picture like they're madly in love. Why can't I meet a guy like that?*

There was something else. The note, yes. She couldn't stop thinking about the note. But there was another memory – of writing up her own *New York Times* announcement with Alex as the groom – that made her feel squeamish now. She must have devised a dozen different versions when they were dating. Andrea Sachs and Alexander Fineman, both graduates of blah, blah, blah. She'd practiced so many times that it was almost strange to see her name beside Max's.

Why couldn't she shake the past lately? First the Miranda nightmare, and now the Alex memories.

Still wrapped in her luxe hotel robe with a diamond wedding band on her left ring finger, Andy reminded herself not to indulge in revisionist history. Yes, Alex had been an amazing boyfriend. More than that, he'd been her confidant, her partner, her best friend. But he could also be astonishingly stubborn and not a little judgmental. He'd deemed her job at *Runway* unworthy almost as soon as she accepted it, and he hadn't been as supportive of her career as she'd hoped. Although he never said it, she couldn't help but feel he was disappointed in her for not choosing a more selfless path, teaching or medicine or something nonprofit.

Max, on the other hand, embraced her career. He had invested in *The Plunge* from day one and claimed it was one of the boldest and best business decisions he'd ever made. He loved her drive and her curiosity; he constantly told her how refreshing it was to date a woman interested in more than the next charity function or who was heading to St Barths over Christmas. He was never too busy to hear story ideas, introduce her to valuable business connections, lend advice on securing more advertisers. No mind that he knew nothing about wedding dresses or fondant cakes: he was impressed with the product she and Emily put out, and he constantly expressed his pride to Andy. He understood busy schedules and crazy hours: never once in all the time she'd known him had he given her hell for staying late or taking an after-hours call, or going in on Saturday just to make sure a layout was perfect before it shipped. Chances were he'd be at work himself, trying to drum up new business, checking on the dwindling portfolio of holdings Harrison Media still controlled, flying somewhere to put out fires or soothe jangled egos. They fit themselves around each other's work schedules, cheer-led for each other, and offered advice and support. They both understood the rules, and they agreed on them: work hard, play hard. And work came first.

The doorbell to her suite rang and Andy was catapulted back to reality. Not yet ready to deal with her mother or Nina or even her sister, Andy sat very still. *Go away*, she silently willed. *Just let me think.*

It wouldn't stop, though. Whoever it was rang three more

times. Summoning her final reserves of strength, she forced a huge smile and swung open the door.

'Good morning, Mrs Harrison!' sang the manager of the estate, a portly, older man whose name she couldn't recall. He was accompanied by a uniformed woman pushing a wheeled room-service table. 'Please accept this celebratory breakfast, with our compliments. We thought you and Mr Harrison might like something to nibble on before your brunch begins.'

'Oh, yes, well thank you. That's lovely.' Andy pulled her robe tighter and stepped back to allow the table to roll past her. She saw the DO NOT DISTURB sign she'd hung the night before on the hallway floor. Sighing, she picked it up and placed it back on the door.

The server rolled the draped breakfast cart into the living room and set it up right in front of the picture window. They made small talk about the ceremony and the reception while the young woman poured the fresh orange juice, uncovered the little pots of butter and jam, and finally, blessedly, gave an awkward mini bow and excused herself.

Relieved that all wedding dieting was officially over, Andy picked up the bakery basket and inhaled the delicious scent through the napkin. She pulled a warm, buttery croissant from the pile and bit into it. Suddenly she was famished.

'Look who's feeling better,' Max said, emerging from the bedroom with mussed hair, wearing only a pair of soft jersey pajama pants. 'Come here, my little drunk bride. How's your hangover?'

She was still chewing when he enveloped her in a hug. The feel of his lips on her neck made her smile.

'I wasn't drunk,' she mumbled through a mouthful of croissant.

'What's this?' He reached for a blueberry muffin and

jammed it in his mouth. He poured them each a cup of coffee, preparing Andy's just the way she liked it, with just a splash of milk and two Splendas, and took a long swallow. 'Mmm, that is *good*.'

Andy watched Max, shirtless, drinking coffee, looking scrumptious. She wanted to crawl back under the covers with him and never come out. Had she imagined the whole thing? Was it an awful dream? Standing before her, holding out her chair and jokingly calling her Mrs Harrison as he laid her napkin in her lap with a flourish, was the man whom up until thirteen hours earlier she'd loved and trusted above all else. Screw the damn letter. Who cared what his mother thought? And so what that he'd bumped into an ex? He wasn't hiding anything. He loved *her*, Andy Sachs.

'Here, look at the announcement,' Andy said, handing Max the Sunday Styles section. She smiled as he snatched it out of her hands. 'It's good, isn't it?'

His eyes scanned the text. 'Good?' he said after another minute. 'It's perfect.'

He came around to her side of the table and knelt down, just as he'd done when he'd proposed a year earlier. 'Andy?' he asked, looking directly into her eyes in that heart-stopping way of his that she loved. 'I know something's going on with you. I don't know what you're jittery about or what's got you worried, but I want you to know that I love you more than anything in the world, and I'm always here for you, whenever you're ready to talk about it. Okay?'

See! He understands me! she wanted to shout for everyone to hear. *He senses something's wrong. That alone means there's no problem, right?* And yet, the words were right there – *I read your mom's letter. I know you saw Katherine in Bermuda. Did anything happen? And why didn't you tell me you saw her?* – but Andy couldn't make herself speak them. Instead, she squeezed Max's hand and tried to push the fear out of her head. This was her one and only wedding weekend, and she wasn't willing to ruin it with insecurity and an argument.

Andy slightly hated herself for copping out. But everything would be okay. It simply had to be.

5

i'd hardly call it dating

She unlocked the door to the West Chelsea loft offices of *The Plunge* and held her breath. Safe. Never had Andy seen another living soul at work before nine – in keeping with typical New York creative hours, most of the staff didn't roll in until ten, often ten thirty – and she was thrilled today was no different. The two to three hours before everyone else arrived were by far her most productive of the day, even if she did feel sometimes slightly Miranda-ish e-mailing and leaving voice mails for people before they'd woken up.

No one, including Max, had blinked when Andy suggested they cut short their post-wedding trip to the Adirondacks. After two days of Andy's puking – and, sadly for Max, no marital consummation – he didn't argue when Andy said they would both be happier back home. Besides, they had a proper two-week honeymoon in Fiji scheduled over the December holidays. It was a gift from Max's parents' best friends, and although Andy didn't know all the details, she'd heard the words *helicopter, private island,* and *chef* thrown around often enough to be very, very excited. Bailing on their three-day getaway in upstate New York when it was already getting too cold to be outside didn't seem like such a big deal.

Andy and Max had fallen into a routine when they'd moved in together the year before, right after he proposed. Weekday mornings they woke up at six. He made them both coffee while she fixed oatmeal or fruit smoothies. They would head to the Equinox on Seventeenth and Tenth together and spend exactly forty-five minutes there; Max did a combination of free weights and the stair treader; Andy bided her time on the treadmill, speed fixed at 5.8, eyes glued to whatever rom com she'd downloaded to her iPad, fervently wishing the time would pass faster, faster. They'd shower and dress at home together, and Max would drop her at *The Plunge*'s office on Twenty-Fourth and Eleventh before zooming in the company car up the West Side Highway to his own offices in midtown west. Both were installed at their respective desks by eight each morning, and barring extreme illness or weather, the schedule was unalterable. This morning, however, Andy had set her phone to vibrate twenty minutes earlier than usual and slithered out from underneath the covers the instant her pillow started to shake. Forsaking a shower and coffee, she pulled on her comfiest pair of charcoal pants, her match-anything white button-down, and her most boring black peacoat and slipped out just as she heard Max's alarm begin-ning to sound. She sent him a quick text saying that she had to get to work early and that she'd see him later that evening for Yacht Party, although her stomach still felt unsettled and her muscles were achy, exhausted. Her temperature last night had been just over a hundred.

Andy's cell rang before she'd even taken off her coat.

'Emily? What are you doing awake?' Andy checked her delicate gold watch, an engagement gift from her father. 'It's, like, two hours too early for you.'

'Why are you answering?' Emily asked, sounding confused.

'Because you called.'

'I only called to leave a message. I didn't think you'd pick up.'

Andy laughed. 'Thanks. Should I hang up? We can try it again.'

'Aren't you supposed to be resting up for a grueling day of wine tasting or something?'

'Leaf-peeping followed by massages, actually.'

'Seriously, why *are* you awake? Aren't you still upstate?'

Andy hit the speaker button and took the opportunity to remove her coat and collapse into her chair. It felt like she hadn't slept in weeks. 'We ended up coming back to the city because I feel like hell. Headache, puking, fever. I don't know if it's food poisoning or the flu or just some sort of twenty-four-hour thing. Besides, Max didn't want to miss Yacht Party tonight, which I have to swing by. So we bailed.' Andy glanced down at her atrocious outfit and reminded herself to leave enough time to run home and change.

'Yacht Party's tonight? Why wasn't I invited?'

'You weren't invited because I wasn't going to go. And now that we're back, I'm planning to be there for exactly an hour before going home to bathe myself in Vicks VapoRub and watch a *Toddlers and Tiaras* marathon.'

'Whose boat is it this year?'

'I can't remember his name. The usual hedge fund billion-aire. More homes than we have shoes. Probably more wives, too. Apparently he used to be friends with Max's father, but Barbara thought he was such a bad influence, she forbade her husband from socializing with him. I think he owns casinos, too.'

'Sounds like a guy who knows how to throw a party . . .'

'He won't even be there. He's just lending his yacht as a favor to Max. Don't worry, you're not missing anything.'

'Uh-huh. That's what you said last year and then the entire *SNL* cast showed up.'

Yacht Life magazine hadn't made a single dime in profits during its ten years in existence, but that didn't stop Max from declaring it one of the most valuable holdings in all of Harrison Media. It gave them prestige and panache; everyone who was anyone wanted their boat featured in the magazine. Every October *Yacht Life* threw Yacht Party to celebrate their Yacht of the Year award, and every year the event drew an impressive stable of celebrities to roam the deck of some totally over-the-top yacht as it sailed around Manhattan and allowed its guests to slurp Cristal, nibble truffle-infused whatevers, and overlook the fact they were on the polluted Hudson in late fall instead of the warm waters of Cap d'Antibes.

'That was kind of fun, wasn't it?' Andy asked.

Emily was quiet for a moment. 'Is that all? You're sick? And Yacht Party? Or is something else going on?'

Say what you will about Emily – she could be brash, aggressive, often downright rude – but she was more perceptive than anyone Andy had ever met.

'Something else? Like what?' Andy's voice pitched higher, the way it always did when she was lying or uncomfortable.

'I don't know. That's why I was calling. You put on a pretty good show all weekend, but I think you're freaking about something. Is it just some perfectly normal buyer's remorse? I'll tell you, I had *panic attacks* the week after Miles and I got married. Cried for days. I just couldn't believe he'd theoretically be the last man I'd ever sleep with. The last one I'd ever *kiss*! But it gets better, Andy, I promise.'

Andy's heart started to beat a little faster. In the two days since she'd found the note, she hadn't breathed a word of it to anyone.

'I found a note from Max's mother in his bag. She basically told him he was making a huge mistake marrying me – *if* he decided to go through with it.'

There was silence on the other end.

'My god, I thought it was something way worse than that,' Emily said.

'Is that supposed to make me feel better?'

'Seriously, Andy, what do you expect? The Harrisons are so old-school. And really, whose mother-in-law likes them? No girl is ever good enough.'

'Apparently Katherine's good enough. Did Miles ever tell you Max saw her in Bermuda?'

'What?' Emily sounded surprised.

'Barbara wrote how Katherine had been so great and didn't Max think it was a *sign* they'd bumped into each other in Bermuda! How *delighted* he'd been to see her.'

'Katherine? Oh please. You can't possibly be worried about Katherine. She used to send him links to her favorite pieces of jewelry before every birthday and anniversary. She wore sweater sets, Andy. Granted, they were Prada – but still, sweater sets. She was our least favorite of all his girlfriends.'

Andy pressed her fingertips to her forehead. Emily and Miles knew Max before she did, knew his entire dating history and had met all the girls over the years. Now, more details Andy didn't really want to hear.

'Glad to hear it,' Andy said, her head beginning to ache.

'He didn't mention it because it doesn't matter,' Emily said. 'Because he's crazy about *you*.'

'Em, I—'

'Head over heels in love with you, not to mention a pretty great guy, despite some poor choices in ex-girlfriends. So she was in Bermuda. Big deal. He wouldn't cheat with her. With anyone! You know it and I know it.'

Two days earlier Andy would've sworn Emily was right. Max wasn't a Boy Scout, but Andy had fallen in love with a man who was, at heart, a genuinely good person. To even consider the alternative was almost too horrible. But she couldn't deny that his omission freaked her out . . .

'It's his ex-girlfriend, Emily! His *first love*! The girl he lost his virginity to. The one he supposedly didn't marry because she wasn't "challenging." He's only ever said nice things about her. I can't help but wonder if he didn't test the waters one last time. For old times' sake? He wouldn't be the first guy to do something stupid at his bachelor party. Maybe a life like his father's, with a sweet little stay-at-home wife, wouldn't be so bad? Instead he decides he wants to rebel and he finds me? How wonderful for him.'

'You're being dramatic,' Emily said, but something in her voice made Andy wonder. Besides, Emily had been the first to use the word *cheated*. Andy hadn't really let herself go there until her friend came right out and said it . . .

'So what do I do now? What if he *did* cheat?'

'Andy, you're being ridiculous. Not to mention hysterical. Just talk to Max. Get the real story.'

Andy felt her throat close. She rarely cried – when she did, it was almost always out of stress and not genuine sadness – but her eyes filled with tears. 'I know. I just can't believe this is happening. If it's true, how could I ever forgive him? For all I know, he's in love with her! I thought we were going to spend the rest of our lives together, and now—'

'Andy! Just talk to him,' Emily said. 'Stop with the water-works for now and talk to him, okay? I'll be in late today,

I have a breakfast meeting with the Kate Spade people. But I'll be on my cell . . .'

Andy knew she had to compose herself before her coworkers arrived. She took a deep, shuddering breath and promised she'd ask Max, although she knew she was going to put it off as long as possible. Suddenly, she couldn't help but entertain the darkest questions: Who would move out of the apartment? Why, she would, of course – it was Max's family money that had bought it in the first place. Who would keep Stanley, their Maltese? What would she tell people? Acquaintances? Her parents? Max's sister? How would they go from being best friends who lived together, slept together, supported each other's dreams and aspirations, to total strangers? They had intertwined their lives together, their home and families and work and schedules, their plans for the future, the magazine. Everything. How could she survive losing him? She loved him.

As though he could sense something forty blocks away, an e-mail from Max pinged in her inbox.

Dear Wife,

I hope your early departure this morning means you're feeling better? I missed our morning together. Can't stop thinking about our amazing weekend and hope you're still smiling, too. I've gotten a hundred e-mails from people saying they had a great time. I'm in meetings until two, but I'll call you then to talk plans for tonight. I want you there, but only if you're up for it. LMK.

Love,

Your Husband

Wife. She was Max's wife. The word reverberated in her head, sounding both strange and wonderfully familiar at the same time. She took a deep breath and reminded herself to stay calm. No one was dying. It wasn't terminal cancer. They didn't have three kids and a crushing mortgage. Plus, despite his oppressive mother, she loved him. How could she not love the man who for last Valentine's Day – a holiday Andy had repeatedly said she hated for all the usual Hallmark, pink-and-hearts-overkill reasons – had draped their tiny balcony in black sheets with stick-on, glow-in-the-dark stars and a table set for two? Who had served grilled cheese sandwiches with anchovies (her favorite) instead of filet mignon, extra-spicy Bloody Marys instead of Cabernet, and her own pint of Häagen-Dazs coffee ice cream to devour instead of some fancy boxed chocolates? They'd sat out there until well past midnight, looking up at the night sky through the industrial-grade telescope Max rented because Andy had once complained, months earlier, that the only thing she hated about city living was not being able to see the stars.

They would get through this.

It was easy enough to repeat this to herself the next couple hours while all was quiet and the office was entirely her own. But she felt her panic ratchet up a notch when everyone arrived at ten, dying to rehash every minute of the weekend, and it escalated even further when Daniel, the art director, showed up at ten with a disk full of digital images that he couldn't wait to go over with her.

'They're gorgeous, Andy. Just breathtaking. You made absolutely the right call going with St Germain for the photo work. He's a diva, I know, but he's so damn good. Here, look at these.'

'You have photos of the weekend already?' Andy asked.

'Unretouched. Don't ask how much we paid to expedite them.'

Daniel, whom Andy had hired last year after interviewing

no fewer than ten potential candidates, slipped a memory card directly into Andy's iMac. Aperture popped open and asked if she wanted to import the photos and Daniel hit yes. 'Here, check these out.' Daniel clicked around and a photo of her and Max filled her twenty-seven-inch screen. She gazed directly at the camera, her eyes intensely blue and her skin flawless. Max had his lips pressed to her cheek; his jaw was defined, his profile perfect. The leaves behind them almost burst out of the background, their oranges and yellows and reds serving as an intense contrast to his black tuxedo and her white dress. It looked like a picture right out of a magazine, one of the most beautiful she'd ever seen.

'Spectacular, isn't it? Here, look at this one.' A couple more clicks and a black-and-white image of the reception filled the screen. Dozens of their guests gathered around the perimeter of the dance floor, smiling and clapping, while Max embraced her for their first dance, to 'Warm Love.' The angle showed Max leaning down to kiss Andy's forehead, his arms wrapped around her middle, her chestnut hair cascading down her back. The button detail they'd decided to add to the train after the last fitting looked fantastic, Andy thought. And she was pleased she'd decided on the shorter kitten heels; it gave them a more clearly defined height difference that looked more elegant in photos.

'Here, check out your solo shots. They're stunning.' Daniel moved his cursor to a folder labeled 'portraits' and opened it to thumbnails. He scrolled for a minute and then clicked on one. The screen came alive with Andy's face and shoulders, dusted just so with a subtle shimmer powder that made her glow. In most of them she'd kept her smile deliberately restrained (according to the photographer, fine lines and wrinkles were harder to mask with a 'full face' smile), but there was a single image of her grinning unabashedly, and

although it made her crow's-feet and laugh lines more noticeable, it was by far the most authentic of the photos. Clearly
it was taken before she'd visited Max's suite.

Everyone had told her St Germain would be an impossible
get, but she couldn't resist trying. It had taken over a month
and no fewer than a dozen calls for St Germain's agent even
to take a message from Andy, repeatedly telling her that *The
Plunge* was much too puny a publication for his world-famous
client to consider, but he'd pass along her info if she would
agree to stop calling. When Andy hadn't heard back after
another week, she wrote St Germain a handwritten letter
and messengered it to his Chinatown studio. In it she promised him two future cover shots of his choosing, all expenses
paid to any far-flung location, and volunteered *The Plunge*
to cosponsor his next fund-raising benefit for the Haiti earth-
quake victims, his favorite charity. That had elicited a phone
call from a woman who identified herself only as St Germain's
'friend,' and when Andy agreed to the woman's request for
The Plunge to do a cover story on St Germain's much-adored
niece, who was engaged to be married next fall, the impos-
sible-to-book photographer signed on the dotted line. It had
been one of her biggest coups at work, and she smiled
thinking about it.

Andy had been terrified to be photographed by such a
famous photographer – and one who specialized in nudes
– but St Germain had immediately put her at ease. She could
see right away what made him so good.

'What a relief!' he had crowed the moment he stepped
into Andy's bridal suite with two assistants in tow. When
they arrived at the estate, Andy remembered feeling inexplicably grateful they'd even shown up. Despite wearing only
a strapless bra and knee-to-chest Spanx, Andy felt nothing
but joy and appreciation at the sight of the photographer.

'What? That you only have to shoot one average bride rather than an entire brigade of swimsuit models? Hi, I'm Andy. It's so nice to finally meet you in person.'

St Germain couldn't have been an inch over five-six, with a slight build and a lily-white complexion, but his voice sounded like it belonged to a linebacker. Not even his indeterminate accent (French? British? A hint of Aussie?) seemed to fit. 'Hah hah! Yes, exactly. Those girls were crazy, completely *aberrant*! But seriously, *ma chérie*, I am so happy we do not need full-body makeup. It is so tiresome.'

'No full-body makeup, I promise. If all goes as planned, you will not be able to tell whether I'm up to date on my bikini wax, either.' Andy laughed. All the drama his booking required had prepared Andy to hate him, but St Germain was irresistibly charming. She knew from his 'friend' that he'd flown in directly from Rio, where he'd been shooting the latest *Sports Illustrated* swimsuit edition. Five days, two dozen models, hundreds if not thousands of inches of tanned and toned legs.

St Germain nodded as though she'd just said something very serious. 'This is good. Ach, I am so tired of looking at skinny girls in bright bikinis. Of course, this is a dream of most men, but you know what they say . . . show me a beautiful woman, and I will show you a man who is tired of . . . well, you probably have heard the rest.' He smiled devilishly.

'It really doesn't sound like you had such a terrible time,' Andy said with a smile.

'Yes, perhaps not.' He reached forward and turned Andy's chin toward the light. 'Don't move.'

Before she knew what was happening, an assistant handed him a camera with a lens the size of a fire log, and St Germain clicked twenty or thirty times.

Andy's hand flew to her face. 'Stop! They haven't done my eyes yet. I'm not even wearing the dress!'

'No, no, you're beautiful just like that. Gorgeous! Does your fiancé tell you you look marvelous when you're mad?'

'He does not.'

St Germain thrust the camera to his left. A black-clad assistant immediately reached for it and exchanged it for another. 'Mmm, well he should. Yes, just like that. Twinkle for me, darling.'

Andy let her shoulders drop and turned to face him. 'What?'

'Go on, twinkle!'

'I'm not sure I know how to twinkle.'

'Raj!' he barked.

One of the assistants leaped up from behind the couch, where he was holding a reflector. He jutted out a hip, pursed his lips, cocked his head slightly to the side, and lowered his eyes in an approximation of a sexy, come-hither look.

St Germain nodded. 'See? Like I tell all the swim babies. Twinkle.'

Andy laughed again now, remembering it. She pointed to one of the thumbnails Daniel was scrolling past. Her eyes were heavy lidded to the point of looking drugged and her mouth was puckered like a duck's. 'See? I twinkled there.'

'You what?'

'Never mind.'

'Here,' Daniel said, enlarging a photo of Andy and Max, midkiss during the ceremony. 'Look how beautiful.'

Andy could only remember the out-of-body anxious sensation that had started the moment the doors swung open. Hearing the first notes to Pachelbel's Canon had confirmed that her window for fleeing was closed. Clutching her father's arm, she spotted her brother-in-law's parents, a pair of her mother's distant cousins, and Max's Caribbean nanny, the woman Max thought was his mother until he was four. Her father led her ever so gently, both pulling her along and, perhaps, keeping her upright. A group of girl-friends from college and their husbands smiled at her from the right. In front of them, Max's gaggle of boarding school friends, nearly a dozen in total, each one irritatingly hand-some with an equally attractive women beside him, all turned and watched her. She briefly wondered why they hadn't divided themselves into the bride's side and the groom's side. Didn't people do that anymore? Shouldn't she, the resident wedding expert, know the answer? But she didn't.

A flash of chartreuse from her right side caught her eye: Agatha, the fashion-forward assistant she and Emily shared, who'd apparently gotten a memo from the great hipster in the sky that neons, in addition to beards and fedoras, were a go. The office staff, nearly twenty in all, flanked Agatha on all sides. Some, like her photography director and her managing director, managed to feign delight at spending Columbus Day weekend at their boss's wedding. The assistants, associate editors, and ad sales girls didn't do as good a job faking it. Andy thought it cruel to invite them all, to obligate them to spend time at a work function when they already clocked in so many hours, but Emily had insisted. She argued it was good for morale to get the whole office together, drinking and dancing. And so, like she had about the florist and the caterer and the size of the wedding, Andy had conceded.

As Andy neared the front of the room, her legs feeling as though she'd trudged through two feet of snow, one face in particular caught her eye. His blond hair had darkened a bit, but the dimples were unmissable. His suit was fitted, crisp, black – not a tuxedo, of course, because he'd never have been caught dead in so pedestrian a costume. He always said dress codes were for styleless people. He always said a lot of things, and Andy remembered hanging on his pontifications as though god himself had decreed them. The post-Alex, pre-Max mistake: Christian Collinsworth. He looked every bit as gorgeous and pompous and confident as the last time she'd woken up beside him in his room at the Villa d'Este five years earlier, still naked and tangled in his sheets, mere moments before he'd casually announced that his girlfriend would be joining him in Lake Como the following day, and would Andy like to meet her? When Emily had asked Andy to invite him as a personal favor to her, Andy vehemently refused, but when Mrs Harrison placed him at the top of her guest list, right alongside Christian's parents, who were very dear friends of the Harrisons, there was nothing she could say. *Oh, Barbara? So sorry, but perhaps it's inappropriate to invite someone with whom I had a fabulous affair to our wedding? Don't get me wrong, he was fantastic in bed, but I'm worried it might make cocktail hour* uncomfortable . . . *You understand, don't you?* So there he stood, a hand on his mother's back, turned toward Andy and giving her that look. The one that hadn't changed one bit in five years and said, *You know and I know that we have a delicious secret.* It was the look Christian gave exactly half the women in Manhattan.

'I'm going to be walking down the aisle and seeing someone I used to have sex with,' Andy had complained to Emily when she first saw Mrs Harrison's guest list. Never mind that Katherine had been lopped off the list at Max's behest. Andy had wanted to cheer when he told his mom over a wedding-planning brunch, 'No Katherine. No exes,' despite her status as 'close family friend.' When Andy had confessed to Max afterward that Christian Collinsworth was also on his mother's list, he looked her in the eye and said, 'I don't give a rat's ass about Christian if you don't.' Andy had nodded and agreed: it was probably best to leave well enough alone and not further upset Barbara.

Emily had rolled her eyes. 'That makes you like exactly ninety-nine percent of brides, excluding your odd religious fanatic and the occasional freaks who met in elementary school and never slept with anyone else. Get over it. I guarantee you Christian has.'

'I know,' Andy said. 'I was probably number one hundred something for Christian. But I still think it was weird to have him at our wedding.'

'You're a thirty-year-old woman who has lived in New York City for the last eight years. I'd be worried if you *didn't* have someone at your wedding you'd slept with besides your husband.'

Andy had stopped marking up the layout in front of her and looked at Emily. 'Which begs the question . . .'

'Four.'

'You did not! Who? I can only think of Jude and Grant.'

'Remember Austin? With the cats?'

'You never told me you slept with him!'

'Yeah, well, it wasn't anything to brag about.' Emily sipped her coffee.

'That's only three. Who else?'

'Felix. From *Runway*. He worked in the—'

Andy almost fell out of her desk chair. 'Felix is gay! He married his boyfriend last year. When did you have sex with him?'

'You're so label-conscious, Andy. It was a one-time thing, after the Fashion Rocks event one year. At one point Miranda made us take drink orders in the VIP room backstage. We both had way too many martinis. It was fun. We ended up at each other's weddings, and who really cares? You've got to relax a little.'

Andy remembered agreeing at the time, but that was before she was zipped into a wedding gown and sent strolling down the aisle to marry someone who'd potentially just cheated on her, while the guy she'd always been a little obsessed with grinned at her (naughtily, she could swear!) from the sidelines.

The rest of the ceremony was a blur. It took the sound of the glass shattering under Max's foot to bring her back to reality. Crash! They'd done it. From here on in, she would never again be just plain old Andy Sachs, herself, whatever that meant. After that split second she would forever carry one of two titles, and neither was particularly appealing at that very moment: married or divorced. How had it happened?

Andy's office line began to ring. She glanced at the clock: ten thirty. Agatha's voice came through the intercom: 'Morning, Andy. Max, line one.'

Agatha came in later and later every day, and still Andy couldn't bring herself to say anything. She reached over to depress her own intercom button, to tell Agatha she couldn't take Max's call, but she simultaneously knocked over her coffee cup and pressed line one.

'Andy? You okay? I'm worried about you, sweetheart. How are you feeling?'

The coffee, now cold enough to feel worse than if it had been hot, slowly streamed off the desk and directly onto Andy's pants. 'I'm fine,' she said hurriedly. She looked around for a tissue or even a piece of scrap paper to mop up the spill. Finding nothing, Andy watched as the coffee slowly soaked through her desk blotter calendar and into her lap, and she began to cry. Again. For someone who rarely cried, she sure was crying a lot lately.

'Are you crying? Andy, what's wrong?' Max asked, and

the concern in his voice only made her tears stream faster.

'No, nothing, I'm fine,' she lied, watching the coffee spread into a circular stain over her left thigh. She cleared her throat. 'Listen, I'm going to have to stop by and change tonight before Yacht Party, so I can walk Stanley. Will you cancel the walker? Are you coming home first or would you rather meet there? What pier does it leave from again?'

They went over details for the evening and Andy managed to hang up without any more talk of her crying jag. She fixed her face in a little desk mirror, popped two Tylenols, chased them with a Diet Coke, and jammed through the rest of her day with barely a breather and, thankfully, no more tears. She even found a half hour to get a blowout at Dream Dry, which in addition to a quick change at home and an ice-cold glass of Pinot Grigio made her feel somewhat human. Max swooped over to her the moment she stepped off the red-carpeted gangplank and into the yacht's open-air living room; his soft kiss and minty, spicy smell made her dizzy with pleasure. And then she remembered everything else.

'You look great,' he said, kissing her neck. 'I'm so glad you're feeling better.'

A wave of queasiness hit Andy like a shovel, and her hand flew to her mouth.

Max's forehead kneaded. 'The wind is making the water rough and the boat roll. Don't worry, it's supposed to calm down any minute. Come on, I want to show you off.'

The party was in full swing, and together she and Max must have fielded a hundred congratulations on their wedding. Could it only have been four days earlier that she'd walked down that aisle? A chilly breeze blew and Andy moved one hand to her hair; with her other hand she tightened the cashmere wrap around her shoulders. More than anything, she was grateful her mother-in-law had some prior social engagement on the Upper East Side and wouldn't be joining them that evening.

'This may be the most gorgeous one yet,' Andy said, looking around the boat's Moroccan-inspired living room. She nodded toward an intricately woven tapestry and ran her fingers across the hand-carved bar. 'So tasteful.'

The wife of *Yacht Life*'s editor, a woman whose name Andy could never remember, leaned in and said, 'I heard they gave him a blank check to decorate. Literally, blank. As in, unlimited.'

'Gave who?'

The woman peered at her. 'Who? Why, Valentino! The owner commissioned him to decorate the entire yacht. Can you imagine? How much must it cost to hire one of the world's preeminent fashion designers to pick fabrics for your couch?'

'I can't even fathom,' Andy murmured, although of course she could. Little shocked her after her year at *Runway*, and what still did was certainly not the extent to which crazy rich people would spend their money.

Once again Andy watched as the woman (Molly? Sadie? Zoe?) scarfed a miniature tartare-topped tortilla and gazed, munching, past Andy.

The woman's eyes grew wide. 'Ohmigod, he's here. I can't believe he's actually here,' she mumbled through her half-chewed food, the hand in front of her mouth doing little to hide it.

'Who's here?' her husband asked with seemingly zero interest.

'Valentino! He just arrived! Look!' The woman managed to swallow her chip and reapply lipstick in one almost-graceful motion.

Max and Andy swiveled toward the red carpet and sure

enough, a tanned, taut, and pulled-tight Valentino gingerly removed his loafers and stepped aboard. A lackey standing just off to the side handed him a snorting, wet-faced pug, which he accepted without comment and began to stroke. He brazenly scanned the party and, appearing neither pleased nor displeased, turned to offer his one free hand to his date. Longtime partner Giancarlo was nowhere to be found; instead, Andy watched in horror as five long fingers with red-lacquered nails reached up from the belowdecks stairwell and wrapped themselves, talonlike, over Valentino's forearm.

Noooooo!

Andy glanced at Max. Had she screamed that aloud or just thought it?

As if in slow motion, the woman materialized inch by dreaded inch: the top of her bob, followed by her bangs, and then her face, twisted into an all-too-familiar expression of extreme displeasure. Her tailored white pants, silk tunic, and cobalt high-heeled pumps were all Prada, and her military-inspired jacket and classic quilted bag were Chanel. The lone jewelry she wore was a thick, enameled Hermès cuff in a perfectly coordinating shade of blue. Andy had read years earlier that the cuffs had replaced the scarves as her Hermès security blankets – apparently she had collected nearly five hundred in every imaginable color and size – and Andy sent up a silent thanks that she was no longer responsible for sourcing them. Watching in a sort of fascinated terror as Miranda refused to remove her shoes, Andy didn't even notice when Max squeezed her hand.

'Miranda,' she said, half whispering, half choking.

'I'm so sorry,' Max said into her ear. 'I had no idea she was coming.'

Miranda didn't like parties, she didn't like boats, and it

stood to reason that she especially didn't like parties on boats. There were three, perhaps five people on the planet who could convince Miranda to board a boat, and Valentino was one of them. Even though Andy knew Miranda would only deign to stay for ten or fifteen minutes, she was panicked at the idea of sharing such a small space with the woman of her night terrors. Had it really been almost ten years since she'd screamed F you on a Parisian street and then fled the country? Because it felt like only yesterday. She clutched her phone, desperate to call Emily, but she suddenly realized Max had dropped her hand and was reaching out to greet Valentino.

'Good to see you again, sir,' Max said in the formal way he always reserved for his parents' friends.

'I hope you will excuse the intrusion,' Valentino said with a small bow. 'Giancarlo was planning to attend on my behalf, but I was in New York tonight anyway to meet with this lovely lady, and I wanted to visit with my boat again.'

'We're thrilled you could be here, sir.'

'Enough with the "sir," Maxwell. Your father was a dear friend. I hear you are doing good things with the business, yes?'

Max smiled tightly, unable to discern if Valentino's question was merely polite or fraught. 'I'm certainly trying. May I get you and . . . Ms Priestly something to drink?'

'Miranda, darling, come here and say hello. This is Maxwell Harrison, son of the late Robert Harrison. Maxwell is currently overseeing Harrison Media Hol—'

'Yes, I'm aware,' she interrupted coolly, gazing at Max with a cold, disinterested expression.

Valentino looked as surprised as Andy felt. 'Aha! I did not realize you two knew each other,' he said, clearly looking for a further explanation.

At the exact same moment that Max murmured, 'We don't,' Miranda said, 'Well, we do.'

An awkward silence ensued before Valentino broke into a raucous laugh. 'Ah, I sense there is a story there! Well, I look forward to hearing it one day! Ha ha!'

Andy bit her tongue and tasted the tang of blood. Her queasiness had returned, her mouth felt like chalk, and she couldn't for the life of her figure out what to say to Miranda Priestly.

Thankfully Max, ever more socially graceful than she, placed his hand on Andy's back and said, 'And this is my wife, Andrea Harrison.'

Andy almost reflexively corrected him – *professionally, it's Sachs* – until she realized he'd deliberately avoided using her maiden name. It didn't matter, though. Miranda had already spotted someone more interesting across the room, and by the time Max's introduction was out of his mouth, Miranda was twenty feet away. She had not thanked Max, nor even so much as glanced in Andy's direction.

Valentino shot them an apologetic look and, clutching his pug, dashed off behind her.

Max turned to Andy. 'I'm so, so sorry. I had absolutely no idea that—'

Andy placed her open palm on Max's chest. 'It's okay. Really. Hey, that went better than I could have ever hoped. She didn't even look at me. It's not a problem.'

Max kissed her cheek and told her how beautiful she looked, how she didn't have to be intimidated by anyone – least of all the legendarily rude Miranda Priestly – and asked her to wait right there while he went to find them both some water. Andy offered him a weak smile and turned to watch as the crew drew up the anchor and began to motor off the pier. She pressed her body into the boat's metal railing and tried to steady her breathing with deep inhalations of the brisk October air. Her hands were shaking, so she wrapped her arms around herself and closed her eyes. The night would be over soon.

6

writing the obit doesn't make it true

The morning after Yacht Party, when Max's alarm went off at six, she thought she might bludgeon it (or him). Only with his prodding was she able to drag herself out of bed and into a pair of running tights and an old Brown sweatshirt. She slowly chewed the banana he handed her on their way out the door and followed him, listlessly, around the block to their gym, where the mere effort of swiping her membership card felt overwhelming. She'd climbed atop an elliptical machine and optimistically set it for forty-five minutes, but that was the extent of her capabilities: as soon as the program moved from warm-up into fat burn, she hit the emergency stop button, grabbed her Poland Spring and her *US Weekly*, and retreated to a bench outside the spin studio. When her cell phone rang with Emily's number, she almost dropped her phone.

'It's six fifty-two in the morning. Are you kidding me right now?' Andy said, bracing herself for the Emily onslaught.

'What, are you not up yet?'

'Of course I'm up. I'm at the gym. What are you doing up? Are you calling from jail? Or Europe? This is, like, the second day this week I've heard from you before nine.'

'You're not going to believe who just called me, Andy!' Emily's voice contained a level of excitement that was usually reserved for celebrities, presidents, or unresolved ex-boyfriends.

'Nobody, I hope, before seven in the morning.'

'Just guess.'

'Really, Em?'

'I'll give you a hint: it's someone you're going to find very, very interesting.'

Suddenly Andy just knew. Why was she calling Emily? To confess her guilty conscience? Defend herself with claims of true love? Announce she was pregnant with Max's baby? Andy had never been more certain of anything in her entire life.

'It's Katherine, isn't it?'

'Who?'

'Max's ex-girlfriend. The one he saw in Bermuda and—'

'Have you still not asked him about that? Seriously, Andy, you're being ridiculous. No, it wasn't Katherine – why on earth would she be calling me? – it was Elias-Clark.'

'Miranda!' Andy whispered.

'Not exactly. Some dude named Stanley who didn't bother much with details or job titles, but I think I figured out from some Googling that he's the general counsel for Elias-Clark.'

Andy leaned over and put her head between her knees for just a moment before 'Call Me Maybe' began blaring from the spin studio. She stood up and placed a hand over her free ear.

'So yeah, I have no idea why he's calling, but he left a message late last night saying it was important and to please call him back at my earliest convenience.'

'Christ.' Andy paced between the women's locker room and the stretching mats. She could see Max doing lat pull-downs in the free-weight area.

'Interesting, no? I have to say, I'm intrigued,' Emily said.

'It must have something to do with Miranda. I saw her last night. First in person and then in my nightmares. It was a very long night.'

'You *saw* her? Where? On TV?' Emily laughed.

'Ha ha. Because my life is so unfabulous you can't even imagine it, right? I saw her at Yacht Party! She was there with Valentino. We actually all had cocktails together and then the four of us went to Da Silvano for dinner. She was quite charming, I have to say. I was surprised.'

'Oh my god, I'm dying right now! How could you not have called me the second you got home? Or from the bathroom of the restaurant? Andy, you're lying right now! This is *insane*!'

Andy laughed. 'Of course it's insane, you lunatic. You think I just happened to share a plate of tagliatelle with Miranda and didn't mention it to you? She was there last night, yes, but she didn't so much as glance in my direction, and my entire interaction was with her Chanel Number Five as she blew past me without a glimmer of recognition.'

'I hate you,' Emily said.

'I hate you, too. But seriously, don't you think that's too much of a coincidence? I see her last night for the first time in forever and she calls you the very next day?'

'She didn't call me. Stanley did,' Emily said.

'Same thing.'

'Do you think they're somehow onto our little habit of dropping Miranda's name to book celebs? That's not a crime, is it?' Emily sounded concerned.

'Maybe they finally figured out that you stole her entire two-thousand-person address book and they're suing you to keep it under wraps?' Andy offered.

'From nine years ago? I don't think so.'

Andy kneaded her aching calf muscles. 'Maybe she decided that she wants you back. That you were the best dry-cleaning dropper-offer and lunch fetcher she's ever had, and she simply can't live without you.'

'Adorable. Look, I'm jumping in the shower now and I'll be out of here in thirty minutes. Meet me at the office?'

Andy looked at her watch, thrilled for the excuse to leave the gym. 'All right. I'll see you there.'

'Oh, and Andy? I'm making the steak tonight. Come early and help me, okay? You can do the zucchini. Miles won't be home until eight.'

'Sounds good. I'll tell Max to get in touch with Miles. See you soon.'

Pan-seared strip steaks and zucchini matchsticks had become their go-to meal for every dinner the girls had cooked for each other in over five years, ever since they'd learned to make it together in a remedial cooking class. It was the only dish either of them had actually mastered the entire semester. And no matter how many times they made the damn steak and zucchini – probably in the neighborhood of two or three times a month – it always made Andy think of 2004, the year after she left *Runway* and her entire world had changed.

Andy wasn't one of those girls who remembered what she wore on every first day of school, third date, or birthday, or even when she had met certain friends or how she'd celebrated most holidays. But the year after Andy left *Runway* was etched forever in her mind: it wasn't every year of your life that you quit your job, your parents got divorced, your boyfriend of six years dumped you, and your best friend (okay, fine, *only* friend) moved clear across the country.

It had started with Alex, a mere month after she returned from her infamous Fuck You Miranda Paris trip. Yes, she cringed inwardly every time she remembered the exchange, aghast at her own bad behavior. Yes, she thought it was just about the most unprofessional and uncouth way of leaving a job, no matter how dreaded said job was. And yes, if she had it to do all over again, could go back in time and relive that moment once more, she probably wouldn't change a damn thing. It had just felt too good. Coming home – to Lily, to her family, and to Alex – had been the right thing to do, and the only part of it she regretted was not doing it earlier, but to her surprise, she didn't just get to snap her fingers and have everything fall back into place. The year she'd spent at *Runway* fetching and finding and learning to navigate the scariest fashion shark tank imaginable had Andy so wrapped up in her own exhaustion and terror that she'd barely had a moment to notice what else was happening around her.

When had she and Alex grown so far apart that year that he no longer thought they had enough in common? He kept claiming everything had changed between them. He didn't know her anymore. It was great she'd quit *Runway,* but why didn't she realize she'd become a different person? The girl he'd fallen in love with answered only to herself, but the new Andy was too eager to do what everyone else wanted. *What does that mean?* Andy would ask, biting on her lip, feeling alternately sad and angry. Alex would just shake his head. They bickered constantly. He always seemed *disappointed* in her. By the time he finally said that he wanted a break, and oh, by the way, he was accepting a Teach for America transfer to the Mississippi Delta, Andy was devastated but not surprised. Officially, it was over, but it didn't feel that way. They talked on the phone and saw each other intermittently for the next month. There was always a reason to call or e-mail, a fleece left behind, a question for her sister, a game plan to sell the David Gray tickets they'd bought months earlier for a concert in the fall. Even the good-bye felt surreal, perhaps the very first time Andy had ever felt awkward around Alex. She wished him good luck. His hug was brotherly. But deep down she was in denial: Alex couldn't live in Mississippi forever. They would take some time, use the distance to think and breathe and figure things out, and then he'd realize he'd made a horrible mistake (both with Mississippi and with her) and come racing back to New York. They were meant to be together. Everyone knew it. It was only a matter of time.

Only Alex didn't call. Not during his two-day drive there, not after he arrived, not once he settled into the cottage house he'd rented because his town was too small for apartment buildings. Andy kept making excuses for him, going through them in her mind like mantras. *He's tired from all the driving, he's overwhelmed with regret about his new life,* and her favorite, *Mississippi must not have cell reception.* But when three days passed, and then a week, and she still hadn't received so much as an e-mail, it hit her: this was for real. Alex was gone. At the very least he was determined to distance himself, and he didn't appear to be coming back. She cried every morning in the shower and every evening in front of the TV and occasionally in the middle of the day, just because she could. Writing for *Happily Ever After,* the

lauren weisberger

up-and-coming wedding blog that had hired her to contribute copy on a freelance basis, didn't help. Who was she to curate the perfect registry list or suggest some off-the-beaten-track honeymoon destinations when her boyfriend found her too hideous even to call?

'Ex-boyfriend,' Lily said when Andy posed this question to her. They were sitting in Lily's childhood bedroom at her grandmother's house in Connecticut, drinking some kind of syrupy citrus tea Lily had bought from the Korean manicurist who had served it at her last nail appointment.

Andy's mouth dropped open. 'Did you really just say that?'

'I'm not trying to hurt you, Andy, but I think it's important you start facing reality.'

'Facing reality? What does that mean? It's barely been a month.'

'A month in which you haven't heard a word from him. Now, I'm sure that won't be the case forever, but I do think he's sending a pretty clear message. I'm not saying I agree with him, but I don't want you to think that—'

Andy held up her hand. 'I get it, thanks.'

'Don't be like that. I know this is hard. I'm not saying it isn't. You loved each other. But I think you need to start focusing on moving forward with your life.'

Andy snorted. 'Is that one of your brilliant pearls of wisdom from your twelve-step meetings?'

Lily leaned back as though she'd been struck. 'I'm only saying it because I care about you,' she said quietly.

'I'm sorry, Lil, I didn't mean it like that. You're right, I know you're right. I just can't believe . . .' As hard as she tried to choke back the tears, her throat tightened and her eyes welled. She sobbed.

'Come here, sweetheart,' Lily said, moving closer to Andy's floor cushion.

In an instant her friend's arms were wrapped around her, and Andy realized this was the first time anyone had hugged her in weeks. It felt good, so pathetically good.

'He's just being a typical guy. Taking some time, doing his thing. He'll come around.'

Andy wiped away tears and managed a small smile. 'I know.' She nodded. But they both knew Alex was no typical guy, and he'd given no indication whatsoever that he was going to come around, not then or ever.

Lily flopped down on the floor. 'It's time you started thinking about having an affair.'

'An affair? Don't you have to be in a relationship before you can cheat on someone?'

'A fling, a one-night stand, whatever. Do I even have to remind you how long it's been since you've had sex with someone else? Because I will . . .'

'I don't think that is really—'

'Sophomore year, Scott whatever his name was, the one with the really unfortunate underbite, who you bonded with one night in the coed bathroom while I puked? Remember him?'

Andy put her hand to her forehead. 'Oh, make it stop.'

'And then he wrote you that card? With "Last Night" on the front and "You rocked my world" on the inside, and you thought it was the sweetest, most romantic thing anyone could ever do?'

'Please, I beg of you.'

'You slept with him for four months! You overlooked his Tevas, his refusal to do his own laundry, his insistence on sending you "Just because" Hallmark cards. You've proven yourself capable of wearing blinders when it comes to men. I'm just saying: do it again!'

'Lily—'

'Or don't. You're in a position to upgrade if you want. Two words: Christian Collinsworth. Doesn't he still crop up every now and then?'

'Yes, but he's only interested because I'm taken. Was taken. As soon as he senses I'm available, he'll go running.'

'If by "available" you mean "open to another relationship," then yes, you're probably right. But if you mean "open to the idea of no-commitment sex purely for pleasure," I think you'll find him willing.'

'Why don't we get out of here?' Andy, desperate to change the topic, scrolled through the e-mails on her BlackBerry. 'Travelzoo is offering four days and three nights in Jamaica, flight, hotel, and meals included, for three ninety-nine over Presidents' Day weekend. Not bad.'

Lily was silent.

'Come on, it'll be fun. We'll get some sun, drink some margaritas – well, not you, but I will – maybe meet some guys? It's been a tough winter all around. We deserve a break.'

Andy knew something was wrong when Lily continued her silence, staring at the carpet.

'What? Bring your books. You can read on the beach. It's exactly what we both need.'

'I'm moving,' Lily said, her voice almost a whisper.

'You're what?'

'Moving.'

'Apartments? You found somewhere? I thought the plan was to finish out the school year here since you only have class twice a week and then start to look for a place in the summer.'

'I'm moving to Colorado.'

Andy stared at her, but she couldn't bring herself to say anything. Lily broke off a microscopic corner of a cinnamon rugelach but left it on the plate. They didn't speak for almost a minute, which to Andy felt like an hour.

Finally Lily took a deep breath. 'I just really need a change, I think. The drinking, the accident, the month in rehab . . . I just associate so many things with the city, so many negative connotations. I haven't even told my grandmother yet.'

'Colorado?' Andy had so many questions, but she was too shocked to say much else.

'UC Boulder is making it really easy for me to transfer my credits, and they'll give me a full ride for only teaching one undergraduate class each semester. They have fresh air and a great program and a whole lot of people who don't know my whole story already.' When Lily looked up, her eyes were filled with tears. 'They don't have you; that's the only part of the whole thing making me sad. I'm going to miss you so much.'

Blubbering ensued. Both girls were sobbing and hugging and wiping mascara from their cheeks, unable to imagine a situation where an entire country separated them. Andy tried to be supportive by asking Lily a million questions and paying close attention to the answers, but all she could think about was the obvious: in a few weeks' time, she was going to be all alone in New York City. No Alex. No Lily. No life.

A few days after Lily's departure, Andy retreated back to her parents' house in Avon. She'd just finished scarfing down three servings of her mother's butter-and-heavy-cream-laden mashed potatoes, washed down with two glasses of Pinot, and was considering unbuttoning her jeans when her mother reached across the table to take Andy's hand and announced that she and Andy's father were getting divorced.

'I can't stress enough how much we love both you and Jill, and how of course this has nothing to do with either of you,' Mrs Sachs said, talking a mile a minute.

'She's not a child, Roberta. She certainly doesn't think she's the reason her parents' marriage is ending.' Her father's tone was sharper than normal, and if she were being honest with herself, she'd have admitted she'd noticed it had been that way for some time.

'It's completely mutual and amicable. No one is . . . seeing anyone else, nothing like that. We've just grown apart after so many years.'

'We want different things,' her father added unhelpfully.

Andy nodded.

'Aren't you going to say anything?' Mrs Sachs's brow furrowed in parental concern.

'What's there to say?' Andy downed the rest of her wine. 'Does Jill know?'

Her father nodded and Mrs Sachs cleared her throat.

'Well, just if you . . . have any . . . questions or anything?' Her mother looked worried. A quick glance at her father confirmed he was about to launch into full shrink mode, start interrogating her about her feelings and making irritating comments like *Whatever you're feeling right now is understandable* and *I know this will take some getting used to,* and she wasn't in the mood for it.

Andy shrugged. 'Look, it's your deal. So long as you're both happy, it's none of my business.' She wiped her mouth with her napkin, thanked her mother for dinner, and left the kitchen. No doubt she was reverting back to teenage brattiness, but she couldn't help herself. She also knew that the demise of her parents' thirty-four-year marriage had nothing to do with her, but she couldn't help thinking, *First Alex, then Lily, now this.* It was too much.

As far as distractions went, logging in the hours researching, interviewing, and writing *Happily Ever After* articles worked for a little while, but Andy still couldn't fill that interminable stretch of time between finishing work and going to sleep. She'd gotten drinks a couple of times with her editor, a tiger of a woman who mostly looked over Andy's shoulder at the recent college graduates milling around the happy-hour bars they frequented, and occasionally she'd see a Brown acquaintance for dinner or a friend visiting New York on business, but mostly Andy was alone. Alex had dropped off the face of the planet. He hadn't called a single time, and the only contact had been a curt 'Thanks so much for remembering, hope you're well' e-mail in response to a long, emotional, and in hindsight, humiliating voice mail Andy left for his twenty-fourth birthday. Lily was happily settled in Boulder and babbling excitedly about her apartment, her new office, and some yoga class she'd tried and loved. She couldn't even fake being miserable for Andy's sake. And Andy's parents officially separated after agreeing that Mrs Sachs would keep the house and Andy's father would move to a new condo closer to town. Apparently the papers were filed, they were both in therapy – although separately this time – and each was 'at peace' with the decision.

It was a long, cold winter. A long, cold, *lonely* winter. And so she did what every young New Yorker before her had done at some point during their first decade in the city and signed up for a 'How to Boil Water' cooking class.

It had seemed like a good idea, considering she only used her oven for storing catalogs and magazines. The only 'cooking' she ever did was with a coffeepot or a jar of peanut butter, and ordering in – regardless of how frugal she tried to be – was way too expensive. It *would* have been a good idea, if New York wasn't the smallest city in the world at the exact times you needed anonymity: sitting across the test kitchen from Andy on her very first day of class, looking supremely hassled and a lot intimidating, was none other than *Runway* first assistant extraordinaire Emily Charlton.

Eight million people in New York City and Andy couldn't avoid her only known enemy? She desperately wished for a baseball cap, oversize sunglasses, anything at all that could shield her from the imminent blaze-eyed glare that still haunted Andy's nightmares. Should she leave? Withdraw? See about attending another night? As she debated her options, the instructor read the class roster; at the sound of Andy's name, Emily jolted a bit but recovered well. They managed to avoid eye contact and came to an unspoken agreement to pretend they didn't recognize each other. Emily was absent the second class, and Andy was hopeful she had bailed on the course altogether; Andy missed the third one because of work. Each was displeased to see the other at the fourth class, but there was some subtle shift making it too difficult for them to ignore each other entirely, and the girls nodded an icy acknowledgment. By the end of the fifth class, Andy grunted a barely discernible 'Hey' in Emily's general direction and Emily grunted back. Only one more session to go! It was conceivable, even likely, that they could each finish out the course with nothing more than guttural sounds exchanged, and Andy was relieved. But then the unthinkable happened. One minute the instructor was reading the ingredient list for that night's meal, and the next he was pairing the two sworn enemies together as 'kitchen partners,' putting Emily in charge of prep work and instructing Andy to oversee the sautéing. Their eyes met for the first time, but each looked quickly away. One glance and Andy could tell: Emily was dreading this as much as she was.

They moved wordlessly into position side by side, and when Emily settled into a rhythm of slicing zucchini into matchsticks, Andy forced herself to say, 'So, how is everything?'

'Everything? It's fine.' Emily still excelled at conveying

that she found every word Andy uttered extremely distasteful. It was almost comforting to see nothing had changed. Although Andy could tell Emily didn't want to ask and couldn't have cared less about the answer, Emily managed to ask, 'How about you?'

'Oh, me? Fine, everything's fine. I can't believe it's already been a year, can you?'

Silence.

'You remember Alex, right? Well, he ended up moving to Mississippi, for a teaching job.' Andy still couldn't bring herself to admit that he'd broken up with her. She willed herself to stop talking but she couldn't. 'And Lily, that friend of mine who was always stopping by the office late at night, after Miranda left, the one who had the accident while I was in Paris? She moved too! To Boulder. I never thought she had it in her, but she's become a yoga fanatic and a rock climber in, like, under six months. I'm actually writing now for a wedding blog, *Happily Ever After*. Have you heard of it?'

Emily smiled, not meanly but not nicely either. 'Is *Happily Ever After* affiliated with *The New Yorker*? Because I remember there was a lot of talk about writing for them . . .'

Andy felt her face grow hot. How naïve she'd been! So young and foolish. A couple of years hitting the pavement, interviewing subjects and writing dozens of pieces that would never get published, cold-calling editors and relentlessly pitching story ideas, had set her straight: it was an enormous accomplishment to be published anywhere, writing about *anything*, in this city.

'Yeah, that was pretty stupid of me,' Andy said quietly. She stole a quick glance at Emily's thigh-high boots and buttery leather motorcycle jacket and asked, 'What about you? Are you still at *Runway*?'

She'd inquired merely to be polite since there was no doubt Emily had been promoted to something glamorous, where she would happily remain until she married a billionaire or died, whichever came first.

Emily doubled down on her zucchini slicing, and Andy prayed she wouldn't nick off a fingertip. 'No.'

The tension was palpable as Andy accepted Emily's matchsticks and sprinkled them with chopped garlic, salt, and pepper before adding them to the sizzling pan. Immediately it began spitting olive oil.

'Turn down that heat!' the instructor called from his perch at the front of the kitchen. 'We're browning zucchini here, not having a bonfire.'

Emily adjusted the stovetop flame and rolled her eyes, and with that barely perceptible movement, Andy was transported directly to their anteroom offices at *Runway*, where Emily had rolled those same, slightly brighter eyes a thousand times each day. Miranda would call out a request for a milkshake or a new SUV or a python tote bag or a pediatrician or a flight to the Dominican Republic; Andy would flounder about, trying to decode what she was saying; Emily would roll her eyes and loudly sigh at Andy's incompetence. Then they'd rinse and repeat, over and over again.

'Em, look, I—' She stopped short when Emily's head whipped around to stare at her.

'It's Emily,' she said tightly.

'Emily, sorry. How could I forget? Miranda called me that for a year of my life.'

Surprisingly, this made Emily snort, and Andy thought she might have even detected a small smile. 'Yeah, she did, didn't she?'

'Emily, I . . .' Andy, unsure how to proceed, stirred the zucchini despite the instructor's command to 'let them stand

and brown without bothering them too often.' 'I know it's been a really long time since that, uh, that year, but I feel badly about how we left things.'

'What, you mean how you weaseled your way onto the Paris trip despite it being my lifelong dream – and despite my working way longer and harder than you ever did – and then you having the nerve to up and *quit* in the middle of it? Never taking a second to consider what a very bad mood that might put Miranda in, or how long it would take for me to hire and train someone new – nearly three weeks, by the way, which meant I was at her beck and call twenty-four/seven, totally solo?' Emily stared down at her zucchini. 'You never so much as e-mailed to say good-bye or thanks for the help or go to hell or anything. So that's how we left it.'

Andy peered at her cooking partner. Was Emily actually hurt? Andy wouldn't have believed it if she didn't see it herself, but it seemed like Emily was actually upset Andy hadn't gotten in touch.

'I'm sorry, Emily. I figured I was the last person you'd want to hear from. It's no secret I didn't love working for Miranda. But I recognize now that it wasn't so easy for you either, and I probably could've been a little less difficult.'

Emily snorted again. 'Difficult? You were a first-class bitch.'

Andy took a deep breath in through the nose and out through the mouth. She wanted to take it all back, call Emily the brown-nosing sycophant she really was, and kiss *Runway* and everyone associated with it good-bye forever. Merely talking about the place for the last sixty seconds had brought back all the old pain and anxieties: the sleepless nights, the endless requests, the forever-ringing phone, the constant belittling and insulting and passive-aggressive comments.

Feeling fat, stupid, and inadequate every morning and exhausted, beaten down, and depressed every night.

But what was the point of engaging now? In an hour and a half the class would be over for good, and Andy would be able to leave, pick up a pint of Tasti D-Lite on her walk home, and hopefully never see her nasty ex-colleague again.

'Here, these zucchini are finished. What's next?' Andy asked, moving the pan to the back burner and coating a clean one with fresh olive oil.

Emily dropped two handfuls of halved Brussels sprouts into the pan and then poured a Dijon, wine, and vinegar mix over it. 'She fired me, you know.'

Andy's wooden spoon clattered to the floor. 'She what?'

'Fired me. About four months after you quit. I'd just finished training the fourth new girl; it was probably eight in the morning on a totally average day, and she waltzed in, barely glanced at me, and told me she didn't need me to come back the next day – or ever.'

Andy couldn't keep her mouth from dropping open. 'Are you serious? And you have no idea why?'

Emily's hand was shaking slightly as she stirred the sprouts. 'None. I worked for her for almost three years – I fucking learned French so I could tutor Caroline and Cassidy in all my free time – and she threw me out like garbage. I was weeks away from a promised promotion to associate fashion editor and bam! Good-bye. No explanation, no apology, no thank-you, nothing.'

'I'm so sorry, that's horrible—'

Emily held up her left hand. 'That was last year. I'm over it. Well, maybe not over it exactly – I still wake up every morning and pray she gets run over by a bus – but after that I can get on with my day.'

Had it not been for the expression of pain on Emily's face,

Andy would have rejoiced. How often had she wondered why Emily didn't recognize all the hideous ways Miranda humiliated and terrorized the people who worked for her? How many times had she wished she had a friend in the office? How much more bearable would it have been if she'd had a partner in crime with whom to commiserate? No one had worked harder or with more dedication than Emily, and Miranda had reneged on all her promises to her anyway. It was so fundamentally unfair.

Andy wiped her hands on her apron. 'I wrote her obit once. Is that weird?'

Emily put down her tongs and stared. It was the first time the entire class they'd made direct eye contact. 'You what?'

'Just as, like, an exercise, you know? I think it's fair to say I didn't exactly dwell on her accomplishments, either. It was surprisingly cathartic. You're not the only one who hopes she meets an untimely death.'

Finally Emily smiled. 'So does that mean you worked at a newspaper? I Googled you for a while after you left, but I never found much.'

Andy didn't know where to start with that one. There was a weird feeling of satisfaction in knowing that Emily tried to keep track of her, too. In the weeks after she left *Runway*, she'd often thought of calling Emily to apologize for quitting so suddenly and putting the first assistant in such a lousy situation, but in the end she always chickened out. You didn't scream *fuck you* at Miranda Priestly and not pay the price with Emily Charlton. So Andy avoided the certain curse-outs and insults and phone slamming and kept her guilt to herself.

'Yeah, that's probably because there wasn't much to find. I lived at home with Lily for a little while she recovered. Helped drive her to physical therapy appointments and twelve-step meetings, that kind of thing. I did a little pitching and writing for my local paper, covering engagements and weddings. When I finally moved back to the city, I sent my résumé to pretty much every listing on Mediabistro and ended up with *Happily Ever After*. So far, it's been pretty okay. I get to write a lot. What are you up to?'

'What do you do for them? It's a wedding website, right? I've read their partner site, the one about home design. It's not bad.'

That was easily the most enthusiastic compliment Andy had ever heard Emily offer, and she ran with it.

'Thanks! Yes, it's anything and everything weddings, from the engagement rings to flowers, dresses, registries, guest lists, venues, honeymoons, accessories, planners, first-dance inspirations . . . you get the drill.' It wasn't earth-shattering, but Andy had carved out a pleasant niche for herself at the website and wasn't altogether unhappy. 'What are you up to?'

'Ladies in the corner!' the instructor bellowed, pointing a silicone scraper in their direction. 'Less talking, more cooking. Despite the name, you actually should learn how to do more than boil water.'

Emily nodded. 'I remember now. You just interviewed Victoria Beckham on what her favorite memories were of her wedding, and if she could advise a bride today to splurge on a single thing, what would it be? And she said the booze, because that's what guarantees people have fun? Was that you?'

Andy couldn't help but smile; it was still such a novelty realizing that people actually read things she wrote. 'Yeah, that was my piece.'

'I wondered if that was you, and then I figured it must be another Andrea Sachs because you were definitely going to be some war correspondent or something. I totally remember it now. I have a Google Alert set up for Posh and I read everything about her. Did you actually get to meet her in person?'

Was Emily really asking Andy questions about her life? Showing interest? Impressed by something Andy had done? It was almost too insane to believe. 'Just for fifteen minutes, but yes, I went to her hotel room when she was in New York a couple months ago. I even got to meet him.'

'No!'

Andy nodded.

'No offense, but how'd you get her to agree to give an interview to a wedding blog?'

Andy thought for a moment, considered how honest to be with Emily, before saying, 'I called her PR woman, said I most recently worked at *Runway* directly for Miranda Priestly, and since Miranda was such a huge fan of Victoria Beckham, I was hoping she would grant me a quick interview about her wedding.'

'And she did, just based on that?'

'Yep.'

'But Miranda doesn't even like Victoria Beckham.'

Emily spooned the sprouts and zucchini slices onto a plate and sat down on a work stool. Andy went over to the platter of cheese and crackers, loaded up a plate, and, placing the plate between them, took the seat next to Emily.

'Irrelevant. It works so long as Victoria – or at least her PR person – likes Miranda, which they always do. So far I have a hundred percent success rate.'

'What? You've done it before? Given the impression that you used to write for *Runway*?'

'I don't lie,' Andy said, popping a cheddar cube in her mouth. 'However they choose to interpret it is up to them.'

'It's brilliant. Just brilliant. Why the hell not? It's not like slaving for her is going to get you anywhere else. Who else have you met?'

'Well, let's see. I got Britney Spears to do a top-ten first-dance playlist, Kate Hudson to tell us how she would elope one day, Jennifer Aniston to describe her dream princess dress, Heidi Klum to talk about wedding-day hair and makeup, and Reese Witherspoon to open up about the pros and cons of marrying young. Next week I'm interviewing J. Lo on how to have an appropriate second or third wedding.'

Emily reached over and created a little sandwich with two cheese cubes and two crackers, and Andy tried to keep her mouth from hitting the floor. *Emily Charlton ate?* 'It sounds great, Andy,' she said through a crunch.

Andy must have been staring at her because she half smiled and said, 'Oh yeah, I eat now. It was the first thing that came back after she fired me. My appetite.'

'Well, you sure don't look it,' Andy said truthfully, and Emily half smiled again. 'Will you tell me what you're up to?'

The instructor materialized out of nowhere. 'Ladies? What's going on here? Because I'm pretty sure "sit around and snack" isn't in the class description.' He clapped his hands together and raised his eyebrows.

'And I'm pretty sure "be a complete jackass" isn't in the teacher description. We were actually just leaving,' Emily said, looking at Andy.

'Yes, we were. Thanks for such a terrific class.' The cheer in Andy's voice made Emily shriek with glee and the rest of the class turn around to watch. The girls gathered their things and stumbled into the hallway before dissolving in laughter.

It should have been awkward a moment or two later, but it wasn't. They may have hated each other before this, but they'd

certainly spent enough time in each other's company to feel
comfortable. Andy tentatively suggested they go get a drink
and continue to catch up, and Emily readily agreed. One
margarita turned into three and three turned into dinner and
dinner into plans two days later. Soon the girls were getting
together regularly for happy hours and Sunday brunches and
quick coffee chats in Emily's office at *Harper's Bazaar*, where
they'd recently promoted Emily to junior fashion editor and
given her a small but windowed space all her own.

Andy became Emily's plus-one to all the fancy fashion
parties; Andy invited Emily along as her 'associate' to cele-
rity interviews. They weighed in on each other's work situations, mocked each other's clothes, and kept their cell
phones turned on at all hours so whoever was out late on
a date would have someone to call when she got home that
night. She still missed Alex and Lily, still got sad thinking
of her parents living apart, and still felt lonely and disconnected, but more often than not, Emily was calling or texting,
wanting to check out the new sushi place that had opened
in SoHo or go shopping for red lipstick or a new espresso
machine or a pair of flat sandals.

It didn't happen overnight, but the unlikeliest thing in
Andy's world had become reality: Emily Charlton, sworn
enemy, was her friend. And not just any friend, but Andy's
best friend, her first phone call for all things good or bad.
Which is why it felt so natural when, a couple years later
– after Emily had left *Bazaar* and Andy was starting to get
bored at *Happily Ever After* – the girls first had the idea for
The Plunge. It was Emily's idea, really, but Andy refined the
magazine's purpose and mission, brainstormed story and
cover ideas, and sourced the first weddings they covered.
With Emily's business contacts and print magazine experience and Andy's writing skills and expertise with all things

wedding related, they conceived and designed a uniquely beautiful product. Enter Max, one of Emily's husband's best friends, as both investor and Andy's future husband, and their lives had become so entwined that sometimes Andy could hardly remember a time when she and Emily had hated each other. With hard work and the passing of time, both she and Emily had managed to leave Miranda in the rearview mirror. Until now.

Andy could hardly believe the fear she felt as she sat in Emily's office, still wearing her running shorts and sweatshirt, her sweaty hands clenched so tight her fingernails left marks on her palms, and listened as Agatha dialed the famous Elias-Clark switchboard.

'Are we really doing this?' Andy moaned, simultaneously desperate to know more and dreading finding out.

'Ah yes, I'd like to speak with Stanley Grogin, please. I'm calling from *The Plunge*.' Agatha nodded to herself, clearly pleased with being the center of the drama, and cleared her throat.

'Mr Grogin? This is Emily Charlton's assistant. She's currently traveling, but she wanted me to get back to you and see if there was anything I could help you with?' Another nod.

Andy could feel a drop of sweat trickle between her breasts.

'Mmm, I see. A conference call. May I ask what it's concerning?' Agatha made a face as though she'd tasted something disgusting and then rolled her eyes, Emily-style. 'Sure thing. I'll pass that along and get back to you. Thanks so much.'

Emily didn't even wait for the girl to put the phone down on the receiver before leaning over and depressing the button to end the call.

'What did he say?' Andy and Emily asked in unison.

Agatha took a sip of her green smoothie and appeared to be enjoying herself. 'He said that he'd like to schedule a conference call between himself and the two of you.'

'A conference call? About what?' Andy asked. Why on earth would an Elias-Clark lawyer be after them after all these years? Unless they really had heard about the ever-so-slightly misleading way in which Andy *might* still invoke Miranda's name to secure celebrities?

'He wouldn't say.'

'What do you mean he wouldn't say?' Emily near-shrieked. 'What did he say when you asked him?'

'Just that he's free most mornings before eleven and that he would only discuss the private matter with both of you . . . and a couple of his colleagues.'

'Oh god, she's back! She's suing us. She's going to make our lives a living hell, I just know it . . .' Andy moaned.

'Miranda couldn't care less about either one of us, I promise you that,' Emily said with her old authority as first assistant. 'If you don't remember a damn thing, remember this: we are dead to her, and she has far more important things to do than dredge up old crap. It's got to be something else.'

Emily was right. It had to be something else. But Andy was struck by the fact that the Elias-Clark exchange popping up on their caller ID could thrust her back to a very dark place of sheer panic. It didn't matter what Elias-Clark *wanted*. Miranda Priestly, Satan herself, waving her devil tail and her Prada bag, filled Andy's world once again with painful memories and fresh anxieties. It was as if the past ten years hadn't happened at all.

7

boys will be boys

It had been a week since the wedding, and if anything, Andy was starting to feel worse, not better. Her head throbbed regularly now, and she felt permanently foggy, sleep-deprived, and at times, queasy. Her fever came and went but never seemed to disappear entirely. It was starting to seem like she'd never get rid of this flu.

When she opened her closet to retrieve her rattiest fleece robe, Max's head popped up. 'Morning,' he said, giving her his cutest sleepy smile. 'Come here and cuddle with me.'

Andy wrapped the magenta rag around herself and cinched the belt. 'I'm not feeling great. I'm going to put on the coffee. I'm not up for working out today, so I think I'll just get an early start at work.'

'Andy? Can you come here a minute? I want to talk.'

For one horrible moment she was convinced he was about

to confess about Katherine. Maybe he'd realized his mother's letter was missing. Maybe—

'What's up?' she asked, perching at the foot of the bed, as far from his reach as possible. Stanley looked at her plaintively, upset his breakfast wasn't as imminent as he thought.

Max pulled on the glasses from his night table and propped his head up with his hand. 'I want you to see a doctor today. I'm insisting.'

Andy didn't say a word.

'It's been nine days you've been feeling like this. Nine days since we got married . . .'

She knew what he really meant. A week already and they'd only had sex once, after which Andy had soaked in the bath for an hour, claiming she felt chilled. Which she did. His patience had worn out, and so had her excuses. Mostly Andy was just desperate to feel better.

'I already made an appointment for this morning. Figured I could cancel it if I was feeling better, which I'm not.'

This seemed to please Max. 'Great. That's great news. Call me right afterward and let me know what he says?'

Andy nodded.

Max pulled the blankets closer around him. 'Is everything else okay? I know you're not feeling well, but you've been . . . I don't know . . . off. This whole week. Did I do something?'

Andy hadn't planned to have the conversation now. She kept waiting for the perfect time, when neither one of them was stressed or rushed or sick, but enough was enough: it was time to get answers.

'I know all about Bermuda.'

Andy didn't realize it, but she was holding her breath.

Max's eyes scrunched in confusion. 'Bermuda? You mean, my bachelor party?'

'Yes,' Andy said. Was he going to lie to her? That was just about the only thing now that could make it even worse.

Max looked at her. 'You must mean Katherine,' he said quietly, and Andy's heart sank. So it was true. Barbara's letter was right: Max had kept secrets from her; there was no denying it now.

'So you did see her there,' Andy said more to herself than to Max.

'Yes, I saw her there. But believe me when I tell you I had *no idea* she was going to be there. I mean, of course her parents own a house there, but I had no clue she and her sister chose that weekend – of all the weekends in a year – for a spa trip. They joined us for cocktails one night. It's not an excuse, but please don't think anything happened, because it didn't. *Nothing.*'

Something about hearing even these limited details was more crushing than she could have imagined.

Then why didn't you mention it? she wanted to scream. *If it was all so sweet and innocent, what's with the note? And the fact that you hid it all from me?*

'How did you find out, by the way? Not that it was a secret, I'm just wondering.'

'I found the letter your mom wrote, Max. The one where she begged you not to marry me. It's not just about Katherine, is it?'

He looked like he might be sick, which gave Andy a small moment of gratification.

'And it obviously is a secret, or you would have told me when it happened. Or shortly thereafter. It meant enough to mention it to your mom, just not to me.' When he said nothing, Andy scooped up Stanley and announced, 'I better get in the shower if I want to make my appointment.'

'I was going to tell you, I swear I was, but I thought it

was selfish to get you worried or feeling weird about something when there's nothing on *earth* to worry about.'

'Worry? I wouldn't have *worried*. I might've taken this ring off!' After so many days of quietly worrying and wondering, the yelling felt wonderful. 'I might've refused to put on that white dress and proclaim my love for you in front of all our friends and families. Especially *your* family, since they don't even like me. They think I'm beneath you. That may have been my choice. So don't you dare sit there and say you were keeping this quiet out of concern for *my* well-being.'

Even as she said it, she knew she was being unfair. Of course she'd had a choice that day. She'd chosen to walk rather than embarrass herself or Max or their families with jealous histrionics. She'd walked down that aisle because she loved Max and trusted him – or at least wanted to – and she was certain there was some sort of logical explanation for everything. Was she supposed to delay a wedding mere minutes before the ceremony because of some undated letter and a bitchy mother-in-law? Did she even want to? Of course not. But Max didn't need to know that quite yet.

'Andy, you're overreacting—'

Clutching the dog to her chest, she slammed and locked the bathroom door behind her. Max knocked furiously and called through the door, but the sound of the shower soon drowned him out. When she walked into the kitchen fully dressed to grab a banana and a bottle of iced tea, Max leaped to his feet and tried to embrace her. 'Andy, nothing happened!' She wrangled herself away so only his hand remained on her shoulder.

She looked around their apartment, a south-facing, three-thousand-square-foot split two-bedroom with home office on the fourteenth floor, with a terrace off the master and a newly renovated kitchen that opened up into a sprawling living and dining room space. The Harrisons had purchased the apartment for Max when he graduated from college, and as expensive as the place was, it didn't come close to comparing price-wise with other Harrison properties. For this reason Barbara had persuaded Max not to sell it when he sold everything else: if nothing else, it was an investment. When he and Andy decided to move in together, Max immediately offered to put his beloved apartment on the market so they could choose somewhere new together, but Andy argued that it was ridiculous to incur all those extra expenses when the apartment was more than enough for the two of them. Max had kissed her and declared how much he loved her lack of materialism. Andy had laughed and announced she was still planning to throw out most of his furniture and hire a decorator. Now, as she glanced around, Andy thought about how beautifully the apartment had turned out, how lucky she was to live there. Thick Berber carpeting, plush velvet couches, and overstuffed chairs invited snuggling. Framed photographs of adventures from around the world she and Max had taken, alone and together, decorated the walls. They'd combined their knickknacks (her slatted, wooden African frog that made a ribbit noise when you brushed a stick across its back; his reclining Buddha bust that he'd dragged back from a trip to Thailand) and all their books and their thousands upon thousands of CDs, creating a warm, welcoming home that felt like a respite.

'Call me as soon as you're done, okay? I'm worried about you. I can pick up an antibiotic or whatever on my way home tonight, just tell me what you need. We have so much more to talk about, I know that, so I'll be home as soon as I can. We're going to get through this, I promise. I should have told you, Andy, I know that now. But I swear to you,

I love you. And absolutely nothing happened in Bermuda. Zero.'

His palm on her shoulder felt like an assault.

'Andy?'

She didn't look at him, didn't respond.

'I love you so much. I'll do anything to win back your trust. I made a bad decision not to tell you I saw an ex, but I didn't cheat. And I'm not my mother. Please come home tonight and talk to me, okay? Please?'

She forced herself to look up and meet his gaze. There, peering at her through worried eyes, looking as anxious as she felt, was her best friend, her partner, the man she loved more than anyone else on earth.

This wasn't the last of it, Andy knew that; they would talk that night, and she would need some more convincing – but not then. She nodded and squeezed his arm and without another word she hoisted her bag over her arm and closed the door behind her.

'Andrea? Good to see you again, dear,' Dr Palmer said as he perused Andy's chart.

He didn't look up. After what, thirty, maybe forty years in practice, how could the man bear to hear another complaint about headaches and a sore throat? Andy almost felt bad for him.

'Let's see here, you had your last physical almost two years ago – you're due, you know that – but you made a sick appointment today, so what's going on?'

'Well, I'm sure it's nothing serious, but I've been feeling pretty lousy for a week now, and it doesn't seem to be getting any better. I've had a nonstop headache, and my stomach's been upset.'

'Sounds like a typical bug that's been going around.

Anything upper respiratory?' He motioned for Andy to open her mouth. She gagged when he depressed her tongue.

'No, not really. But a fever on and off.'

'Mmm. Take a deep breath for me? There.'

In quick succession he checked her eyes and ears and then kneaded her belly and asked how it felt. She replied 'fine' but had an irrational desire to punch him in the face for gathering her skin (fat?) rolls into bunches.

'Well, I'll take a strep culture because you're here and your throat is irritated, but I'm almost certain that's not what it is. Honestly, I think it's just a virus that needs to work its way through your system. I would recommend getting the flu vaccine, so long as you're here. Take Tylenol as needed, drink plenty of fluids, and rest, and call me if your fever spikes.'

He was talking quickly now, making notes and folding up her file and getting ready to leave. Why were they always in such a rush? She'd waited almost an hour to be seen, and now he was bolting out after four minutes.

'You don't want to be tested for any sexually transmitted diseases, do you?' Dr Palmer asked, not even bothering to look up from his paperwork.

'Pardon?' Andy asked. She coughed.

'Strictly protocol. We ask all unmarried patients, give them the option.'

'Actually I am married,' Andy said. 'As of a week ago.' She marveled at how strange it still felt to say it. Married.

'Congratulations! Well, then, if that's all, I'll be getting on my way. Good to see you, Andy. I think you'll be feeling better soon.'

He turned to leave the exam room, and before Andy could think anything through, she blurted, 'I'd like to be tested for everything, please.'

Dr Palmer turned around.

'I know it's probably all in my head, and there's nothing to worry about, but I did just find out that my husband saw his ex at his bachelor party. I mean, I know it's his ex-girlfriend and not some prostitute, and of course I don't actually think anything happened – he swears it didn't, but . . . better safe than sorry, I guess?' She paused for just a moment to take a deep, gasping breath. And then, more calmly, she said, 'We just got married last weekend.'

Ninety-nine percent of Andy knew she was being completely and utterly ridiculous. She was almost certain Max hadn't cheated on her with Katherine or anyone else. He'd never been anything but loving and up-front with her, and while he'd made a mistake in not mentioning the run-in, she really did believe him when he claimed nothing happened. And even if by some unlikely chance something had happened, what were the chances he was going to get a sexually transmitted disease from Katherine von Herzog, the virgin princess herself? Von Herzogs didn't do herpes. Period. All that said, on the teensy, tiny chance her current illness had something to do with Max and Katherine, she should know once and for all.

He nodded. 'The lab is down this hall to your left. Go there now and they'll draw your blood. Leave a urine sample in the bathroom. When you return, take everything off. There's a paper gown by the chair over there, opening in the front. I'll be back with a nurse momentarily.'

Andy tried to thank him, but he disappeared too quickly. She scooted off the exam table and headed toward the lab, where a large, unsmiling woman quickly and near-painlessly drew her blood without ever making eye contact and then directed Andy to the bathroom. She returned to the exam room and, as directed, changed into the front-opening gown and climbed back up on the table. The ancient copy of *Real Simple* magazine on the chair caught her eye, and she had managed to stay focused on a ten-step plan for cleaning out your laundry room when the doctor and another man entered.

'Andy, this is Mr Kevin, our nurse-practitioner,' Dr Palmer said, motioning toward the Asian man who appeared not a day older than seventeen. 'I'm sorry we don't have any women available right now. You don't mind, right?'

'Of course not,' Andy lied.

The exam was blessedly fast. While she couldn't see what the doctor was doing and he didn't bother to explain, she felt a tiny bit of pressure and some familiar swabbing, perhaps like a Pap smear. She tried to ignore Mr Kevin staring between her spread legs as though he'd never seen anything like it before. Just as she was starting to feel supremely uncomfortable, Dr Palmer pulled the paper firmly over her lower body and patted her ankle.

'All done, Andrea. Depending on how backed up the lab is, I'll have some of these results by today, some by tomorrow. Make sure with the receptionist on your way out that your phone number is up-to-date. If you don't hear from me by five tomorrow, feel free to call the office.'

'Uh, okay. Is there anything else I—'

'We've got it all covered. Talk to you soon.' And before she could utter another word, or even ask what tests he'd conducted, the doctor was gone.

It wasn't until she'd counted out her co-pay in cash and shrugged on her coat and swiped her MetroCard for the subway that she realized he hadn't said anything even remotely reassuring. No 'I'm sure there's nothing to worry about,' or 'It's good to be cautious, but I'm sure everything's fine,' or even 'I don't see anything down here to be concerned about.' Just a vague 'all done' and a speedy exit. Was he merely afraid of another hysterical breakdown, or had he seen something that raised a red flag?

Andy could barely concentrate at work. Barbara, Katherine, Bermuda, and chlamydia on one hand. Miranda on the other. She honestly didn't know which was scarier. She tried to distract herself with a quick glance through 'Page Six' online, but a photo of Miranda's daughters stared back at her. No longer the little girls who had tormented Andy years ago, the twins looked no less miserable. In the photo, from some gallery opening the previous evening, Caroline was dressed in head-to-toe black and draped across some guy sporting a waxy mustache and acne. Cassidy had attempted – and pulled off, Andy had to admit – the half-shaved-head look. Her skintight, glossy leather pants accentuated her frightening thinness and, combined with her ruby-red lipstick, gave her a goth china-doll appearance. The caption told her both girls were currently freshmen, home for their fall breaks, Caroline from RISD and Cassidy from some French-run university in Dubai. Andy couldn't help but wonder how Miranda felt about her daughters' choices, and the thought made her smile for a moment.

Emily knocked on Andy's office door and walked in without waiting for a response. 'Hey, you look horrible. Are you still sick? More to the point, did you talk to Max?'

'Yes on both counts.' Andy plucked a Hershey's Kiss from the glass bowl she kept on her desk before pushing the bowl toward Emily.

Emily sighed, unwrapped one, and popped it in her mouth. 'So, what did he say? I asked Miles, by the way, and he swears there were zero girls hanging out with them. And I believe him. Not that he won't lie to me, but I can usually tell . . .'

117

'It's true, Em. Katherine was there. He admitted it.'

Her friend's head snapped around like a rubber band. Andy stared at the tiny smear of chocolate on Emily's lower lip and wondered why she felt dead inside.

'What do you mean he admitted it? Admitted what, exactly?'

Andy's cell pinged and a text popped up on the screen. Both girls leaned forward to see if it was from Max, which it was, and Emily looked questioningly at Andy.

What did doc say?

The thought of lying on that cold table, having her lady privates swabbed while two men watched, came rushing back, and Andy was filled with an overwhelming desire to murder Max. In all the years since high school that she'd been sexually active – including a number spent dating in the shark tank that was New York City – Andy had never once worried she'd caught some sexually transmitted disease. She was careful, bordering on obsessive, and proud of it. How unfair that now, when she finally felt secure enough to let her guard down, to give herself completely to her *husband*, for god's sake, she was being tortured waiting for STD results to come back.

She began typing with her thumbs. *Test results later today or tomorrow. Probably just a bug.*

'Andy?'

Andy unwrapped another Kiss and bit the tip off before popping the whole thing in her mouth.

'Can you lay off the bingeing for a second here and tell me what's going on?' Emily snatched the candy bowl from Andy's reach and put it on the floor. 'Whatever way this all shakes out, you're not going to be happy packing on ten pounds of cheap candy, I promise you that.'

'There's really not much to report. I told him I knew

what happened in Bermuda, and he broke down and apologized.'

Emily cocked her head to the side. Women the world over would have killed for those reddish-brown waves, and all she could talk about was dying them blond. 'Okaaay. But you *don't* know what happened in Bermuda. You just know that he bumped into his ex-girlfriend.'

Andy held her hand up. 'Please stop. It's not even up for debate. I know you're trying to make me feel better, but Max apologized a thousand times, assured me it wasn't planned in advance, that Katherine was just there with her sister and they all ran into each other and she hung out with them. He claims he was going to tell me, but in some fucked-up way he thought it was more selfish to do that, so he just kept his mouth shut and hoped it would all go away.'

'Oh, Andy, I can't even believe—'

'Well, believe it,' she snapped, irritated at even the suggestion her best friend would doubt her story. 'I spent the morning getting tested for STDs.'

Emily's mouth fell open in the most inelegant, non-Emily way. And then she started to laugh. 'Andy!' she cackled, her shoulders shaking. 'You've got to be kidding me. Max didn't give you some disease. And I assure you, Katherine didn't give him one, either.'

Andy shrugged. 'I don't know what to tell you. He claims nothing happened. But he was in Bermuda six weeks ago coincidentally with his ex-girlfriend, and now I'm sick with all sorts of weird symptoms and no explanations. What would you think?'

'That you're the biggest drama queen on earth. Seriously, Andy. STDs?'

The girls were silent for a minute, listening to their staff begin to trickle in, and then Andy heard Agatha going through the messages from the night before.

'Can I be a really bad friend for a second? Promise you won't hate me for asking?'

'I can't promise, but I'll try,' Andy said.

Emily opened her mouth to say something and then closed it again. 'No, sorry, forget it, it's not important.'

'You want to know about the Elias-Clark call, right? What our next move is?' It had been four days since the call and Emily had asked Andy what she wanted to do a half dozen times. Meanwhile, Elias-Clark had called again to schedule the conference call and Agatha said they'd get back to them ASAP. 'I guess we have to return the call.'

Emily nodded but it was obvious she was pleased. 'Okay, sounds good.' Emily's phone buzzed, and she glanced down. 'That's Daniel. I'm sure he's been bugging you too, but he wants to know what we decided with the February cover.'

'We didn't decide anything,' Andy said, knowing she wasn't being helpful.

'Well, are you still okay with putting your wedding on the cover? If I were you, I'd do it in a heartbeat.'

Andy sighed. She'd almost forgotten about that. 'We got the film back and it's gorgeous, and we blew almost our entire editorial budget on St Germain, and we don't have anything half as good to sub in. The whole issue is riding on that spread. I get it.'

'All true.'

Without warning, Andy's throat tightened. 'What do I do, Em? It feels like everything's spinning out of control. I can't believe his family hates me. And this whole Katherine thing is just unnerving.'

Emily flicked her hand. 'I've seen the way you two look at each other. My god, if Miles and I had half of what you and Max have, we'd be golden. He worships you, and I know him – he's kicking himself right now, wondering why he was an ass, and he's terrified he's going to lose you. But you know what that makes him? A guy. A guy who screwed up by not telling you, but still the same guy you fell in love with, the one who always said he'd never met anyone he wanted to settle down with. Until he met you.'

Andy gave Emily a look. 'If this is his way of settling down, I'd hate to see what playing the field looked like.'

'Do you remember him begging you to move in with him six months after you met? He wanted to go ring shopping for your first anniversary! And if that man mentions "starting a family" one more time, Miles is going to kill him. He really does love you, Andy, and you know it.'

'I do know. I just need to keep telling myself.' Andy coughed and dabbed her eyes with a tissue. 'It's fine to run the wedding in the February issue,' she said before she could chicken out.

'Really?' The look of relief on Emily's face was almost comical.

'Really. The pictures really are beautiful. There's no reason to waste them.'

Emily nodded and then hightailed it out of Andy's office, probably before either one of them could say something to screw it up.

By the time Andy walked to her block, she was feeling if not calm, then some similar approximation of it. Max played in a basketball league after work once a week, but Andy knew he planned to skip it that night so he could come home and take care of her. If he left work at the usual time, he'd be home in the next thirty minutes. What should she do? Accept her husband completely lied to her about seeing his first love? Wasn't she old enough to know that where there's smoke, there's fire? If he omitted the information that he'd seen Katherine, there had to be more, right? And if there was more, what would she do? *Leave him?* Wouldn't Barbara just love that one – Andy up and gone two weeks in. A man in a suit turned around to look at her. Had she said it aloud? Was she losing her mind?

She tossed her oversize Louis Vuitton tote bag – one of those behemoth schleppers that claimed it could hold five hundred pounds without snapping a strap – onto the hallway bench and kicked off her shoes. She checked her watch. Twenty-five more minutes. Sourcing and eating a slice of whole wheat slathered in peanut butter and an ice-cold Diet Coke took another eight. How would she start? *Max, I love you but I feel like we should take a few days to think about things.* It sounded straight out of a movie. Deep breath. When the time came, she would just say whatever was on her mind.

Her screen lit up with a text message.

Home in 10. You need anything?

Fine, thx. See you then.

She thought about calling someone, anyone, to fill the time but didn't know what she could possibly say. *Oh, hi, Lily. Did you have a good time at the wedding? Flight back okay? Terrific! Yes, I'm just waiting for Max to get home so I can tell him I want a day or two to think things through. A week after our wedding, no less!* She bit her cuticles and stared at the time on her phone, until it rang and she almost jumped out of her seat. It was a blocked number, but she'd long ago given up on screening them.

'Hello?' The sound of her voice shaking surprised her.

'Andrea Sachs, please.'

'This is she. May I ask who's calling?'

'Oh, hello, Andrea. This is Mr Kevin, from Dr Palmer's

office? I'm calling with some test results. Is now a good time?'

Is it ever? Andy thought. *I can combine a confirmation of some vile genital affliction with my 'I need some space' request. Now is actually a terrific time.*

'Yes, now is just fine, thank you.'

'Okay, let's see here . . . your strep culture came back negative, but I think we were expecting as much. As for the STD panel, I've got good news. Negative for chlamydia, gonorrhea, hepatitis, herpes, HIV, HPV, syphilis, and bacterial vaginosis.'

Andy waited, eager for him to continue, but there was an awkward silence.

'That is good,' she said, wondering why he was being so weird. 'Right? So negative for everything?'

Mr Kevin coughed. 'Well, not exactly negative for *everything* . . .'

Andy racked her mind, trying to remember if anything was missing from the list. *He said HIV, right? And herpes?* Was there something new, some new cutting-edge disease she hadn't even heard of yet? Was he scared to tell her because she was going to die? She would take Max with her, she swore to herself . . .

'Your HCG levels are actually quite high, Andrea. Congratulations! You're pregnant.'

Somewhere in the back of her brain she'd understood where he was going with his announcement, probably right around the word 'congratulations,' but she felt totally incapable of processing it. It was as though someone had reached out and placed a gigantic black sheet over the lens of her life. Just black. She was conscious and breathing but unable to feel or see or hear anything at all. She had questions, so many questions, but more than anything else, she felt a quiet, stunned disbelief. Pregnant? It couldn't be true. Wasn't true. It must have been a mistake. No matter that a tiny voice inside her head was saying, *You suspected it all along. The nausea, the irregular periods, the aches and heaviness and general misery. You knew, Andy, but you couldn't deal with it.*

Stanley's barking brought her back to attention. He only barked when the front door opened, which meant Max was home.

'Andrea? Are you there?' For a moment, she wasn't sure if Mr Kevin or Max had asked the question.

'Yes, yes, I'm here,' she said into the phone. 'Thank you for the information.'

'Do you have an obstetrician or do you need a referral for one? I can't tell how far along you are without an ultrasound, but judging from your levels, I wouldn't say this is a brand-new pregnancy. It would probably be best to get in for an appointment as soon as possible.'

'Andy? Are you home?' Max called, the front door slamming behind him. Stanley went into a barking frenzy.

'Thank you, Mr Kevin. I will handle it,' she lied for what felt like the thousandth time that day. *Not a brand-new pregnancy.* What did that even mean?

'Hey,' Max whispered, coming up behind her and kissing her neck. 'Who are you on with?'

She clamped her hand over the microphone. 'No one.'

'Andrea? Is there anything else I can help you with?' asked the disembodied voice through her cell phone.

'Is that why I'm sick?' she asked.

Mr Kevin cleared his throat. 'That would certainly explain the nausea and the fatigue. Dr Palmer thinks your other symptoms – the sore throat, the fever, the muscle aches – are unrelated. A virus, stress, perhaps just being run down. You should feel better shortly.'

'Yes, I'm sure I'll feel great shortly. Thanks for calling.' She pressed the 'end' button, took a deep breath, and tried to calm her runaway pulse.

'Everything okay?' Max asked. He opened the refrigerator, took out a green Gatorade, and swallowed half of it in three seconds.

Andy didn't answer. She wasn't sure her voice still worked.

Max wiped his mouth and offered Andy an apologetic look. 'Sorry I'm late. I know we need to talk tonight. What's going on? Did you hear from the doctor? Come here. Sit with me.'

Andy allowed him to lead her to the couch, where she mentally calculated the distance from the living room to the hallway powder room in case she vomited. Max began to stroke her hair, and Andy didn't have the energy to make him stop.

'Talk to me, sweetheart. I know this has been a really long week for you, what with the wedding and being sick and . . . the whole Katherine thing. Which I need to tell you again, because I don't think I was clear enough this morning. Nothing happened. Nothing. I've been doing a lot of thinking, and I want you to know that I'll do anything – anything on *earth* – to work through this with you and make you feel better.'

Andy tried to speak but couldn't. A baby. Her and Max's child. A Harrison. She wondered if Barbara would disapprove of her grandchild, too.

'What's happening in that head of yours? What did the doctor say? Are you on antibiotics? Should I go pick up a prescription? Tell me what's going on.'

She didn't know where she mustered the energy, but before she could think anything through, Andy forced herself to smile. *Pregnant. Pregnant. Pregnant.* The word kept reverberating through her mind, and it was all she could do not to scream it. How badly she wanted to tell Max! But no, she needed some time to think.

She reached over to pat Max's hand and said, 'Let's talk about everything another time, okay? I still don't feel great. I think I'm going to lie down for a while, okay?'

And before he could say another word, she was gone.

8

no david's bridal, no baby's breath, no dyeable shoes of any kind

In the week since Mr Kevin had called with the news that had changed her life, Andy hadn't told a soul. Not Emily, not Lily, not her mother or sister, and certainly not Max. She needed time to think, not a lot of unsolicited advice and opinions, and certainly not the excited congratulations and happiness that would surely follow. On one hand, it was thrilling. A baby! She'd never been one of those little girls who could spout off every detail of her dream wedding starting at her tenth birthday, from the material of the gown to the shade of the bridal bouquet, but she most definitely had always envisioned her future as a mother. Back then it had been two kids by thirty, a boy and a girl (the boy first, of course). As she got a little older and began to understand that two kids by thirty – hell, *any* kids by thirty – felt way different than she'd thought, Andy altered the equation. In her mid to late twenties, she'd spent quite a bit of time thinking about it, and she had come to the conclusion that two, maybe three kids, at some point between thirty and forty would be perfect. The first two, an older boy and a younger girl, would be two years apart, guaranteeing their closeness and friendship later in life despite their different genders. The third, a girl, would come three years later, long enough to give Andy a bit of a breather but not so long that Andy would be too old or the new baby wouldn't be the best of friends with her big sister and the apple of her big brother's eye.

What she'd failed to envision, of course, was the piece of this puzzle that kept it from being 100 percent fantastic news (never mind the nagging little detail that she'd been pregnant at her own wedding, and anyone with a kindergarten education could do the calculations): namely, she wasn't sure she could trust the father of her child, her baby's grandmother hated her, and she had been thirty seconds away from suggesting a break when she found out she was pregnant. Talk about a game-changer. All the perfectly logical rationalizations that had convinced her she should leave if he'd cheated with Katherine – they weren't bound to each other by anything more than a legal document, they didn't have any children whose lives they would be wrecking – had gone up in smoke with a plastic cup of pee and a lone phone call from a male nurse.

The lights dimmed and Andy's mother emerged from the kitchen carrying a cake, its entire surface alight with candles. They all began to sing.

'Had to make sure you had all forty-two on there, didn't you, Mom?' Jill asked.

'Forty-three. One for good luck,' Mrs Sachs said.

128

The boys and Kyle finished their screeching rendition of happy birthday and then insisted Jill make a wish.

'I wish my husband would get a vasectomy,' Jill murmured under her breath as she leaned over her cake.

Andy almost choked on her coffee. The sisters dissolved in laughter.

'What did you say, Mommy?'

'I wish for health and happiness for my children, my husband, my sister, and my mother,' Jill said, and blew out the candles.

'Hey, you okay?' Kyle asked, nudging Andy's arm with his elbow. Her brother-in-law offered her a slice of cake on a paper plate, but Jonah grabbed it out of his hand before Andy could reach for it.

'Jonah! Give that back to your aunt right now. You know the rules – ladies first!'

Jonah glanced up, fork poised over the icing, a desperate look on his face. Andy laughed. 'Leave him be, I'll get the next one.'

Jonah's fork immediately plunged into the icing. He shoveled a large bite into his mouth and gave Andy a chocolatey thank-you grin.

Kyle handed her another piece, one that didn't get intercepted, and looked right into her eyes. 'Seriously, Andy, is everything okay? You look a little . . . tired.'

'Tired.' The great euphemism for *You look like shit and I don't know why*. Yes, she supposed she was tired. For about a thousand different reasons.

She forced herself to smile. 'Just a tough time at work, what with the wedding and everything. Not really up for a work trip right now. At least it's Anguilla.'

Kyle looked at her questioningly.

'Harper Hallow and Mack? They're getting married at the

lauren weisberger

Viceroy in Anguilla this weekend and I'm covering it. Apparently he wanted to have the whole thing on some converted soundstage in Fresno – I think they met on tour there or something? – but she overruled him. Thankfully.'

He said, 'Quite the job perk. What, literally the entire universe wants to see that wedding, and you're *going* to it?'

'It's incredible, isn't it? She has the best job on earth,' Jill said, dabbing at something chunky and gross on her shoulder.

Although Andy still got instinctively anxious when anyone talked about her having 'the best job on earth,' even she had to agree it was pretty spectacular. She loved the feeling of creating something from scratch, of getting to shepherd new ideas from pitches to polished layouts to finished issues. It was tremendously satisfying to brainstorm one day and write the next, and then perhaps spend a few days editing followed by a week of issue planning. The variety kept things exciting and there were always new challenges. But most of all, she loved being her own boss.

When Emily had pitched Andy the idea of starting their own print wedding magazine together, Andy flatly refused. The girls were on their second annual spa weekend away together, a tradition Andy had proposed when she realized she'd scrimped and saved all year to afford a vacation but had no one to go with. Despite Emily's recent and (Andy thought) impulsive marriage to Miles, a reality TV producer five years older who'd just had a huge, surprise hit, Emily agreed to leave her new husband for four days of spa treatments, sun, and sand with Andy. They were sitting together in the warmest of three indoor hot tubs at the Mandarin Oriental's spa on the Mayan Riviera. Naked. They'd just completed a hot-stone massage in the romantic couples' room that overlooked the ocean and retired to the women's relaxation area, where Emily had tossed her towel on a

130

chaise longue and did a little happy dance before sipping her ginger tea, taking a nibble of a dried apricot, and then slowly – ever so slowly – lowering herself into the steaming hot water. It was all Andy could do not to stare enviously at Emily's textbook waist-to-hip ratio, her perfect breasts and toned legs and rounded bum without a teaspoon of cellulite. Andy herself was thin, granted, but her body didn't have any of the ripeness of Emily's – she was all straight lines and angles. She wondered why on earth she was so self-conscious in front of her best friend, but she couldn't help dropping her towel right at the edge of the tub and submerging herself in three seconds flat. As Emily chatted animatedly, Andy focused on keeping her shoulders below the swirling eddies of water, feeling exposed despite being entirely covered.

'What do you mean "no"? You haven't even heard my idea yet.' Emily whined in the charmingly petulant way that Andy knew meant she wasn't really upset.

'I don't have to hear your idea. I'm done with print. So is the rest of the world. Believe it or not, I actually *like* my job.' At the time Andy had a sane boss, was writing four days a week for *Happily Ever After*, and had the germ of an idea for a novel percolating. With her clips and flexible hours, she was sure she could start writing enough weekly to get an agent. She was on her way . . . possibly to a hand-to-mouth existence salary-wise, but still.

'Yes, but it's just a *job*! What I'm talking about is a *career*. It's entrepreneurship. We'll launch it together and it will be our baby. You can't tell me you're not ready for something more than top-ten updo lists! *Happily Ever After* is a lovely little website with some occasional cute content and a whole lot of trite filler shit. You know it and I know it.'

'Thanks.'

Emily hit the water with her hand. 'Oh, don't be so sensitive, Andy. You're being underutilized there. You're so much more talented than that. I want you to write full-length cover stories, work with brilliant photographers who will execute your vision, assign your ideas to other writers and edit them, mentor them, oversee them. You'll travel to far-flung destinations and interview celebrities, and of course we'll accept swag and free trips and every imaginable discount because we won't claim to be even remotely impartial. How *fun* does that sound?'

Andy jutted out her lower lip. 'Not terrible.'

'You can say that again. Very not terrible. I'll be the public face of the magazine and do all the stuff you would hate. I'll throw the parties and court the advertisers and do all the hiring and firing. I'll find the office space and buy all the equipment and supplies. We'll find really terrific people who can oversee a lot of these things so we can focus on making it the premier wedding magazine in the country. Did I mention health insurance? And enough of a salary to actually eat out on your own dime? Can you even imagine it?'

Andy felt herself relax into the hot tub, her shoulders finally beginning to unknot. She had to admit she *could* imagine it. It sounded pretty freaking amazing, actually. But she couldn't help wondering what qualified either of them to launch and run a real live magazine. A few combined years of low-level assistant and associate editor work together with an additional few years writing for a website? How would their wedding magazine be any different from the dozens of other frothy confections that wrote breathlessly of filmy veils and form-fitting dresses? And how, exactly, were they going to pay for all this? Office space in Manhattan? Andy's studio barely fit the console table that doubled as her desk, and although the brownstone duplex Emily shared with Miles was larger and way more posh, there was hardly room for a light box, much less an *art department*. It sounded fantastic, but could it actually work?

Emily threw her head back in delight, drenching her piled-on, glamorous bun. 'Andy, you're much too logical for your own good. No effing fun, I tell you. Leave everything to me – I've got it all covered.'

'Oh, well that makes for terrific business plan. When we're applying for bank loans and they ask what we need the money for, I can just tell them that Emily's got it all covered.'

'I do! Miles has a dozen friends, maybe more, all New York bankers or Hollywood types, who are always looking to invest in this kind of thing. They just love throwing extra cash at creative start-ups, especially when it's something media or publishing related. They can't help it – they automatically think sex, models, and glamour. And we will feel very free to encourage that type of thinking. Because the way I see it, our magazine is going to be different from every other wedding rag out there.'

Andy was still trying to process the information about their dozen potential investors and how much money they were willing to throw around, but this part about how their magazine would distinguish itself sounded like even more of a fantasy. 'Really? Because I've become pretty familiar with the whole wedding universe, and trust me, it's not easy to come up with fresh material all the time. Not a whole lot changes from year to year.'

'Irrelevant!' Emily scoffed. The bubbles began to slow. Emily bounded out of the tub, her perfect skin slicked with water. Settling back on her bench opposite Andy, she sipped her tea and said, 'Ours is going to be überstylish. Upscale. The luxe version of weddings. The phrase "sample sale" will never appear in our pages. Nor will "affordable honeymoons," "smart ways to save money," or "beautiful bouquets for less." There will be no articles on where to find good deals . . . on anything. No David's Bridal, no baby's breath, no dyeable shoes of any kind.'

'You do realize we're in the midst of a worldwide recession, don't you?'

'Which is exactly why our readers will want something aspirational! You think ninety-nine percent of the people who read *Runway* can afford so much as a single pair of stockings featured in the issue? Of course not,' Emily said.

Despite her pragmatic streak, Andy could feel herself getting excited. 'That's true,' she said. '*Runway* isn't their catalog – it's their inspiration. It gives smart, style-savvy women who don't necessarily have the funds to dress in couture anything a muse when designing their own style, when it comes time to choose things they *can* afford. It would make sense that all those women who are inspired by the out-of-reach looks in *Runway* would be just as inspired by the out-of-reach weddings we'd feature in *The Plunge*.'

Emily beamed. '*The Plunge*?'

'Don't you love it? "Take the plunge," "plunging necklines" . . . it's simple, dramatic, effortless. It's perfect.'

'I do. I freaking love it. *The Plunge*. You're brilliant, that's exactly what we're calling it!' At this point Emily stood up and actually did a little naked jig. 'I knew you'd get it. Why don't you start thinking of where you want to go for our inaugural issue. Maybe Sydney? Or Maui? Provence? Buenos Aires? Trust me, this is going to be fabulous.'

Emily, impulsive, crazy Emily, had been right. Of course there had been roadblocks and obstacles along the way (the raw loft space that wasn't ready until six months after the promised date; more difficulty securing a printer than either of them had anticipated; sifting through the no fewer than *twenty-five hundred* résumés they'd received after posting eight separate positions), but for the most part, the path from brainstorming to execution had been relatively smooth, thanks almost exclusively to Emily's blind faith and ambition and Miles's well-connected and well-financed friends – Max being the biggest contributor of the whole lot, with an $18\frac{1}{3}$ percent stake in the company. A group of five other investors shared 15 percent, which left Andy and Emily with a third each. They were the clear owners with $66\frac{2}{3}$ percent between them; they could outvote anyone else and ensure that they had the ultimate say over all major decisions concerning the magazine.

The Plunge was edited with a nod to high fashion and refinement: one of-a-kind designer dresses; diamond jewelry worthy of being passed down through the generations; guides on how to select the most elegant silver servers, rent a private island for your honeymoon, curate unique and finely crafted registry lists. It started out small, a quarterly with only forty pages or so an issue, but within two years Andy and Emily were publishing seven times a year (every other month with a June special issue) and had more subscribers and newsstand buyers than they'd projected at the outset.

As Emily had predicted, very few of their readers could afford the lifestyle proposed by *The Plunge*, but they were all savvy and stylish and luxury-aware enough to use the gorgeous photos and detailed articles as inspirations for their own weddings. The first few months of the magazine's existence hadn't been quite as splashy. They covered any weddings with the least hint of glamour or sexiness that they had access to: one of Emily's colleagues at *Bazaar* who married a hedge fund guy at a yacht club; a friend of Emily's from college whose fiancé had directed a dozen famous action flicks; Emily's celebrity dermatologist, who agreed to have her wedding to a well-known on-air news personality covered so long as *The Plunge* also mentioned her new Restylane-like filler by name. The brides and grooms may not have been household names, but the weddings were always lavish and the resulting photographs lent the magazine a hint of prestige it couldn't have attained through registry suggestion lists and ring guides alone.

Ironically it was Andy's connection who got them the couple that launched *The Plunge* from semiobscurity into a national curiosity. Max was invited to the wedding of a socialite he'd grown up with, a beautiful girl with a trillionaire Venezuelan father who was engaged to marry the son of a Mexican 'businessman,' nod-nod, wink-wink. It had only taken a single call from Max and the promise that the bride could have final say over which photos were used. The resulting feature, with all its gorgeous, insider photographs of compounds in Monterrey and stunning Latina women dripping in diamonds, had gotten a lot of attention at all the gossip and entertainment sites online, and even a mention in a *60 Minutes* story about the FBI, the Mexican 'businessman,' and his security team's arsenal of automatic weapons, which made the Navy Seals look underprovisioned.

From there it had been easy to book weddings. Both Andy and Emily had copies of Miranda's contacts' numbers from *Runway*, and they weren't shy about using them. They developed a routine as finely choreographed as a ballet. Both girls would scour websites, blogs, and gossip magazines for news of engagements, give it a few weeks for all the excitement to die down, and then call either the star directly or their publicist, depending on how close either's relationship was with *Runway* or Miranda. At that point they would blatantly drop Miranda's name, mention that they'd collectively worked under her for *years* (not a lie), and explain (in not too much detail) how they'd 'branched out' to a high-end wedding magazine. They would follow up each phone call with a FedExed copy of the Mexican wedding issue, wait exactly one week, and then call once more. So far, seven out of eight of the celebrities they'd contacted had agreed to have *The Plunge* cover their wedding for a future issue, so long as they were still free to sell pictures to a weekly in the interim. Andy and Emily never argued with this provision; their photography, the in-depth interviews they conducted with their couples, and the homey, accessible way Andy wrote the articles set them worlds apart from the grocery aisle competition. Plus each issue that featured a famous actress, model, musician, artist, or socialite made it easier to persuade the next celebrity to sign on, usually without a lot of the *Runway* name-dropping. The formula had been working beautifully for years now, and they were running with it. These real-life celebrity weddings had become not just the highlight of each issue but also the magazine's defining feature and selling point.

Sometimes she could still barely believe it. Even now, flipping through the just-published November issue with Drew Barrymore and Will Kopelman on the cover, it was hard to comprehend that the entire magazine existed because of Emily's vision a few years earlier and all their mutual brainstorming and ideas and hard work and mistakes since then. Andy had gone into it hesitantly, yes, but the magazine was her love, her baby. They had built something from scratch that they could be proud of, and every day she was grateful to Emily – for the magazine, and for its happy dividend, her introduction to Max.

'Do you think Madonna will be there?' her mother asked, bringing her paper cake plate to join Andy, Kyle, and Jill at the table. 'Don't she and Harper go to the same Kabbalah studio or something?'

Jill and Andy turned to stare at their mother.

'What? I can't read a copy of *People* in the dentist's office?' she asked, picking at her cake. Since she and Andy's father had gotten divorced, Andy's mother had grown increasingly careful about what she ate.

'I actually wondered that myself,' Andy said. 'I don't think so because she's in the South Pacific for something right now. But the publicist has confirmed that Demi will be there. Not as fun now that she's sans Ashton, but interesting nonetheless.'

'Personally, I would like confirmation that nothing on Demi Moore's body is real,' Mrs Sachs said. 'That would make me feel better.'

'You and me both,' Andy said, shoveling in the last bite of cake. It was all she could do not to scoop her entire hand into the cake toddler-style and shovel it into her mouth. She'd choose nauseated over famished any day.

'Okay, crew, fun's over. Jake and Jonah, please bring your plates to the kitchen and kiss everyone good night. Daddy's going to fill the tub now and give you both your bath while I give Jared his bottle,' Jill announced, looking meaningfully at Kyle. 'Then because it's my birthday and I get to do whatever I want, I'm going directly to sleep and Daddy is going to be your point person tonight should anything come up, okay?' She hefted Jared onto her hip and kissed his cheek. He swatted at her face. 'Any bad dreams, "I'm thirsty"s, "I'm cold"s, "I want a hug"s, you wake up Daddy tonight, okay, my loves?' Both boys nodded solemnly and Jared squealed and clapped his hands.

Jill and Kyle corralled all three boys, thanked Andy's mom for the cake, kissed everyone good night, and disappeared upstairs. A moment later Andy heard the bathtub begin to run.

Mrs Sachs disappeared into the kitchen for a moment and came out with two mugs of decaf English Breakfast tea, still steeping but already fixed with milk and Splenda. She pushed one across the table toward Andy.

'I heard Kyle ask you earlier if everything is okay . . .' Andy's mother concentrated on wrapping her tea bag around a spoon.

Andy opened her mouth to say something and quickly closed it again. She wasn't one of those girls who called home three times a day from college or would recount the intimate details of her romantic relationships to her parents, but it was harder than she thought – damn near impossible – not to tell her own mother that she was expecting a child. She knew she should tell her, *wanted* to tell her. It felt totally unnatural that besides her doctor and the lab techs, she and Mr Kevin were the only two people on the planet who knew that she was pregnant, but she still couldn't bring herself to say the words. It didn't feel real, and as conflicted as she was over everything with Max, it certainly didn't seem right to tell anyone, even her own mother, before she told him.

'Everything's fine,' she said, not meeting her mother's gaze. 'I'm just tired.'

Mrs Sachs nodded, although it was clear she knew Andy was withholding something. 'What time is your flight tomorrow?'

'Eleven, out of JFK. I'm getting picked up here at seven.'

'Well, at least you'll have a couple days somewhere warm. I know you don't really get to relax when you're covering a wedding, but maybe you'll find an hour or two to sit outside?'

'Yeah, I hope so.' She briefly considered telling her mother about the call from Elias-Clark but knew a huge conversation would ensue. Better she got some rest than wind herself up for a night of Miranda nightmares.

'How's Max? Is he upset you're headed out so soon after your wedding?'

Andy shrugged. 'He's fine. He's going to the Jets game on Sunday with the guys, so he probably won't even notice I'm gone.'

Mrs Sachs was quiet at this, and Andy wondered if she'd gone too far. Her mom had always liked Max and loved seeing Andy happy, but she didn't pretend to understand the Harrison family wealth and what she saw as their need to be constantly social.

'I ran into Roberta Fineman last week at that federation luncheon I went to in the city, did I tell you that?'

Andy tried to feign indifference. 'No, you didn't mention it. How is she?'

'Oh, she's doing really well. She's been dating someone for years now; I think it's serious. I heard he's a dentist, a widower, and that they'll probably get married.'

'Mmm. Did she mention Alex at all?'

She hated herself for asking, but she couldn't help herself. Even after more than eight years apart, with only a single run-in since then, it still shocked Andy how little she knew about Alex and his current life. Google failed to provide anything but the basic biographical information she already knew and a lone article three years back that quoted Alex raving about the live music scene in Burlington. Andy could see that he'd gone to grad school at UVM and from what she could tell, he still lived in Vermont. He'd mentioned a girlfriend, a fellow skier, when they'd run into each other but hadn't given many more details. He wasn't on Facebook, which didn't surprise Andy. Lily either didn't know much more or chose not to tell her – probably the former, since she knew Lily and Alex only mailed each other holiday cards and, once, when he was considering matriculating there, he had e-mailed about her experience at UC Boulder.

'She did, yes. He's finished his master's and he and his girlfriend are moving back to New York. Or maybe they already did? She has a creative profession, I can't remember what exactly, but she has a good opportunity in the city, so I guess Alex will be looking for something there.'

Interesting. Alex and the creative, pretty skier were still together, three years later. Even more interesting: he was moving back to the city.

'Yeah, he told me about his girlfriend when I ran into him at Whole Foods. My god, that must have been, what? I had just started dating Max . . . three years ago. I guess it's serious with them.'

She said this last part wanting her mother to deny it, rationalize it, come up with some ridiculous analysis or opinion that of course Alex wasn't serious about the girl, but Mrs Sachs merely shook her head and said, 'Yes, Roberta hopes they'll be engaged by the end of the year. Of course, she's only in her midtwenties, so I don't think there's any rush. But I'm sure Roberta is as eager for grandchildren as I am.'

'You have grandchildren. Three, actually. Treasures, each of them.'

Andy's mom laughed. 'They're a handful, aren't they? I wouldn't wish three boys on anyone.' She took a sip of her tea. 'I don't remember you bumping into Alex. Did I know about it?'

'I was still working at *Happily Ever After* and I had just met Max. You were on that riverboat cruise with your book club. I remember because I wrote you about it and your reply was from some funky keyboard that replaced every *y* with a *z*.'

'Your memory never ceases to amaze me.'

'Alex was in the city for the summer doing some sort of educational internship through Columbia. I still don't know why he was at Whole Foods that day, but of course Max and I had just gone for a run and stopped in to pick up some water. I looked like hell, and Alex was dressed for an interview. The three of us got coffee for ten minutes upstairs, which was every bit as awkward as you'd think. He mentioned then he was dating a master's student, but that it wasn't serious.'

Andy omitted the part of the meeting where her heart was racing through the entire too-short latte, how she laughed a little too hard and nodded a little too vigorously every time Alex cracked a joke or made an observation. She didn't tell her mother how she wondered if he was excited to see his girlfriend later that night, if he loved her, if he thought of this new girl as the one person who truly understood him. Andy didn't mention how desperately she hoped he'd follow up their accidental meeting with a phone call or e-mail, and how she'd been hurt – despite her excitement over her new relationship with Max – when she didn't hear from him. How she had cried that night in the shower remembering all the years they'd spent together, wondering how they'd become such strangers, before yelling at herself to put Alex out of her mind once and for all and concentrate on her feelings for Max. Handsome, sexy, funny, charming, *supportive* Max. She didn't say any of it, but something told her her mother understood.

Andy helped her mother clean up the dishes and put away the cake. Mrs Sachs provided a highly detailed running commentary on every interaction she had during Andy and Max's wedding, opinions on what people wore, how much they drank, whether or not they appeared to be having a good time, and how it compared to all the weddings of her friends' children she'd attended in the past few years (superior on all counts, of course). She was careful not to mention the Harrisons either way. Jill reappeared briefly to pour two cups and one bottle of milk, and Andy felt like she was betraying both her mother and sister by not telling them the news. Instead, she wished Jill a happy birthday, kissed them both good night, and retreated to her childhood bedroom, the one farthest from the stairs on the second floor.

Plans were under way to update Andy's bedroom now that she was all grown up – she'd helped her mother choose a queen bed with a leather headboard, plus a set of those hotel-style sheets and a duvet, crisp white with a straight line of espresso stitching – but nothing was ready yet. Her white shag carpet, colored gray from years of illegally wearing her shoes inside, and her purple-and-white-flowered quilt felt a thousand years old. A half-dozen bulletin boards were covered with remnants of her high school years: the tennis schedule for the fall 1997 season, assorted magazine tear-outs of Matt Damon and Marky Mark, a *Titanic* movie poster, a phone list for the yearbook staff, a shriveled stem from some dance's corsage with its flower long dropped, a postcard from Jill's postcollege trip to Cambodia, a pay stub from the TCBY she worked at the summer after graduation, and pictures, so many pictures. And almost every one of them featured Lily, smiling right alongside Andy, whether the girls were in taffeta dresses for prom, jeans for volunteering together at Avon's no-kill shelter, or matching tracksuits for the single season they went out for the cross-country team. Andy removed a pushpin and pulled one of the pictures

lauren weisberger

from the board: she and Lily at the state fair with a group of friends, walking off the Gravitron, each looking greener than the next. She remembered rushing into the bushes to puke mere moments after that shot was snapped and trying to convince her parents for the next three days that her reflexive vomiting was only the result of too many go-rounds on that evil ride and not a rebellious act of teenage drinking (although there was that, too, of course).

She flopped on her twin-size bed, now slightly sagging in the center from so many years of use, and dialed Lily's phone number. It would be ten to nine in Colorado, and Lily would probably have just put Bear down for the night. She answered on the second ring.

'Hey, beautiful! How's life as a newlywed?'

'I'm pregnant,' Andy said before she could talk herself out of it.

There were three, maybe five seconds of silence before Lily said, 'Andy? Is that you?'

'It's me. I'm pregnant.'

'Oh my god. Congratulations! You people don't waste much time, do you? Wait, that would be impossible . . .'

Andy held her breath as Lily did the math. She knew the entire world would do the exact same thing and that it would drive her crazy, but Lily was different. It was such a relief to tell someone. 'Yeah, totally impossible. They think it's not a "new" pregnancy, whatever that means, and obviously we haven't even been married two weeks. I'm scheduled for an ultrasound next week. I'm freaking out . . .'

'Don't freak out! It's scary, I know, I remember that part. But it's so wonderful, Andy. Are you going to find out what you're having?'

There it was: the quintessential normal question to ask a newly pregnant friend. It made Andy choke up with its innocence, and for a moment she was doubly upset to realize that this conversation with her oldest friend in the world couldn't be solely a celebration. They wouldn't get a chance to debate whether Andy was having a boy or girl, or list favorite names, or discuss the pros and cons of one ridiculously expensive stroller versus another one. There were other things to say.

'How excited is Max? I can't even imagine! He's been talking about babies since the day you met.'

'I haven't told him.' Andy said this so quietly she wasn't sure Lily heard her.

'You haven't *told* him?'

'Things are weird between us. I found a letter from Barbara the day of our wedding, and I can't stop thinking about it,' Andy said.

'Weird how, exactly? Weird enough to make you not tell your husband you're carrying his baby?'

Once she started talking, she couldn't stop. She told Lily everything, absolutely everything, including some of the details she hadn't even admitted to Emily. How she debated asking for some time apart to think and was five seconds away from telling Max when she got the call from Mr Kevin. How she didn't want to touch him. Andy even managed to articulate, for the very first time, how she couldn't stop wondering if Max was telling her the entire truth about Katherine.

'So . . . there you have it. Pretty picture, isn't it?' Andy pulled the elastic out of her ponytail and shook her hair. She laid her cheek against her pink floral pillow and inhaled: it was probably just the same Tide or Bounce or whatever, but it smelled like her childhood, and she didn't ever want it to change.

'I don't even know what to say. Do you want me to come

there? I can leave Bear with Bodhi, probably, and be on a plane tomorrow . . .'

'Thanks, Lil, but I'm headed to Anguilla for work in the morning. And you were just here. But I appreciate it.'

'You poor thing! And screw Barbara! What a witch. But god, you must feel so vulnerable! I distinctly remember being pregnant with Bear and having these fears, terrors really, that Bodhi was going to leave me stranded, pregnant, alone. I don't know what it is, but there's something about expecting a baby that puts you in this . . . this *mind-set*. I can't explain it.'

'No, you just did, and I know exactly what you mean. A week ago I was considering a time-out to think things through. Give us a chance to be honest with each other and really figure things out. It wasn't going to be easy, but I was doing it. Now? There's a *baby*! Max's baby. And I want to be upset with him, but I already love his baby.'

'Oh, Andy. I know. It's just the beginning.'

Andy sniffed. She hadn't even realized she'd been crying.

'You think you love that baby now? Just wait.'

'I . . . I just thought it would be different.'

Lily was quiet for a moment. Andy knew her friend well enough to know that Lily was debating bringing up her own experience, as worried as she probably was about turning the focus back to her. But then she said, 'I know, sweetie. You have this vision that you're going to wake up one day next to your adoring husband of two years, and you're going to stroll into the bathroom together to look at the stick you just peed on, and you're both going to collapse back onto the bed together in joy and excitement, hugging and laughing and thrilled. And he'll come to every appointment with you and rub your feet and buy you pickles and ice cream. Well, you know how often that happens? Like, never. But I'm here to tell you that it doesn't make it any less wonderful.'

Andy thought of the day, almost four years earlier, when Lily called and announced she was pregnant. She'd been living in Boulder for two years already and had decided to slow down on her PhD path in order to teach more. The girls didn't speak that often, but when they did, Andy was always envious of how happy Lily sounded. At first Andy thought Lily's new yoga obsession was like her own long list of short-lived interests, all of which she'd embarked on passionately and discarded quickly: tennis, pottery, spinning, cooking. When Lily announced she'd be punching class cards in exchange for a small stipend and discounted classes, Andy shook her head knowingly. So Lily. When she'd announced she'd signed up for the five-hundred-hour teacher-training course, Andy laughed to herself. But then, when she'd completed it in record time and spent the following four months at an ashram in Kodaikanal, India, taking courses like 'Yoga for Emotional Imbalances' and 'Yoga for a Strong Heart' under world-famous swamis with unpronounceable names, Andy began to wonder. Soon after her return to the States, Lily began dating the owner and head teacher of her yoga school, a converted Buddhist named Bodhi, originally Brian, from Northern California, and a year after that, Lily called to give Andy the big news: she and Bodhi were expecting a baby in six months. Andy could barely believe it. A *baby*? With *Bodhi*? She'd met him once when Lily brought him to Connecticut, and she'd had a hard time getting past his thick dreadlocks and even thicker muscles and his penchant for sipping green tea from a thermos, hot or cold depending on the season, every minute of every day. He seemed like a nice enough guy, and he was clearly in love with Lily, but none of it gelled for Andy. She hadn't asked many questions, but Lily knew her well enough and said, 'This wasn't an accident, Andy. Bodhi and I are committed to being lifelong partners, and we don't need some legal whatnot to make it official. I love him, and we want children together.'

She guiltily harbored doubts all through Lily's pregnancy, wondering what her friend was thinking, why exactly she'd dived off the deep end. But from the moment she laid eyes on Lily nursing her infant son a couple weeks after his birth, Andy knew Lily was doing exactly the right thing for herself, her partner, and her son. There had been distance between them for a little – Andy couldn't begin to understand everything Lily was feeling in her new role as mother and (sort of) wife – but she was grateful her friend had created this new life for herself. And now she was grateful that Lily knew exactly what she meant.

'Foot rubs and ice cream? Hell, I'd settle for just a few weeks of no chlamydia scares.'

'I'm glad you can laugh about it,' Lily said, and Andy could hear the relief in her voice. 'I know this is an incredibly hard time, but I'm still allowed to be happy for you, aren't I? You're having a baby!'

'I know. I wouldn't believe it myself if it weren't for the crushing exhaustion and constant nausea.'

'I thought I had cancer before I found out,' Lily confessed. 'I literally could not keep my eyes open for longer than a three-hour period. I couldn't think of another explanation.'

Andy was quiet, processing how wonderful and strange it was to be talking about her pregnancy with her oldest friend on earth, and she must have drifted off, because Lily said, 'Andy? You there? Did you just fall asleep?'

'Sorry,' she mumbled, wiping a touch of drool from the corner of her mouth.

'I'll let you go,' Lily said.

Andy smiled. 'I miss you, Lil.'

'I'm here for you, sweetie. Call *anytime*. And give yourself permission in Anguilla to get a little sun and drink a virgin piña and forget about everything for a day, okay? Can you promise me that?'

'I'll try.' They exchanged a few more good-byes, and Andy told herself not to feel guilty for failing to ask after Bear or Bodhi. If there was ever a time to be a little self-centered, Andy figured, it was then. She yanked off her jeans, which were already starting to feel uncomfortably snug, and pulled her sweater over her head. Teeth brushing, face washing, flossing . . . it could all wait, she thought as she returned her head to her cool floral pillow and pulled her girlhood quilt up to her chin. Everything would look better in the morning.

9

virgin piñas all around

Eleven A.M. flight. A three-hour delay with an unplanned stop in Puerto Rico. A 'ferry' boat ride from Saint Martin that felt like riding a Jet Ski through a hurricane. And finally a long wait at an un-air-conditioned customs gate followed by a ride on dusty, bumpy local roads. Traveling was tough when you weren't knocked up, but pregnant it was almost intolerable.

The hotel made it all worthwhile, although *hotel* didn't come close to accurately describing the place. It was a wonderland. A charming, villagelike wonderland, with little individual thatched-roof villas tucked into lush greenery around a crescent-shaped beach. The 'lobby,' an open-air pavilion with marble floors and Balinese-style wood carved furniture, was filled with elaborate birdcages and singing tropical birds and looked on an ocean so clear and blue Andy

150

momentarily thought she was hallucinating. When she'd stepped onto her own suite's private balcony, Andy had spotted a monkey swinging in the tree above her.

Now she pushed herself to sit on the bed and surveyed her surroundings. Her king platform bed was draped with all-white linens, and the mattress was magically firm and plushly soft at the same time. There was a coconut-wood table and chairs near the front door and a sectional sofa with glass coffee table and a Bose stereo system to the left of the bed. The bamboo-frame thatched roof, in addition to walls of sliding glass that opened completely on three sides, made it feel like the suite was outdoors. The plunge pool hung precipitously over the balcony, its green water blending into its surroundings, and its two teak chaise longue chairs with striped cushions and a coordinating umbrella created the chicest private sun lounge she'd ever seen. White marble covered nearly every surface in the cavernous bathroom, including the double vanities and the glass-enclosed rain-forest shower that was almost as large as the second bedroom in her New York apartment. Towels so fluffy and white they looked like spun sugar hung from heated bars; fresh frangipani flowers adorned the dressing area; softly scented shampoo and conditioner sat in small clay bottles labeled with miniature rope signs around their necks. At the far end of the bathroom, surrounded by palm trees and lush vegetation, rested a massive soaking tub. It was surrounded on three sides by eight-foot-high walls, but it was completely open to the outside air, and miraculously, it was already filled with warm, fragrant water. A small clay pot of bath salts rested on its edge, subtle music wafted from somewhere, and the scent of greenness, of plants and trees and soil, combined with heat from the afternoon sun, filled the outdoor room.

She wriggled out of her leggings, and her T-shirt hit the ground before Andy was even fully awake. She sank into the fragrant water, just warm enough in the humid, outdoor air, and closed her eyes. Automatically, her hands ran over her belly, prodding it, still unable to believe there was a tiny life growing inside her. Although she hadn't let herself think about it until right now, she suddenly realized she wanted a son. Why, she couldn't say. Maybe it was seeing both her sister and Lily with boys, the only small children she knew well and loved. Or maybe it was the idea of a mama's boy, a sweet little thing with floppy long hair and a security blanket, who got dressed up in miniature blue blazers and neckties and curled into her lap. She wasn't sure, but Max had long ago announced he was certain they would only ever have girl babies. He claimed he couldn't wait to teach their daughters all about tennis and football and golf, to dress them in miniature uniforms and coach their T-ball team. He predicted blond babies, despite the fact that neither of them was blond, and that they'd love their daddy more than any man in the whole world. It was one of the things that drew Andy to him – the reputed playboy was a softie at heart, a man who wanted hearth and home more than any she'd met and was unafraid to admit it. Andy hadn't known him to be any other way, but his sister had immediately remarked about how meeting Andy had changed Max into the man he was always meant to be. He was going to die of happiness when she told him the news.

Somewhere a room phone rang, and Andy looked around in a panic before spotting an extension discreetly mounted on the wall near the tub.

'Hello?'

'Mrs Harrison? Yes, hello, this is Ronald, from the concierge desk? Ms Hallow asked me to let you know that the rehearsal dinner will begin in an hour on the beach. May I send someone to escort you?'

'Yes, thank you. I will be ready then.'

She turned on the hot water and stuck her feet directly under the stream. Her entire body felt exhausted, but her mind was awake and racing. In one hour she'd be attending the rehearsal dinner of music's most powerful couple. Harper Hallow had racked up no fewer than twenty-two Grammys over the course of her career – a tie with U2 and Stevie Wonder – although she'd been nominated for nearly a dozen more; her intended, a rapper born Clarence Dexter who now went by the one-word name Mack, had made hundreds of millions parlaying his musical career into a lucrative shoe and clothing line. Their wedding would make them among the richest, most famous couples in the world.

After a few more minutes of soaking, Andy forced herself to climb out of the luxurious tub and made a beeline for the rain-forest shower, where she happily rinsed and shaved her legs using the thoughtfully provided teak bench. She pulled on a pair of white linen pants, a silky turquoise and orange top, and flat silver sandals, thinking Emily would be proud. As she was packing her notebook and phone into the hotel-provided straw tote bag, the villa's doorbell rang. A young, shy Anguillan boy wearing a crisp short-sleeved shirt greeted her quietly and motioned for Andy to follow him.

They walked for three minutes and arrived at a pavilion that housed a casual poolside bar. The sun was just beginning to set over the water; the air was cooler now, and a sliver of moon was visible. Hundreds of people milled about, holding cocktails in coconut shells and bottles of Caribbean beer. A twelve-piece reggae band played island tunes and a group of children, all dressed in designer everything, giggled and danced in front of them. Andy surveyed the scene but didn't immediately spot either Harper or Mack.

Her phone rang just as she accepted a glass of sparkling water from a uniformed waiter.

Andy walked toward the side of the tent and pulled the phone from her bag. 'Em? Hey. Can you hear me?'

'Where are you exactly? You know the rehearsal dinner started twenty minutes ago, right?'

Emily's voice was so loud that Andy had to hold the phone away from her ear. 'I'm standing right in the middle of it, chatting up the most charming people. There's nothing to worry about.'

'Because you know we need some details to person-alize everything and all the good, gossipy toasts happen tonight . . .'

'That's why I'm here, notebook in hand . . .' Andy said as she glanced at her tiny clutch and realized she'd forgotten so much as a pen. If this is what it was like to be in the first trimester, what was going to happen six months down the road?

'What's Harper wearing?' Emily asked.

'Em? I can barely hear you. It's so windy here.' Andy blew into the phone for effect.

'Uh-huh. Hang up and send me a picture. I'm dying to see what everything looks like.'

Andy blew some more. 'Will do! Gotta run.' She clicked her phone off and returned to the party. Tiki torches surrounded the entire area where guests were choosing items off a massive raw bar in the center of the open-air tent. Andy was just about to speak a few notes into her phone's recorder when a woman wearing a headset and carrying an overflowing leather folio stepped directly into her path.

'You must be Andrea Sachs,' the woman said, looking relieved.

'And you must be Harper's publicist . . .'

'Yes, I'm Annabelle.' She grabbed Andy's arm and pulled her toward the tables in the sand. 'There are flip-flops in that basket if you'd rather wear those. There's the raw bar and passed hors d'oeuvres for cocktail hour, and of course the waiters can get you anything you'd like to drink. Mack had all the food and wine flown in especially for the weekend, so please do try to sample everything. I can provide a menu, too, if you need it for fact-checking.'

Andy nodded. Publicists to the stars tended to be tightly wound with a talking speed three times faster than that of average people, but they certainly made her job easier.

'We'll be serving dinner soon, followed by thirty minutes of toasts, emceed by Mack's agent, who's also a dear friend, which will be followed by dessert and after-dinner drinks. Cars will be waiting after the festivities to bring the young people to the island's best discotheque and home again. Naturally, Harper will retire to her suite immediately after dessert, but you're more than welcome to join the after-party if you'd like.'

'Discotheque? Oh, I think I'll probably just—'

'Okay, sounds good,' the woman said, continuing to pull Andy along. They arrived at a round table of eight with a dramatic bird-of-paradise centerpiece and seven chattering, attractive guests. 'Here we are. Everyone, this is Andrea Sachs from *The Plunge* magazine. *The Plunge* will be covering the festivities, so please show her a good time.'

Andy could feel her face redden as everyone turned to look at her. And then her stomach did a little flip-flop as she heard a familiar voice, one that transported her back ten years in an instant.

'Well, well, who do we have here?' the voice sang, sounding both amused and predatory. 'What an *interesting* little surprise!'

Nigel beamed back at her, his too-perfect teeth almost glowing in the night.

Andy tried to say something, but her mouth was too dry to talk.

Annabelle laughed. 'Oh, that's right, I almost forgot you two used to work together. How perfect!' she trilled, motioning for Andy to take a seat. 'It's like a little *Runway* reunion!'

It was only then that she noticed that Jessica, the event planner during Andy's tenure at *Runway*, and Serena, one of the junior editors, flanked Nigel on either side. Both managed to look younger, thinner, and all around more confidently gorgeous than they had a decade before, not that she should have been surprised . . . it was classic *Runway*.

'Well, aren't I the luckiest girl in the world!' Nigel trilled. 'Andrea Sachs, come sit right here by me.'

He was wearing a cross between a robe and a dress, all white, over pants that could possibly have been skinny jeans but more closely resembled leggings. A fringed silk scarf hung from his neck all the way down to his knees and it featured a none-too-subtle Louis Vuitton logo print the entire length. Despite the tropical heat, the ensemble was topped off with a mink Cossack hat and purple velvet slippers.

Andy had no choice but to take a seat next to Nigel. He grinned widely but not nicely. 'I won't even mention how you abandoned me! I took you under my wing and *this*' – he pulled on the fabric of Andy's tunic and scrunched his face up in distaste – 'is how you repay me? By leaving? And without so much as a good-bye?'

After the Paris debacle, Andy hadn't returned to the

Runway offices to collect as much as a pencil, but she'd written a long, appreciative letter to Nigel, apologizing for disrespecting Miranda and thanking him for mentoring her. No response. In the following months Andy had e-mailed him a copy of the letter, sent a couple other 'How are you, I miss you!' notes, and even posted on Nigel's style blog. Nada. Meanwhile, Emily claimed she'd fled to his office within seconds of being fired, only to be met with a closed door and an uncooperative assistant. She, too, had e-mailed him and, once, invited him to a private dinner party honoring Marc Jacobs that *Harper's Bazaar* was hosting but had never received a response.

Andy cleared her throat. 'I'm so sorry. I really did try to get—'

'Please!' Nigel screeched, waving his hand. 'Let's not talk shop at a party. Girls, you remember Andrea Sachs, I'm sure?'

Serena and Jessica. Neither nodded nor offered so much as a halfhearted smile. Jessica appraised Andy's outfit with icy disapproval while Serena took a sip of her wine and stared at Andy over the top of her glass. Andy listened to Nigel prattle on about Harper's outfit and Mack's sport coat. Andy sipped her Pellegrino and listened. He was crazy, no doubt about it, but a small part of the old Andy loved him. Eventually Nigel gave Andy a knowing look and turned to speak with the model seated to his left; Serena and Jessica began working the room, and Andy knew she should get up to mingle. It had been years since she'd felt so socially awkward. Ten years to be exact. She nibbled some corn bread and sipped her lemon water, all the while rubbing her belly under the table. Was it the old *Runway* vibe that was making her so queasy or the fact – the one she kept trying to forget – that she was unexpectedly pregnant and not even her husband knew the truth?

lauren weisberger

The toasts began. Harper's best friend, a hairdresser who was famous not just for her styling skills but also for her transgender advocacy work, gave a touchingly sweet and tad-too-boring tribute to the happy couple. She was quickly followed by one of Mack's brothers, a professional basketball player who made numerous references to Mack and Magic Johnson, not one of them remotely interesting. And then there was Nigel, who wove the most beautiful tale of knowing Harper since she was a gawky tween, unrecognizable to the zillions who worshipped her today, thanks entirely to Nigel's handiwork. The entire party laughed uproariously.

Finally, after everyone else had moved on to dessert, Andy excused herself and stepped outside the tent. She fumbled through her clutch for her phone and dialed, barely even considering the price of international roaming. This was an emergency.

Emily picked up on the first ring. 'Is everything okay? Please tell me they haven't called off the wedding.'

'They're still getting married,' Andy said, relieved to hear her friend's voice.

'Then why are you calling me in the middle of the dinner?'

'Nigel's here! With Serena and Jessica. And I'm seated with them. This is literally my worst nightmare.'

Emily laughed. 'Oh come on, they're not so bad. Let me guess, Nigel pretended you never reached out to him? That you cut him out of your life?'

'Exactly.'

'Just be thankful *she's* not there. It really could be worse,' Emily said.

'Twice in two weeks would put me over the edge. As in, I'd completely lose my mind.'

Emily was silent on the other end.

'You there? What? Thanking your lucky stars you're not

158

here with me? I'm telling you, Anguilla's not looking so great right about now.'

'So, I don't want you to freak out, Andy . . .' Emily's voice got quiet.

'Oh no. Please. What's wrong?'

'Nothing's wrong! My god, you're always so dramatic.'

'Em . . .'

'It's incredible news, actually. Maybe the best I've ever heard.'

Andy took a deep breath.

'I spoke to the lawyer at Elias-Clark – he totally tracked me down, by the way, found my cell and called me thirty minutes ago, which is really late for a business call. It shows how eager they are! I mean, can you even believe he would—'

'Eager for what, Emily? What did he want?' Andy could hear someone giving a toast over the microphone somewhere behind her, and she suddenly wanted nothing more than to be at home, in her bed, snuggled next to Max the way they used to before she found the note.

'Well, at first he just reiterated that he wanted a meeting. So I'm thinking total lawsuit, right? Like, we've been misrepresenting ourselves or some total bullshit and Miranda is going to—'

'Emily. *Please.*'

'But it's not that, Andy! He didn't want to give any specifics until we were face-to-face, but he said something vague about being interested in "the business of *The Plunge*," as he put it. You know that can only mean one thing!'

Andy nodded to herself. She knew exactly what that meant. 'It sounds like they're interested in acquiring us.'

'Yes!' Andy could tell Emily was trying to keep the excitement out of her voice, but it wasn't working.

'I thought we agreed that we weren't going to sell for the

first five years, that we were going to take our time to really build the product and give it a great foundation. We're barely three years in, Emily.'

'You know as well as I do that you don't pass up an opportunity like this!' Emily all but shrieked. 'This is Elias-Clark we're talking about here. Only the biggest and most prestigious publishing company in the world. This could be the opportunity of a lifetime.'

Andy felt a little jolt. There was an excitement, a profound satisfaction, to the idea that Elias-Clark would be interested. There was also real terror. 'Do I need to say it, Em? Do I? Have you forgotten that Miranda is the editorial director of all of Elias-Clark now in addition to editing *Runway*, and that would make her our boss again?' Andy paused to calm her voice. 'Just a minor little detail, but perhaps one you may want to consider.'

'I'm really not worried about it,' Emily said, and Andy could almost picture her friend waving her off as though they were discussing where to pick up sandwiches.

'Well you're not here right now, seated with those *Runway* Stepford Clackers. I think you'd be worried about it if you were.'

Emily sighed as though this was exactly the reaction she'd expected. 'Look, Andy, can you just agree to keep an open mind? At least until we hear what they want? I promise we won't do anything you're not comfortable with.'

'Okay. Because I'm not comfortable working for Miranda Priestly again. I can tell you that right now.'

'We don't even know what they're offering! Go have a drink, try to enjoy the party, and leave everything else to me, okay?'

Andy looked around at the gorgeous setting. Maybe another virgin colada would be nice.

'It's just a meeting, Andy. We'll deal with it then. Repeat after me: it's just a meeting.'

'Okay. It's just a meeting,' Andy replied. She repeated the phrase to herself three more times, and she tried to believe it, she really did. But who was she kidding? It was all so much more terrifying than that.

10

one half of a robe made for two

How long had it been since they kissed? She tried to remember. It seemed impossible, but she couldn't recall Max's lips on hers more than a few times since they'd exchanged vows and kissed in front of three hundred wedding guests. It felt familiar but exciting, and when Max had picked her up from work in a cab, unannounced, it felt uncomplicated: she was happy to see him. She was also relieved to be back from Anguilla, away from Nigel and the *Runway* crew, and she felt safe snuggling into Max's arms in the taxi's backseat, all familiar smells and expert kisses. It felt like coming home should, at least until an ad came on Taxi TV for JetBlue's Bermuda route.

Max followed her eyes to the screen. He knew exactly what Andy was thinking, but he tried to distract her with more passionate making out.

She tried to kiss him back, but suddenly that note was all she could think about.

'Andy . . .' Max could feel her retreating. He tried to hold her hand but she pulled it away. Pregnancy hormones surely weren't helping Andy get past this. She'd read somewhere that expectant moms began to hate their husband's smell. Could that be happening already?

Max swiped his credit card when the cab pulled up to their building at Sixteenth and Eighth. He held the door open for Andy and exchanged niceties with the evening doorman. Andy walked ahead into their apartment, and Stanley descended on them in a frenzy. The pup trailed after her to the master bedroom, with its canopied king-sized bed and chaise reading chair. She made kissing noises at him, and he obliged, following her into the bathroom, where she locked the door, turned on the tub, and scooped up her dog.

'Uch, you reek,' she whispered in his floppy ear, her face buried in his warm neck. Stanley was addicted to chewing bullies, some sort of cracklike chew stick that was supposedly made out of bull penis, a fact that made Andy retch whenever she considered it, pregnant or not.

He licked her face, managing to stick the very tip of his tongue in her mouth, and Andy gagged. Stanley woofed apologetically.

'It's okay, boy. You're certainly not the only thing that makes me puke these days.'

She stripped off her wrap dress, black tights, bra, and underwear and turned to examine her profile. Aside from the angry red mark around her midsection where the tights had constricted her all day, Andy had to admit that her belly looked pretty much the same as always. Not totally flat, she could see as she rubbed a hand over it. But the slight bulge she saw certainly wasn't anything new. Perhaps her waist was a tad thicker, not quite as defined as it had been a month or two earlier. Soon it would disappear entirely. She knew this, and yet it seemed impossible to fathom – almost as hard to imagine as the lima bean with the beating heart inside her.

With the lights dimmed and Stanley stretched out on a towel on the tub's side platform (where he'd occasionally dip his snout into the water and help himself to a drink), Andy sank into the water and exhaled. Max knocked on the door to ask if she was okay.

'I'm fine, just taking a bath.'

'Why did you lock the door? I want to come in.'

Andy looked at Stanley, who was panting, head suspended, just above the hot water.

'I didn't mean to,' she said. She heard his footsteps pad away.

She soaked a washcloth and stretched it over her chest. Deep breath in, long exhalation out. She allowed herself to float, weightless, for just a few minutes. The weekly e-mail from BabyCenter that highlighted her baby's development had reminded her that baths while pregnant should be warm, not hot, and since she couldn't stand a bath that was anything less than scalding, Andy compromised with herself by only remaining submerged for five minutes. It wasn't the long, leisurely relaxation session she usually indulged in before bed, but it would have to do.

As the water loudly drained from the tub, Andy slipped into her plush terry-cloth robe. It was half of an engagement gift from Max's maternal grandparents. Andy's was apple red and read 'Mrs Harrison' in white embroidery on the left breast; Max's was white and had 'Mr Harrison' in red. As she tied the belt she thought about the argument that had ensued when she'd shown Max the gift.

'Cool,' he'd said, setting down the infamous tatty duffel he toted everywhere – even back then.

'It's a very nice thought, but they didn't even ask whether or not I'm going to change my name,' Andy said.

'So?' Max asked, pulling her in for a kiss. 'She's assuming it. She's ninety-one. Give her a break.'

'No, I hear that. It's just that . . . I'm not going to change my name.'

Max laughed. 'Of course you are.'

His cocky confidence prickled her more than anything he could have said or done.

'My name's been Andrea Sachs for over three decades, and I want to keep it that way. How would you feel if someone asked you to change your name at this point in your life?'

'It's different . . .'

'No, it's not.'

He looked at her, really looked at her. 'Why don't you want to take my name?' he asked in a voice so genuinely hurt she almost changed her mind on the spot.

She squeezed his hand. 'It's not some sort of political statement, Max, and it's absolutely nothing personal. Sachs is just the name I grew up with, the one I'm used to. I've worked hard to build a career, and Sachs is the name I've used along the way. Is that so hard to understand?'

Max was quiet. He shrugged his shoulders and sighed. Andy understood that it was probably only the first of many conversations. This was marriage, right? Discussions and compromises? She hugged him and kissed his neck and they both seemed to set it aside, but it quickly became one of those arguments that came to represent so many other, bigger issues. *Who doesn't take their husband's name?* he kept asking, the disbelief in his voice. He played the parental card

('My mother loves you like her own daughter'), which now made Andy want to scream; the grandparent card ('This name has been in our family for countless generations'); and the guilt card ('I thought you'd be proud to have me as your husband – I'm proud you're going to be my wife'), and when all else failed, he halfheartedly tried a threat: 'If you don't want to take my name for the world to see, maybe I shouldn't wear a wedding ring for the world to see,' but when Andy had just shrugged and said he was welcome to wear a ring or not, he apologized. He admitted he was disappointed but he would try to respect her decision. She immediately felt ridiculous for taking a stand on something that was obviously so important to him, especially when she didn't feel *that* strongly about it. When she wrapped her arms around his neck and said she would still use Sachs professionally but would be happy to change it to Harrison for everything else, Max looked like he might collapse with gratitude and relief. She'd been secretly pleased to do it, too: it might have been antifeminist and old-fashioned and whatever else, but she *liked* sharing a name with her husband. Now their baby would be a Harrison, too.

'Hey,' he said, looking up from his copy of *GQ* when Andy walked toward the bed. He was wearing only a pair of Calvin Klein boxer briefs. His skin tone was that perfect olive color that always looked just a little bit tan; his stomach was tightly toned without being obnoxious and his shoulders were comfortingly broad. She felt a swell of attraction, despite herself. 'Nice bath?'

'Always.' She poured herself a glass of water from the carafe she kept on her bedside table and took a sip. She wanted to turn around and admire Max's body, but she forced herself to pick up her book.

Max sidled up next to her. His biceps flexed as he wrapped

his arms around her from behind and kissed her neck. She felt a familiar jolt of excitement in her belly.

'Your skin is so warm. You must have been cooking in there,' he murmured, and Andy immediately thought of the baby.

She felt him kiss her neck again, and before she realized what was happening, Max had shimmied her robe over her shoulders and down to her waist. His hands reached around to gently cup her breasts. She slid away from his touch and rewrapped her robe.

'I can't,' she said, looking away.

'Andy.' His voice was heavy, disappointed. Defeated.

'I'm sorry.'

'Andy, come here. Look at me.' He touched her chin between his thumb and his fingers and gently turned her face to his. He kissed her lips softly. 'I know I hurt you, and it kills me. This whole situation' he gestured in circles with his hand – 'my mom, you not being able to trust me, not wanting to be near me . . . it's my fault, and I understand why you're feeling this way. But it was a note and *nothing* happened. Nothing. I'm sorry, but only for not telling you, nothing more.' He paused, annoyed now. 'You need to let this go. Maybe the punishment doesn't fit the crime.'

Andy could feel her throat constrict and she knew the tears would follow soon.

'I'm pregnant,' she said, her voice a mere whisper.

Max froze. She could feel him staring at her. 'What? Did I—'

'Yes. I'm pregnant.'

'Oh my god, Andy, that is the most incredible thing.' He jumped up and began to pace, a look of anxious excitement on his face. 'When did you find out? How do you know? Have you been to a doctor? How far along?' He fell to his knees by the bed and clasped both her hands in his own.

Max's obvious joy was comforting. This was hard enough; she couldn't imagine what it would be like if he was ambivalent (or worse) about the news. She felt him squeeze her hands, and she was grateful for it.

'When I went to Dr Palmer last week, remember? Before Anguilla? They did a urine test and called that night with the news.' Andy decided it was best to omit the part where she asked for an entire STD workup.

'You've known since last *week* and you haven't told me?'

'I'm sorry,' she said again. 'I needed some time to think.'

Max gazed at her with an inscrutable expression.

'So anyway, they don't think it's a "brand-new" pregnancy, whatever that means. They can't tell for sure until I have an ultrasound, but I'm guessing it happened that one time in Hilton Head . . .'

She watched as Max remembered. The house they'd rented for an Indian summer week with Emily and Miles. That one night in the outdoor shower, just before dinner, when they'd sneaked in together like two teenagers. When Andy had sworn to Max it was a safe time, that she'd just had her period the week before, and they'd gotten carried away.

'The shower? Is that when you think it happened?'

Andy nodded. 'I was switching pills that month and took a few weeks off, and I guess I calculated wrong.'

'You know what this says, don't you? It was meant to be. This baby was meant to be.' This was Max's favorite line. Their meeting – meant to be. The success of her magazine – meant to be. Their marriage – meant to be. And now the baby.

'Well, I don't know about that,' Andy said, but couldn't help smiling. 'I think it means that we have solid proof that the rhythm method doesn't work, but yeah, I guess you could look at it like that, too.'

'When can you have the ultrasound? To know when the baby is due?'

'I made an appointment with my gynecologist for tomorrow.'

'What time?' Max asked, almost before she could finish her sentence.

'Nine thirty. I wanted earlier but it was all they had.'

He immediately picked up his phone. Andy wanted to hug him as she listened to him leave instructions for his secretary to cancel or reschedule all of his morning meetings.

'Can I take you to breakfast tomorrow morning before our appointment?'

Why had she waited so long to tell him? Here he was, her Max, the man she had *married*. Of course he was thrilled with the news that they were going to have a baby. Of course he'd cancel everything without a moment's hesitation to be at the first – and every, if she had to bet – appointment. Of course he had immediately, instinctively, switched to *our* and would undoubtedly use phrases like *We're pregnant* and *our baby*. She hadn't thought he'd be any other way, but it was still an intense relief to experience it firsthand. She wasn't all alone.

'Well, I was thinking of running to the office for an hour or two beforehand. I've gotten so behind lately. First the wedding, then the nausea, and now the whole Elias-Clark thing . . .'

'Andy.' He squeezed her hand again and smiled. 'Please.'

'Yes. Breakfast sounds nice.'

A wave of nausea overcame her. It must have registered on her face, because Max asked if she was okay. She nodded, unable to speak, and moved quickly toward the bathroom. As she retched, she heard him ordering ginger ale, saltines, bananas, and applesauce from the corner bodega. When she returned to bed, he looked at her sympathetically.

'You poor thing. I'm going to take such good care of you.'

Her head throbbed with the aftermath of vomiting, but she felt strangely better than she had in weeks. 'Thank you.'

'Come here, give me your feet.' He motioned for her to sit next to him, and he pulled her legs into his lap.

The kneading felt heavenly. She closed her eyes. 'There goes our honeymoon in Fiji,' she said, remembering it for the first time. 'Although I guess there's no reason we couldn't still go in December as long as everything looks normal.'

Max stopped kneading and peered at her. 'You are not flying halfway around the world away from your doctor. Putting your body under all the stress of jet lag and travel? No way. We'll have time for Fiji later.'

'You're not upset to miss it?'

Max shook his head. 'We're going to give our baby everything, Andy, you'll see. You're going to create the perfect nursery, and fill it with stuffed animals and adorable little clothes and lots of books, and I'm going to learn everything there is to learn about babies so I know exactly what I'm doing from day one. I'm going to change diapers and give bottles and take her for walks in a stroller. We're going to read to her every day and tell her stories about how we met and take her on vacations to the ocean where she'll feel the sand in her feet and learn to swim. And she's going to be so loved. By both our families.'

'Her, huh?' Her whole body had relaxed, and for the first time in weeks, her stomach quieted.

'Of course her. She's going to be a gorgeous little blond girl. It's meant to be.'

When she opened her eyes again, the clock read six forty-five A.M. She was under the duvet, still wearing her robe, Max snoring softly beside her. The lights were dimmed but not off; they must have both fallen asleep midconversation.

After they both showered and dressed, Max hailed a cab and directed it to Sarabeth's on the Upper East Side, a charming little breakfast nook near her gynecologist's office and convenient to exactly nothing else. Andy could only manage toast with homemade jam and a cup of chamomile, but she enjoyed watching Max devour his cheese omelet, home fries, extra-crispy bacon, two glasses of orange juice and large latte. He talked animatedly as he ate, excited for the appointment ahead, chattering about possible due dates and questions for the doctor and ideas for making the announcement to their families.

They paid the bill and walked the six blocks up Madison Avenue. The waiting room was busy; Andy could count at least three obviously pregnant women, two with husbands, and a handful of women most likely too young or too old to be expecting. How had she never noticed before? How strange to be there with Max, holding his hand, giving both their names at the front desk. Andy was shocked when the receptionist barely looked up. She had just announced she was there for an ultrasound. Her first! Wasn't this news to *everyone*?

Fifteen minutes later a nurse called her name and handed her a plastic sample cup.

'Restroom is down the hall, on your right. Please bring your sample into exam room five. Your husband can wait for you there.'

Max smiled at Andy, shot her a *good luck* look, and followed the nurse toward the exam rooms. When Andy met him there three minutes later, he was pacing the cubicle-sized room.

'How'd it go?' he asked, raking his hand through his hair.

'I peed on my hand. Like always.'

'Is it really that hard?' Max laughed, looking relieved at the distraction.

'You have no idea.'

Another nurse arrived, a heavyset woman with a kind smile and silvery hair. After dipping a stick in Andy's urine and declaring it perfect, she measured her blood pressure (also perfect) and asked when she'd had her last menstrual period (Andy could only ballpark it).

'Okay, love. Dr Kramer will be in shortly. Weigh yourself – be sure to deduct a pound for clothing – strip from the waist down, and cover yourself with this.' She handed Andy a paper sheet and gestured toward the exam table. Both Max and Andy watched in fascination and revulsion as she covered a probe attached to the ultrasound machine with something that looked exactly like a condom and then squirted it with a glob of K-Y Jelly. She wished them a good morning and closed the door behind her.

'So that's how this is going down,' Max joked, staring at the now-more-than-ever-phallic probe.

'I have to say, I thought this was going to be an over-the-belly thing. That's always how it is on TV . . .'

The door opened, and Dr Kramer must have overheard because she smiled and said, 'I'm afraid we're a bit too early for the abdominal ultrasound. Because your fetus is still so small, only the transvaginal can pick it up.'

Dr Kramer introduced herself to Max and began prepping the machine. She was a petite, pretty woman in her late thirties, and her movements were quick and sure. 'How are you feeling?' she asked over her shoulder. 'Any nausea or vomiting?'

'Both.'

'Totally normal. Most women find it abates by twelve or fourteen weeks. You can keep down clear beverages, crackers, that type of thing?'

'Most of the time,' Andy said.

'Don't worry too much about what you're eating right now. The baby is getting everything it needs from your body. Just try to eat small, frequent meals and get plenty of rest, okay?'

Andy nodded. Dr Kramer eased the paper sheet up a bit and instructed Andy to scoot down on the table and place her feet in the socked stirrups. Andy felt the slightest bit of pressure and a quick feeling of coldness between her legs, and then nothing. It was far less invasive than even a pelvic exam, she thought with relief.

'There we go,' Dr Kramer said, moving the probe ever so slightly. The screen filled with the familiar sight of black and white blobs, like they'd seen in the movies so many times. The doctor pointed to a particular blob in the very middle of what appeared to be a black vacuum. 'There. You see? That flickering right there? That's your baby's heart beating.'

Max was out of his chair and gripping Andy's hand. 'Where? That right there?'

'Yep, that's it.' She paused, examined the screen, and said, 'And it looks like a strong, healthy heartbeat. Wait, one sec . . . there.' She moved the probe a bit and turned up the volume knob. The heartbeat sounded like a rhythmic, underwater pulse and was as fast as a horse galloping. It filled the room.

Andy was lying flat on her back, only able to lift her neck a few inches from the table, but she could see the screen and the blob and its flickering little heart perfectly: her baby. It was real and it was alive and it was growing inside her.

Her tears were silent and her body stayed still, but she couldn't stop herself from crying. When she looked over at Max, who was still death-gripping her hand and staring at the screen, she saw that his eyes were filled as well.

'You're measuring at ten weeks, five days, and everything looks absolutely perfect.' The doctor picked up a plastic cardboard wheel and began sliding its two discs around one another. 'We'll continue to date the pregnancy with ultrasounds since you're not positive of your timing, but according to what we see today, your due date is June first. Congratulations!'

'June first,' Max breathed reverently, as though it were the best day in the entire world. 'A spring baby. It's perfect.'

They didn't just vanish, all the doubts and fears and anger over the letter – Andy wasn't sure they ever would – but seeing that little living bean inside her, knowing that she and Max had made it together, and would meet it soon, and would, god willing, be its parents forever, made all that fade into the background. And when the doctor told them to meet in her office and left them alone, and Max nearly jumped on the table with her in joy and happiness, and he shouted, 'I love you!' so loudly Andy laughed out loud, it faded even a little bit more. She would make it work with Max. She would forgive him and move past any doubts. It was the only way forward. She would do it for their baby.

11

more or less famous than beyoncé?

The building that housed *The Plunge*'s offices was, thankfully, different in every way from Elias-Clark's, or even the West Village walk-up *Happily Ever After* called home. Originally a lumberyard in the 1890s, the building had gone through a few incarnations – meatpacking plant, food-processing mill, fabric warehouse, and furniture workshop – before becoming, predictably, a converted loft space with floor-to-ceiling windows, exposed brick walls, salvaged wooden floors, and much-hyped Hudson River views (a.k.a. views of Jersey City). Andy could still remember Emily's excitement three years earlier when the broker who'd been showing them office spaces brought them to Twenty-Fourth and Eleventh. The fortresslike building was impressive, but Andy had wondered: didn't the neighborhood feel a little too . . . raw?

Emily scoffed as she gingerly stepped over a man passed out near the entrance. 'Raw? It's got character, and character is exactly what we need!' she'd said. Character rather than good heat, air-conditioning, and reasonable assurances that they wouldn't be murdered still bothered Andy, but she couldn't deny that the office interiors were a thousand times nicer than anything they'd seen, and they were cheaper, too.

She yanked the metal cage door of the elevator open, stepped inside, and closed it behind her, a move she had perfected even with an armful of hot coffees. Every day Andy swore she'd use the stairs; every day she stepped in the elevator and thought, *Tomorrow.* On the fourth floor she smiled at *The Plunge*'s current receptionist, inevitably an overqualified recent college graduate who only stayed long enough to ensure she or Emily was forever interviewing new candidates.

It was nice getting in late every once in a while.

'Morning, Andrea,' Agatha said. She was wearing a navy dress with cream-colored tights and chunky red patent heels, and Andy was left to wonder, as she always did, how her assistant kept, constantly, on fashion's cutting edge. It must have been exhausting.

'Good morning!' Andrea sang loudly.

Agatha stood waiting like a guard dog as Andy walked past her into her office, a larger, glass-enclosed version of the cubicles near it, and said, 'Follow me.' Immediately thinking that sounded too harsh and commanding, she added with a forced laugh, 'If you have a minute.'

'So listen, Emily's been calling for you, like, every three seconds. I promised her I'd send you right over there.'

'I told her I'd be late this morning. It's the first morning in six months she gets in before me and she's hysterical, huh?' Andy said, thinking it had to be the Elias-Clark call that had Emily in a snit. 'Okay, I'm headed there now. Will you please forward any calls from the Harper wedding people to her office?'

Agatha nodded. She looked supremely bored.

What *The Plunge* did have in common with *Runway*: long-legged, stiletto-favoring, designer-donning girls. Per their working agreement, Emily had been responsible for the office hiring, with the single exception of Carmella Tindale, Andy's part-features editor, part-managing director, whom she had poached from *Happily Ever After* and strongly felt she couldn't live without. Noticeably, Carmella was slightly overweight with unruly brown hair and inch-thick gray roots. She favored shapeless pantsuits paired with Merrell clogs in the winter and FitFlops in the summer, and her lone stab at style was a genuine (according to Emily) Prada backpack that she had bedazzled herself with an interesting array of puffy paint, rhinestones, and colored thread. Carmella was an undeniable fashion disaster of epic proportions, and Andy loved her dearly. The rest of them, though, were close cousins of the *Runway* Clackers, each leggier and skinnier and prettier than the next. It was downright depressing.

'Good morning, Andy,' said Tal, a willowy Israeli with pale skin, jet-black hair, and a figure that could have stopped a tank. She was wearing a pair of skinny cargo pants paired with a cropped blazer and high-heeled suede booties.

'Morning, Tal. Did you ever get in touch with OPI's people? We need a definite yes or no by the end of the week.'

Tal nodded.

Andy's cell phone rang. 'Great. Let me know as soon as you hear.' She turned her attention to her phone. 'Max? You there?'

'Hi, love. How are you feeling?'

Until he'd said anything, she'd been feeling fine, but the moment she thought of how she felt, a wave of nausea rolled over her.

'I'm okay. Just about to head into Emily's office for a meeting. What's going on?'

'I was thinking. What if we invite my parents and sister, and your mom, and Jill and Kyle, and your dad and Noreen, over to our place for dinner? We can tell them it's to go over the wedding proofs and help us choose pictures for our album. And then we'll break the news.'

She'd wanted to tell her mother and Jill so badly when she last saw them, but now that Lily and Max knew – and Emily, too; she was planning to tell her right then – it somehow felt like enough.

'Oh, I don't know . . .'

'It'll be great. We have that first-trimester screening, what'd she call it?'

'The nuchal translucency.'

'Right. So we have that the beginning of next week and make sure everything's a go, which of course it will be, and then we make our families the happiest people on earth. I can have the company's party planner find a caterer. They'll bring everything, cook, clean up . . . you won't have to lift a finger. What do you say?'

Andy smiled at an art department Clacker who cruised by her wearing thigh-high boots and what must have been ten pounds of expertly knotted and twisted gold chains around her neck.

'Andy?'

'Sorry. Um . . . okay? That sounds good.'

'It'll be great! Next Saturday night?'

'No, Jill and Kyle and the boys head back to Texas that morning. Maybe Friday?'

'Sure. I'll talk to everyone and figure out the details. Andy?'

'Hmm?'

'It's going to be great. They're going to be so happy for us . . .'

Andy couldn't help but wonder what Barbara would think. The dreaded daughter-in-law giving her a much-hoped-for grandchild. What a dilemma! Her hyper-Botoxed face would probably reveal nothing. But maybe the news of a baby would change everything for the better . . .

'I love it,' she said. 'It's a perfect way to tell them.'

'I love you, Andy.'

She paused for just a moment, a fraction of a second really, and then said, 'I love you too.'

'Andy? Get in here!' Emily commanded from within her glass cubicle. It was a phrase that sounded eerily familiar.

'I can hear you're being summoned. I'll talk to you later,' Max said and hung up. Andy could practically hear him smiling.

Andy entered Emily's office, took a seat in one of the leather sling chairs, and kicked off her moccasins to bury her feet in the fluffy sheepskin rug. Flouting the magazine's frugal decorating budget, Emily had spent a fortune of her own money to make her office look like something out of *Elle Decor*. The red lacquer desk, white leather chairs and sheepskin rug were just the beginning. A sleek, low-profile cabinet housed Emily's magazine and book collection, filmy white curtains adorned the dramatic windows, and canvas-stretched photos of all *The Plunge*'s covers since the magazine's inception filled the single exposed-brick wall. On the two glass partitions that separated the office from the rest of the loft, Emily had hung a collection of stained glass figurines and ornaments that caught the light and threw beams of color in every direction. A modern, life-size sculpture of two Dalmatians frolicked in the corner and a miniature Sub-Zero fridge built into the side of a horizontal bookcase kept Emily's supply of Evian, rosé champagne, and Honest Teas well chilled. A dozen elegantly framed personal pictures perched on every surface. Andy was reminded that Emily had aspired to be Miranda's assistant from age twelve. Or perhaps she'd aspired to be Miranda?

'Thank god, you're finally here!' Emily said, glancing up from her computer. 'I'm just going to finish this e-mail, give me two seconds . . .'

Andy noticed a pile of proofs from her own wedding off to the side. She plucked the top one and studied it. She'd loved it when she saw it online, and she loved it even more in hard copy. It was perhaps one of the only pictures taken of the whole wedding where she felt her smile was entirely genuine. Just as the music began playing for their first dance, Max had come up from behind and wrapped his arms around her. He kissed her on the side of her neck, which tickled, and she threw her head back onto his shoulder, laughing with surprise and delight. The photo was completely natural, totally unposed. It was a nontraditional cover choice, but both Andy and Emily were batting around the idea of doing something different.

'Can you even believe we're getting ready to close the March issue?' Andy asked, staring at the photo of herself and Max.

'Mmm,' Emily murmured, her eyes glued to her screen.

'Do you really think we can use a candid for the cover? Is it too . . . flighty?'

Emily sighed. 'It's still a St Germain. It's hardly something one of your cousins forwarded us from Shutterfly.'

'True. I do like it . . .'

Emily opened the top drawer of her desk, extracted a pack of Marlboros and a lighter, took one for herself, and offered the pack to Andy.

'This is our *office*, Emily,' Andy said, hating that she sounded like someone's mother.

Emily touched the cigarette tip to the lighter's flame, inhaled deeply, and exhaled a long, neat smoke stream. 'We're celebrating.'

'It's been six years,' Andy said, looking at the cigarette longingly. 'Why does that still look so freaking good?'

Emily held out the pack again but Andy merely shook her head. She knew she should probably leave the office until Emily finished – she had the baby to think about now – but Emily would have killed her.

'What are we celebrating?' Andy asked, transfixed by Emily's long, sensual exhalations.

'You're never going to guess who I got a call from this morning,' Emily said, doing a strange little jig in her chair.

'Beyoncé?'

'No. Why her?'

'More or less famous?'

'Who's more famous than Beyoncé?'

'Emily, just tell me.'

'Guess. You have to guess. You're *never* going to guess, but just try.'

'That sounds fun. Let's see . . . Jay-Z?'

Emily groaned. 'You're so uninspired. Who would be maybe the last person in the known universe to call our office and request a meeting?'

Andy blew on her hands to keep them warm. 'Obama?'

'You're unbelievable. You have no imagination whatsoever!'

'Emily . . .'

'Miranda! Miranda fucking Priestly called for us this morning.'

'No she didn't.' Andy shook her head. 'Factually impossible. Unless there's been some sort of people's revolution at *Runway* that we haven't heard about, Miranda did not call here. Because Miranda doesn't call anywhere. Because last time I checked, Miranda was physically, mentally, and emotionally incapable of dialing numbers on a phone without help from someone else.'

Emily took a quick inhale and stamped the cigarette out in an ornate stained glass ashtray she kept stashed away in her desk. 'Andy? Are you listening?'

'What?' Andy looked at Emily, who stared back at her in shocked disbelief.

'Do you hear anything I'm saying?'

'Of course. But tell me again. I'm having a hard time processing it.'

Emily sighed dramatically. 'So no, she did not actually call herself. But her senior assistant, some South African chick named Charla, called and asked if you and I would come to the office for a meeting. In two weeks. She stressed that it would be with Miranda herself.'

'How'd you know she was South African?' Andy asked, solely to piss off Emily.

Emily looked like she might explode. 'Did you not hear what I just told you? We – you and I – are meeting with Miranda!'

'Oh, I heard you. I'm trying to keep from hyperventilating right now,' Andy said.

Emily clasped her hands. 'There's only one explanation. It's got to be to discuss a possible acquisition.'

Andy glanced at her cell phone and tossed her phone back in her bag. 'You're crazy if you think I'm going.'

'Of course you're going.'

'I am not! My weak heart can't handle it. To say nothing of my self-respect.'

'Andy, that woman is the editorial director of Elias-Clark. She's the final editorial arbiter over every single magazine at the company. For god knows what reason, she has requested our presence at eleven a week from Friday. And you, my friend and cofounder, are going to be there.'

'Do you think she knows we use her name to book celebrities?'

'Andy, I really don't think she cares about that.'

'Didn't I read somewhere that she authorized that famous historian, the really intellectual one, to write her biography? Maybe she wants him to interview us?'

Emily rolled her eyes. 'Uh-huh. That sounds likely. Of the three million people she's worked with over the years, she wants one she fired in front of thirty staffers for no reason and the one who told her to fuck off in Paris. Try again.'

'I have no idea. But guess what? I'm really comfortable with never knowing.'

'What do you mean, never knowing?'

'Just what I said. I think I can live a full and complete life not knowing why Miranda Priestly suddenly wants to see us.'

Emily sighed.

'What?'

'Nothing, I just knew you'd be difficult. But I confirmed the meeting anyway.'

'You did not.'

'I did. I think it's important.'

'Important?' Andy was aware she sounded vaguely hysterical, but she couldn't stop. 'In case you don't realize it, we haven't been enslaved by that lunatic for years. Through lots of hard work and dedication, we have built our own successful magazine, and we did it without terrorizing our staff or wrecking anyone's life. I will never again step foot in that woman's office.'

Emily waved her off. 'It's not the same office; she moved floors. And you can declare you'll never go there again *after* our meeting. I, for one, need to know what she wants, and I can't go alone.'

'Why not? You're so enamored with her. Go by yourself and tell me about it. Or don't. I don't really care.'

'I'm not enamored with her, Andy,' Emily said, clearly growing exasperated. 'But when Miranda Priestly calls you in for a meeting, you go.' Emily reached her arm across the desk and held Andy's hand. She pouted and her eyes looked sad. 'Please say you'll come.'

Andy snatched her hand back. She was silent.

'Pretty please? For your best friend and business partner? The one who introduced you to your husband?'

'You're really pulling out all the stops, aren't you?'

'Please, Andy? I'll take you out for Shake Shack afterward.'

'Wow. You're bringing your A-game.'

'Please? For me? I'll be forever indebted.'

Andy sighed heavily. Visiting Miranda on her own turf sounded about as appealing as a day in prison, but Andy had to admit to herself that she too was curious.

She pressed her hands into the desk and made a big show of heaving herself to stand. 'Fine, I'll do it. But I want a Shack T-shirt in addition to my burger, fries, and shake, and I want a onesie for my new baby.'

'Done!' Emily sang, clearly delighted. 'I'll buy you the whole damn—' She stopped and looked at Andy. 'What did you just say?'

'You heard me.'

'No, I don't think I did. I thought you said something about a baby, but you've been married for less than five minutes, and there's no way . . .' Emily stared into Andy's eyes and moaned. 'Oh my god, you're not kidding. You're knocked up?'

'Very.'

'What's with you people? What the hell is your big rush?'

'It's not like we planned this . . .'

'What, you don't know how babies are made? You've spent the last fifteen years of your life managing *not* to get pregnant. What happened?'

'Thanks for being so supportive,' Andy said.

'Well it's not like running a magazine and newborns go hand in hand. I'm thinking how this is going to affect *me*.'

'It's still a ways off. I'm only just now starting my second trimester.'

'Already with the lingo and everything.' Emily looked to be computing the numbers. She flopped into her desk chair and grinned evilly. 'Wow. You really didn't plan this.' Her voice lowered to a delighted whisper. 'Is it even Max's?'

'Of course it is! What, you think I went back out after my bachelorette day at the spa and had crazy sex with one of the yoga instructors?'

'You have to admit, that would be pretty cool.'

'Don't you want to ask me any normal-person questions? Like when I'm due, or if I know what I'm having? Maybe how I'm feeling?'

'Are you sure it's not twins? Or triplets? Because *that* would be a story.'

Andy sighed.

Emily held her hands up. 'Okay, okay, I'm sorry. But you have to admit, this is pretty unbelievable. You got married, what? A month ago? And you're already three months

185

preggers? It's just not a very Andy move, is all. And what will Barbara say?'

The mother-in-law comment stung, probably because Andy was wondering the exact same thing. 'You're right, it's not a very me move at all. But it's happening, and not even Barbara Harrison can stop it now. And when you overlook all the other stuff and just focus on the baby part, it's pretty great. Earlier than we'd hoped, but still great.'

'Mmm.' Emily's lack of enthusiasm wasn't surprising. She'd never come out and said she didn't want children, but despite her being married for nearly five years and a semicompetent aunt to Miles's nieces, Andy had always assumed it. Children were messy. They were sticky and loud and unpredictable, and they made you fat and unstylish, at least for long stretches of time. They were decidedly un-Emily.

There was a knock on Emily's door and Agatha walked in. 'Daniel wants to know if you can run to his office for, like, two seconds. He said he needs to show you something but he's waiting for a phone call.'

'Go. We can talk about this later,' Andy said, relieved to have finally shared the news.

'Damn right we will. But let's stay focused on the meeting too, okay? We need to discuss what you're going to wear . . .' She walked around the desk and pulled open Andy's cashmere cardigan. 'No obvious bump per se, but definitely something we need to be careful about. I think you should wear that A-line wool dress, the one with the gold epaulets? It's nothing great, but at least it has a little drape around the middle . . .'

Andy laughed. 'I'll take that under advisement.'

'Seriously, Andy. Big news and all, I get it, but we have to be a hundred percent for Miranda. You're not, like, going to be puking or anything, right?'

'I'll be fine.'

'Great. I'll let you know how it goes with the Vera people. Don't forget to touch base with St Germain – they're waiting for your call.'

Emily grabbed her trench coat and tote bag and waved back at Andy over her shoulder. 'Congrats again!' she shouted, and Andy cringed, wondering if Emily knew not to blab her news to the entire office.

Then again, what did it matter? She was pregnant, and if all went well – and Andy found herself fervently hoping it would – in six months she would be having a baby. A baby. The Miranda meeting, the idle gossip, it all melted away when she stopped for a moment and imagined herself holding a soft-skinned, sweet-smelling infant. She placed two hands over her belly and smiled to herself. A baby.

12

trumped-up harassment charges plus a straitjacket or two

Andy walked into the Starbucks closest to Elias-Clark and had to hold on to the counter to steady herself. She hadn't been there in ten years, and the flashbacks were so vivid and unpleasant she thought she might faint. A quick glance around confirmed none of the faces behind the register or manning the espresso machines were familiar. She caught sight of Emily waving from a corner table.

'Thank god you're finally here,' Emily said, taking a long sip of her iced coffee with obvious care to avoid smudging her lipstick.

Andy checked her watch. 'I'm almost fifteen minutes early. How long have you been here?'

'You don't want to know. I've been getting dressed and redressed since four in the morning.'

'Sounds relaxing.'

Emily rolled her eyes.

'It was worth it, though,' Andy said, looking approvingly at Emily's fitted bouclé pencil skirt, skintight cashmere turtleneck sweater, and sky-high stiletto boots. 'You look fantastic.'

'Thanks. You too,' Emily said automatically, without looking up from her phone.

'Yeah, I thought this dress I borrowed looks pretty good. Not bad for maternity, right?'

Emily's head whipped up, a panicked expression on her face.

'Hah, just kidding. I'm wearing the dress you told me to, and it's not maternity.'

'Adorable.'

Andy suppressed a smile. 'When do you think we should head over there?'

'Five minutes? Or maybe now? You know how much she loves it when someone's late.'

Andy reached over and helped herself to a sip of Emily's coffee. It was sludgy with sugar, almost too thick to pull through the straw. 'How do you drink this crap?'

Emily shrugged.

'Okay, let's remember this: We don't owe Miranda a thing. We are there to listen and listen only. She can't wreck our lives anymore with a single wave of her wand.' The words all sounded good, but Andy wasn't sure she believed them herself.

'Oh, don't kid yourself, Andy. She's the editorial director of all of Elias-Clark. She remains the most powerful woman in both fashion and publishing. She could absolutely wreck our lives for no reason other than she feels like it, and I'm sure you've been awake since three A.M., too.'

Andy stood up and buttoned her puffy down coat – she

189

had wanted to wear something more elegant, but the day was arctic, and she wasn't prepared to feel freezing in addition to terrified. She had spent her standard thirty minutes getting ready this morning, had donned the dress with the epaulets, as Emily had advised. Not winning any awards, but not objectionable either. 'Come on, let's go. The sooner we get there, the sooner we can leave.'

'Great attitude,' Emily said, shaking her head. But she stood and zipped up her gorgeous, cropped fur jacket.

They didn't exchange a single word on the walk to Elias-Clark, and Andy felt reasonably okay until they entered the lobby and made their way over to the visitors' desk to check in, something neither of them had done since the day they were each first interviewed.

'This is surreal,' Emily said, stealing glances around. Her hands trembled.

'No Eduardo at the turnstiles. No Ahmed at the magazine stand. I don't recognize anyone . . .'

'You recognize her, don't you?' Emily said, motioning over her shoulder with her eyes as she shoved her visitor badge into her purse.

Andy followed her gaze and immediately saw Jocelyn, *Runway*'s recently promoted beauty director and all-around society darling, crossing the lobby. She knew from the gossip blogs that Jocelyn had had a busy decade – two kids with her millionaire banker husband, a divorce from him, and a remarriage to an old-money billionaire with an additional two children – but no one could have ever known from merely looking at her: she appeared every bit as young, thin, and fresh-faced as she had when Andy roamed the halls. If anything, she had settled beautifully into her thirties and she carried herself with a calm, confident regality she hadn't possessed as a younger woman. Andy couldn't help but stare.

'I don't think I can do this,' Andy murmured. A wave of anxiety washed over her. What was she doing, thinking she could just show up here after everything that had happened and waltz into Miranda Priestly's office like nothing was wrong? This was a horrible idea, a disastrous one. Her urge to flee was overwhelming.

Emily grabbed Andy's arm and practically yanked her through the turnstile and onto the elevator, where they were somehow, blessedly, alone. She punched the button for the eighteenth floor and turned to Andy. 'We're going to get through this, okay?' she said, her voice trembling slightly. 'Look on the bright side – at least we don't have to go to the *Runway* floor.'

There was no time to answer before the doors swept open and they were faced with the familiar white starkness of every Elias-Clark reception area. Miranda had moved to a sweeping office on the corporate floor after her big promotion, although her *Runway* digs remained perfectly intact as well. Apparently she could sweep, unhindered, between both offices, terrorizing double the number of people in half the time.

'Guess they haven't redecorated,' Andy muttered.

The receptionist, a lithe brunette with an almost too-severe bob and a jolting shade of red lipstick, forced a smile that looked more like a smirk. 'Andrea Sachs and Emily Charlton? Right this way.'

Before either of them could confirm their identity – or even unwrap their scarves – the girl touched her card to the keypad, pushed open the enormous glass doors, and blazed through them, her four-inch heels not slowing her in the least. Emily and Andy had to run to keep up.

They exchanged looks as they followed the receptionist through a labyrinthine hallway, past palatial glass-enclosed offices with stunning Empire State Building views and expensively suited executives in various states of executing. This was happening so fast! There wasn't going to be even a moment to sit, catch their breaths, offer each other comforting words. The receptionist hadn't offered them water nor taken their coats. For the very first time, Andy understood – really, completely understood – how it had felt for all the editors, writers, models, designers, advertisers, photographers, and regular old *Runway* staffers who left the relative safety of their own offices to brave a visit to Miranda's. No wonder they'd all looked like the walking dead.

A moment later they arrived at a suite similar to the setup Miranda had occupied at *Runway*: an anteroom with two immaculate assistant desks fronting open French doors that revealed a massive office with sweeping views, elegantly decorated in muted shades of gray and white with occasional pops of soft yellow and turquoise, which lent the whole room the feel of a sunny beach house. Painted driftwood frames that managed to look both antique and modern held photos of now-eighteen-year-olds Caroline and Cassidy, each one appearing pretty and vaguely hostile in her own distinct way. The carpet stretched wall to wall in an expanse of shocking white, its only color a lone wild streak of turquoise. Andy had just noticed the enormous tapestry on the far wall, a stitched fabric creation meant to look like a painting, when a door within Miranda's office opened and the woman herself emerged. Without looking at Andy or Emily or either of her assistants, she strode toward her desk and began issuing the all-too-familiar directives.

'Charla? Can you hear me? Hello? Is anyone there?'

The girl who must have been Charla had just been preparing to greet Andy and Emily; she motioned toward them with her pointer finger to wait; grabbed a clipboard, which was presumably the Bulletin; and bolted into Miranda's office.

'Yes, Miranda, I'm right here. What can I—'

'Call Cassidy and tell her to ask her tennis coach to join us this weekend while we're away, and then call the coach and ask her yourself. No is not an acceptable option. Let my husband know we will be leaving tomorrow from the apartment at exactly five. Inform the garage and the Connecticut staff of our arrival time. Messenger a copy of that new book, the one they reviewed last Sunday, to my apartment before we leave, and schedule a phone call with the author for first thing Monday morning. Make a reservation for lunch today at one and inform Karl's New York staff. Find out where the Bulgari people are staying and send flowers, lots of them. Tell Nigel I'll be ready for my fitting today at three, not a minute later, and make sure the dress and all the accessories are ready. I know the shoes won't be finished yet – they're custom-making them in Milan – but find out the dimensions and make sure I have an exact replica for our run-through.' It was here that she finally took a breath, eyes to the ceiling in an apparent effort to recall a final command. 'Oh yes, and get in touch with the Planned Parenthood people to schedule a meeting to go over details for the spring benefit. Is my eleven o'clock here?'

Andy was so wrapped up in the minutiae of Miranda's requests, her mind so automatically and instinctively concentrating on remembering and assimilating the information, that she barely even heard the last sentence. Emily's elbow in her side rib jolted her back to reality.

'Get ready,' Emily whispered, removing her coat and tossing it on the floor beside an assistant desk.

Andy did the same. 'How do you suggest I do that?' Andy hissed back.

'Miranda can see you now,' Charla announced, her unsmiling face surely a bad omen.

She didn't escort them into Miranda's office. Maybe she figured they knew the protocol, or maybe she'd decided they weren't important enough, or maybe the system had changed in the last few years, but when Charla waved them forward, Andy felt herself take a deep breath at exactly the same time Emily inhaled, and side by side, they walked as confidently as they could manage into Miranda's office.

Thankfully, miraculously, she did not look them up and down. She didn't look at them at all. She didn't invite them to sit, or greet them, or in any way acknowledge their existence. Andy had to fight the urge to report some sort of progress or accomplishment, let Miranda know that her lunch had been properly scheduled or the tutor successfully wrangled. She could feel the tension emanating from Emily, too. Unsure of what to do or say, they just stood there. For what may have been the most uncomfortable forty-five seconds of silence ever experienced anywhere, by anyone, for any reason. Andy glanced at Emily, but her friend appeared frozen in terror and uncertainty. And so they stood.

Miranda sat perched on her cold metal chair, back ramrod straight, signature bob as smooth as a wig. She wore a charcoal-colored pleated skirt, made of wool or possibly cashmere, and a patterned silk blouse in stunning shades of red and orange. A delicate white rabbit-fur capelet rested elegantly on her shoulders and a single large ruby, the size of a small candy egg, hung from a chain around her neck. Her nails and lips were varnished in the same red wine color. Andy watched, mesmerized, as those thin, lacquered lips wrapped around the cardboard coffee cup, drank, released. She ran her tongue slowly, deliberately, across the top lip first and then the bottom. Like watching a cobra devour a mouse.

Finally – finally! – Miranda turned her gaze upward from her papers and toward them, although there wasn't the least glimmer of focus or recognition. Instead, she cocked her head slightly to the side, looked from Emily to Andy and back again, and said, 'Yes?'

Yes? *Yes? Yes* as in *What can I help you with, you office intruders?* Andy felt her heart begin to race even faster. Did Miranda really not comprehend that *she* had invited *them* there? Andy almost fainted in appreciation when Emily opened her mouth to speak.

'Hello, Miranda,' Emily said, her voice sounding steadier than she looked, a wide, fake smile plastered on her face. 'It's good to see you again.'

Andy reflexively proffered her own wide, fake smile and nodded enthusiastically. So much for calm, cool, and collected. To hell with remembering that this woman couldn't hurt them now, that they didn't need her for anything, that her hold over them had long since evaporated. Instead, the two of them stood there, grinning like chimpanzees.

Miranda peered at them without a flicker of recognition. Nor did she seem to understand that she had initiated the appointment.

Emily tried again. 'We were both so pleased when you requested this meeting. Is there something we can help you with?'

Andy could hear Charla inhale sharply from the anteroom. This had the potential to go very wrong very quickly.

But Miranda merely looked puzzled. 'Yes, of course, I called you here to discuss your magazine, *The Plunge*. Elias-Clark is interested in acquiring it. But what did you mean when you said it's good to see me *again*?'

Andy whipped around to look at Emily, but her friend was staring straight at Miranda, frozen. When Andy hazarded a glance at Miranda, she saw the woman staring daggers at Emily.

Andy had no choice. 'Oh, I think Emily just means that it's been so long since we worked here together. Already almost ten years! Emily was your head assistant for two years, and I—'

'Two and a half!' Emily barked.

'And I was here for a year.'

Miranda touched a red nail to an uncomfortably moist red lip. Her eyes narrowed in concentration. After another awkward silence, she said, 'I don't recall. Of course, you can imagine how many assistants I've had since then.'

Emily looked like she was filled with murderous rage.

Terrified of what her friend might say, Andy powered forward. She forced a little laugh, which sounded tinny and bitter, even to her own ears. 'Yes, I'm relieved you don't recall, as my . . . uh . . . tenure here didn't end on the best terms. I was so young, and Paris, while wonderful, was just really overwhelming . . .'

Andy could feel Emily glaring at her now, willing her to shut up, but it was Miranda who interrupted her.

'Were either of you that sorry girl who turned completely catatonic and needed to be carted off to a psychiatric hospital?'

Both girls shook their heads.

'And neither of you were that lunatic who repeatedly threatened to burn down my apartment . . .' This appeared to be more statement than question, although Miranda did glance at them to see if it elicited any reaction.

Again, they shook their heads.

Miranda's brow furrowed. 'There was that plain girl with the terribly cheap shoes who tried to have me arrested on some sort of trumped-up harassment charge, but she was a blonde.'

'Not us,' Andy said, although she could feel Miranda's gaze burning into her booties, not offensively cheap but not designer either.

'Well then, you must not have been that interesting.'

Andy smiled, this time for real. *I guess you're right*, she thought. *Merely telling you to fuck off on a Parisian street corner and deserting you in the middle of the shows isn't even worth remembering. Noted.*

Andy's shock was interrupted by Miranda's shrill voice, unchanged after all this time, still exactly the same pitch and tenor that it was in Andy's memories and nightmares.

'Charla! Helloooo! Is anyone out there? Helloooo!'

A young girl who clearly wasn't Charla but an even younger, prettier, more nervous version of her materialized in the doorway. 'Yes, Miranda?'

'Charla, get Rinaldo in here. I need someone to run through the numbers.'

This request clearly panicked the girl. 'Oh, um, well, I think Rinaldo is out today. On vacation. Is there someone else I should call?'

Miranda sighed so deeply and with such disappointment, Andy wondered if Charla Lite would be summarily fired. She stole another look at Emily, desperate for some sort of connection, but Emily was standing beside her, hands clasped together in some sort of death grip, appearing nearly comatose.

'Stanley then. Get him in here immediately. That's all.'

Non-Charla scurried out of the office, her expression twisted in anxiety and fear, and Andy wanted to hug her. Instead she thought of her Stanley, safe and snuggled right then, probably chewing a bully stick, and she missed him terribly. Or maybe she just missed anywhere but there.

Moments later a middle-aged man in a surprisingly

unfashionable suit materialized in Miranda's office and, without being greeted or invited, strode past their little cabal to take a seat at Miranda's round table. 'Miranda? Would you care to introduce me to your visitors?'

Emily's mouth dropped open. Andy was so surprised she almost laughed out loud. Who was this brave soul in a bad suit who spoke to Miranda as though she were a mere mortal?

Miranda appeared momentarily ruffled, but she motioned for Andy and Emily to follow her to the table. Everyone sat.

'Stanley, may I introduce you to Andrea Sachs and Emily Charlton? They are the editor and publisher of *The Plunge*, the newest addition to the bridal magazine market, as I brought to your attention a few weeks ago. Ladies, this is Stanley Grogin.'

Andy waited for an explanation of what Stanley Grogin did, but none was forthcoming.

Stanley shuffled around some folders, muttered to himself, and pulled three stapled packets of papers from a leather folio and slid one each to Andy, Emily, and Miranda. 'Our offer,' he said.

'Offer?' Emily squeaked, her very first word in many minutes sounding more like a plea for help.

Stanley gave Miranda a look. 'Did you run through the basics with them?'

Miranda merely glared at him.

'Miranda mentioned she, uh, you . . . Elias-Clark, I guess, was interested in acquiring us?' Emily said.

'*The Plunge* has shown solid growth, both in subscription and advertising, since its inception three years ago. I am impressed by its level of elegance and sophistication, two qualities that are hardly synonymous with bridal magazines. The celebrity feature each month is especially appealing. You

should both be commended for what you accomplished.'
Miranda clasped her hands over her paperwork and peered
at Andy.

'Thank you,' Andy croaked, her voice cracking. She
couldn't even risk a glance at Emily.

'Please take some time to consider the offer,' Stanley said.
'You'll want your people to look it over, of course.'

It was at this point that Andy realized how bush-league
they must have seemed, to arrive sans 'people.' She picked
up her packet and began to leaf through it. Next to her,
Emily did the same. As phrases popped out at her – *current
editorial team, transition, relocation of premises*, blah, blah, blah
– her focus softened and all the words began to blur together.
It wasn't until the second-to-last page that her gaze lasered
in on the purchase price, a number so astonishingly high
that she snapped back to reality. Millions. It was hard to get
past *millions.*

Stanley clarified a few points that Andy didn't completely
understand, gave them copies of the proposal to pass along
to their legal team (*Note to self,* Andy thought, *get legal team*),
and suggested they could perhaps schedule another meeting
in a couple weeks to discuss any remaining questions they
might have. It was phrased to convey that this entire deal
was a fait accompli, that the girls would be certifiably insane
if they didn't accept such a generous offer from such a prestigious publisher. It was just a matter of when.

Non-Charla appeared in the office door and announced
that Miranda's car to lunch had arrived and was waiting
downstairs. Andy was desperate to ask if Igor was still her
driver, and if so, how he was doing, but she forced her
mouth shut. Miranda commanded the girl to bring her an
iced Pellegrino with a lime, giving no indication as to whether
she actually heard about the car or not, and stood up.

lauren weisberger

'Emily, Ahn-dre-ah,' Miranda announced. Andy waited for a 'pleasure to meet you' or a 'nice to see you again' or a 'have a lovely afternoon,' or 'we look forward to hearing from you,' but a few ensuing seconds of silence soon indicated that nothing further would be forthcoming. Miranda nodded at them both, murmured something about not waiting around all day for their answer, and strode out. Andy watched as Non-Charla handed Miranda a lush mink coat and a crystal goblet of Pellegrino, both of which Miranda snatched without slowing. It was only after she'd disappeared down the hallway that Andy realized she hadn't breathed in at least sixty seconds.

'Well, always an adventure, isn't it?' Stanley said, gathering his papers. He handed each of the girls a business card. 'We look forward to hearing your thoughts as soon as possible. Call me with any questions. You'll have better luck reaching me than her. But of course you already know that.'

He stuck out his hand, perfunctorily shook each of theirs, and disappeared down the hallway without another word.

'He's a real personality plus,' Emily muttered under her breath.

'Do you think he knows who we are?' Andy asked.

'Of course he does. He freaking knows our zodiac signs, I'm willing to bet. He works for Miranda.'

'Well the two of them together are a dream team,' Andy whispered back. 'How long did that entire meeting last? Seven minutes? Nine? So much for wining and dining.'

Emily grabbed Andy's wrist and squeezed so hard it hurt. 'Do you even *believe* what just happened? Let's get out of here. We *need* to discuss.'

They thanked Charla and Non-Charla, and Andy thought for a moment how incredible it was that Miranda had called

200

her by her own name for an entire meeting. She wanted to sit down with those two young, miserable-looking girls (Charla appeared only mildly downtrodden, as though her spirit had been squeezed but not crushed; Non-Charla had the lifeless eyes and listless expression of the clinically depressed), and reassure them that, should they choose to pursue it, there was life after Miranda Priestly. That they would one day look back on their year of servitude and, despite occasional PTSD-like flashbacks, be proud they'd survived the hardest assistant job on earth. Instead, she smiled kindly, thanked them both for their help, accepted her coat, and fled as quickly after Emily as they could manage while still maintaining a shred of dignity.

'Are we going to the uptown Shake Shack or the original?' Andy asked the moment they hit the sidewalk, suddenly ravenous.

'Seriously, Andy.' Emily sighed. 'You're thinking of burgers right now?'

'We had a deal! ShackBurgers, fries, and shakes. A baby onesie. It was a condition of this meeting!'

Emily ran-walked back to the Starbucks they'd met in a mere hour earlier. 'Can you focus on something besides food for a second? I owe you, okay? Here, drink this.'

Emily ordered an iced tea for Andy and a plain cup of coffee for herself. They picked up their drinks and Andy, irritated but unwilling to make a scene, followed her to a table in the farthest corner.

Emily's eyes were glowing with excitement; her hands shook. 'I can't believe that just happened,' she shrieked. 'I mean, I'd *hoped*. Miles was convinced, but I certainly wasn't. They want to buy us! Miranda Priestly is *impressed* with our magazine. Elias-Clark wants to acquire it. Can you even comprehend this?'

Andy nodded. 'Do you believe she didn't even recognize us? Here we were, so worried about what she was going to say, and she had zero idea that either one of us used to—'

'Andy! Miranda fucking Priestly wants to buy our magazine! *Our* magazine! Buy it! Is this even registering for you?'

Andy noticed her own hands were shaking as she sipped her tea. 'Oh, it's registering. It's the most insane thing I've ever heard. Flattering, of course, but mostly just insane.'

Emily's mouth dropped open in the most unattractive way. She sat staring at Andy, lower jaw near the table, for what felt like an eternity before slowly shaking her head. 'My god, it never even occurred to me . . .'

'What didn't?'

'But of course, it makes perfect sense.'

'What does?'

Emily's mouth turned down and her forehead crinkled in . . . what? Disappointment? Despair? Anger?

'Emily?'

'You don't want to sell to Elias-Clark, do you? You have reservations.'

Andy could feel her throat tighten. This was not going well. There was that part of her that felt a swell of pride. They were successful enough to have caught the attention of the world's preeminent publisher. Elias-Clark wanted to add them to its portfolio. Could there be a greater endorsement of their product? But. Elias-Clark was synonymous with Miranda Priestly. Could Emily possibly *want* to sell *The Plunge* to Elias-Clark? With barely a word spoken, the vibe between them had instantly changed.

'*Reservations?*' Andy coughed. 'Yes, I guess you could say that.'

'Andy, don't you realize that this is what we've been working toward since the moment we started? Selling the magazine? And that we now have an offer *years* before we ever thought possible, a great offer from literally *the* most prestigious magazine publisher on the planet? What can you possibly not like about that?'

'I like everything about it,' Andy said, speaking slowly. Measured.

Emily broke into a wide smile.

'I'm every bit as flattered as you are, Em. The fact that Elias-Clark wants to buy our little magazine is totally mind-blowing. It's incredible on every level. And did you see that purchase price?' Andy smacked her own forehead. 'I never thought I'd see a payday like that in my entire life.'

'So why do you look like your dog just died?' Emily asked. She pressed 'ignore' on her phone when Miles's picture popped up.

'You know why. You saw it, too.'

Emily feigned confusion. 'I didn't get a chance to examine every single word, but for the most part, it—'

Andy pulled out her packet and turned to page 7. 'Remember this little clause, right here? The one that states the entire senior editorial team must stay in place for at least one calendar year to help with the transition?'

Emily waved. 'It's just a year.'

'*Just a year?* Gee, I can't remember where I heard that before.'

'Oh please, Andy. You can do anything for a year.'

Andy stared at her friend. 'That is factually untrue, actually. The one thing I cannot do for a year is work for Miranda Priestly. I think I've already proven that.'

Emily stared at her. 'This isn't just about you. We're partners here, and this is a dream come true.'

The offer itself was gratifying, no doubt, but how could she possibly agree to sell their baby to Elias-Clark of all

lauren weisberger

places, not to mention agree to work there again for another year? It was inconceivable, and they hadn't even gotten to enjoy any of the celebratory gossip or rehash what they'd just witnessed – Miranda Redux, her office, her shell-shocked assistants, the whole deal.

Andy rubbed her eyes. 'Maybe we're both overreacting. Why don't we contact a publishing lawyer and ask him to negotiate on our behalf? Maybe we can get rid of that year-long-transition clause? Or maybe someone else will want to acquire us, now that an offer's been made? If Elias-Clark is so keen on it, chances are others will be, too.'

Emily just shook her head. 'It's Elias-Clark. It's Miranda Priestly, for god's sake. It's like they're anointing us.'

'I'm trying here, Em.'

'Trying? I can't believe you're not *jumping* at this opportunity.'

Andy was quiet. 'What's our rush?' she asked. 'This is the first offer, and it's years earlier than we expected. Why race into it? Let's take our time, think it through, and make the best decision for both of us.'

'Seriously, Andy? We would be certifiably insane not to accept this offer. I know it, and you know it.'

'I love *The Plunge*,' Andy said quietly. 'I love what we've built together. I love our offices and our staff and getting to hang out with *you* every day. I love that no one tells us what to do or how to do it. I'm not sure I want to give all that up just yet.'

'I know you love it. I do too. But this is an opportunity a million people would kill for. Certainly anyone and everyone who's ever grown a business from scratch. You need to see the big picture, Andy.'

Andy stood up and gathered her things. She reached out and squeezed Emily's arm. 'We just found out five seconds

204

ago. Let's give ourselves a little time to think it through, okay? We'll figure something out.'

Emily's hand reflexively hit the table in frustration. Not hard, but enough to stop Andy in her tracks. 'I sure hope so, Andy. I'm willing to talk about this more, but I'm telling you now, we cannot squander this opportunity. I won't let us stand in the way of our own success.'

Andy slung her bag over her shoulder. 'You mean me. You won't let *me* stand in the way of *your* success.'

'That's not what I said,' Emily said.

'But that's definitely what you meant.'

Emily shrugged. 'You may hate them, but they are the very best and they are offering to make us rich in our own right. Can't you take the long view for once?'

'What, you mean like the worshipful view you've always taken of Elias-Clark? And let's be honest, of Miranda too?'

Emily glared at her. Andy knew she should end it there, but she couldn't help herself.

'What? I'd be willing to bet anything that you still blame yourself for getting fired. That even though you were the best goddamn assistant she ever had, you still think Miranda was in some way justified for throwing you out like last week's garbage.'

Anger flashed across Emily's face, and Andy knew she'd gone too far. But all Emily said was, 'Let's not do this now, okay?'

'Fine. I'm headed to run some errands over lunch. I'll see you back at the office,' Andy said, and walked out without another word. It was going to be a very long day.

13

i could easily be dead by then

Andy rested her head against the taxi seat and inhaled the not-unpleasant vanilla scent of the dangling air freshener. It was the first time in weeks she could remember smelling something and not wanting to vomit. She was breathing deeply when her phone rang.

'Hi,' she said to Max, and hoped he wouldn't bring up the meeting. She was looking forward to telling their families about the baby that night, and she didn't want to keep thinking about Miranda.

'Where have you been? I must have left a thousand messages with Agatha. How did the meeting go?' His tone was urgent.

'Me? Oh, I'm fine, thanks for asking. You must have been worried!' Andy said. She had kept Max up most of the night, thrashing with anxiety over the meeting.

'Seriously, Andy, how'd it go? They want to buy you, don't they?'

This made her sit straight up. 'Yes, they do. How did you know that?'

'What else could they have wanted?' he crowed, sounding triumphant. 'I knew it, I just *knew* it! Miles and I have a bet about how much. You both must be so excited.'

'I'm not sure *excited* is the word I'd use. Maybe *terrified* is a little closer.'

'You should be proud as hell, Andy! You did it. You and Emily, against all odds, built this thing from scratch, and now the most prestigious magazine publisher on earth wants to buy it from you. It doesn't get any better than that.'

'It is an honor,' Andy said. 'But there are definitely some worrisome details.'

'Nothing you can't work out, I'm sure. I can recommend a great lawyer, someone from an entertainment firm we use. They can iron out any issues.'

Andy kneaded her hands. Max was making it sound like a done deal when they'd only just gotten the offer that morning.

'So when's everyone getting there?' she asked, trying to change the subject. 'And do you think they suspect anything?'

'I told you, I've got it all under control. There's a husband-and-wife chef team here now, and they're whipping up a feast. Everyone's getting here in an hour. They're all going to flip when we tell them about the baby, and now we have this incredible news to share, too.'

'No, I don't want to mention anything about—'

'Andy? Can you hear me? Look, I've got to make a few calls. I'll see you soon, okay?'

She heard the phone click and once again allowed her head to rest against the seat. Of course, her husband was an investor, a substantial one. It was perfectly understandable he'd be thrilled; it made him look like a genius, not to mention help line the Harrison coffers. But she wasn't yet ready to share the news. The baby was one thing – that was exactly the kind of news you shared with future grandparents, even the Barbara Harrisons of the world – but an entire evening spent discussing Miranda Priestly? No thank you.

Despite her initial reservations, by ten P.M. Andy had to admit that the evening had been a success. Everyone was still going strong. Unsurprising for her family, who interpreted 'time to leave' as 'time to begin saying good-bye, hugging, rehugging, asking last-minute questions, visiting the bathroom, offering once again to clean up, and kissing each and every person in the room,' but this was very unusual for Barbara, who was always fashionably but never rudely late, a tidy and considerate guest, and quick to thank her host and leave. With the exception of Eliza, who had left an hour earlier to meet friends, each and every one of their immediate family members was still planted in the living room, chatting animatedly, drinking voraciously, and laughing like teenagers.

'I'm so delighted for you both,' Mrs Harrison said in a way that indicated nothing about her true feelings. But maybe she meant it? Maybe a baby – the promise of a new Harrison – was enough to win Andy some respect and acceptance? They sat side by side on the backless chaise. 'A grandchild, my, my. Naturally I'd always hoped, but so soon! Quite the surprise.'

Andy tried to ignore the 'so soon' part. Max had insisted they leave out the details about the baby being unplanned – he didn't want everyone thinking it was some sort of mistake – but Andy was sure his mother was no more thrilled with the idea that she and Max had deliberately conceived this child two months before getting married. Wouldn't that be just like her low-class daughter-in-law?

'Of course you'll name him after Robert if it's a boy,' Mrs Harrison said, clearly intending it to be a statement and not a question. Even more infuriating, Barbara directed her stipulation to Max, as though he were the sole name decider.

'Of course,' Max said without so much as glancing in Andy's direction.

She had no doubt they'd name a baby boy after Max's father, and probably even a little girl – Andy wouldn't want it any other way – but still she bristled at the presumption.

Jill caught Andy's eye and coughed. Loudly.

'You never know, I have a feeling these two will have a girl. A tiny, perfect, sweet little girl. All sugar and spice and everything my three boys aren't. At least, that's what I'm hoping.'

'A girl would be lovely,' Mrs Harrison said in agreement. 'But we'll want a boy at some point to carry on the family business.'

Andy refrained from pointing out that she, a female, was perfectly capable of running a business and any daughter of hers would be the same. Nor would she mention that Max's father, a male, hadn't exactly shown a whole lot of business acumen when making decisions on behalf of Harrison Media Holdings.

Max caught her eye and sent her a silent thank-you.

Andy's grandmother piped up from the couch opposite Andy. 'That child won't be born for another six months. I could easily be dead by then, in which case I'll insist they name the child for me. Ida's due to come back again, isn't it? All the old-timer names are in favor again.'

'Grams, you're only eighty-eight and you're strong as an ox. You're not going anywhere,' Andy said.

'From your lips to god's ears,' her grandmother replied, then spit three times in quick succession.

'Enough with the naming,' Jill said, clapping her hands together. 'Does anyone want some more decaf? If not, I think we should get going and let the parents-to-be get some rest.'

Andy shot her sister a grateful smile. 'Yep, I'm pretty tired, so . . .'

'No one in our family has lived past eighty,' Grams called to Andy. 'You're crazy if you don't think I'll be dead any day now.'

'Mom, stop that. You're perfectly healthy. Come on, let's get our stuff together.'

Andy's grandmother waved her hand dismissively. 'I lived long enough to see this one married off, which I never thought would happen. And not just married off, but pregnant. Will wonders never cease.'

There was a moment of uncomfortable silence before Andy burst out laughing. It was so vintage Grams. She hugged her grandmother and whispered to Jill, 'Thanks for getting them all out of here.'

'Before everyone goes, we have another exciting announcement . . .' Max said, standing to get the room's attention.

'Oh Christ, it's twins,' Andy's grandmother moaned. 'Two identical little rug rats at the same time.'

'Twins?' Mrs Harrison asked, her voice rising by at least three octaves. 'Oh, my.'

Andy could feel Jill turn to her questioningly, but she was too busy shooting Max a warning look to respond. He didn't catch her eye.

'No, no, it's not twins. It's about *The Plunge*. It seems Andy and Emily got—'

'Max, please don't,' Andy said quietly, her voice as hard and even as she could manage without creating a scene.

He either didn't hear her or didn't care.

'—an incredible offer from Elias-Clark to acquire *The Plunge*. An outrageously generous offer, to be more precise. Those two pretty much accomplished the impossible in getting such a young start-up noticed and courted like that so soon. Let's all raise a glass to all of Andy's hard work.'

Exactly no one raised a glass. They all began talking at once.

Andy's father: 'Elias-Clark? Does that mean you-know-who all over again?'

Barbara: 'Well, it couldn't have come at a more auspicious time! You'll be able to unload that little vanity project and move on to something more rewarding, like spending time with your baby. And perhaps I could get you involved with some boards . . .'

Jill: 'Wow, congratulations! Even if you don't want to sell it to them, the offer itself is such an honor.'

Andy's mother: 'I can't abide the idea of you working with . . . with . . . oh, what's her name again? The one who tortured you for a year?'

Grams: 'What, you work all this time to build the whole damn thing and now you just turn around and sell it? I don't understand you kids today.'

Andy glared at Max until he walked across the living room and enveloped her in a bear hug. 'Wonderful, isn't it? I'm so proud of her.'

Jill must have caught the look on Andy's face, because she sprang to her feet and announced to everyone that they'd all had enough excitement for one night, and they should all leave immediately so Andy and Max could sleep.

'I'll call you from the airport tomorrow, okay?' Jill said,

211

standing on tiptoe to wrap her arms around Andy's neck. 'I'm so incredibly excited for you guys. It really is the greatest thing ever. And I won't even give you shit about telling me at the same time you told your mother-in-law. I'm not offended, don't worry.'

'Good,' Andy said with a grin. 'Because pregnant people can do no wrong, as I'm quickly finding out.'

Jill shrugged on her down coat – it was bracingly cold, even for November – and said, 'Enjoy it while it lasts. People only care when it's your first. You can be nine months and ready to pop with your second, and no one's even going to offer you a seat. And your third?' She snorted. 'They outright ask if it was planned or not. Like they couldn't imagine anyone doing that voluntarily . . .'

Andy laughed.

'Not that we did do it voluntarily . . .'

'Details.' Andy reached out and tucked Jill's hair behind her ear. She'd almost forgotten what it was like to spend a quiet moment or two with her sister. Living across the country, they saw each other so rarely, and when they did, the kids and Kyle and Max and Andy's mom were almost always there, too. They hadn't been that close growing up – the nine-year age difference meant Jill had left for college when Andy was only a little girl herself – but in the last five or six years, the girls had begun talking regularly on the phone and tried to plan more frequent visits. There was even more to chat about when Andy got engaged, from wedding planning to all the ways husbands and fiancés were maddening, mysterious creatures, and Jill had been a supportive and loving matron of honor. Nothing could have put them in the same frame of mind faster than Andy's getting pregnant, she realized as she watched her sister pull on a pair of brown equestrian-style boots. For the last decade

Jill's life had revolved around parenting her boys, something Andy understood intellectually but couldn't relate to in any real way. Now, about to become a mother herself, Andy could sense she and Jill were about to have more in common than at any other point in their lives, and she suddenly couldn't wait to share the experience with her sister.

It took everyone another twenty minutes to gather their shoes and coats and hug good-bye and say congratulations one last time. When the door finally closed, Andy thought she might collapse.

'Tired?' Max asked, massaging her shoulders.

'Yes. But happy.'

'Everyone seemed legitimately pleased. And your grand-mother was in rare form tonight.'

'Not rare enough. But yes, they were all so happy.' She turned around to face Max, who was standing behind the couch. She made a conscious decision not to say anything about the Elias-Clark announcement. Max had worked so hard to plan the perfect evening, and he was obviously just excited for her. Andy forced herself to focus on the positive. 'Thank you for tonight. It was really special getting to tell everyone together.'

'You had a good time? Really?' Max asked with such hopefulness that it made her inexplicably sad.

'Really.'

'I did too. And they were all so thrilled with your *Plunge* news, too. I mean, how incredible. Barely three years out and already an offer from—'

Andy held up her hand. 'Let's talk about it another time, okay? I just want to enjoy tonight.'

Max moved forward to kiss her, pressing her body into the kitchen island with his own, and Andy felt a familiar jolt of excitement. It took her a moment to realize that for the first time since their wedding, she didn't feel exhausted or nauseated. Max nibbled her lower lip, gently at first, and then pressed into her with more urgency. She glanced at the husband-and-wife chef team, who were now tidying up the kitchen. Max followed her gaze.

'Follow me,' he said gruffly, wrapping his hand around her wrist.

'Don't you have to pay them?' she giggled, walk-running to keep up with Max as he led her to their bedroom. 'Shouldn't we at least say good-bye?'

Max pulled her into the room and quietly shut the door behind them. Without another word, he undressed her and wrapped his arms around her. They fell, kissing, onto the bed together, Andy on top of Max. She pinned his hands by his ears, kissed his neck, and said, 'I remember this.'

Max flipped Andy onto her back and lowered himself onto her. It all felt wonderful – the weight of his body against hers, the smell of his skin, the feel of his hands. They made love slowly, sweetly. When they were finished, Andy rested her head on Max's chest and listened as his breathing became regular and rhythmic. She heard Stanley bark as the chefs let themselves out, and she must have drifted off because when she next opened her eyes, she was shivering atop the covers and Stanley had wedged himself between her and Max.

Andy snuggled under the duvet and lay there ten minutes, fifteen. Sleep didn't come again, although she was so tired she felt like she could barely roll over. This, too, was a new pregnancy-induced misery: the bone-weary exhaustion coupled with inexplicable insomnia. Beside her, Max's breathing slowed and then evened out, his chest rising and falling with steady predictability. For as energetic and active as he was during the day, at night he slept soundly on his back, hands folded corpselike over his chest, rarely moving or readjusting. A 747 could have landed in their bedroom and he would have done little more than sigh, turn his head a few inches, and resume his strong, steady breathing. It was maddening on every level.

Climbing carefully out of bed, Andy pulled on her Mrs Harrison robe and the fluffy travel socks she'd purchased at the newsstand at JFK. She scooped a groaning Stanley into her arms and padded down the hallway toward the couch, where she collapsed in an ungraceful heap. Their DVR was disappointing: mostly old football games that Max had recorded but ended up watching online; a few NFL commentary shows; an ancient episode of *Private Practice*; a *60 Minutes* she'd already seen; a *Modern Family* that she'd promised Max they would watch together; and the final hour of the *Today* show's special wedding episode from two weeks earlier, when Andy and Emily had both checked out all the vendors and trends that Hoda and Kathie Lee discussed. Live TV wasn't much better: the usual late-night shows, some infomercials, a repeat of *Design Star* on HGTV. Andy was about to call it quits when something in the midnight slot caught her eye: *The High Priestess of Fashion: The Life and Times of Miranda Priestly*.

Oh shit, she thought to herself. *Do I have to?* Unlike everyone she knew, Emily included, Andy had refused to see it in the theater when it was out a year earlier. Who needed the flashbacks? The voice, the face, the constantly disappointed tone and reprimanding words. Andy could remember them all like they'd happened yesterday – why did she need to watch it in living color? Yet here, in the safety of her own living room, curiosity overtook her. *I have to.* Her thumb hesitated for only a moment before selecting the program. An angry-looking Miranda, adorned in a cream-colored Prada dress, gorgeous heels with a subtle gold buckle adornment, and of course, the ever-present Hermès bangle, glowered back at her.

'I don't think this is the time nor the place,' her icy voice said to whatever poor soul held the camera.

'Sorry, Miranda,' a disembodied voice replied before the screen went temporarily black.

And then, a second later, still in her office but now wearing a wool skirt suit, probably Chanel, with ankle booties. Appearing no more pleased than she had in the last scene.

'Aliyah? Can you hear me?'

The camera swiveled to a tall and exceedingly thin girl, not a day over twenty-one, who wore shiny white leggings, ankle booties that were eerily similar to Miranda's, and a gorgeous cashmere vest over a silk, man-styled shirt. The girl's wavy hair was messy and tangled in that sexy, Giselle-like way Andy could never pull off, and her eyes were smudged with kohl. She looked as though Miranda had just interrupted her having sex right on the assistant desk in the anteroom – seductive, sultry, naughty. And of course, terrified.

'Let everyone know that I'm ready for the run-through. It was scheduled for this afternoon, but I'll be leaving the office in twenty minutes. Make sure the car is waiting. Call Caroline's cell phone and remind her of her appointment this afternoon. What happened to that tote bag you were having fixed? I'll need it by three o'clock. As well as the dress I wore to the New York Public Library event last year or the year before. Or perhaps it was the pediatric AIDS dinner? Or that party in that dreary loft space on Varick after the fall shows last year? I can't recall, but you know the one I mean. Have that at my place by five, with the right sandals. And some earring options. Make a reservation for tonight, early dinner, at Nobu, and tomorrow, breakfast, at the Four Seasons. Make sure they have an adequate supply this time of pink grapefruit juice, not just the white, which is vile. Tell Nigel to meet me at James Holt's studio this afternoon at two; cancel my hair appointment but confirm the manicure and pedicure.' Here, she stopped for just a moment to catch her breath. 'And I'll need the Book tonight after eleven but before midnight. Do not, I repeat, do not leave it with the idiot doorman, and do not bring it into my apartment unless I'm there. We have . . . *houseguests* staying with us this evening, and they aren't to be trusted with it. That's all.'

The girl nodded in a way that didn't inspire confidence. Andy could tell instantly she was new and hours, if not minutes, from being fired. She had no pen or paper, no ability to remember all the requests or ferret out all the answers. Andy's own mind was reflexively firing questions. *Which 'everyone' exactly needs to know about the run-through? Where's the driver right now and can he get back there on time? Where is she going? What appointment does Caroline have this afternoon, and does she already know about it? Which tote bag? Will it be ready by three o'clock and if so, how do I get it to the office? Will she even be at the office, or will she already be at home? Which dress? I know for a fact she wore different dresses to each of those events, so how on earth do I know which one she means? Did she give me any color/cut/designer clues to narrow it down? Which sandals? Is there an accessories editor in right now and can she get earrings on time? What kind will look best with the mystery dress? What time exactly should I make the Nobu reservation? Tribeca or Fifty-Seventh Street location? And breakfast at the Four Seasons? Seven? Eight? Ten o'clock? Remember to send the general manager a thank-you gift for accommodating the grapefruit juice request. Find Nigel, relay blessedly specific information, and follow up on*

217

all grooming appointments. Preemptively make suite reservations at the Peninsula for when Miranda inevitably calls me in the middle of the night complaining about her houseguests (friends of her husband's, no doubt) and demands an immediate escape. Warn driver of probable late-night transport from Miranda's apartment to hotel. Stock hotel suite with Pellegrino, the Book, and an appropriate workday outfit for tomorrow, including all accessories, shoes, and toiletries. Plan to sleep not one wink as you see Miranda through this trying time. Repeat.

The camera left Miranda and followed the girl back to her desk – the same desk Andy had sat at ten years earlier – and watched as she frantically scribbled notes on miniature Post-its. The camera zoomed in as a single tear slid down her peachy cheek. Andy felt her own throat close up and she hit 'pause.' *'Get a grip!'* she hissed to herself, noticing that her fingernails were digging into her palm as she death-clutched the remote control and her shoulders were practically wedged in her ears. She was scared to glance up, despite the frozen frame on the television, her terror nearly the same as when she'd watch movies with young girls running alone in heavily forested areas, headphones on, blissfully unaware that a deranged serial killer was about to leap from behind a tree. This was why Andy had refused to see the movie when it first came out, despite everyone else's prodding and mocking. She had felt this way twenty-four hours a day for an entire year. Why did she need to subject herself to it again?

Stanley woofed at his own reflection in the window and Andy pulled him close. 'Should we make a cup of tea, boy? What are you in the mood for? Mint?'

He stared at her dumbly.

She stood up, stretched, rewrapped her robe. Not wanting to wait for the kettle to boil, she dug around in the gigantic bowl of coffee and tea pods Max kept on the counter until she found one for herbal tea. She popped it in the machine, added a packet of real sugar (no more artificial sweeteners!) while it steeped and a dash of milk, and was back on the couch in under a minute.

Emily was still in touch with a handful of people at *Runway* and so was privy to countless current and ridiculous Miranda requests, outrageous firings, and public humiliations. It seemed age had not humbled or slowed the woman whatsoever. She still went through assistants faster than steak lunches. She still punctuated nearly every command with *that's all.* She still called her staff night and day, berating them over the phone for not reading her mind or divining her needs before slamming down the receiver and calling again. Andy certainly hadn't needed to watch that snippet to bring it all back – to this very day, a certain old-school Nokia cell phone ring, heard on the crosstown bus or across a crowded bar, could send her into paroxysms of panic. Now the screen in front of her brought it all rushing back in stark color.

It had taken months after that fateful afternoon in Paris before Andy could sleep through the night again. She'd wake with a gasp imagining some task she'd failed to complete – she'd lost the Bulletin again or sent Miranda to the wrong restaurant for a lunch meeting. Andy had never picked up another copy of *Runway* from the moment she'd left, but of course it taunted her from bodegas, hair salons, doctors' waiting rooms, mani-pedi places, everywhere. When she was offered the job at *Happily Ever After* by a girl only a few years older than herself who promised Andy 'loads of writing independence' so long as she wrote on generally approved topics and delivered them on time, it felt like a new start. Lily was moving to Boulder. Alex had broken up with her.

Her parents had announced their separation. Andy had turned twenty-four a few months earlier and was living alone in what felt like, for the first time in almost two years, an overwhelmingly huge city. For company she had her television and the odd college friend, if she reached out. And then, thankfully, Emily.

The sound of Miranda's shrill voice snapped her back to reality. The live television pause had run out, and the documentary had snapped back onto the screen. Andy watched for just a moment as Miranda's soon-to-be-ex-assistant tried fruitlessly to remember the list of things that had just been dumped in her lap. Andy saw the expressions of surprise and panic followed by realization and defeat, and her heart went out to the girl. Her firing would come as a surprise only to her, convinced as she surely was that this job was her ticket to a bigger and better world. The girl couldn't possibly understand that in eight or ten years she'd be sitting in her own living room, with perhaps a husband to call her own and a baby on the way, and she would still want to throw up or murder someone every time she heard a certain ringtone or spotted a white scarf or accidentally surfed past a certain show on the television.

As though on cue, text at the bottom of the screen announced that one day had elapsed since the last scene. Here, Miranda was seen wearing a stunning Burberry coat with an Yves Saint Laurent bag flung over her shoulder as she walked into the anteroom on her way out to lunch or a meeting.

She stared at the senior assistant, another girl Andy didn't recognize but whom she could identify because of her spot in Emily's seat, until the girl dared to look up.

'Dismiss her,' Miranda said, not bothering to lower her voice a decibel.

'Pardon?' the Emily assistant asked, out of shock, not because she was unable to hear.

'Her,' Miranda said, motioning her head in the direction of the junior assistant. 'She's a moron. I want her gone before I return. Begin interviewing immediately. I expect you'll do a better job this time.'

Miranda cinched her trench around her microscopic waist and strode out of the office. The camera swiveled to the desk of the junior assistant, whose face registered the same shock it would have if she'd been struck. Before the girl's huge, sweet eyes could dissolve into tears, Andy shook her head and clicked off the TV. She had seen enough.

14

miranda priestly all but called you gorgeous

Andy laughed as Emily white-knuckled the chair's armrests and gingerly lowered herself into the front-row, courtside seat.

Emily shot her a look. 'I don't know what you're laughing at. At least I'm only injured, not huge.'

Andy looked down at her belly, now solidly rounded and unquestioningly obvious at five months along, and nodded, smiling. 'I'm huge.'

'These seats are like Jay-Z style,' Emily said, looking around. Max and Miles were sitting courtside on the player's bench watching warm-ups, in guy heaven. Their heads turned as each seven-foot-something player ran, shot, dribbled, and dunked. 'Every now and then, Miles actually comes through with something good.'

'I wish I cared the least bit about the Knicks or basketball in general,' Andy said, rubbing her belly. 'I feel like we don't really appreciate it.'

The crowd behind them roared when Carmelo Anthony ran onto the court for his warm-up.

'Please,' Emily said, rolling her eyes. 'I'm here for the front-row VIP experience, and you're here for the food. So long as we're clear on that, it's fine.'

Andy shoved a forkful of truffled mac and cheese into her mouth. 'You should really have some of this . . .'

Emily blanched.

'What? Doctor's orders to gain thirty pounds . . .'

'Isn't that for the whole nine months and not just the first half?' Emily asked, looking at Andy's piled-high plate in disgust. 'I mean, I'm no pregnancy expert, but you look clear on your way to pulling a Jessica Simpson.'

Andy smiled. She'd been enjoying the occasional extra cupcake and slice of pizza now that the nausea had subsided, yes. It definitely wasn't only her belly that was looking bigger either – both her face and her butt had filled and rounded out – but she knew it wasn't anything out of the ordinary. Only when she was talking to Emily, who still referred to pregnant women as 'fat' or 'really packing it on,' did she even think about it. Andy had come to accept that her only real pleasure these days came from food and that no one ever looked at a pregnant woman and thought she was large or small, fat or thin, even tall or short; she was just pregnant.

The guys turned around and waved; Emily winced as she waved back and touched her abdomen. 'Christ, this hurts. And no decent painkillers! A few losers go and get themselves hooked on Oxy, and it means a lifetime of Advil for the rest of us.'

'I told you it was crazy to come tonight. Who goes to Madison Square Garden the week they discharge you from the hospital?'

'What was I supposed to do?' Emily asked, genuinely puzzled. 'Sit home in my pajamas and watch a Lifetime movie when you're all here? Besides' – she nodded toward the front row across the court – 'I wouldn't see Bradley Cooper at home.'

'And he wouldn't be able to admire your golden tan,' Andy said.

Emily ran her fingertips across her cheekbones. 'Exactly.'

The New Year's trip to the island of Vieques with Emily and Miles had been nothing short of fabulous: a gorgeous beachside villa with two master bedroom suites, a private pool, a bartender who seemed to specialize in fruity rum drinks, and plenty of swimming, tennis, and lazy beach time. Not only did they never once get dressed up to go anywhere, but some nights they didn't even bother changing out of their bathing suits and cover-ups for dinner. Andy and Emily had agreed not to discuss the Elias-Clark offer or any business on vacation, and with the exception of one dinner mention about investing in beach property post-payout, they'd kept that pact. Andy knew they were delaying the inevitable, and they had a conference call with Stanley scheduled for the first Monday back. But for the duration of the week? They slept late, drank heavily (Andy allowed herself the occasional glass of champagne and then plenty of calorie-laden virgin piña coladas; being pregnant, she finally realized what it felt like for Max, who even now, after all these years, never had a single drink), read trashy magazines, and sunned themselves eight hours a day. It was the most relaxing vacation Andy could remember, right up until Emily had gotten appendicitis.

'I'm sure it's just food poisoning,' she'd announced their eighth morning, when she showed up at the breakfast table looking pale, sweaty, and traumatized. 'And don't for one single second think I'm pregnant, because I am not.'

'How do you know? If you're puking, you're probably—'

'If the pill on top of my IUD can't prevent pregnancy, then I should go on the road as some sort of fertile freak show.' Emily doubled over and struggled to catch her breath. 'I am *not* pregnant.'

Miles shot her a sympathetic look but didn't stop shoveling French toast into his mouth. 'I told you those mussels were bad news . . .'

'Yeah, but I shared them with her, and I feel fine,' Max pointed out, pouring himself and Andy cups of decaf coffee from a stainless carafe.

'All it takes is one,' Miles said, his eyes scanning the *Times* on his iPad.

Andy watched as Emily carefully stood up, held her abdomen, and walked as fast as she could back to her room. 'I'm worried about her,' she said to the guys.

'She'll be fine by tonight,' Miles said, not looking up. 'You know how she gets.'

Max and Andy exchanged a look. 'Why don't you go check on her?' he said to Andy quietly. She nodded.

She found Emily writhing atop the covers, curled in a ball, her face twisted in pain. 'I don't think this is food poisoning,' Emily whispered.

Andy called the resort's front desk to ask about a doctor, and they assured her they would send the on-staff nurse immediately. The woman took one look at Emily, pressed a few times on her belly, and declared it appendicitis. She texted something on her phone, and a few minutes later, a hotel van appeared to take Emily to the local clinic.

After allowing Emily to stretch out on the middle bench, they all piled in. They'd been in Vieques over a week, and with the exception of a quick jaunt to another hotel for lunch, not one of them had been off the resort grounds. The ride to the clinic was short but bumpy – only Emily's whimpering punctuated the silence as they all gazed out the window. When they finally pulled into a parking lot, Max was the first to say what they were all thinking.

'This is the clinic?' he asked, staring at the dilapidated structure that appeared to be a cross between an unfinished grocery store and military airplane hangar. The words *Centro de Salud de Familia* appeared in neon on the front, although more than half the letters were burned out.

'I'm not going in there,' Emily said, shaking her head. She looked like she might pass out from the effort.

'You don't have a choice,' Miles said. He wrapped one of Emily's arms over his shoulders and motioned for Max to do the same. 'We need to get you some help.'

They half carried Emily through the front door and were greeted with a scene of total silence. With the exception of a lone teenager watching what appeared to be an episode of *General Hospital* from the early eighties on an overhead black-and-white television, the place was completely deserted.

Emily moaned. 'Get me out of here. If I don't die first, they'll kill me.'

Miles rubbed her shoulders while Max and Andy went in search of help. The desk toward the back of the room was empty, but the nurse who'd accompanied them from the resort felt free to walk behind it, open a side door, and shout into it. A woman wearing scrubs and a surprised expression appeared.

'I have a young woman with probable appendicitis. I'll

need a blood test and an abdominal X-ray immediately,' she said authoritatively.

The woman in scrubs took one look at the nurse's ID badge and nodded wearily. 'Bring her back,' she said, and motioned for the group to follow her. 'We can do the blood test, but the X-ray machine is down today.'

As they were led down the hallway, the lights flickered on and off at unpredictable intervals. Andy could hear Emily begin to cry and realized this was the first time in the decade she'd known Emily that she'd seen her lose her cool.

'It's just a blood test,' Andy said as soothingly as she could.

The woman dropped their entire group in an exam room, left a cotton gown of questionable cleanliness on the table, and walked out without a word.

'They will be back soon to draw your blood. There is no need to change your clothing,' the hotel nurse said.

'Well, that's good, because there is no chance I was going to,' Emily said, clutching her abdomen.

Another woman in scrubs appeared and, staring at her clipboard, said, 'You the Lyme disease?'

'No,' Miles said, looking concerned.

'Oh. Here, I'm going—'

The hotel nurse interrupted. 'Suspected appendicitis. I just need a white blood cell count and an X-ray to confirm. Her name is Emily Charlton.'

After another five minutes where each of them double- and triple-checked to make sure the needle she was using was brand-new in sealed packaging, Emily proffered her left arm and winced as the woman took a sample. The hotel nurse then took her to another room for an X-ray, where the machine had supposedly just been fixed, and returned with the news: it was appendicitis, as she suspected, and it would require immediate surgery.

lauren weisberger

With the word *surgery,* Emily swooned and nearly toppled over onto the table from her sitting position. 'No fucking way. Not happening.'

Max turned to the hotel nurse. 'Is there a hospital on the island? Perhaps somewhere . . . a little more modern?'

The nurse shook her head. 'This is only a clinic. They are not equipped for surgery, and I wouldn't recommend it even if they were.'

Emily started to cry harder; Miles looked like he might faint, too.

'Well I'm sure other guests of the resort have needed minor surgeries before, right? What's our next step?'

'We would need to have her transferred to San Juan by helicopter.'

'Okay. How quickly can we do that? Is that what your other guests have done?'

'No, I'm afraid not. We had a woman go into early labor once, and another with a horrible case of kidney stones. Oh, and there was that elderly gentleman who had a minor heart attack, but no, none of them went to San Juan. They always fly to Miami.'

'How long before she needs surgery?' Max asked.

'Depends. Sooner is better, of course. You want to avoid the appendix rupturing. But considering she hasn't had pain for very long and her white blood cells aren't through the roof, I'd say you could possibly make it.'

That was all Andy needed to hear before she kicked into planning mode *Runway*-style. Working her phone and Max's simultaneously, shouting out commands to Miles, Andy managed to charter a small prop plane in under an hour – all the while driving the bumpy roads to the airport. She organized an ambulance to meet their plane at Miami International, and called a general surgeon at Mount Sinai in Miami – one of Alex's old friends from college – to arrange for someone to operate on Emily immediately. Andy and Max would see off Miles and Emily and then return to the hotel to pack up everyone's belongings before jumping on the first commercial flight to Miami they could find.

Andy was saying her good-byes on the plane when Max said, 'You're incredible. You're like a professional fixer. I've never seen anything like that.'

'That's my girl,' Emily said with a weak smile. 'I trained her myself.'

'Yeah, well, as much of a crazy bitch as you are, you still don't hold a candle to Miranda,' Andy said, gently tapping Emily's forehead. 'Next time challenge me.'

The surgery had gone smoothly, all things considered. Since Emily's appendix did partially rupture, the doctors kept her in the hospital for nearly a week, but there were no major complications. Andy and Max stayed for a day or two, long enough to witness the outrageous arrangement of flowers with a note that merely read 'From the office of Miranda Priestly.' Emily's convalescence meant rescheduling their call again, date TBD. Andy happily went back to the business of editing *The Plunge* without the specter of another Elias-Clark conversation for an entire blissful week. She browsed a few baby boutiques in her neighborhood, test-drove some strollers, and chose the perfect gender-neutral bedding in the sweetest lime green and white elephant pattern. When Emily called Andy two minutes after landing at JFK and announced Miles had gotten them 'sick tickets' to the Knicks game that night, Andy could only shake her head. Who else would walk off a flight – looking absolutely fabulous, by the way – and directly to a basketball game mere days after having an organ removed?

They watched the team warm up a little while longer and

then, at Andy's insistence, visited the private club room for some reinforcements. Andy piled her plate high with shrimp and cocktail sauce, crab legs and butter, barbecued chicken, corn on the cob, and enough salty, flaky biscuits to feed four people. She dropped all the food on a corner table before leaving again to retrieve a huge cup of Coke (oh, it wouldn't hurt anything just this once!) and a heaping piece of chocolate mousse cake.

'You're really going for gold, huh?' Emily asked as she nibbled from her tiny plate of crudités.

'I'm five months pregnant and on my way to being the size of a house. I'm going to live a little,' Andy said, and bit off the end of a shrimp.

Emily was too intent on trying to spot celebrities in the intimate VIP lounge to really pay much attention. Her eyes moved slowly, subtly, around the room as she investigated every face, every bag, every pair of shoes until Andy saw her eyes widen.

Andy followed Emily's gaze and inhaled so sharply, the piece of shrimp became lodged in her throat. She could still breathe, but all her coughing was failing to move it either up or down.

Emily glared at her. 'Can you keep it down, please? Miranda is here!'

Andy breathed in as much oxygen as she could manage and coughed powerfully. Finally, after a few more panicked coughs, the food flew out of her mouth and into Andy's waiting hands, where she wrapped it in a napkin and tossed it on their table.

'That's the most disgusting thing I've ever seen,' Emily hissed under her breath. 'Why don't you just puke all over the place next time?'

'Thanks for asking, I'm just fine. I appreciate your concern.'

'What the hell is she doing at a Knicks game? Miranda is no basketball fan.'

Emily stole another glance. 'Ah, I see. She's with her boyfriend. He must like basketball.'

Andy squinted across the room and saw that Rafael Nadal was seated next to Miranda. They were both drinking coffees, and Miranda was laughing at every word he uttered. Her teeth were perfectly straight and normal sized – absolutely nothing noteworthy about them either positively or negatively – but the very few times Andy had seen Miranda smile, she had gotten goose bumps. The pale skin stretched across her face; those thin, white lips pulled into even tighter little lines; and the teeth looked like they'd reach out and bite you if you got too close . . . Andy shivered just thinking about it.

'God, he's gorgeous.' Emily sighed, not bothering to hide her gaze now.

'Do you think they're sleeping together?' Andy asked.

Emily looked at her, eyebrows raised to the ceiling. 'You're joking, right? He's her muse. Her little crush. She would eat him alive.'

Andy dunked a crab leg in butter. 'Let's go find the guys. I don't want to risk a Miranda run-in. I've had enough excitement the last few days, and you have, too.'

'Don't be ridiculous,' Emily said, standing up with an obvious wince. She smoothed her hair and pulled some imaginary lint off her cashmere sweater. 'Of course we're going to say hello. She sent flowers to the hospital! It would be downright rude not to thank her for them.'

'*She* didn't send them, Emily. You remember how—'

But it was too late. Emily had already dragged Andy by the forearm to stand, doing so in such a way that it appeared she was helping a bottom-heavy pregnant lady out of her seat. Emily wrapped her hand around Andy's wrist and began to pull her across the room. 'Just follow my lead,' she said as they quickly covered the carpeted room. In less than ten seconds the girls were standing in front of Miranda's table.

Andy glanced down at her wrist, where Emily's hand kept a viselike grip. She prayed for a five-alarm fire to spontaneously break out and force them all to run for their lives. But there was only stupefied silence on all fronts until the even-more-handsome-in-person tennis player cleared his throat.

'Do you have something you'd like me to sign? Or should I just sign this napkin?' he asked, looking at Emily since Andy's eyes were pointed at the ground.

'Oh no. No, no, no,' Emily said in a flustered, very un-Emily-like way.

Nadal laughed. 'Silly me. Look at you two. You probably aren't here for my autograph, are you? You want Ms Priestly's.' With this, he turned to Miranda and said, 'I wish I had as many beautiful young women worshipping me as you do.'

'Oh, Rafa!' Miranda laughed, her skin pulling across her teeth in that ghoulish way. 'You flatter me.'

Me too, Andy thought. Had Rafael Nadal just called them beautiful?

Miranda reached out and placed her hand on Nadal's arm. She giggled again.

Emily and Andy exchanged glances. Miranda was flirting!

Thankfully Emily found her voice before things got even more awkward.

'Actually, I'm Emily Charlton and this Andy – Andrea – Sachs. From *The Plunge*?'

Not to mention various periods of indentured servitude, Andy thought.

'Thank you so much for the flowers! They were gorgeous, and that was so thoughtful of you.'

Miranda evaluated them both coolly, although Andy *knew* Miranda recognized them. No matter – it didn't stop her cheeks from burning when Miranda slowly ran her eyes from Andy's head to her toes. It still made Andy want to amputate both feet when Miranda's eyes came to rest on her shoes (today's, incidentally, were a pair of dirty Converse sneakers she'd unearthed from the dregs of her closet – she deserved to be comfortable). But it was when Miranda's gaze rose again and stopped on Andy's belly that she truly wanted to run.

'My, my,' Miranda said, her eyes fixated on Andy's midsection as though it were an IMAX screen. 'Expecting, are we?'

'Yes, uh, my husband and I are having a baby,' Andy rushed to say, some inexplicable force impelling her to name-drop Max's existence. 'I'm a little more than halfway through.'

Andy braced herself for what would inevitably come next – most likely an eyebrow-raise and a comment like 'Only halfway, hmm?' – so no one was more stunned when Miranda broke into another smile. And this one somehow wasn't creepy.

'How lovely for you,' she said with what sounded like sincerity. 'I just adore babies. Is this your first? You're carrying beautifully.'

Andy was so shocked that she found she was unable to respond. She simply stared at Miranda, nodding, and rubbed her bump protectively. She wasn't quite sure she'd heard the woman correctly.

'Yes, it's her first, and they're not finding out what they're having. But don't worry about a thing, Miranda. Andrea's not due until late spring, which leaves us plenty of time to iron out the details of—'

Miranda's eyes flashed coldly and her lips curled into thin, hissing cobras. 'Did I never teach you it's rude to talk business in social situations?' she snarled, her entire demeanor changing in a second.

Teach you.

Emily recoiled as though she'd been slapped. 'I'm sorry, I wasn't—'

'Miranda, go easy on them.' Rafael laughed. He caught the eye of a friend or a fan standing near the bar and excused himself. 'Nice meeting you two. Good luck with . . . everything.' Andy couldn't help but hear the warning in his voice.

'I'm sorry, Miranda, I just thought th-that—'

Miranda interrupted Emily's stammering. 'You may call Stanley on Monday morning if you'd like to discuss it.'

Emily nodded. Andy was about to announce a need to visit the ladies' room or an urgent desire to find their husbands, anything at all to get them out of there, but Miranda once again peered at Andy.

'And you, Ahn-dre-ah. I'll have my assistant get you a copy of my baby list. I think you'll find it most useful.'

Andy coughed. 'Oh, thank you,' she said, not knowing what else to say. 'That sounds nice.'

'Mmm. And do let me know if you need any recommendations for nanny agencies, baby nurses, and the like. I have some wonderful resources.'

It was all Andy could do not to faint. This was surely the longest conversation she'd ever had with Miranda Priestly where the woman didn't berate, command, or humiliate her. For a moment, Andy even felt guilty for thinking, *Of course Miranda has the best recommendations on hiring other people to raise your children.*

Instead, she smiled at Miranda and thanked her.

'It was great seeing you, Miranda,' Emily said, a note of

desperation apparent in her voice. 'Hope to speak to you again soon.'

Miranda ignored her entirely. She nodded to Andy and went to retrieve Rafael.

'Is it me, or was that the weirdest exchange ever?' Andy asked Emily, after they both watched Miranda and Nadal depart the VIP room.

'What? I thought it went perfectly,' Emily said, although Andy could see she was upset.

Andy stared at Emily. 'She didn't even ask how you were feeling.'

'What? That's just her personality – it isn't personal,' Emily said. 'She was downright sweet about your pregnancy. She said you're carrying beautifully! That's practically a love pronouncement in Priestly land.'

'And then she almost took your head off with her fangs! So even Satan has a soft spot for unborn babies. Great. But I can't stay pregnant forever, Em. If we sell to Elias-Clark, you're going to have to pull your weight around here and get knocked up, too.'

The color drained from Emily's face. 'Don't even.'

Andy laughed. 'I'm serious! The only way Miranda Priestly acts like a human being is around pregnant people. Otherwise she's a monster. I know we've been tiptoeing around this but please: you can't possibly still be considering selling to her.'

Emily's large eyes widened even more. 'Considering it? Hell yes, I'm *considering* it. I'm in! And if you had even a shred of business sense about you, you would be, too.'

'And if you had a shred of self-preservation, you'd be just where I am: running for the hills.'

'You're so dramatic!' Emily sighed dramatically.

'You call ten years of therapy and nightmares and flashbacks dramatic? If you and she want to cover the cost of my shrink and throw in an unlimited supply of sleeping pills and biweekly massages, I'll consider it. Anything short of that, and I wouldn't survive.'

The guys materialized before them. 'You won't believe who we just saw,' Max said with more excitement than would be possible for him if he'd seen Miranda Priestly.

'A certain famous fashion editor?' Emily asked seriously.

Max frowned. 'No. Megan Fox and her husband, the one from *90210*? They're sitting right next to us.'

'And she's even hotter in real life,' Miles added helpfully.

When neither girl responded, the guys exchanged a look. 'What's going on here?' Miles asked.

'We just had a Priestly run-in,' Andy said, looking to Max for sympathy. She was surprised to see how animated he became.

'Priestly as in Miranda? Really? Did she mention the buyout? Is she upset that so much time has passed since the initial offer?'

Andy glared at him. 'It's hardly been "so much time." The first call came after our wedding, and they wanted to see our numbers for the final quarter. Miranda's the one who all but takes off from Thanksgiving to New Year's. And here we are, a week into the new year. We're hardly procrastinating.' Andy knew she sounded defensive, but she couldn't help herself.

Miles thumped Max on the back. 'Let's go get a drink. Things sound stressful here.'

Max nodded. 'I just think if you're going to do it, you should really make a move on it sooner than later so she doesn't think—'

'We've got it covered,' Andy said with more irritation than she'd intended.

Max raised his hand in surrender. 'Just offering an opinion.'

Every time they discussed it, Max went on and on about the prestige of being acquired by Elias-Clark, the honor of receiving such an impressive offer after so little time in business, and how it would free Andy up to try something else she really loved – after a year of hell, of course. Andy couldn't help but suspect he was thinking with his wallet, thinking of boasting about his smart investment and his smart wife, both. She knew Harrison Media Holdings was floundering even more this year than last, and Andy's income was Max's and vice versa: he'd insisted they both enter the marriage without a prenup, on equal terms – an arrangement that far favored Andy, and enraged Mrs Harrison – so Andy was happy that both she and Max would benefit financially from a sale. What she wasn't delighted about was the constant low-grade pressure Max subtly but continually put on her. She didn't presume to weigh in on his business decisions.

'We'll be at the bar when you girls are done. No cat fights, okay? The game's starting any minute,' Miles said.

Emily turned to her, but Andy couldn't bring herself to meet Emily's eyes.

Finally she looked up. 'What?'

'You really aren't going to agree to this, are you? Not now, and not ever.' Emily intertwined her fingers and appeared to be exerting intense effort to keep her hands in her lap. She had the wiry anticipation of a tiger about to spring.

Andy opened her mouth to try to explain herself once again, but she shut it before she said a single word. 'It's just more than I can handle right now, Em. I know you can

237

understand that. I'm trying to stay on top of everything at work, I lost weeks and weeks to puking and exhaustion, and this baby is coming like a freight train in just a few more months. I have so much to do to get ready. It would be a lousy time to sell to anyone, much less to *her* . . .'

'So, no. You're saying no, right?' Emily's devastation was palpable.

Of course Andy was saying no, and if she had the nerve she would say what she really meant, which was: *I'd sooner die or go broke or not work anywhere than spend so much as a single additional day working for that woman*. But because she was Andy and she hated conflict, despised disappointing people, she said, 'I'm not saying no forever, just no for right now.'

A glimmer of hope flashed across Emily's face. 'Okay. I can understand that. It's just a little too much now. We'll obviously have an amazing spring season of weddings. Stanley mentioned even doing a brainstorming session to see how we'd work conceptually with Elias-Clark . . .'

'Yeah, let's revisit it after I've had the baby.' Andy felt guilty for misleading her friend, and she couldn't help but wonder when Emily had spoken to Stanley without her.

'So long as they're still interested,' Emily said poutily.

'I'm sure they'll still be interested. We'll have even more issues by then, more subscribers, and because you do your job so well, even more advertisers. We've grown every quarter since inception, and there's no reason to expect this will be any different. Plus, who knows better than you that playing hard to get just makes them want you more, right?'

'I'm not sure it works that way with Miranda Priestly. She's not really the playing-hard-to-get type. But if it's this or nothing, I guess I don't have a choice,' Emily said with uncharacteristic resignation.

'That's the spirit!' Andy said, trying to make her friend laugh.

Emily's look of defeat only lasted a moment before she said, 'I'm hoping the baby softens you. Or you get so fat I can just roll you over. I'll call Stanley this week and tell them we're taking a brief hiatus from negotiations. Just until you've had the baby.'

Andy nodded.

'Come on, let's get a drink and toast ourselves.'

Emily helped pull Andy out of the seat and they both winced in discomfort.

'What exactly are we toasting?' Andy asked.

'I survived a backwater island clinic. Miranda Priestly all but called you gorgeous. And we're probably going to sell our little magazine that could to the world's preeminent publisher. If that doesn't deserve a virgin mojito, nothing does.'

Andy watched as Emily made her way toward the guys, looking pleased and fabulously stylish once again. She knew she'd just made a huge mistake – she'd only pushed off the inevitable – but she vowed to put it out of her mind. For as long as she possibly could.

15

i'm here to tell you that not not-trying is trying

When she awoke from an intense, black sleep, the first thing Andy noticed was the distinctive smell of lavender and the sound of piped-in ocean waves.

'I'm glad to see you were able to relax,' the masseuse said softly as she tidied the counter with its assorted oil bottles and warm towels. 'Do you want some help down?'

Andy struggled to focus, but her contact lenses felt like glass.

'No, I'm fine, thanks,' she said, sending out a silent thank-you to Olive Chase for choosing to have her bachelorette party at the Surrey's hotel spa, and for insisting that Andy join them in the festivities. When Andy had protested, saying she needed only an hour or so to interview Olive, the actress showcased her million-dollar laugh and told Andy she would schedule her for a deluxe prenatal treatment that included a salt scrub, milk bath, and full-body massage using a specially designed donut pillow contraption that allowed pregnant women to lie facedown. If there was ever a time she loved her job, it was right then. Let the *New Yorker* writers be sticklers for journalistic integrity. She would get an afternoon of bliss.

Andy pushed herself to a sitting position using both arms and allowed the sheet to fall to her waist. Her belly was officially massive, tight as a drum and situated in such a way that lying down, sitting, and standing were all equally uncomfortable. The only time she felt any relief from the pressure and heaviness was when fully submerged in water, so Andy had taken to spending as much time as possible in the tub. At eight and a half months pregnant, she was no longer going to the office every day. But when Olive had invited *The Plunge* to attend her bachelorette festivities, Andy jumped at the chance: the actress's wedding would be after Andy gave birth, and Andy didn't want to miss all the action.

Carefully lowering her feet to the floor, Andy gathered her clothes and began the tedious task of dressing herself: full-panel maternity leggings, followed by a highly unattractive combination nursing/sports bra, and topped off with a ruched tunic in a hideous eggplant shade. There was simply nothing cute or stylish left at this stage of the game. She slipped her swollen feet into Birkenstocks (she could no longer reach her feet well enough to buckle or tie any real shoes by herself) and sent a silent thank-you that Emily wasn't there to witness this particular getup.

Andy thought about the previous workday's drama. Completely out of the blue they'd received a call from Elias-Clark — the first one since Emily had put them off back in January. Andy was at the OB, getting a standard checkup

– one of her last; she could barely believe it – when Emily called her, hysterical.

'Stanley left me a voice mail,' Emily said breathlessly. 'He said it's important and we need to call back *immediately*. When are you in today?'

'I don't know,' Andy said truthfully. 'I was supposed to be done by now, but the doctor is concerned that the baby isn't moving enough. I think I need more testing.'

'So, like by eleven? Twelve? You *are* coming in, right?'

Andy tried to ignore Emily's complete lack of interest in the health of her unborn child.

'I'll be in,' she said, her teeth gritted. 'I'll be in as soon as I can.'

Dr Kramer was worried that Baby Harrison was acting too 'snoozy.' There had already been an exam, followed by an ultrasound and, finally, a stress test – all with inconclusive results. Andy and Max were instructed to go get some lunch, including a sugary soda or dessert to give the baby a little jolt, and return an hour later to repeat the stress test. Dr Kramer had casually said, 'This is not an emergency, so don't worry. You're far enough along now that even if we have to induce you today, everything will be perfectly fine.' Max and Andy exchanged looks: induce *today*? Thankfully all tested normal the second time around and Andy felt like she could breathe again. Emily had been less understanding.

'Here, we're calling Stanley back this second,' Emily said, following Andy into her office. 'Don't even take your coat off.'

'I'm fine, and so is the baby. Thanks for asking,' Andy said.

'Of course everything's fine or you wouldn't be here. What is not fine is ignoring Miranda Priestly.'

The secretary put their call through and Emily fell all over herself trying to explain what had taken them so long.

Stanley pretended he didn't hear. Or maybe he really didn't. Instead he said, 'On behalf of Elias-Clark, we would like to increase our proposed purchase price by twelve percent. Miranda would, of course, like an answer immediately.'

Emily glanced at Andy, who shook her head violently. 'Not now!' she mouthed, pointing to her enormous bump. 'We agreed we wouldn't talk about this now.'

Emily looked like she was about to have a heart attack. She gripped the phone as if she could better emphasize her point. 'We'll be back to you *so* soon,' she said. 'Andy's about to pop. I mean, as soon as the baby's born, we'll be much better situated to—'

Stanley's response was not encouraging. 'I'll let Miranda know,' he said. 'I know I don't need to tell you two how much patience she has for delays.'

'Andy won't be out on leave long,' Emily said, her knuckles turning white. 'I mean, it may mean putting off the conversation for a couple months, but that won't change—'

'Miranda doesn't care about maternity leave,' Stanley said. 'She herself only missed seventy-two hours for the birth of the twins.'

'Yes, that really was remarkable,' Andy murmured into the speakerphone, swirling her finger near her forehead to indicate Miranda's lunacy.

Stanley cleared his throat. 'I just want to be transparent here – waiting isn't her forte. But you've made it clear what your timetable is. Good-bye now.'

After he disconnected, Emily looked at Andy wildly. 'We may lose this whole thing, Andy!'

Andy stared at her. 'We made an agreement. No talk until after the baby.'

lauren weisberger

'Maybe we should just send our lawyer to talk. To smooth things over. Buy us a little time.'

'That's not a solution. Seriously, Em, they just upped their offer. They're dying to buy *The Plunge*. Waiting has only improved their terms. Another couple months won't hurt a thing.'

'This pregnancy is becoming an excuse for everything.' Emily said this quietly, but Andy could feel her frustration.

That very afternoon two signature orange boxes with brown ribbons arrived via messenger from Hermès: three bangles apiece, each one different and ornately beautiful. Emily couldn't put them on fast enough. Andy looked at her with a smile. Maybe playing hard to get *was* enticing to Miranda.

Andy shuddered now just thinking about it. The masseuse led Andy to the relaxation room and helped settle her into a terry-cloth-swathed chaise longue. A minute later, a robe-clad Olive appeared, her already perfect skin literally glowing from a facial. No redness or irritation for her.

'How was it?' she asked Andy, helping herself to a small plate of dried apricots and almonds.

'It was heaven. Pure heaven,' Andy said, the same way she might to a friend.

It was surreal to be chatting so casually with perhaps the most famous woman on the planet. Olive Chase's movies had netted $950 million worldwide. She was recognized everywhere from the Bedouin sands of Egypt to the ice plains of Siberia to the remotest villages of the Amazon. Her romantic trials and tribulations had been the subject of endless coverage and analysis, all of her failed relationships lined up like roadkill behind her. The world had given up on her finding a man, or loving a man, or keeping a man, and her status as Most Gorgeous Single Woman Ever had been firmly cemented – much to the dismay of hundreds of thousands of regular guys, all of whom swore they were perfect for her – when she stepped onto the red carpet with just that . . . a regular guy. No amount of after-the-fact burnishing or all-out fiction writing could make Clint Sever, an engineer by training but a website designer by passion, anything more than the guy next door. When they'd met the year before under vague circumstances (Andy's entire goal for her upcoming interview was to ferret out more details of the first meeting), Clint was living in Louisville, Kentucky, a universe away from the glitz of Hollywood, and apparently the only Olive Chase movie he'd ever seen was a Christmas special she'd starred in twenty years earlier. He was twenty-nine, of completely average height, weight, and appearance, and in all the interviews Andy had watched, he seemed completely unfazed by his new life and megastar fiancée. He had willingly signed a prenup that would leave him exactly zilch if they ever divorced, regardless of how long the marriage lasted, how many children they had, or what Olive earned during its tenure. He submitted to interviews and walked red carpets and attended A-list parties when required but didn't appear impressed, intimidated, overwhelmed, or even really all that interested in any of it. Olive, on the other hand, couldn't shut up about her 'new man,' 'the sexy new guy' in her life, calling him 'the person who makes me happier than I ever thought possible.' Despite being ten years Clint's senior and having shared a bed with nearly every famous actor, athlete, and musician in existence (she didn't discriminate between men and women, it was rumored), Olive was reputedly head over heels in love with her average joe, and she wanted nothing more than to talk about it.

'Good! I just love it here.' Olive curled her coltish legs under her and settled into the chaise next to Andy's. 'No one else should be done for a little while, so I thought we could chat now.'

'Great,' Andy said, pulling out her notebook, but Olive clearly wasn't in a rush to start the interview.

She motioned for an attendant standing discreetly by the door and said, 'Darling, do you think you could break the rules and bring us some real drinks? I don't think tea is going to cut it today.'

The woman beamed at Olive. 'Of course, Miss Chase. What may I bring you?'

'I'd love a Patrón margarita, no salt.' She paused and shook her head. 'Actually, extra salt. Bloating be damned.' Olive turned to Andy. 'Do you want a Shirley Temple? No, probably not with all those fake red dyes and chemicals. Aren't maraschino cherries, like, automatic cancer? I think it's Pellegrino for you!'

Andy was instantly charmed.

'I ditched Daphne, my PR chick,' Olive said, leaning in conspiratorially. 'She's going to be so pissed! But my god, what can really happen? You write for a wedding magazine! This is not, like, a *60 Minutes* interview.'

'That is most definitely true,' Andy said, relieved to have a few unscripted minutes alone with Olive. If she could keep the girl drinking like this, she'd be able to ask anything she wanted. *US Magazine* had already purchased the rights to the first wedding pictures, but Andy hoped she'd be able to get the most complete story and accompany it with dozens of additional and varied pictures beyond the quickie four-page spread *US* would have to race to publish thirty-six hours after the event.

'So when are you due? By the looks of it, any second.'

Andy laughed. 'By the feel of it, too. But really not for another few weeks.'

Olive gazed longingly at her belly. 'I can't wait to get pregnant. What are you having?'

'I don't know yet,' she said. 'I like the idea of a surprise at the end of all that work.'

A look flashed across Olive's face, an expression Andy couldn't quite place. Something told her she should change the subject immediately, but Olive beat her to it.

'So, where do we begin?' she asked. 'Do you, like, want to hear about my entire childhood? Should I start with conception?'

Andy laughed. Olive was unlike any other celebrity she'd ever interviewed. There had been Harper Hallow and Mack, who had set a new bar (at least for Andy) in terms of fame. There was the well-known stylist with her own television show; the infamous woman chef who berated employees with a string of curse words and insults; the young country singer marrying the much older pop singer; the number-one-ranked female tennis player in the world; the reality TV star who'd transcended the *Housewives* franchise and become a worldwide name brand; the Oscar-winning, Spanish-speaking actress with the most jaw-dropping figure. Many of them were household names. Most were crazy as loons. All of them were attractive and intriguing in their own often weird ways. And here was Olive Chase, undoubtedly the most famous and successful of all of them, and she seemed so . . . normal. Killer body, gorgeous hair, great skin, addictive laugh . . . check, check, check. But disarmingly sweet? Willing to discuss anything (and without a publicist!)? The kind of person who immediately feels like a best friend in the making? Not what Andy was expecting.

'Let's maybe start with how you guys met,' Andy said,

pen poised above paper, praying to herself that Olive would offer something more than vague platitudes.

'Oh, that one's easy. We met the same way everyone does these days – online!'

Andy tried to control her excitement; she hadn't read about Olive dating online anywhere. 'Yes, but I wouldn't imagine a whole lot of celebrities meet people online. Weren't you concerned about privacy?'

Another long pull of her margarita and a brush-back of her silken hair. Olive appeared to consider this. She nodded. 'Of course I was concerned about it. But I had to find a way! I can't tell you how many actors and athletes and male models and musicians and hedge fund guys and just general all-around assholes I was set up with over the years. I think I dated every dickhead in North America, and quite a few in Europe. But then I'd be sitting home, late at night, alone as usual, and surfing the ordinary-people websites. There were so many great guys out there! Funny, charming, lovely men. Men who wrote poetry or loved fly-fishing or built homes from scratch or taught high school. I e-mailed with one guy in Tampa who was raising three kids all by himself after his wife died of ovarian cancer. Can you imagine?'

Andy shook her head.

'Me neither! I never met anyone like this, only men who wanted to be the first to tell you how talented or gorgeous or rich or powerful they were. And I have to say, I was over it. I created a profile where I was completely honest about my personality, very forthcoming, and didn't include a picture or any mention of acting. I didn't think anyone would ever e-mail me back without a picture, but they did. You'd be surprised. Clint was one of the first men I started corresponding with, and we hit it off immediately. Sometimes we'd e-mail ten, twelve times a day. We started talking on the phone after two weeks. We got to know each other in, like, the most organic way you could ever imagine, because appearance or money or status had nothing to do with it.'

'I can certainly see the appeal,' Andy said, not untruthfully.

'He fell in love with the real me, not some media creation of me.'

'How'd you meet for the first time?' Again, Andrea reminded herself not to appear too eager. She had no idea why Olive was confiding details to her that she hadn't shared with anyone else, but she was desperate to keep them coming.

'Let's see, it was probably about five or six weeks of talking every day. By then he knew I lived in L.A. and was an aspiring actress, and he offered to come out to visit me, but I couldn't risk getting chased by photographers the whole time. Not to mention that my house might have been a little intimidating. So I went to Louisville.'

Olive said this like a native, *Loo-ah-ville*.

'You went to Louisville?' Andy tried, but it came out sounding more like *Looey-ville*.

'I went to Louisville. Flew commercial, connected in Denver, the whole nine. I didn't let him pick me up at the airport in case there were paparazzi waiting. He came to my hotel.'

'Isn't there a really lovely, famous old hotel in Louisville that they've recently—'

'Oh, I stayed at the Marriott.' Olive laughed. 'No penthouse, no presidential suite or private butler, no special treatment. Just a pseudonym and a regular old room at the Marriott.'

'And?'

'And it was fantastic! I mean, don't get me wrong, the

bathroom was kind of gross, but our first meeting was amazing. I had him come up to the room so I wouldn't get recognized in the lobby, and he joked on the phone about how forward I was being, but when he knocked on the door, I just knew that everything was going to be okay.'

Andy sipped her water.

'And was it?'

Olive all but squealed. 'It was more than okay, it was perfect! Of course he knew who I was the moment he saw me' – somehow, and Andy wasn't sure how, Olive managed not to sound obnoxious saying this – 'but I just explained that I was still the person he'd e-mailed with and talked to for all those weeks. He was surprised, or I guess pretty shocked – he had nightmares I'd be a four-hundred-pound man or something – but we opened a bottle of wine and kept talking about all the things we had before – places we wanted to visit, our dogs, his relationship with his sister and mine with my brother. We just, like, totally opened up to each other, as real people. I knew right then I would marry him.'

'Really? Right then? That's amazing.'

Olive leaned forward conspiratorially. 'Well, not right then, but definitely a couple hours later after we had the best sex you could ever imagine.' Olive nodded, as though agreeing with herself. 'Yes, that's when I knew.'

'Mmm,' Andy murmured, looking at her notes. She prayed her phone was recording everything clearly, because there was no way anyone was going to believe this. Andy checked Olive's half-full margarita and wondered if she'd been drinking earlier, but Olive appeared sober. Andy's phone rang. She clicked off the ringer and apologized.

'Get it!' Olive implored. 'I've been yakking my head off all this time. Let someone else have a chance.'

'Oh, it's fine. I'm sure it's nothing.'

'Answer it!'

Andy looked at Olive, who had turned on her full-wattage Hollywood smile, and knew she had to obey her. She pressed 'talk' and said hello, but the caller had already hung up.

'Must have just missed them,' Andy said, and turned back on the recording feature.

'So are you married? Knocked up by accident? Single girl using a spcrm donor? I was this close to doing the sperm-donor thing myself.'

Andy smiled, her mind immediately going to her grand-mother. 'No, just plain old married. Although yes, I guess you could say I was knocked up by accident.'

'What, were you like totally not using anything but still telling everyone you weren't trying? That's my favorite. I'm always like, sweetheart, if you're not playing defense, you're playing offense. Not not-trying is *trying*, you know?'

'Up until a few months ago I would've agreed with you.' Andy laughed.

The attendant appeared and asked if they'd like another drink.

'I know a lot of people think seven months isn't long enough to *really* know someone, but with us it is. It feels like we've known each other since birth. I can't explain it, really. There's just this connection, and it has nothing to do with my job or his. You know?'

'I do,' Andy said, although she didn't. Andy was in the camp that said making a lifelong commitment to another person after knowing them seven months was insane.

This time it was Olive's phone that rang. 'Hello? Oh, hi, sweetie.' She continued to nod and murmur and at one point giggled like a teenager. 'Don't be naughty, Clint! I'm here with a reporter. No, you can't. It's a girls' day! Okay. Love you too.'

251

Olive clicked her phone closed and turned to Andy. 'Sorry, love, what were you saying?' Her phone buzzed again, and this time Olive reached to read a text message. 'It looks like the other girls are finishing up. Did you get everything you needed? You're welcome to come meet everyone if you want . . .' Olive offered this sweetly, but Andy could tell the actress would prefer she didn't take her up on it.

'Um, okay. I, uh, I was just hoping to go over some of the wedding details. I won't be at the wedding because of maternity leave, but my colleague Emily will be there.'

Olive pouted. 'I want you to come.'

It was all Andy could do not to swoon. 'I'd love to, trust me. Santa Barbara is just gorgeous, but I don't think I can leave the baby. Maybe you could give me some advance details on the dress, the flowers, how you chose the food, the decorations, that sort of thing?'

'Oh, you can just talk to my stylist about that stuff. She picked everything.'

'Everything? She picked your dress?'

Olive nodded and stood up. 'The dress, the food, the flowers, the music we'll walk to, the whole thing. She knows me so well. I told her to choose whatever she liked best.'

In years of covering weddings, Andy had never heard anything like it. Olive Chase didn't want any input into the biggest day of her life? Really?

Andy's expression must have registered the disbelief she felt, because Olive laughed. 'I found the *guy*! After more than twenty years of being single and jerked around and cheated on and alone, I found my soul mate. Pardon my French, but you think I give a shit about the *flowers*?'

Andy stood up too, less gracefully than Olive, and smiled. She could've just written it off to the difference between a bride who was thirty-nine and one who was twenty-five, but part of her believed it was because Olive Chase, famous for her fantastic boobs and ability to cry on command, had figured something out the rest of them hadn't.

'Fair enough,' Andy said, although she wanted to say so much more.

'Okay, well, thanks for the drink and the chat. I'd better go find my girls. It was really great meeting you.' Olive stood and smiled.

'Thanks,' Andy said, giving Olive, who had already turned to walk away, a half wave. 'Good luck with everything.'

Olive was already digging her cell phone out of her bag and laughing happily into it. Andy sank back into her chair and exhaled. She had gossipy ammunition on the world's most famous celebrity, and all she could think about were Olive's parting words. *I found my soul mate . . . you think I give a shit about the flowers?*

Andy stretched her legs and stared out onto the tops of the neighboring buildings. She sipped her water with lime and inhaled deeply, hoping the attendant would leave her alone for a few more minutes. She wanted to steal a bit more time before racing out into the frantic city, to the baby planning tasks and the work phone calls and Emily's relentless panic, to sit and reflect on everything Olive had just said. If she let herself, Andy would think back to her own wedding, how obsessed she'd been with every last detail, how much attention and time and effort she'd invested into making sure everything was perfect. How she'd gone steadfastly through three years of dating and engagement to Max, because he was handsome and successful and charming and it was easy and her family and friends approved and because of course she loved him, too. She was in lockstep – doing what she was supposed to do. And with a guy as close to perfect as she could imagine: rich, handsome, kind, wanting kids. But had she missed something along the way? Did this marriage have a feeling of inevitability? She loved Max, of course she did, but was he really her *soul mate*? Did she love Max as much as Olive loved Clint?

She sighed and set down her drink. Why did she insist on torturing herself like this? Max was perfect – as a husband, and a soon-to-be-father, and yes, as a soul mate. It was natural to feel anxious and unsettled right before giving birth, right? All pregnant women felt this way. Andy glanced around to make sure she was alone, and then she dialed Max's number. He didn't pick up, but the sound of his recorded voice reassured her.

'Hi, baby,' she said, her voice a low whisper. 'I just wanted to say hi. I'll be home in a little and I can't wait to see you. I love you.' Andy clicked off the phone and smiled. She rubbed her belly. It wouldn't be long now.

16

give him a test drive

'Ohmigod, she's gorgeous! Come here, sweetheart, your auntie Lily's been wanting to meet you for so long. Wow, don't you look *just* like your daddy!'

'Yeah, it's almost uncanny, isn't it?' Andy said. She held the baby out to Lily. 'Lily, please meet Clementine Rose. Clem, this is your aunt Lily.'

'Look at her eyes! Are they green? And all that black hair! What lucky baby is born with so much hair? It's like staring at a very cute, tiny little feminine version of Max.'

'I know,' Andy said, watching her daughter study her oldest friend. 'Supposedly she looks like Max's father, too. Rose is for Robert. It's like I was merely a vessel for producing Harrison clones.'

Lily laughed.

She missed Lily more than ever since she'd had Clementine.

She'd made a few casual acquaintances in the new-moms support group she'd joined a month before, but more often than not, Andy was lonely. Unaccustomed to endless stretches of unscheduled maternity-leave time, she staggered from chore to chore in a sleep-deprived haze, each day bleeding into the next with a near-identical mix of breast-feeding, pumping, diaper changing, bathing, dressing, rocking, singing, strolling, cooking, and cleaning. Activities Andy used to wedge into small snippets of stolen time in her hectic day – laundry, grocery shopping, a trip to the post office or drugstore – now ate up hours, sometimes entire days, since Clementine and her nonstop demands always took precedence. She loved spending time with her daughter, and while she wouldn't have given up those moments spooning in bed together, or eating a sandwich on the High Line in the middle of a warm summer day while Clem had a bottle, or slow-dancing together to Chicago's *Greatest Hits* in the privacy of their living room, the daily drudgery was harder than she'd ever imagined.

Mrs Harrison was aghast that Andy refused to hire a baby nurse – there had never been a Harrison baby in history without her own dedicated hired caretaker – but Andy held her ground. 'Your mother would hire me a wet nurse if I'd let her,' she'd said to Max after one particularly unpleasant visit from her mother-in-law, but he had only laughed. Andy's own mother came in once a week to keep them company and help with the baby, and Andy lived for those days, but otherwise there wasn't a lot of outside interaction. Jill was back in Texas. Emily always remembered to ask after Clementine when she called, but Andy certainly knew, and understood, that she was not calling for an update on how many times Clem pooped that morning or whether she'd enjoyed tummy time. Emily wanted one thing – to restart the Elias-Clark conversations. Miranda and Stanley were circling like sharks; Emily was literally counting down the days of Andy's maternity leave. The only person who would and could talk endlessly about four-in-the-morning feeds and the pros and cons of pacifier use was Lily, and she was thousands of miles away, busy with one child and expecting another.

Andy could see Lily watching her as she gingerly sat down on the couch. It was one in the afternoon, but Andy was still wearing a pair of Max's sweatpants, furry slipper-socks that resembled indoor Uggs, and a pullover hooded sweatshirt so voluminously huge that it must have, at some point, belonged to a linebacker.

'Still not feeling normal down there?' Lily asked, sympathy in her voice.

'Not even close.' Andy nodded toward the lemonade she'd placed in front of Lily.

Lily smiled and sipped. 'They say you forget it all, and I never believed that was possible, but I swear I can't remember a thing. Except the pain from the stitches afterward. That I remember.'

'I'm still not sure I can forgive you for not preparing me better. You're supposed to be my best friend. You've been through this before. And you didn't tell me a goddamn thing.'

Lily rolled her eyes. 'Of course I didn't! It's the code of women everywhere, and it must be followed. It's even more important than not sleeping with your friends' exes.'

'It's bullshit is what it is. I will tell anyone who wants to know all the gory details. Women deserve to know what to expect. This whole secret society of birthing mothers is ridiculous.'

'Andy! What would you have liked to be told about in greater detail? That pushing feels like you're going to split in two? Would that have really helped you get through it yourself?'

'Yes! Maybe then I wouldn't have thought I was dying. Let's see, it would've been nice to know that it's normal to be ankle-deep in blood the first time a nurse helps you pee, that they put stitches in places you didn't even know existed, that breastfeeding feels like having an actual piranha clamp down on your nipple and chew.'

Lily grinned. 'And that the epidural, like, hardly ever works on both sides? Or that you'll seriously wonder if you'll ever be able to wear anything but the disposable mesh granny panties you stole from the hospital? Is that what you mean?'

'Yes! Exactly.'

'Uh-huh. Keep dreaming. You would've had a nervous breakdown if I told you any of that, and besides, you wouldn't have had the joy of discovering it yourself.'

'It's all so wrong,' Andy said, shaking her head.

'It's how it has to be.'

Andy could still remember her shock – her absolute disbelief – when Dr Kramer reached between Andy's legs, retrieved a wailing and blood-covered infant after sixteen hours of labor, and declared, 'Baby Girl Harrison looks great!' It had taken dozens of diaper changes and endless pink onesies, blankets, teddy bears, and tutus before the reality had finally settled in. Andy had a daughter. A little girl. A perfect, sweet, incredible baby girl.

As if to punctuate this point, Clementine let out a cry that sounded more like a mew. Andy scooped her up from Lily's arms and walked her back to the nursery.

'Hi, my love,' she crooned. She gently laid the baby on the changing table and removed her swaddle, her purple onesie, and a soaked diaper. She wiped the baby's bottom, patted it with A&D, affixed a new diaper, and changed her daughter into a pink-and-gray striped T-shirt with matching leggings and a coordinating striped pink hat. 'There you go, sweetie. Doesn't that feel better?'

Andy scooped her up and, cradling the baby expertly in her arms, walked toward the living room, where Lily was busy gathering her things.

'Don't go,' Andy said, feeling like she might cry. The unpredictable weeping jags had leveled off recently, but she couldn't deny the knot in her throat.

'I don't want to,' Lily said. 'I'm going to miss you two so much. I'm meeting my old supervisor all the way uptown, though. I've got to leave now or I'm going to be late.'

'When am I going to see you again?' Andy asked, already doing the calculation in her head.

'You'll have to come visit me when this baby's born,' Lily said, wrapping a sweater around her shoulders.

The girls hugged and Andy could feel Lily's hard bump between them. She placed both her hands around it, bent down, and said, 'You take it easy on your mama, okay? No somersaults in there.'

'Too late.'

They embraced again and Andy watched as her friend disappeared down the hallway. She wiped away a few tears, assured herself it was just the hormones, and began to pack the diaper bag; if she and Clem didn't leave immediately, they too would be late.

She walked as fast as her injuries and the stroller would allow as Clem cried.

'We're almost there, chickie. Can you hold out a little longer?'

The walk to the kiddie play-gym where the weekly new-moms support group met was mercifully short, which was fortunate because Clementine's cries had increased from a complaint to all-out wailing. The other mothers looked on sympathetically as Andy pulled the baby from her stroller, collapsed with her on the padded floor, and un-self-consciously pulled out her left breast. Although Clem's eyes were clenched shut and her body was rigid with crying, she found the nipple as if by sonar and clamped on with all her might. Andy breathed a sigh of relief. A quick glance around the room confirmed she wasn't alone: three other mothers were in various stages of breast-reveal, two more were changing dirty diapers, and three were slumped on the floor, looking alternately dazed and near tears, hunched over their flailing, uncooperative, and unhappy babies. Only one woman appeared showered and appropriately dressed in real, nonmaternity clothes: a baby's aunt.

The group leader, a curly-haired woman named Lori who claimed 'life coach' as her job title, took a seat in the circle of harried mothers and, after taking a moment to smile somewhat maniacally at each and every baby, greeted the group by reading a quote.

'"Motherhood: all love begins and ends there." A beautiful sentiment by Robert Browning, don't you think? Would anyone like to share their thoughts on that?'

Theo's mother, a tall, elegant black woman who was tortured trying to decide whether or not to leave her legal career in order to raise him full-time, sighed deeply and said, 'He slept six hours straight every single night this week, and then the last two nights he woke up every forty-five minutes, inconsolable. My husband tried to take a few shifts but he's started falling asleep at work. What's happening? Why are we going backward?'

Heads bobbed all around. This was how every session began. Hippie-dippy life coach Lori read a beautiful and inspirational quote. Not a single mother in the room even feigned interest, and a couple resorted to outright hostility. Inevitably, one of them asked the question that was burning in her mind, completely and entirely ignoring Lori's contribution, and the other mothers jumped right on the bandwagon. It was an unchanging, unspoken agreement to reclaim the group as their own, and it made Andy smile every time.

Andy couldn't help but imagine Emily sitting in on a session. She would stare at them all in pity, no doubt – frazzled, makeup-less, covered in spit-up and poop, living without showers and sex and exercise and sleep – as they sat in a semicircle and their life coach read them kumbaya stories. And yet something about the whole scene was an incredible relief to Andy: these women may not have been her closest friends, but at that moment in her life, they understood her in a way no one else did. She couldn't believe she was capable of bonding so quickly with a group of complete strangers, but Andy secretly loved the group meetings.

'I hear you. We're in the same boat,' Stacy said, in the process of hooking her nursing tank. Her daughter, Sylvie, an eight-week-old with more hair than most toddlers, let out a man-sized burp. 'I know it's too early to even think about sleep training, but I'm losing my mind here. She was up from one to three last night, and she was happy about it! Smiling, cooing, grabbing my finger. But the second I put her down, she freaked.'

Bethany, a marketing director for a cosmetics company who, by her own admission, didn't know her way around a lip gloss, said, 'I know how you feel about co-sleeping, Stacy, really I do, but I think in this case you should consider it. I can't tell you how much easier it is to have Micah right beside us, all night long. You just roll over, pop in a boob, and go back to sleep. Forget all the developmental, bonding crap that surrounds it – I do it out of sheer laziness.'

Stacy tucked Sylvie's blanket under her arms. 'I just feel like I can't do that to Mark. Already Sylvie takes up ninety-nine point nine percent of my time and energy. Don't I at least have to pretend I still have a marriage?'

'Marriage? With a two-month-old?' shrieked Melinda, mother to Tucker, who'd just had surgery for some sort of an eye problem. 'What, your sex life is so hot you don't want to jeopardize it by having a baby in your bed?'

Everyone laughed. Andy nodded her agreement: she and Max hadn't managed sex yet, and she was perfectly fine with that.

Rachel, the newest mother of the group, a petite blonde with blotchy red skin and a long, winding scar on her right hand, leaned forward. 'I just had my six-week postpartum exam,' she near-whispered.

'Oh dear. Did they clear you?' Sandrine asked in her faint French accent. Her daughter, a waifish four-month-old with dual citizenship, began to cry.

Rachel nodded. An expression of abject terror crossed her face before she, too, began to sob. 'It's all Ethan can talk about – he's had a countdown calendar on the fridge for weeks now – and just the thought of it panics me. I'm not ready!' she wailed.

'Of course you're not ready,' Bethany said. 'I couldn't even *think* about it until three months out. And a friend of mine said it killed until six months.'

'Max comes at me with that look in his eye, and he just doesn't get it,' Andy offered. 'I swear even my OB was horrified by the scene down there at my six-week checkup. How can I let my husband see it?'

'Simple. You don't,' chimed in Anita, a quiet girl who usually revealed very little.

'My sister, who has three kids of her own, swears it gets better. You recover at least enough to work on conceiving the next one,' Andy added.

'Sounds hot. Something to look forward to,' Rachel said with a smile.

'I'm sorry, but you guys are scaring the hell out of me,' said Sophie, the only nonmom in the room. 'All of my friends with kids swear it's not that bad.'

'They're lying.'

'Through their teeth.'

'Which they'll continue to do right up until you have a child of your own and can call them out on it. It's just how it's done.'

Sophie swung her thick auburn hair, freshly cut in perfect, face-framing layers, and laughed. She was the only one among them not wearing leggings, an empire-waist dress, or a sweatshirt. Her nails were newly manicured. Her skin looked healthy and tanned. Andy was willing to bet anything that her legs were shaved and her bikini line waxed and that under the snug-fitting V-neck she was wearing a bra made of lace instead of industrial-grade spandex. Probably even a thong. It was almost too much to bear.

Even her charge was beautifully turned out. Baby Lola, all of nine weeks, was dressed in head-to-toe Burberry plaid: smocked dress, tights, headband, and booties. She rarely cried at the meetings, appeared never to spit up, and, according to Auntie Sophie, was sleeping through the night by seven weeks. Sophie brought Lola each week while Lola's mother, Sophie's sister-in-law, clocked in long hours between her pediatric private practice and the peds unit at Mount Sinai. Apparently Lola's mom thought the new-moms support group was really a playgroup of sorts for the little ones – despite the fact that none of them were even old enough to sit up – and had asked Sophie to take Lola in her place. So each and every week, the slim and attractive Sophie with an undoubtedly intact vagina brought an adorably dressed Lola to listen to Andy and her new-mommy friends complain, cry, and beg for advice. The worst part was Andy wanted to hate her, but Sophie was just too damn sweet.

'I don't know if I can handle hearing about a normal sex life right now,' Rachel said as she hoisted her baby to her shoulder.

'Don't worry, I don't have anything resembling a normal sex life,' Sophie said, staring at the floor.

'Why not?' Andy asked. 'I thought you lived with your adoring boyfriend. Trouble in paradise?'

At this, Sophie began to cry. Andy couldn't have been more shocked if the girl had stood up and started to do a striptease.

'Sorry,' she whimpered, looking dainty and sweet even while she cried. 'This isn't the place.'

'Why don't you tell us what's happening,' Group Leader Lori said in an irritatingly reassuring voice, clearly happy for the chance to contribute at all. 'We've all felt free to unburden ourselves. I'm sure I speak on behalf of everyone when I say that this is a safe place, and you should feel welcome here.'

It looked as though Sophie hadn't heard her, or merely chose, like the rest of them, to ignore Lori, but a moment later, after delicately blowing her nose and giving Lola a kiss, she said, 'I've been cheating on my boyfriend.'

There were a few seconds of silence in the padded gym room where not even a baby squawked, and Andy tried to hide her shock. From everything Sophie had said, she adored her boyfriend. According to Sophie, Xander was sweet and solicitous, a sensitive guy who could ask after her feelings but still spend six straight hours on a Sunday watching football. They'd been dating for years and had recently moved in together, which, at least as of a few weeks ago, she thought was going really well. They didn't talk about it much directly, but she felt it was assumed they would get married and have children, and although she was younger than him by six years, she was starting to feel ready.

'Define *cheating*,' Bethany said, and Andy was relieved someone had broken the silence.

'Well, nothing too crazy,' Sophie said, staring at her hands. 'We haven't, like, slept together or anything.'

'Then you're not cheating,' Sandrine declared. 'You Americans get so hung up on the nuances – on all of it really – but if you love your boyfriend and he loves you, this little fling will pass.'

'I thought so too, but it's not passing!' Sophie said, her voice almost a wail. 'He's a student in one of my photography classes, so automatically I see him three times a week. It started out with lots of flirting, mostly on his part, although I admit I was flattered. To have someone pay attention like that . . .'

'Does Xander not pay attention?' Rachel asked.

Sophie wrung her hands. 'Barely anymore. Ever since we got a place together . . . I don't know what it is, but I feel like furniture.'

'I can't tell you how many of us *wish* our husbands looked at us like furniture,' Andy said.

The group laughed and nodded.

Sophie didn't crack a smile. 'Yes, but we don't have a child together. We're not married. We're not even engaged! Don't you think it's a little premature to be living like roommates?'

'So what's happened? Just some flirting? Trust me, Xander's not racked with guilt every time he shares a laugh with some girl at work and you shouldn't be either,' Anita said.

'Last night we grabbed dinner after class. With a few other people too,' Sophie rushed to add. 'But then they left and he insisted on walking me home. At first I wouldn't let him too near because I knew Xander was at home, but we ended up making out on my block. Which is just the craziest thing ever, because Xander could've walked right by. My god, what was I thinking?'

'So I'm guessing it was good?' Stacy asked.

Sophie raised her eyes to the ceiling and groaned. 'Good? It was *fantastic*.'

A few of the girls cheered. Sophie showed the slightest hint of a smile before smacking her forehead rather aggressively with the inside of her palm. 'It's never going to happen again. Do we agree it would be worse to tell him just to relieve my conscience than it would to pretend it never happened?'

'Of course you should not tell him!' Sandrine announced regally. 'Don't be such a prude.'

A few of the other women nodded in agreement, although it wasn't clear if they agreed with Sandrine because she was right or because she was French.

'I just feel so guilty. I love Xander, I really do. But I'm starting to wonder what this means . . .'

'Well have you decided what's going to happen the next time you see . . . what's his name?' Anita asked, always the practical one.

'Tomás. Tomorrow in class. Of course I told him it was a mistake and it could never happen again, but I can't stop thinking about him. And . . .' Sophie paused here, looking around the room nervously. 'He e-mailed me. He said he can't wait to see me. Am I the worst person ever?'

One of the babies began to wail uncontrollably, and yet another breast was freed from its zip-up sweatshirt. The cries quieted.

'Give yourself a break, Soph,' Andy said while she draped Clementine across her knees and rhythmically pounded her back. 'You're not married, you don't have kids, you're attractive as hell. Live a little! You can all hate me for saying it, but I think you should go right ahead and give Tomás a test-drive. And then you should come in here next week and tell us every detail.'

Once again, everyone laughed. What was it about not exchanging vows with someone or creating an offspring together that suggested Sophie's relationship with Xander wasn't as serious as their own? Andy wasn't sure. She felt a little guilty encouraging Sophie to cheat, but not as much as she probably should have. Sophie's little exploratory make-out with Tomás (sexy-sounding from just his name, no less) sounded exciting, adventurous, the exact kind of wild fun you were supposed to have before conversations about breast pumps and stool softeners and diaper creams claimed your life. Sophie would figure it out – either she'd return to Xander more confident in what they shared, or she wouldn't. Maybe Tomás was right for her, or maybe it was someone totally different she hadn't even met yet. Andy knew it was a double standard, was acutely aware that someone – namely, Xander – stood to get very hurt, and yet she couldn't help but think the stakes just weren't that high.

A couple more babies started fussing as the time drew close to three o'clock, and Lori announced that the session was over for the week. 'Some interesting things to think about, ladies,' she said as everyone began packing up bottles, pacifiers, teething rings, burp cloths, blankets, nursing covers, and stuffed animals. 'Next we'll have a sleep specialist from Baby 911 in to tell us how and when to set the little ones up on a schedule. Please let me know by e-mail if you can't make it. As always, I'm inspired by all of you! Have a great week.' She left the room to give them all a few moments to talk among themselves.

The moment the door closed, Andy heard one of the women next to her groan audibly.

Bethany muttered, 'Does she really find it so inspiring that we sit around in our sweatpants all day covered in puke and baby shit? I mean, seriously.'

'Did you see her face when I said we'd made out? She was definitely searching for an inspirational quote about that one,' Sophie said.

Andy packed up Clementine and said good-bye to the other women. Already they were starting to feel like friends.

Andy didn't notice Max was home until she wheeled the stroller into the living room and began to unpack.

'Who do we have here?' he asked, giving Andy a peck on the cheek and immediately turning his attention to Clementine. In response, Clem gave her daddy a wide, tooth-less grin and Andy felt herself instinctively grinning back. 'Look at this happy girl,' he said, hoisting Clementine out of her stroller and tucking her snugly into the crook of his arm. He lightly kissed her nose and handed her back to Andy.

'Want to take her for a little? I'm sure she'd love some daddy time.'

'I really need to lie down for a few minutes,' Max said, heading toward the bedroom. 'It's been the longest week. Very stressful.'

Andy followed him and deposited Clem on the bed. 'I'm

sorry to hear that. But I could really use thirty minutes to take a shower and maybe eat a bowl of cereal.' She kissed her daughter and laid the baby on Max's pillow.

'Andy,' Max said in that tone he sometimes took with her. The one that conveyed through a single word that he was *this close* to losing his patience. 'I'm under a lot of pressure right now.'

'Well, there's nothing better than some baby gurgles to cure that. Enjoy your daughter,' Andy said, and closed the bedroom door behind her.

She rinsed off quickly in the guest bathroom and got back in her yoga pants and fleece. There wasn't any milk left in the refrigerator, but she made herself a peanut butter and banana sandwich, grabbed a Diet Coke, and collapsed onto the couch. How long had it been since she'd watched a show without a baby hanging on her breast? Or eaten a meal uninterrupted? It was bliss. She must have nodded off, because she woke to Max and Clementine beside her on the couch. Max had pulled open Clem's pajamas and was tickling her belly. As a reward, Clem was giving the best, most beautiful smiles imaginable.

'You okay?' Max asked as he tickled under Clem's arms.

'I am now,' she said, feeling infinitely more relaxed than she had before. That's how it always seemed these days with the mood swings: highs and lows, ups and downs.

Clem punctuated her toothless grin with some sort of delighted squeal.

'Was that a laugh?' Max asked. 'I thought she was too young to laugh.'

Andy squeezed his arm. 'It sure sounded like a laugh.'

She'd always imagined herself head-over-heels in love with her child, but she'd never pictured her husband every bit as smitten. Max was a wonderful father – engaged, involved, affectionate, and fun – and there was little she loved more than watching her husband and daughter interact. Andy knew nothing was wrong, despite little territorial skirmishes like the one just witnessed. Everything was right, actually, for the first time in so many months. Her daughter was healthy and happy, her husband was sweet and, for the most part, solicitous, and she was enjoying these few exhausting but priceless months of being with her newborn baby. Mrs Harrison's letter to Max, the fact that Max had seen and hidden the fact of seeing Katherine – these were distant memories. Whatever lingering anxiety she felt was from the hormones, or the sleep deprivation, or both. She turned her attention to her family. They were together, tired but happy, enjoying their new baby, and she was going to savor every second.

17

james bond meets *pretty woman*, with a little dash of *mary poppins*

'Are you almost ready?' Max called from the living room, where Andy knew he was leisurely enjoying a bottle of root beer. She could picture him draped across the couch in his dark European-cut suit and expensive Italian loafers, sipping his drink and idly checking his iPhone. His hair was newly trimmed and his face freshly shaven, and he would smell of shampoo and minty aftershave and, inexplicably, of chocolate. He would be excited for the party, eager to get there and begin making the rounds of people he knew and liked. Perhaps his foot would be tapping impatiently. Meanwhile, down the hall, Clementine was being fed by Isla, the twenty-two-year-old Australian babysitter Andy had hired based on a recommendation from the mommy group and a Google background check. In other words, a complete stranger.

The doorbell rang. For a moment she thought it was the television, but when Stanley started barking and a quick glance at the baby monitor showed Clem and Isla snuggled together on the glider, she figured it was a food delivery of some sort. For Isla, probably. The landline rang and Andy grabbed it.

'It's okay to send them up,' she said hurriedly into the phone.

'Oh, Andrea? Sorry, I just wanted to let you know that—'

A shrill voice from inside Andy's foyer interrupted the doorman. 'Hello! Anyone home? Hello . . .'

'—Mrs Harrison is on her way up. She said you were expecting her.'

'Yes, of course. Thank you,' Andy said, glancing down at her own nakedness. She heard Max greeting his mother in the hallway outside the bedroom. A moment later, his head popped in the door. 'Hey, so my mom's here,' he said, almost like a question. 'She was invited to a gallery opening tonight and it's just around the corner. She thought she'd stop in and say hello to the baby.'

Andy stared at him, noting his sheepish smile. 'Seriously?' *I need your mother like I need two broken legs right now,* Andy thought.

'Sorry, baby. She was literally around the corner. And she's got some other event uptown that starts in like thirty minutes, so it really is just a quick hello. I thought we could all have a drink together before both parties.'

'I'm not even dressed, Max,' Andy said, waving to the tangle of towels, black dresses, and support undergarments on their bed.

'Don't worry about it, she's here to see Clem. Take your time, I'll pour you some champagne. Come out whenever you're ready.'

She wanted to scream at her husband for not consulting with her on this most unwelcome surprise, but instead she just nodded and motioned for him to close the door. She could hear Max introduce Barbara to Isla – 'Oh, Australia, you say? What an *interesting* place' – and then their voices faded as they headed toward the living room. Andy turned her attention to a pair of nonmaternity Spanx shorts, size small. She worked them inch by inch over her thighs, and they resisted every step of the way. Clearing the widest part of her leg was cause for celebration, but it was short-lived: she had to focus on getting them over her butt and stomach. They dug and pinched up and down her entire lower body, and by the time she had finally yanked them into place, beads of perspiration ran uncomfortably down her back and between her breasts. Her hair, professionally blown out for the first time since Clementine's birth, now stuck to her face and neck. Grabbing a magazine to fan herself and clad only in nude-colored, too-tight shaper shorts and a heavy-duty nursing bra, her body spilling out of both, Andy started to laugh. If this wasn't sexy, she didn't know what was.

Her cell phone rang from the nightstand. She rolled like a greased piglet across the bed and grabbed it.

'Bad time,' she said automatically, the way you could only do when you were a new mother.

'I'm just calling to wish you good luck tonight.' Jill's voice was warm and familiar, and immediately Andy felt herself calm ever so slightly.

'Good luck being a postpartum, leaking, lactating, over-weight cow among a sea of gorgeous people, or good luck leaving my baby girl with a stranger I essentially found on the Internet?'

'Both!' Jill said brightly.

lauren weisberger

'How am I going to do this?' Andy moaned, acutely aware she was already late.

'Same way everyone else does: wear all black, check your cell phone every four to five seconds, and drink as heavily as the situation will allow.'

'Good advice. Drink, check. Cell phone, check. Now I just need to cram my ass into the long-sleeved black dress. Remember, with the cutout in back? The one I used to wear all the time pre-baby?'

Jill laughed. Not nicely. 'You're barely four months out, Andy. Don't expect a miracle.'

Andy stared at the dress laid out next to her on the bed. Depending on whether she was a four or a six, it either looked elegantly fitted or sexily curve-hugging, and depending on accessories, it was perfect for everything from a quick drinks date to a ballroom wedding. Tonight, however, it looked better suited for a doll, or maybe a tween.

'It's not going to happen, is it?' she asked, her voice a near whisper.

'Probably not. But who cares? You'll be back into it in another couple months, what's the difference?'

'The difference is I don't have anything to wear!' Andy didn't want to sound hysterical, but her sweating had increased and the clock was ticking. Dress-wise, there was no Plan B.

'Of course you do,' Jill said, her tone the same one she used with Jonah when he was being particularly petulant. 'That black dress, with the three-quarter-length sleeves? That you wore to Grandma's brunch in March?'

'That's maternity!' Andy wailed. 'Not to mention it was appropriate for an eighty-nine-year-old's birthday party.'

'Think of how much thinner you'll look in it now.'

Andy sighed. 'I've got to run. Sorry I can't ask anything

274

about your life right now. Plus Barbara's here to visit Clementine. I swear it's on purpose, the one night I cannot afford to get upset because I'm already a wreck—' Andy stopped herself. 'Is everything okay with you?'

'Everything's fine. Get rid of Barbara, and go have fun. It's your first night out in ages, not to mention a hugely exciting professional night, and you deserve it.'

'Thanks.'

'But remember – keep drinking.'

'Got it. Black, phone, booze. Good-bye.' She hung up and smiled at the phone. She missed her sister desperately sometimes, especially on nights like these.

Max appeared in the doorway. 'You're still not dressed? Andy, what's wrong?'

Andy grabbed a damp towel from the floor and held it up to her chest. 'Don't look at me!'

Max walked over and stroked her sweaty hair. 'What's going on with you? I see you naked every day.'

When Andy didn't say anything, Max pointed to the dress beside her. 'That one looks too corporate,' he said kindly, although Andy knew he must have overheard at least part of her conversation and probably said *corporate* when he meant *small*. He opened her closet and rifled through her dress section. He pulled the exact same dress Jill had suggested. 'Here,' he said, holding it aloft. 'I always love you in this one.'

Andy sniffled, close to tears, and clutched the towel closer.

Max removed the hanger and laid the dress on the bed. 'Why don't you put this on and touch up your makeup? The car's waiting for us downstairs, but it's early. Come say a quick hello to my mother, and we'll be off.'

'Sounds great,' Andy mumbled as Max dabbed the tiniest bit of shaping mold into his hair and adjusted an imperceptible

lauren weisberger

flyaway. She put on the maternity dress. Jill and Max were right, it was the only possible choice, and it didn't look terrible. Sleek? No. Sexy? No. But it contained her gigantic nursing bra and covered her jiggly tummy and concealed her not-quite-back-to-normal bum, and honestly, that was more than she could have hoped for. She paired it with super-sheer stockings, the kind with the seam up the back, and a pair of stacked three-and-a-half-inch Chloé heels that had hurt a decent amount pre-baby and now made her feet feel like they were wedged into Chinese binding slippers. Ignoring the dull ache in her calves that would surely become shooting pains before the night's end, Andy slicked on a new rich red lipstick she'd purchased for the occasion, smoothed her blowout as best she could, and thrust her shoulders back. Was she her pre-baby self? Not exactly. But, at least for someone who had just birthed a child, she wasn't half-bad.

Max whistled appreciatively from behind her as he checked her out in the mirror. 'That is one hot mama,' he said, wrapping his arms around her from behind.

For a moment she let him touch her jiggly belly, saying, 'These little rolls here turn you on, don't they? Come on, just admit it.'

Max laughed. 'You look fantastic.' He reached out and lightly cupped a breast. 'These are a dream.'

Andy smiled. 'The rack alone is almost worth it, isn't it?'

'That and the kid. Between the boobs and the baby, I'm fully on board.' He led her into the hallway, helped her on with her silk wrap, and squeezed her hand tightly when Isla emerged from the nursery holding a heavy-lidded Clementine. Barbara trailed behind her, looking absolutely fabulous in a tailored sheath dress with a coordinating blazer and nude patent pumps.

'Hello, Barbara,' Andy said, suddenly feeling like a towering,

276

graceless tank next to her coiffed and elegant mother-in-law. 'How lovely of you to stop by.'

'Yes, dear, well I hope it's not an intrusion, but I realize it's been weeks since I've seen my granddaughter, and I was in the neighborhood . . .'

Barbara paused and glanced around the hallway. 'Did you do something different here? Is that painting new? Or perhaps that mirror? What a relief! I have to say, I never did like that . . . that *collage* you chose to display so prominently.'

'Mother, that "collage" was a mixed-media piece from a very hot new artist whose work has been displayed all over Europe,' Max said. 'Andy and I found it together in Amsterdam, and we love it.'

'Mmm, well, you know what they say! There's no accounting for taste, is there?' Barbara trilled.

Max shot Andy an apologetic look. Andy shrugged in response. They'd been married for a year, and while she'd hardly forgotten about the letter Barbara had written to her son about his choice of wife and wasn't exactly *used* to her – she didn't think she'd ever be – Andy was no longer surprised by her either.

In the living room, Barbara perched on the edge of an armchair as though it was teeming with bedbugs.

Andy couldn't resist. 'Oh, Max, remind me to call the exterminator first thing Monday morning. He hasn't been here in *forever*. We're overdue.'

Max looked at her questioningly. Barbara leaped to her feet. Andy tried not to laugh.

'How did she do on her bottle?' Andy asked Isla, wanting nothing more than to grab her daughter from this stranger's arms.

'Great, she drank all five ounces. I changed her dirty nappy, and I'm going to put her down now. She wanted to say good night to her mama first.'

'Oh, come here, my love,' Andy said, relieved at the chance to hold Clementine one last time without appearing as psychotic as she actually felt. For this, she was already grateful to Isla. 'You be good for your new babysitter, okay?' Andy kissed her daughter's chunky cheeks once, twice, three times before handing her back.

Isla settled Clementine comfortably on her shoulder and nodded. 'I'll read her *Goodnight Moon* now and rock her to sleep. Then—'

'Don't forget to put her in her sleep sack,' Andy interrupted.

Max squeezed her hand again.

'What?' She looked at him. 'It's important.'

Isla rushed on. 'Of course. Put her in her sleep sack, read *Goodnight Moon*, rock her to sleep. Dim the lights without making it completely dark and put on the white-noise machine. She will probably wake up around nine thirty or ten to eat again, but even if she doesn't, I should dream-feed her the four-ounce bottle in the fridge, right?'

Andy nodded. 'If you can't remember how to use the bottle warmer, just put it in a mug of hot water for a few minutes. But please remember to test the temperature before you give it to her.'

'Okay, Andy, it sounds like everything's great here,' Max said, kissing Clem on the forehead. 'Come, sit for a minute and visit and then we'll head out.'

'You have both our cell numbers, just in case? And the sheet on the counter with all the emergency contact numbers? My mother's in Texas right now so she won't be much help . . .' She glanced at Barbara, who was intently reading something. 'Better yet, just call 911 as fast as—'

'I promise I'll take wonderful care of her,' Isla said with a quiet, reassuring smile that nonetheless made Andy wish she had a nanny cam.

Andy stopped, frozen, wondering how this had happened. She'd sworn every which way that she would be the cool mom, the relaxed one, the mom who didn't freak out over germs or babysitters or organic everything. The one who could go with the flow and not go crazy. But one look at the tiny, vulnerable being who was entirely dependent on her for everything had changed all that. Andy had only left Clementine with her mother or, once, out of sheer desperation, with Max's sister, and that was only when she had doctor's appointments and didn't want to subject Clem to the filthy waiting rooms. She'd returned all the sleepers and onesies they received as baby gifts unless she could confirm, beyond a doubt, that none contained poisonous flame-retardant fabric; also returned were all plastic baby toys that read 'Made in China' or could not be proven BPA, PVC, and phthalate free. Against every promise she'd made herself, her husband, and anyone who would listen, Andy moved heaven and earth to stick to Clem's schedule, a carefully choreographed routine of feedings, naps, playtime, and walks that was prioritized over everyone and everything. It wasn't like she wanted to be the lunatic helicopter mother, but she felt helpless to control it.

Andy took a deep breath, exhaled quietly through her mouth, and forced a return smile. 'I know you will. Thank you.' She watched as Isla carried Clem to the nursery.

The sound of Barbara's voice brought her back to reality. 'Andrea, dear? What is this?' her mother-in-law asked, holding aloft a small sheaf of papers.

Andy sat on the couch and grabbed her champagne glass, liquid courage. Barbara must have decided that the couch had a higher likelihood of being vermin-free, because she sat down next to Andy and crossed her legs. 'Here, this. It says, "Miranda's Ultimate Baby List." This isn't from Miranda *Priestly*, is it?'

It had been tacked to the bulletin board above her desk, a funny place for Barbara to snoop, but Andy didn't have enough fight in her to bring it up.

'Ah yes, Miranda's list. She sent it to me right after Clementine was born. Miranda doesn't really like *people* per se, but apparently she has a soft spot for babies.'

'Is that right?' Barbara murmured, glancing through the pages, her eyes alight. 'My, my, it's quite comprehensive.'

'That it is,' Andy said, glancing over Barbara's shoulder. She'd nearly fainted in shock when it first arrived a couple of weeks after Clem's birth, accompanied by a box wrapped in pink paper and festooned with white ribbons and a silver Tiffany baby rattle. Inside the box was a note on Miranda's letterhead that read, 'Congratulations on your new addition!' Beneath that, under a half-dozen layers of tissue paper, nestled the most exquisite mink blanket Andy had ever seen. Or really, the *only* mink blanket she'd ever seen. It was silky-soft and enormous, and Andy immediately folded it and draped it across the foot of her own bed, where she snuggled with it almost every night. Clem had yet to puke or poop or drool on it, and as far as Andy was concerned, she never would. Mink! For a baby! Andy smiled to herself now and remembered what Emily had pointed out: clearly Miranda had chosen this gift all by herself, because no assistant would ever send a full-sized mink throw as a baby gift. For anyone. Ever. And if that hadn't been fabulous enough, there was also 'Miranda's Ultimate Baby List.'

Twenty-two pages, single-spaced. A table of contents with subjects like 'Items Needed for Hospital,' 'Items Needed at

Home: First Couple of Weeks,' 'Baby Toiletries,' 'Baby Medical Needs,' and 'Safety Checklist.' Naturally, Miranda gave her recommendations for putting together the perfect layette (preferably from Jacadi, Bonpoint, and Ralph Lauren): short-sleeved onesies, long-sleeved onesies, footed pajamas, socks, booties, knit caps, hand mitts, pants-and-top outfits for boys, dresses or rompers with leggings for girls. Washcloths, towels, crib sheets. Swaddle blankets, stroller blankets, mono-grammed nursery blankets. She even had a favorite brand of hair accessories. But it didn't stop there. There were Miranda's recommendations for pediatricians, lactation consultants, children's nutritionists, allergists, pediatric dentists, and doctors willing to make house calls. She listed all the resources one might need to put on a bris, a chris-tening, or a baby-naming service: acceptable synagogues, churches, mohels, caterers, and florists. Decorators who specialized in nursery design. A contact at Tiffany who would place the baby's monogram on silver spoons, cups, and commemorative plates. A diamond specialist where Daddy could buy Mommy the perfect push present. And most important of all, a list of people to aid in the raising of said babies: night nurses, nannies, babysitters, tutors, speech therapists, occupational therapists, educational consultants, and at least a half-dozen agencies, all of which were chosen and vetted by Miranda herself for providing 'the right kind' of caregivers.

Barbara finished reading the list and set it down on the table. 'How considerate of Ms Priestly to share her list with you,' she said. She cocked her head to the side and peered at Andy. 'She must really see something in you.'

'Mmm,' Andy murmured, unwilling to shatter Barbara's newfound respect for her. Assistants had compiled and organ-ized the list, Andy knew that, and the only flattering fact was that Miranda had directed her staff to send it to her. That, and the mink blanket, which Andy shamelessly showed to her mother-in-law.

'Spectacular!' Barbara breathed as Andy placed it across the woman's knees. Barbara stroked it reverently. 'What a unique and thoughtful baby gift. I'm sure Clementine simply adores it.'

Max emptied the last drops of champagne into Andy's glass. He refilled his and his mother's with Pellegrino. 'Mother, you're welcome to stay, but Andy and I must have to go. The car's been waiting downstairs for twenty minutes, and we're now officially late.'

Barbara nodded. 'I understand, dear. I just couldn't pass up an opportunity to see my granddaughter.'

Andy smiled magnanimously. 'Clem enjoyed it too,' she lied. 'You're welcome anytime.' She refrained from pointing out that Barbara hadn't so much as held her beloved grand-daughter, nor even patted the baby's head. From everything she'd seen, her mother-in-law had admired Clem as she lay in the safety of her babysitter's arms, and for the first time, Andy understood a bit what it must have been like for Max to grow up with this woman as his mother.

She and Barbara stood; Andy gave her an obligatory kiss on the cheek and turned to find her clutch, but Barbara's hand closed over her own. 'Andrea, I'd like to tell you something,' she said in her Park-Avenue-accented voice.

Andy panicked. Max was already halfway down the hallway, getting their coats. She couldn't remember the last time she had been alone with Barbara Harrison, and she was in no place to—

Barbara's hands tightened over both of Andy's, and she felt herself being drawn closer to her mother-in-law. So close that she could smell her delicate perfume and see the deep indentations around her mouth, so ingrained that not even the latest and greatest fillers could tackle them. Andy held her breath.

'Dear, I just wanted to tell you that, for whatever it's worth, I think you're a wonderful mother.'

Andy felt her mouth fall open. She couldn't have been more shocked if Barbara had confessed that she had a vicious meth addiction.

Was it merely because Miranda Priestly had deemed her an important-enough person with whom to share her list? Probably. But Andy didn't care. She didn't care because it was still nice to hear from the mother-in-law who thought Andy unworthy of her son, and it was nice to hear because Andy knew Barbara was right: she had flaws like anyone else, but she was a damn good mom.

'Thanks, Barbara,' she said, squeezing her mother-in-law's hands. 'That means a lot to me, especially coming from you.'

Mrs Harrison wrenched her hands away and brushed an imaginary hair from her eye. Moment over. But Andy smiled nonetheless.

'Yes, well, I'd better be on my way,' Barbara sang. 'I simply can't be late tonight. Everyone will be there.' She accepted Max's help putting on her coat and then held her cheek out for a kiss from her son.

'Bye, Mom. Thanks for stopping by,' he said. His expression said he'd overheard their conversation.

Andy waited for the door to close behind Barbara. 'Well, will wonders never cease?' Andy asked with a smile, wrapping a cashmere scarf around her shoulders. 'She all but told me she loves me.'

Max laughed. 'Let's not get carried away,' he said, but Andy could see he was pleased, too.

'She loves me!' Andy cheered, laughing. 'Mrs Barbara

Harrison the almighty worships Andy Sachs, mother extraordinaire!'

Max kissed her. 'She's right, you know.'

'I know,' Andy said with a smile.

Isla joined them in the hallway. 'I promise I'll take great care of her,' she said.

And before she could say another word or kiss her baby one final time, Max whisked her into the hallway, then the elevator, and finally into the backseat of a Lincoln Town Car that smelled like new leather and reminded her, as Town Cars always did, of her year at *Runway*.

'She's going to be fine,' Max said, squeezing her hand once again.

When they pulled up to Skylight West at Thirty-Sixth and Tenth Avenue, they joined a long line of chauffeured Town Cars. Drivers idled in some; attractive couples and friends in party attire climbed out of others. Andy swung open her door before they'd rolled to a stop.

'Do you believe Emily pulled this together so quickly?' she asked Max under her breath as he helped her out. 'Just having a party to celebrate our three-year birthday is a great idea, but getting Vera Wang and Laura Mercier to underwrite the whole thing was a stroke of brilliance.'

Max nodded. 'It's great for publicity. Knowing Emily, she'll get all the boldfaced names here tonight, and you know who loves a party like that . . .'

Andy looked at him blankly. 'Who?'

'Elias-Clark! Events like this are right out of their playbook. Throw a splashy party, get a bunch of famous faces to show up, and get mentions of it plastered all over the gossip pages tomorrow. It does terrific things for the magazine's profile, and not just with readers. Emily knows that tonight will raise *The Plunge*'s profile and make it even more desirable to Miranda.'

Max said this factually, the way a businessman familiar with the industry would, but it rankled Andy. While she'd certainly seen the benefits of an advertiser-funded fancy soiree in terms of publicity and profile, she hadn't considered how it would translate to their acquisition position. It was so Emily. It bothered her even more that Max didn't seem to understand why it bothered her.

They'd reached the elevator that would whisk them to the rooftop, but Andy pulled Max's hand and motioned for the other guests – all of whom looked fabulous but none of whom looked familiar – to go ahead without them.

'You okay?' he asked.

Andy felt her throat tighten. Her phone buzzed and a text popped up on the screen. 'Emily wants to know where we are,' she said.

'Come on, let's go up and enjoy tonight, okay?' Max reached for Andy's hand, and she allowed herself to be pulled into the elevator.

A very young woman wearing a sexy red dress ducked into the elevator just before the doors closed. 'Rooftop?' she asked.

'For the *Plunge* party?' Max asked, and the girl grinned.

'I wasn't even invited,' she said. 'My boss was, but I begged her to let me come when she couldn't make it. This is *the* event to be at tonight.' The girl's face flashed recognition. 'Wait, you're not Max Harrison, are you? Wow, it's so great to meet you.'

Max and the girl shook hands. She looked like she'd just met Ryan Gosling.

The elevator doors swung open and Max gave Andy a raised-eyebrow look and a mischievous smile. She made a mental note to find Emily immediately and report this juicy tidbit but forgot the instant she stepped onto the rooftop. It was magic, pure magic. The open-air space stretched for what seemed like miles in every direction with only the twinkling lights of the skyline creating a dramatic boundary between the party and the entire island of Manhattan. Straight ahead the Empire State Building shone blue and silver, cresting from behind the red neon *New Yorker* sign. To the right, the sun had just set over the Hudson, casting it in dramatic shadows of deep purple and orange, the lights of New Jersey gleaming behind it. In every direction she looked, lights were turning off in office buildings and shops, and turning on in apartments and bars and restaurants as the entire city made its daily transition from work to relaxation; the cacophony below – the usual mix of sirens, taxi horns, music, and people, so many people – rose from the street. The city was alive and humming on a warm night in early October, and Andy thought there was no better place on earth.

'Do you fucking believe this?' Emily materialized out of nowhere and grabbed Andy's arm. Her criminally gorgeous figure was swathed in a neon-pink Hervé bandage dress, and her hair cascaded in perfect red waves over her bare shoulders. 'How insane does this place look?'

It was hardly surprising that Emily didn't ask about Clementine or inquire how Andy was doing. Emily had visited when Andy got home from the hospital and brought Clementine an outrageously expensive and hugely impractical cashmere gown, hat, and mitten set (in June), but she'd been pretty much absent since then. The girls held conference calls with various staffers to discuss work, and they e-mailed multiple times a day, but a noticeable coolness had settled over their friendship. Andy wasn't sure if it was the baby or her refusal to discuss the Elias-Clark offer, or if Andy was just being hypersensitive, but it felt like something between them had changed.

Max motioned that he was heading to the bar and would return in a minute.

Andy turned to Emily and tried joking. 'Did you have that dress shortened and taken in? Was the corsetlike wrapping just not tight enough for you?' she asked.

Emily pulled back for a moment and looked down at her belly. 'Is it too tight? Am I having mirror delusion? Because I thought it looked good!'

Andy cuffed her on the arm. 'Shut up, you look amazing and that's nothing but jealousy talking from the whale wearing the shower curtain.'

'Really? Good. I thought so too, but you never know.' She waved her arms. 'You're looking better too.'

'How generous. Thanks.'

'No, really, it's true. Your boobs are, like, almost normal sized and I love the Chloé shoes.' Emily motioned toward the crowd. 'Do you believe this place?'

Andy spun slowly around and took in the rooftop. Cast-iron fire pits boasted dancing flames. Miniature white string lights crisscrossed overhead. Beautiful people milled everywhere, laughing and sipping the specialty drink, a heavenly muddled mix of Patrón, simple syrup, cilantro, and lemon juice. They moved effortlessly between the dimly lit bar and the low, white leather couches and acrylic coffee tables that had been arranged in living-room-like configurations. Groups stood along the railings, admiring the endless views in every direction.

Emily took a drag from her cigarette and slowly exhaled. Andy wasn't pregnant anymore. Just one wouldn't kill her. Andy motioned toward the pack.

'You want one?' Emily asked, and Andy nodded.

The first inhalation burned her throat and tasted terrible, but it improved quickly after that. 'My god, this is good.'

Emily leaned closer. 'Patrick McMullan is here photographing. Supposedly Matt Damon and that cute wife of his are here, but I haven't seen them yet. There's a whole slew of Victoria's Secret models, and they're keeping the guys happy. And Agatha just got a message from Olive Chase's publicist that she and Clint may be stopping by after another event in Tribeca. I'm not exactly sure how it happened, but this is turning into the party of the year.'

Max returned, handing Andy one of the cilantro tequila drinks and holding a water for himself. 'Sorry, Em, I didn't know what you wanted.'

She made a beeline for the bar before Andy could blink.

'I haven't seen you smoke in years,' Max said, eyeing her cigarette.

Andy took another drag. She was enjoying it immensely now, both the cigarette and Max's look of surprise.

In a nearby couch area, Miles was talking to a few people from *The Plunge*'s staff, specifically to Agatha, who was wearing a sleeveless white crepe romper, cinched at her nonexistent waist with a gold snake-shaped belt and punctuated with kick-ass gold lamé heels that on anyone else would have looked cheap and trying too hard but on Agatha just looked fierce. Andy didn't like how friendly they appeared, but before she could think too much about it, Miles spotted her and jumped to his feet.

'I propose a toast,' he announced, holding his beer stein aloft. 'To Andy and Emily, wherever she is. They managed to make weddings something beautiful and interesting. Something with style. And apparently, we're not the only ones who think so.'

With this everyone at the table cheered.

Miles waved his glass, clinked it first with Andy's and then with Agatha's. 'Happy birthday to *The Plunge*. Three years never looked so good.'

Andy did her best to smile and clink her glass with the others. After a couple minutes' small talk, she excused herself to find Emily and make sure the enormous Sylvia-Weinstock-designed wedding cake Andy had ordered – her only task for the evening – was being prepped for its grand appearance.

She was walking past the smaller corner bar when she heard a familiar voice call her name. *It can't be,* she thought to herself, and refused to look. *He lives in London now. He's barely ever in New York. He isn't on the invite list.* It wasn't until she felt the warm hand wrap around her bare forearm that she knew for certain.

'What? Not even a hello?' he said, pulling her close to him. As always, he was wearing a European-tailored – that is to say, tight – suit, a crisp white shirt opened one button too many, and no tie. He had a day's worth of stubble and perhaps an extra etching or two around his eyes, which did absolutely nothing to detract from his sexiness. And he was staring at her with an expression that said he knew it.

There was only one thing to do: forget about her melting blowout and lack of accessories and relocated baby weight (ass, thighs, boobs), and just *own* it. She stuck her sizable chest forward as Christian Collinsworth let his eyes run over the length of her body.

'Christian,' she murmured. 'What are you doing here?'

He laughed and sipped his drink, which she knew was an extra-dry gin and tonic. 'You think I could be in New York and hear about the party of the year and not stop by? Especially when we're all here to fete my Andy's accomplishments?'

Andy tried to match his casual laugh but hers sounded

more like a donkey bray – guttural, honking, and much too loud. 'Your Andy?' She held up her left hand. 'I'm married now, Christian. Remember the wedding you attended a year ago? We have a daughter now.'

His dimples came out in full force; the smile that caused them was amused and perhaps a bit condescending. 'I heard as much but I wasn't sure whether to believe it or not. Congratulations, Andy.'

Wasn't sure whether to believe it or not? Why, because the idea of me as a mother is just too far-fetched for comprehension?

In an instant his hand was on her, right at the spot where her lower back and hip met, the location of some Spanx-busting back-and-love-handle-combo fat rolls that had proven stubborn beyond belief. He gave her a squeeze and she turned to him in horror.

He threw his hands into the air. 'What? Are you Mormon now in addition to being married? Is your husband going to materialize out of thin air and punch me in the face because I touched his property?' And again, there was that smile. 'Come on, let's get you a drink, and you can catch me up on what else has been happening.'

Somewhere far away, Andy knew she should excuse herself to help Emily, check in with the babysitter, find a bathroom, anything at all except blindly follow Christian Collinsworth to the bar, but she was incapable of leaving him. She accepted the tequila drink Christian handed her and did her best to lean against the bar in a manner that conveyed confidence, aloofness, and sexiness all at once. At this point she could only hope to remain upright and not spring a leak from her now-heavy breasts.

'What's your daughter's name?' Christian asked. He gazed directly into Andy's eyes and yet still managed to convey that he couldn't have cared less.

'Clementine Rose Harrison. She was born in June.'

'Nice. And how have you been adjusting to motherhood?'

It had gone too far, and Andy was pleased to discover she'd found her voice. 'Oh, save it, Christian. You really want to talk sleep schedules and swaddle blankets? Why don't we talk about your real favorite subject. How have *you* been since we last saw each other?'

He sipped his drink and appeared to think about this. 'I have to say, I've been good. Did you know I'm living in London?' He didn't wait for Andy to respond. 'And it's really been working for me. Lots of time to write, good opportunities to do some traveling in Europe, plenty of new faces. New York was just getting so . . . tired.'

'Mmm.'

'Right? I mean, aren't you at the point where you would rather be anywhere but here?'

'Actually, I—'

'Andy, Andy, Andy.' He leaned toward her, tilting his chin down and blinking his unfairly long lashes. 'Didn't we have such a good time together? What happened to us?'

Andy couldn't help but laugh once again. 'What happened? You mean when we woke up one morning in your suite at the Villa d'Este and you asked if I wanted to meet your girlfriend? Who just so happened to be arriving later that day? Never mind that we'd been dating for nearly six months at that point?'

'I wouldn't say—'

'Sorry. *Sleeping together* for nearly six months.'

'It's never that simple. She wasn't my girlfriend per se. It was a complicated situation.'

A flash of chartreuse caught her eye.

'Andy?' Christian pushed up even closer to her, but Andy was barely aware of him.

291

lauren weisberger

She could now see that the chartreuse was actually a poncho – a fur poncho – and it sashayed closer and closer to Andy. Before she had a second to compose herself, Nigel had wrapped his arms around her and pushed her face into his furry shoulder.

'Darling! I was hoping I'd see you here. Quite the little soiree you girls threw here tonight. I'm very impressed.'

Christian leaned over and whispered in Andy's ear. 'You might want to say hello.' Andy glanced at his grin and dimples and, for a split second, wanted to stick her tongue in his mouth.

Nigel didn't seem to notice Andy's shock. Instead, he thrust her backward by the shoulders, kissed both her cheeks, and said, 'We brought the whole team tonight. No one wanted to miss out on such a delicious party!'

With this pronouncement, Andy thought she might faint. Was this the price of success? To have Miranda constantly, persistently, miserably resurfacing in her life? On her first public outing since giving birth, did she really need to deal with Miranda Priestly on top of a disappointed friend, a cheating ex-boyfriend, and soon-to-be-leaking breasts?

Thankfully, Christian stepped in and greeted Nigel. Almost instantly the two were discussing the schedule of the upcoming Fashion Week, and Andy was able to sneak a look at the *Runway* crew: Serena, Jessica, and three or four Clackers were all in various states of fabulousness, with miles of thick, shiny, blown-out hair; skimpy dresses; high heels; toned arms; flat stomachs; tanned legs; and sparkly jewelry. There wasn't a single misstep among them; individually each looked gorgeous, and together they made a cabal so attractive it just seemed wrong.

'Miranda's not here?' Andy blurted out, completely unaware that she was interrupting Christian and Nigel.

Each turned to stare at her. Christian's look was one of sympathy, the type of expression you gave to a ranting crazy person on the subway. Nigel's was one of amusement. 'Why no, dear. You think Miranda had nothing better to do tonight than come here? If it weren't so self-involved, it would almost be sweet . . .' He smiled magnanimously.

Andy stared at him in horror. 'No, it's not that I *wanted* her to be here . . .'

Nigel slowly nodded and turned back to Christian, who made no attempt to smooth over her awkwardness. Max's approach and a slug from her drink saved the day.

'Hi, baby,' Andy said, perhaps a bit unnecessarily, but she appreciated the quick flash she saw across Christian's face. 'Max, you remember Christian Collinsworth. And of course, you've met Nigel.'

'Good to see you,' Max and Christian said in unison as they shook hands. Andy was proud to see Max reach around and pat her ex on the back, looking confidently taller and manlier than Christian.

Nigel snagged a pink umbrella cocktail off a passing tray and held it up in Max's direction before taking a delicate sip. 'Lovely seeing you again, Mr Harrison,' he sang.

'Great party, isn't it?' Max asked, taking a drink from his club soda. 'Who would ever believe a magazine that's only three years old could draw a crowd like this?'

Andy blushed, realizing that Max was trying to sell the scene to Nigel, but Nigel didn't seem to notice.

'Every girl loves a wedding, don't they? Even this one!' he trilled, pointing to himself.

Max and Christian merely stared at Nigel, but Andy immediately understood.

'Are you and Neil making it official?' she asked.

Nigel grinned. 'I've already got Karl working on my outfit.

293

Picture James Bond meets *Pretty Woman*, with a little dash of *Mary Poppins* thrown in for good measure.'

The three of them nodded enthusiastically.

Christian took that moment to excuse himself, and Andy caught Max staring after him.

'That sounds amazing,' Andy said to Nigel, though she hadn't the faintest clue what he meant.

'It's going to be the wedding of the year,' he said without the least bit of irony or modesty.

Andy had a flash of brilliance. It was so obviously perfect that she could barely get the words out. 'You know, I'm ashamed to say it, but *The Plunge* has never covered a same-sex marriage. I'll have to talk to Emily first, but I'm sure we would both love it if you'd consider letting us feature your wedding. We would guarantee you the cover, of course, and do a great in-depth interview covering all aspects of how you met, started dating, got engaged, the works. I can't make any promises, but maybe we could even arrange for St Germain, or perhaps Testino, to shoot—'

Something about the way Nigel smiled at her – slyly, knowingly, but also with sympathy – stopped Andy midsentence.

'It's quite amazing, it really is,' he said, shaking his head. 'It's like destiny!'

'So you like the idea?' Andy asked hopefully, already imagining Emily's ecstatic reaction to the news.

'Love it, darling. Miranda and I discussed it this morning, and we both agreed it would be cover-worthy. Although she prefers Demarchelier, I still think it would work with Mario. Regardless, it's going to be smashing. I just adore when an idea comes together!'

'You and Miranda discussed it?' Andy asked, searching for an explanation. The disappointment set in almost immediately.

'I didn't realize it would be the type of thing *Runway* would—'

Nigel screeched. 'You're too sweet, darling! Of course it's not right for *Runway*, but it's absolutely perfect for *The Plunge*.'

Andy looked at him in confusion. 'So you want to talk about featuring it? Because I know we would be so excited to—'

Again, Nigel's expression silenced her. 'No need to talk about anything at all, my love. It's all been decided.'

Andy's eyes flew to Max, who was staring at the ground.

'Oh, you must mean the proposal for Elias-Clark to acquire *The Plunge*, right?' Andy asked, truly puzzled and trying to recover a modicum of control.

No one said a word. Nigel stared at her as though she'd just offered him a test ride on her spaceship.

'I know it's on the table, and we're very much entertaining the idea,' she lied again. 'But nothing's been decided yet.'

Another long, excruciating period of silence ensued.

Nigel smiled patronizingly. 'Of course, dear.'

Max cleared his throat. 'Well, however it happens, I think we can all agree it'll make a great story. Congratulations again! Now, will you please excuse me while I steal Andy away for a moment?'

Nigel was back in the mix of the *Runway* crew before Max even had a chance to steer Andy toward the bar.

'Was that just what I think it was?' Andy asked, numbly accepting the glass of wine Max handed her.

'What? Nigel just being overenthusiastic? I think it's a great sign he's so excited about having his wedding in *The Plunge*, don't you?'

'Of course I do. But he made it sound like this was all a fait accompli, like Miranda already owns us and gets to make all the calls. Doesn't he know we've tabled that conversation for the time being?' *And by* tabled, *I mean squashed forever,* Andy thought.

'I wouldn't worry about it,' Max said. 'You've always said Nigel was just really excitable.'

Andy nodded, although she couldn't ignore the feeling of cold dread that had settled over her. The mere suggestion that Miranda would be deciding which weddings they would cover and who would shoot them was enough to make her sweaty with anxiety and fear. She knew then, even more certainly than she had before, that she would *never* allow that to happen.

'Hey, love, I'm saying good-bye,' Christian said into her ear as he swooped up behind her. Andy instantly felt self-conscious when he placed his hands on her hips and kissed both her cheeks. He turned to Max, who was staring daggers at him, and said, 'Good to see you again, man. And congratulations on your lovely wife. She's the best.'

Max had already tightened his grip around Andy's shoulder and merely nodded at Christian before directing Andy back toward their table.

'You didn't have to be rude,' Andy said, although she was secretly delighted with Max's unspoken reaction: *Back off my wife, and take your too-tight suit and your dimples with you.*

'Oh please. Rude would have been telling that douchebag to stop openly hitting on my wife and get the fuck out of my face. I can't believe you *dated* that guy.'

Andy wisely decided not to correct Max's perception that she and Christian had done anything besides sleep together. Instead, she took her husband's hand and joined the crowd in a rousing rendition of 'Happy Birthday' for *The Plunge.* Everyone cheered.

The next three hours passed in a blur of hors d'oeuvres,

music, and chatter, even a little dancing. Andy talked to dozens, maybe hundreds of people, and although she wasn't the least bit drunk – she'd stopped drinking early in anticipation of her late-night nursing session – she barely remembered a single word exchanged except those between herself and Nigel. Why did he think the acquisition was so imminent? She wanted to ask Emily but watching her actually eat a piece of the Weinstock cake, she knew she could refrain from an Elias-Clark conversation for one night. Andy had to admit she was still hoping – irrationally, she knew – that the whole thing would just fade into the woodwork. Instead, she kissed her friend good night, congratulated her on a hugely successful party, and followed Max into the backseat of a taxi.

When the cab pulled up in front of their building, Andy practically bolted into the lobby. This was the longest since Clem was born that Andy had left her side, and she couldn't bear another second. She scooped her just-awakened daughter into her arms and pressed her lips to the baby's warm, red cheeks. It was all she could do not to chew them, she thought with a smile as Clem's face began to scrunch up in a telltale wail.

'How is she?' Max asked, having paid Isla and seen her into a taxi.

'Delicious as ever. Perfect timing – she just woke up for her midnight feed.'

Max held Clem while Andy kicked off her heels and stripped off her dress and her insanely painful Spanx, which she deposited directly in the trash. Climbing naked under the cloudlike covers and collapsing back into the pile of pillows, she groaned in pleasure. 'Give me my baby,' she said, arms extended.

Max handed her the whimpering bundle and the entire

world of Nigel and Emily and *The Plunge* and Miranda Priestly disappeared into blissful nonexistence. Lying on her side, Andy unzipped Clem's pajamas. She placed her hand directly on her daughter's warm belly. She stroked her chest and her back, whispering quietly in her ear as she guided her breast to Clem's mouth, and exhaled in relief as the baby began to suck. Max pulled the covers up over the pair as Andy pressed her lips to Clem's head and continued to rub her back in slow, steady circles.

'Beautiful,' Max said, his voice gruff with emotion.

Andy smiled up at him.

Max crawled, fully dressed, beside them in bed.

Andy watched her daughter suckle for another couple of minutes and saw Max close his eyes, a slight smile on his lips, and without a second thought, she reached out and squeezed his upper arm. His eyes didn't open but she knew he was awake. A surge of peace, hope, comfort coursed through her. It had been forever since she'd told him, unsolicited, and she wanted him to know.

'I love you, Max,' she whispered.

18

stop talking and step away

Andy covered Clem's face in kisses before handing her over to Isla. She watched as the baby flashed a smile and reached out for her, and the waterworks began. And it wasn't the baby who was crying. Was Andy going to sob like a crazy person every day for eternity? Would Clementine leave in the morning, backpack on and pigtails bobbing, on her way to fourth grade, with Andy a blubbering wreck at the bus stop?

'It's only your third day back,' Max said reassuringly as he watched the emotional good-bye. 'It'll get easier.'

'I can't believe it's only Wednesday,' Andy said, carefully dabbing her eyes.

Max held the front door open for her and Andy willed herself to walk through it. It was such a bittersweet thing: she desperately missed Clem and hated leaving her all day, but it did feel good getting back to work. To adult conversations and spit-up-free clothes and using her mind again for something other than singing 'You Are My Sunshine.'

'Share a cab?' Max asked. He walked to the curb and thrust out his arm.

'I can't, I have to run a couple errands before work. There's never any time afterward.'

A cab pulled up. Max kissed Andy and ducked into the backseat. 'Keep me updated, okay?'

Andy frowned. 'Isla texts you with updates too, doesn't she?'

'About your conversation with Emily, I meant.'

Andy knew exactly what he meant but feigned confusion.

'Aren't you guys having your big sit-down today? To discuss your next move?'

'Mmm,' Andy murmured, suddenly desperate to get away. 'Have a good day.'

Max pulled the door shut and the cab took off like a race car. She checked her watch. Eight A.M. Gone were the days of leisurely coffees and fresh-made smoothies and gym visits – although Max still got there at least three days a week without her – but Andy didn't mind. She'd so much rather spend those couple of hours with her daughter, snuggling in bed together, playing on the fluffy nursery rug. It was now the best part of the whole day.

Andy was sorting her clothes when the dry cleaner's receptionist, a fortysomething Ecuadorian man who always gave Andy Tootsie Rolls, shouted a greeting over her shoulder.

'Hey, man, new customer! Welcome, mister!'

Andy didn't turn around.

'How much will it cost to shorten this skirt?' she asked.

'Just an inch, inch and a half? I'd like it to hit right above the knee instead of at it.'

The receptionist was nodding, but it was the voice behind her that caught her attention. 'You can go shorter than an inch. You've got the legs to pull it off.'

The voice vibrated in her toes, and Andy knew it was Alex before she turned around.

Her Alex. Her first love, the man she always thought she'd marry. He had been there through all four years of college and the craziness of life at *Runway* and the fallout period after it. Alex had joined her on family vacations. He'd attended holiday dinners and birthday parties and celebratory drinks of every kind. Alex knew she hated sliced tomatoes but loved tomato-based everything, didn't laugh when she death-gripped his hand when their flight had turbulence. For nearly six years, he'd known every inch of her body as though it was his own.

'Hey there,' she said, collapsing into his open arms for the most natural-feeling hug in the world.

He kissed her on the cheek like an exuberant uncle – rough, excited, platonic. 'I'm serious, Andy. Don't go getting all conservative on me in your old age.'

'Old age?' she said, feigning outrage. 'The last time I checked, you were two months older than me.'

He pushed her back but held her upper arms and made a long, slow show of carefully looking her up and down. The obvious affection, the wide smile, that adorable head nod – it made her instantly comfortable. Confident even. Despite still being eight or ten pounds above her pre-pregnancy weight and overall jigglier than usual, she felt attractive.

'You look terrific, Andy. Glowing. And I hear I owe you a huge congratulations on baby Clementine.'

Andy looked at him, caught off guard by the warmness

of his smile. He appeared genuinely happy for her. 'Your mom?'

He nodded. 'I hope it doesn't freak you out, but she sent me those pictures of you in the hospital the first few days. I guess your mom was so excited she forwarded them to everyone in her address book. Anyway, your daughter is beautiful and you and your husband looked very, very happy.'

'Anything else I can do for you two?' the receptionist asked.

'Sorry, we're leaving. Thanks for everything.'

She followed Alex outside. She tried to focus on the present moment, but her mind kept cycling through the hospital pictures from Clem's birth: Andy, minutes postpartum, looking all sweaty and makeup-less and pale; Clementine first covered in blood and vernix and then cleaned up but still ruddy and cone headed; a stubble-faced Max looking alternately like he wanted to throw up and kiss someone. They were photos of possibly the most intimate time of their entire lives, and Alex had seen them. She wanted to kill her mother, really punish her, even while a tiny, deeply buried part of her was happy Alex had gotten to share that.

'Where are you headed?' he asked. 'Do you have time for a coffee?'

Andy glanced at her watch, but she knew full well she would agree no matter the time. Besides, why get to work before everyone else? 'Um, yeah, that would be great. I'm only just back at work full-time, so it probably doesn't matter if I'm a little late.'

Alex smiled and offered his arm, which Andy accepted. In one block they passed a Starbucks, an Au Bon Pain, and a Le Pain Quotidien, and Andy wondered where they were headed.

'How has it been being back to work?' Alex asked as they walked. It was already getting cold, and Andy could see her breath form little clouds, but the sun was bright and shining and the morning felt a little bit hopeful.

In his very first question, Alex had hit on the topic at the forefront of Andy's every waking moment. Three days in and it was still torturous leaving Clem. Still, she felt she shouldn't complain. Being her own boss, the hours were reasonable and flexible, and she would never have to miss a doctor's appointment or a sniffly nose. Isla was an absolute dream whom Andy trusted completely, and her mother planned to spend an afternoon a week caring for her granddaughter and making sure all ran smoothly at home. She had the financial means to hire great help, the support of family and an involved husband, and an easy, adaptable baby who stuck happily to her schedule of eating, sleeping, and playing. And it was *still* hard to balance it all. How did women do it with multiple children, grueling hours, low pay, and minimal or no help? Andy couldn't even fathom it.

'It's been good,' she said automatically. 'I'm really lucky to have a great husband and nanny. They've both made it a lot easier.'

'I would imagine it's never easy leaving that little person every day. Of course it must be wonderful to get out of the house, talk to adults, focus on your own work every day. But you must miss her.'

He said it plainly, with empathy and no judgment. Andy's throat threatened to close.

'I miss her so much,' she said, trying not to cry. She thought of Clementine right then, most likely spending a little time kicking around on her play mat before getting a warm bottle and going in for her first nap of the day. She would wake up happy and cooing, her face pink and warm and pressed from sleep, her hair mussed in the most adorable way. If she closed her eyes, Andy could smell her neck, feel her velvety skin, picture those perfect apple cheeks. And although he obviously didn't have children of his own, something told her Alex understood.

Alex ushered her down a flight of stairs and into a nearly hidden bakery that felt like a combination of an illicit speakeasy and a Parisian café. They claimed the lone empty table and Andy checked her phone as Alex ordered at the counter for them.

'The usual?' he asked, and she nodded.

'Here you go.' He set a frothy decaf latte in front of her, the kind that looked more like a soup bowl than a coffee mug, and took a sip from his iced Americano. It felt like not a single minute had elapsed since the last time they'd seen each other.

'Thank you,' Andy said, licking the foam as delicately as she could manage. 'Okay, now it's your turn. You can start by telling me how you know about this adorable little coffee shop that's exactly six blocks from my apartment when I've never even seen it.'

'I wish there was a story that made me seem cooler, but I actually read about it in a guidebook.'

Andy raised her eyebrows.

'I moved back to the city this past fall and felt totally out of the loop. So I bought one of those *Not for Tourists* guides or whatever you call them, the ones that are totally for tourists? And they suggested this place as somewhere only locals and insiders go.'

'I'm buying the damn guide the second I get to a computer,' Andy said with a grin. She paused, took another sip. 'So where do you live now?'

'In the West Village. Christopher and the highway? I guess it used to be kind of seedy, but it's completely gentrified now.'

'And you do your dry cleaning in Chelsea?' Andy couldn't help asking.

Alex gave her a look, an amused one that seemed to say *I'm onto you*. 'No, I don't do my dry cleaning in Chelsea. I'm going to see an exhibit at the Rubin Museum. I just happened to see you from the sidewalk and came in.'

'The Rubin Museum?'

'Himalayan art? Seventeenth and Seventh? Don't tell me you've never heard of that one either.'

'Of course I have!' Andy said, too indignantly, especially since she walked by it nearly every day and had yet to step inside. 'So what brings you back to the city? You just finished your degree, right? I think my mom mentioned that. Congratulations!'

If it felt as strange for Alex as it did for Andy that they knew details about each other's lives through their mothers, he didn't let on. 'Yeah, I finished in the spring and stayed in Vermont over the summer to just hang out and relax. I moved back at the end of August, which was every bit as hot and hellish as you'd imagine, and I've been getting reacquainted with the city. I can't get over how much has changed since . . . since the last time I lived here.'

They were both quiet for a moment, remembering. 'Yeah, but New York never really changes. It just feels different living downtown, I think,' Andy said.

'Maybe. Or maybe you and I were both working so much then that we didn't get to explore a lot. I've had a couple months now with nothing to do but wander. I start work next week. I thought I'd be excited, but I'm actually kind of bummed.'

Andy sipped her coffee and tried not to think about the fact that Alex had yet to reference any kind of significant other. He'd stuck solely to the *I* pronoun and hadn't mentioned the girlfriend as a reason to stay in Vermont for the summer, a reason to move to New York, or someone who had factored into his months of seemingly solo city wandering. Andy's mother had insisted they were close to getting married, but it sure didn't seem that way now. Maybe it was over between them?

'Why are you smiling like that?' Alex asked, smiling right back at her.

Horrified at the thought that he might be able to read her mind, she quickly shook her head. 'No reason. You said you're starting work on Monday? Whereabout?'

'A new school in the West Village. It's called Imagine. I'll be helping design their curriculum before they open, and then I'll be the vice principal.'

'Imagine, Imagine . . . why do I know that name?' Andy racked her brain. 'Is that the elite private international school where a kid can move from New York to Shanghai to wherever else bond traders live and not miss a single class?'

'That's the one.'

'Yeah, they just had a big article about it in the *Times*. Isn't there some thousand-person wait list even though it costs like fifty grand for kindergarten?'

'It's on par cost-wise with other private schools in Manhattan. It just sounds like more because they've instituted a year-round schedule. Studies show that summer break causes students to fall drastically behind their Asian counterparts, who do not take three months off a year.'

Andy reached across the table and poked him in the upper arm. She couldn't help but notice it felt rock-hard. The old

Alex occasionally went for a jog or played a pickup game of basketball, but it looked like the new Alex actually worked out. 'Are you telling me that you're the vice principal of the fanciest, snootiest, most expensive for-profit preparatory school in the United States, Mr Teach for America?'

Alex smiled ruefully. 'It's actually the third-most expensive in the world. And the first two are ours, too – one in Hong Kong and one in Dubai. They cost even more. But I have to say, it's a really amazing program.'

Andy looked down at the table and then back up at Alex, who was fiddling with a straw wrapper. She was torn between treading carefully with this person she hadn't seen in years and laying it all out on the line in the honest, straightforward way she and Alex had always prided themselves on. 'Sounds like a change from what you're used to. Are you happy about it?'

Her words must have hit harder than she'd anticipated, because Alex visibly flinched. 'Like I said, it's a great program and a good opportunity. Would I have preferred to stay in the nonprofit realm? Probably. But I was earning barely enough to support myself, and . . . I'm getting too old for that.'

So there it was. He hadn't stated it explicitly yet, but he didn't really need to. Alex needed to take a job that paid because he either was, or wanted to be, someone's husband.

She almost said a thousand things, but not one of them sounded right or appropriate. Just as she was about to murmur a 'hmm' or an 'I understand,' Alex said, 'Ever since my girlfriend's brother had a baby, it's all she can talk about. And from what I hear, babies are pretty expensive.'

'They sure are' was all she could think to say, and she was surprised she had managed even that. They'd been doing so well . . . flirty without crossing any lines, mutually excited to see each other, equally interested in one another's lives. *But a baby?* Considering she was married herself with a healthy baby girl, Andy knew she was hardly entitled to be deflated by this news. Any reasonably decent person would be happy that Alex, whom she would always love and adore, had found his own happiness. And yet she felt a bit sick.

Her phone rang, and never before had she been so grateful, but when she saw it was Emily calling, she hit 'ignore' and tossed it in her bag.

'Did your caller ID just say that was Emily Charlton?' Alex asked.

'The one and only.'

'I still can't believe you two became friends – it blows my mind. All I remember is you hating each other.'

'Not only friends – best friends. And business partners. We reunited in a cooking class and had a powerful thing in common: she hated Miranda as much as I did.'

Andy stopped. She suddenly realized what had changed between them. The cooking-class Emily would have called Miranda exactly as she saw her: a stark-raving-mad tornado of a woman who was intent on leaving devastation and destruction in her wake. Someone to be avoided at all costs. Now, instead of sharing Andy's misery at the idea of once again working for that lunatic, Emily had reverted back to her *Runway* self: the girl who had worshipped Miranda and aspired to work for her from childhood. Emily's stay on the anti-Miranda train had been brief: once Miranda showed the slightest bit of interest in *The Plunge*, Emily had instantly forgiven the woman for firing her, humiliating her, and crushing her dreams. Emily was actually looking forward to meeting with Miranda and the Elias-Clark people to brainstorm and see how they might work together. When Andy joked she might open fire at the meeting and take everyone

down with her, Emily had shrugged her shoulders and said,
'What? Have you ever considered that maybe we've been
overreacting all these years? That she's not going to win any
charm awards, but she's really not the devil incarnate?'

Andy's phone bleated again. She checked, unwillingly.
Emily.

'Maybe you should get that?'

Andy checked her watch. It was only a little after nine.
She knew Emily would be calling to see when they could
begin discussions.

'I'll see her at the office in a little.'

Now Alex looked at his watch. 'I need to hear more about
your magazine. I've bought a bunch of the issues, do you
know that? Look, the Rubin doesn't open until ten. Do you
have time for a quick breakfast?'

Andy must have looked dumbfounded or, at the very
least, generally confused, because Alex continued. 'There's
a decent diner around the corner where we could get something more than a muffin. What do you say? Do you have
a few more minutes?'

All she wanted to ask was if he'd seen the issue that
featured her own wedding, but instead she said, 'Sure.
Breakfast sounds great.'

They settled at a booth in the back of the Chelsea Diner,
and Andy tried to suppress the weird feeling of being there
with Alex. Just the weekend before she and Max had brought
Clementine there at six thirty on Saturday morning; it was
the only neighborhood place that was open. Now she looked
across the way to the table they had occupied, almost willing
Clementine to appear, kicking and grinning in her infant car
seat, to snap her back to reality. The phone buzzed again.
Emily. Again, she pushed 'ignore.'

Before Andy could even taste her cheddar cheese omelet,

she blurted, 'So, tell me about this mysterious girlfriend.' She came precariously close to saying, 'My mother tells me it's serious,' but was able to show some much-needed restraint.

At the mere mention of her, Alex smiled. And if that wasn't irritating enough, it appeared to be genuine. 'She's a handful,' he said, shaking his head. Andy almost spit out her coffee. *In bed? Is that what he means?* 'She definitely keeps me on my toes.'

What did that mean? That she was spirited? Feisty? Clever? Ballsy? Funny? Charming? *All of the above?*

'How so?' Andy coughed.

'Just a woman who knows her own mind, you know?' Implying, obviously, that Andy wasn't one of them.

'Mmm.' Another bite. Another reminder to herself to chew slowly and swallow. That she was happily married. A mother. That Alex was certainly allowed to have a girlfriend, however spunky she might be.

'She's an artist, a real free spirit. She does a lot of freelance work, some consulting, a little teaching, but mostly she's locked away in her studio or searching for inspiration.'

'You moved back to New York because of her work, is that right?'

Alex nodded. 'Not that it was anything specific, just that there are so many more opportunities. She grew up in the city, and she's got a huge group of friends here, her parents, and her brother and his family. So it's like a whole network. She definitely made it clear from the day I met her in Burlington that she'd be back in New York the first chance she had.'

Her phone rang again, somewhere under their table, but Andy felt as though she were in those final seconds before a car crash, where your mind sees nothing except the image right in front of your eyes, your hearing is momentarily shut down, and every ounce of attention is laser-focused on the present second.

'Do you think you'll marry her?' Andy asked. She set down her fork and looked directly into Alex's eyes. The frisson she felt was undeniable; she couldn't even fake indifference or a touch of aloofness.

Alex laughed, a little uncomfortably. 'Do you want to get that?'

'What? Oh, no, I'm sure it's just Emily again. She can be like that. You were saying . . .'

But the spell was broken. Alex quickly changed the subject back to Andy, asking if the baby was sleeping and whether or not they had any upcoming travel plans. Their ease had turned to awkwardness. He seemed as nervous as she felt, and she couldn't pinpoint why. Of course it was always unnerving catching up with an ex, especially one as meaningful as Alex. How did you go from knowing someone so intimately, sharing every fear and thought and dream with them, to becoming practical strangers? It happened all the time, but it didn't make it feel any less surreal. Andy was sure she could bump into Alex on a street corner in sixty years and still feel that same strong connection to him, but most likely they would never be confidantes, or even truly friends, ever again.

Alex somehow paid for the check before it was even brought to the table, and Andy's profuse thanks made things even more awkward.

'Hey, don't mention it,' Alex said, holding the door to the street open for her. 'I'll be employed by a for-profit as of next week. I'm going to be rolling in it.'

Andy swatted his arm. It was a relief to be out the diner, back outside, not staring into each other's eyes.

311

'Are you cabbing or taking the subway to the office?'

Her phone noted five missed calls from Emily. 'I better jump in a taxi.'

Alex held his arm out, and within seconds a yellow cab screeched to a stop in front of them.

'That's probably the fastest I've ever gotten a cab all the time I've lived in the city,' Andy said, wondering if he heard the undertone: *Too fast; I wasn't ready to say good-bye yet.*

Alex held open his arms for a hug. Hesitatingly, Andy stepped into them. It was all she could do not to collapse against him and bury her face in his neck. His smell was so familiar, as was the affectionate way he rubbed her back between her shoulder blades. She might have stood there all day but the taxi driver honked.

'This was great,' Alex said, an indeterminate expression on his face. 'Really great to see you.'

'You too, Alex. And thanks again for breakfast. Next time we'll have to go out, the four of us. I'd love to meet your girlfriend,' Andy lied. *Shut up!* she yelled at herself in her head. *Stop talking and step away!*

Alex laughed. It wasn't mean, but it wasn't agreeable either. 'Yeah, maybe one day. Keep in touch, okay? Let's not go so long next time . . .'

Andy tucked herself into the backseat. 'Of course!' she called brightly. The taxi began to pull away before Alex had even closed the back door. They both laughed and waved good-bye.

It was blocks before Andy exhaled. Her hands were shaking. When her phone rang again, she could barely compose herself enough to locate it in her bag.

'Hello?' she asked, surprised to find herself thinking it would be Alex.

'Andy? Are you okay? I called you at the office but Agatha

said you weren't in yet, and Emily's been calling you all morning.' Max.

'I'm fine. What's going on?'

'Where are you?'

'What, are you keeping tabs on me?' Andy asked, suddenly unreasonably incensed.

'No, I'm not keeping – yes, I guess I am. I left you over two hours ago, and your office tells me you haven't been in yet and haven't been answering your phone; yes, I guess you could say I got worried. So kill me.'

Andy softened. 'Sorry. I was just running errands. I'm in a cab on my way to the office now.'

'Errands for two hours? You never take cabs to work.'

Andy sighed as audibly as she could. 'Max, I have a bit of a headache,' she said, feeling guilty for lying – about the headache, by omission about seeing Alex, about the errands – but she desperately wanted to hang up. Was this how Max had felt when he decided not to tell her about running into Katherine in Bermuda? That some things deserved to be left unsaid, especially when no one had technically committed any crimes: the way that person could still make your stomach drop; the feeling you got when he or she touched your arm or laughed at your joke. First loves were powerful and private, and they stayed with you a very long time. A lifetime. You could love your current partner more than anyone else on earth, but there would always be a small, intimate piece of your heart tucked away for the person you loved first. She felt it for Alex, and she suddenly understood that Max must have felt it for Katherine, too.

She softened. 'What were you calling about, love?'

'I just wanted to wish you luck! I know this is a big decision day.'

Elias-Clark. That's why Max had been checking up on

her. Emily had probably called *him* to track her down. Once again they were teaming up. Andy took a deep breath to quell her annoyance.

'Thank you, Max,' she said, and realized how formal and annoyed she sounded. Before he could reply, her call waiting beeped. 'It's Emily calling for the thousandth time. I'll talk to you later, okay?' She clicked over without saying good-bye.

'Hey,' she said.

'Where the hell are you?' Emily screeched. 'I've been calling you all morning.'

'I'm fine, thanks, and you?'

'Seriously, Andy. It's late, and you know we have lots to discuss. Where *are* you?'

The cab pulled up to the front of the building and Andy saw Emily, back to the street, sans coat, and wildly waving an unlit cigarette.

'I'm here.'

'Where?' Emily screamed to be heard over the din of nearby construction.

Andy paid the driver and got out of the cab. She could immediately hear Emily yelling through both the phone and across the sidewalk.

'Are you going to smoke that, or are you just standing outside because you enjoy listening to that incessant jackhammer?'

Emily whipped around and upon seeing Andy, slammed her phone shut. She lit her cigarette, inhaled deeply, and sprinted to the curb. 'Finally! I had Agatha clear my entire day. We've waited a long time to have this conversation, and we're going to give it the attention it deserves.'

'Good morning to you too,' Andy said, feeling the cold dread return.

'Where were you?' Emily demanded, punching the elevator button.

Andy smiled to herself. She wasn't going to share Alex with anyone. 'Just some errands,' she said, her mind back at breakfast: the coffee, the conversation, the laughs. He'd left her mere minutes earlier, and already she missed him. It was a very bad sign indeed.

19

ceviche and snakeskin: a night of terror

Andy stood at her kitchen counter, diluting Pedialyte with warm water, when her cell phone rang. 'Agatha?' she asked, tucking the phone between her face and her shoulder. 'Is everything okay?'

As usual, her assistant sounded weary and put upon from the moment she opened her mouth. 'Emily called from Santa Barbara. I guess she had bad reception in the mountains or the valley or wherever she is, but she wanted me to give you the heads-up that Olive and Clint are fighting. The ceremony's already been pushed back by an hour, and Emily is worried they're going to call it off completely.'

'No,' Andy whispered, pressing the phone to the side of her face so hard her cheek hurt.

'I don't have any more details than that. She kept cutting

out,' Agatha said with intense irritation, as though Andy had asked her two dozen questions. How horrible could the girl's day be with both her bosses gone and nothing to do but drink coffee and field a few phone calls?

She heard Clem begin to cry from the nursery.

'Agatha? I've got to run. I'll call you back in a little.'

'Do you know how long? Because it's already after five here and . . .'

How many times had she wanted to say that to Miranda, but instead she'd bitten her tongue and waited another hour, three, five? Miranda never felt guilty, though. Andy had regularly waited until ten, eleven o'clock at night, sometimes even midnight if the art department was running late with the Book. Now her own assistant was irritated at five P.M.?

'Just sit tight, okay?' Andy hung up without further explanation, although she wanted to yell something about being stuck in her apartment with an infant who'd been puking around the clock for twenty-four hours, while her business partner was trying to feed them information from the communication blackout that was a celebrity wedding in the Santa Barbara foothills. It wouldn't kill the girl to sit at her desk and surf Facebook for another thirty minutes.

Andy gathered Clem into her arms and kissed her face and head. She felt warm but not too feverish. 'You okay, sweet girl?' she murmured.

The baby wailed.

The landline rang somewhere in the distance. She wanted to ignore it, but on the off chance it was either Clem's pediatrician returning her call or Emily trying her home instead of her cell, she ran to find an extension.

'Andy? Can you hear me?' Emily's voice screeched through the phone.

'Loud and clear. You don't have to scream,' Andy said,

wiping ineffectually at a puddle of vomit that clung to her shoulder.

'Let's see if you're still saying that when I tell you that the wedding is off. Bam! Over! I'm sitting here at the Biltmore with no fewer than eight hundred wedding guests and there's not a bride in sight!' The volume of Emily's voice increased with every word.

'What do you mean, no bride?'

'She's already delayed the wedding twice. She's not here. No one's seen her!' Emily hissed.

Andy inhaled sharply. Not good. Very not good.

'She's Olive Chase,' Andy said with more calmness than she felt. 'She found the world's most perfect guy. Don't you think she's just running a little late?'

'It's been two fucking hours, Andy! There were rumors circulating before, something about a fight last night that carried over to this morning. Nothing concrete. But then someone's husband caught a late puddle jumper from L.A. and claims he saw Olive, her mother, and her make-up artist waiting to board an American Airlines flight back to L.A. at the Santa Barbara Airport. It's over, Andy. They haven't officially called it yet, but I'm telling you she's gone and so is our entire issue.'

'What do we do?' Andy whispered, unable to hide her panic.

'I get the hell back to New York, and we rework everything. Those two country singers who met in Nashville – what are their names? Where he's so much hotter than she is? Their wedding from six weeks ago can take the cover, I'm not worried about that. It's all the editorial we had planned around Olive that is totally freaking me out right now.'

Andy thought of how every single article in the entire issue was somehow themed to coincide with Olive: how to choose wedding makeup that complements 'mature' brides, where to honeymoon to escape prying eyes, city guides to both Santa Barbara and Louisville, including interviews with local shop owners, party planners, and hoteliers.

Andy moaned. 'Oh, god. It's too much. We won't be able to do it.'

'And don't even get me started on the advertising. I'd say sixty percent of this issue's advertisers bought space based solely on the Chase wedding. Maybe more. And at least half of those are first-time buyers we desperately need to retain.'

Andy heard a noise from the hallway, and then the front door slammed.

'Hello? Who's there?' she called, trying to keep the panic from her voice. She wasn't expecting anyone, but she'd clearly heard the door open and close. Isla was off work to take the GREs, and Max had already left for the airport for an overnight business trip.

Andy heard footsteps in the hallway. She clutched Clem to her chest and pressed her mouth to the phone. 'Emily, someone's here! Call 911! What do I—'

'Relax,' Emily said, sounding irritated. 'It's your nanny. I told her to come in as soon as possible.'

'Isla?' Andy asked, confused. 'But she took a—'

'She can take the damn test another time, Andy. We need you in the office now!'

'But how did you know—'

'Remember who you're talking to? If I can find Miuccia Prada while she dogsleds without cell reception in the Canadian Rockies on New Year's Day, I can sure as hell locate your damn nanny. Now get dressed and get to the office!'

The phone clicked, and despite herself, Andy smiled.

Isla appeared in the nursery. 'Hey,' she said. 'How's Clemmie feeling?'

'I'm so sorry about all this!' Andy said. 'I had no idea Emily was going to call you like that. She had no right to contact you without my permission and suggest that you come in today. I never would have—'

Isla smiled. 'It's fine, I totally understand. Plus with the extra two weeks' salary she said you'd pay me, it will help defray my school costs. So I really appreciate it.'

'Oh, well you know Emily – always with the great ideas,' Andy said cheerily as she imagined all the ways she might kill her friend and enjoy it. She kissed Clem's cheek and handed her to Isla.

'Her fever's down, but please check her again in another couple hours, and if it's above a hundred and one, call me. She can have as many bottles of breast milk as you can get her to eat, and some Pedialyte mixed with water, too. Just keep her drinking. I'll be back as soon as I can, but it may be late.'

Isla snuggled Clem and waved Andy off. 'Emily told me you needed me to stay over tonight, so I brought a bag. Don't worry about a thing, I've got it covered.'

'Of course she did,' Andy muttered. She desperately wanted to shower but knew she didn't have time. Instead, she swapped her puke-stained shirt for a clean one, threw her hair into a ponytail, and pulled on a pair of sneakers she would normally never have worn to work. She was out the door in under ten minutes. Her phone bleated the moment she fell into the backseat of a taxi.

'Do you have me chipped or something? I just got in a cab.'

'What took you so long?' Emily asked, her annoyance apparent.

'Seriously, Em? Tone it down.' Andy said this as playfully as she could manage, but she didn't appreciate Emily's brusque, *Runway*-reminiscent tone.

'I'm racing to get the last red-eye out of L.A., and I'll obviously come right from the airport tomorrow morning. I've already gotten in touch with everyone else; they're all on their way in, or will be soon. I told Agatha to order dinner for everyone. Chinese, because it's fast. It should be there in twenty minutes. Oh, and I also told her to hide all the decaf coffee pods. I want everyone drinking full caffeine tonight – it's going to be a long one.'

'Wow. Would you like to tell us what time we all take bathroom breaks, or should we decide that for ourselves?'

Emily sighed. 'Mock all you want, but you and I both know there's no choice. I'll call you back in five.'

Again she hung up without saying good-bye, another unwelcome remnant from the *Runway* days. Andy knew she had to be in the office all night, and that Emily had actually helped her by doing all the legwork, but she couldn't shake the old feeling of being bullied and ordered around by Miranda's ex-first assistant.

Andy paid the driver and made her way up to the office. An unhappy Agatha glanced up from her desk.

'Sorry, Agatha, but tonight is—'

The girl held up her hand. 'I know. Emily already told me. I've ordered the food, started on the coffee, and called everyone in.' She stated this with such listlessness, such obvious misery, that Andy almost felt badly for her. But then she remembered her own sick child left home with a babysitter, the red-eye that Emily now faced, and the impossibly long night they all had ahead of them, and merely thanked her assistant and closed her door.

Andy worked without interruption for nearly two hours, reviewing the text for the two country singers, making notes about details that needed fleshing out or fact-checking. She was about to head to the art department to discuss the photography when Max called. She looked at the clock: eight P.M. He must have just landed in Boston.

'I got your e-mail. Christ, it sounds like a nightmare,' he said.

'It sure is. Where are you now?' Andy asked.

'I'm still at the airport. Wait, my car's pulling up right now. I've got to meet the Kirby people downtown in thirty minutes.' Max greeted the driver and gave him some instructions and then said, 'I just spoke to Isla. She said Clem doesn't have a fever, and she's getting her bottle ready right now.'

'Did she nap well?'

'I don't know, it was a quick call. Isla said something about staying over tonight?'

'Yes, Emily arranged it. I'm going to be here all night.'

'Emily arranged it?'

'Don't ask.'

Max laughed. 'Fair enough. So you want to tell me what happened? It sounds bad.'

'I don't know much more than what I wrote you, just that Olive called off the wedding at the very last second. I really never saw this coming. Thankfully we have another couple we can plug in, but it screws up the issue in more ways than I can count.'

'Geez. I'm sorry, Andy. Do you think it's going to affect the potential sale?' Max asked this in his trying-to-tread-carefully tone.

'Potential sale?'

'The Elias-Clark offer,' Max said quietly. 'I thought I remember Emily saying something about the deadline coming up for that. Obviously I don't know all the details, but I imagine it would be better to accept the offer before there's a problem with an upcoming issue.'

Andy bristled. 'Elias-Clark is the furthest thing from my mind,' she lied, thinking how very Elias-Clark this whole nightmare of a day was becoming. 'Anyway, you know how I feel about that offer.'

'I know, Andy, I just really think—'

'I'm sorry, Max, but I've got to run. I have hours of work ahead of me, and it's not getting any earlier.'

There was a moment of silence before he said, 'Call me later, okay?'

Andy agreed and hung up. She looked at the sea of pages in front of her – storyboards on the floor, assistants and editors and designers running around outside her office – and knew it was going to take every last ounce of energy to face this night.

When her phone rang again instantly, she didn't even wait for Agatha to answer it. 'What?' she asked, more rudely than she intended.

'May I speak with Andrea Sachs, please?' the voice asked in a pleasant but indeterminate accent.

'This is she. May I ask who's speaking?' Andy felt a wave of irritation. Who besides Max or Emily would be calling her at work at eight o'clock in the evening?

'Andrea, this is Charla, Miranda Priestly's assistant?'

Andy's irritation quickly turned to anxiety. Miranda Priestly's office was calling? Her mind instantly began to cycle through the possibilities, none of them appealing.

'Hello, Charla. How are you doing tonight?'

There was a pause, and Andy knew the girl was shocked into silence that someone had inquired after her well-being. She remembered all too well the feeling that people she spoke to every single day, some of them every hour, wouldn't have so much as noticed – never mind cared – if she simply ceased to exist.

'I'm fine, thank you,' the girl lied. 'I'm calling on behalf of Miranda.'

At the sound of Miranda's name, Andy reflexively cringed.

'Yes?' she managed to croak.

'Miranda kindly requests your presence at a dinner party this Friday evening.'

'A dinner party?' Andy asked, unable to hide her disbelief. 'This Friday?'

'Yes. She'll be hosting at her home. I assume you remember the address?'

'At her home?'

Charla said nothing. Andy shivered from the icy silence and after a long, quiet moment said, 'Yes, I certainly remember.'

'Great, well then it's settled. Cocktails at seven, dinner at eight.'

Andy opened her mouth to respond, but no words came out. After what felt like an eternity of silence, Andy said, 'I'm sorry, I won't be able to make it this Friday.'

'Oh? Ms Priestly will be sorry to hear that. I'll let her know.'

The line went dead. Andy shook her head at the weirdness of the whole interaction.

It made no sense. Miranda wanted her to attend a dinner party? For what reason? With whom? As her anxiety increased, Andy realized the invitation could be issued for only one reason. She dialed Emily.

'Yes?' Emily asked breathlessly.

'Where are you? Don't you have a red-eye to catch?'

'Why do you think I'm running right now? The traffic from Santa Barbara was hell and I just got to LAX. What's up?'

'So, you're not going to believe this for a single second, but I just got a call from Miranda's office.'

'Oh yeah?' Emily asked, sounding not the least bit surprised. Excited, perhaps. But definitely not surprised. 'Was she calling to invite you to dinner?'

'Yes. How did you know that?'

Andy heard a voice over the intercom announce final boarding for a flight to Charlotte. 'But, ma'am, you're not going to Charlotte,' a man's voice said.

'I'm crazy fucking late, can't you see that? Do I really have to take my peep-toe wedges off for a security check? Really? Because that just seems asinine.'

'Ma'am, I'm going to have to remind you that swearing at a TSA agent is—'

Emily made some noise that sounded like a growl and hissed, 'Fine, here, take my goddamn sandals.'

'I don't know how you're not getting arrested right now,' Andy said.

'So, I got the same call from Miranda's assistant,' Emily said, barely missing a beat.

Andy almost dropped the phone. 'What did you tell her?'

'What do you mean, what did I tell her? I told her you and I would be happy to attend. She said Miranda thinks it would be a good opportunity to see if we're on the same page editorially. It's a working dinner, Andy. We can't say no.'

'Well, I did. Say no. I told her I couldn't make it.'

There was some more rustling. Andy braced herself for Emily's anger, but it never came. 'Don't worry about it,' Emily said. 'I told her we'd both be there, ready and willing to talk all about *The Plunge*'s future.'

'Yes, but I told her—'

'Charla texted me ten seconds ago. I guess you must have just hung up with her. She said you couldn't make it. I told her you absolutely could. Come on, Andy, we agreed to listen. And think about this experience. *Dining at Miranda's!'*

Agatha peeked her head into Andy's office, but Andy waved her away. 'You RSVP'd for me? You said YES?!'

'Oh, Andy, stop being such a loser! I think it's a lovely gesture that Miranda has invited us to a dinner at her home. She only does that for the people she likes and respects the most.'

Andy couldn't help herself; she snorted. 'You know as well as I do that Miranda likes exactly no one. She wants something from us, plain and simple. She wants *The Plunge*, and this is part of her strategy for getting it.'

Emily laughed. 'Of course it is. So what? Does it sound so terrible to enjoy a meal prepared by a Per-Se-trained chef in a gorgeous Fifth Avenue penthouse overlooking Central Park, surrounded by all sorts of interesting and creative people? Come on, Andy. You're going.'

'I feel sick, but I can't very well call back and contradict you, can I? Do we bring Max and Miles? What do we wear? Is it just us or will there be other people? I can't deal with this, Em, I really can't.'

'Look, I'm boarding now. Stop stressing. I'll get you something to wear and we'll figure it all out. Right now you've got to focus on salvaging this issue, okay? I'll call as soon as I land, or earlier if the plane has Wi-Fi.' And with that, Emily hung up.

The entire staff of *The Plunge* worked through the night, the next day, and the following night, taking turns catching cat naps on an Aerobed set up in the supply closet and showering at a nearby Equinox. Emily worked the phones relentlessly, begging, pleading, and convincing advertisers who'd purchased space based solely on Olive's name that it was still worthwhile to run their ads; the art department scrambled to lay out an entire cover and feature in less than a day; and Andy spent hours crafting an editor's letter that explained the situation to readers in a clear, concise way without sounding accusatory of Olive or insensitive to the bride they had currently chosen to feature. They were all exhausted, overworked, and unconvinced that their efforts would result in even a decent issue.

Salvation came at one in the morning on the second night – ten o'clock Los Angeles time – in the form of a call from Olive's publicist, who promised every which way that the wedding was back on. Neither Andy nor Emily believed her at first, but the girl, who sounded every bit as hysterical and exhausted as they felt, swore on her life and that of her firstborn that everything down to the doves they would be releasing at 'I do' had been rescheduled for the following afternoon.

'How can you be sure?'

'If you saw her face after they flew back to Santa Barbara on their helicopter, you'd be sure, too. Hair and makeup is scheduled to begin at nine. After that, it's bridesmaids' brunch at eleven, photos at two, ceremony at five, cocktails at six, reception from seven to midnight, afterparty until last man standing. Trust me, I'm sure.'

Andy and Emily's eyes met over the speakerphone. Emily raised her eyebrows questioningly and Andy violently shook her head no.

'I'll be there,' Emily said with a huge sigh. She yelled to a bleary-eyed Agatha to book her a ticket on the first flight out in the morning and to notify the L.A.-based photographer that he would need to head back to Santa Barbara. Andy tried to thank her, but Emily just held her hand up.

'You'd do it if you didn't have a kid,' Emily said, gathering her things to go home and repack for the next couple hours.

'Of course,' Andy said, although she wasn't sure she

would. The days and nights spent at the office had been hell, and she couldn't fathom getting on a plane. She wouldn't admit it aloud, but if the decision had been hers, she might have taken the easier way out and run with the new, reworked issue. Emily was doing the right thing, and Andy was grateful she had the perseverance to see it through.

The chaos of scrapping, reworking, and ultimately reinstating the Olive issue was probably the only thing on earth that could have distracted Andy from the looming Miranda dinner, but as soon as Emily confirmed that Olive really did walk down the aisle this time, Andy found she could think of nothing else. Miranda. Her apartment. Who else would be there? What would they discuss? Eat? Wear? It was totally unfathomable that after so many nights slipping in and out as an indentured servant, Andy would be *dining at Miranda's table*. Andy *should* cancel, but ultimately she decided to take a deep breath, accept a borrowed dress from Emily, and be a grown-up about the whole thing. It was one night, only one night.

Which is exactly what she kept telling herself until the cab pulled up to Miranda's opulent Upper East Side building and the uniformed door attendant swept them into the elevator. 'You're here to see Ms Priestly,' he said, his words somewhere between an order and a question.

'We are indeed,' Andy replied. 'Thank you.'

Andy glanced at Emily, who shot her the same warning look an exasperated mother might give her obnoxious toddler.

'What?' Andy mouthed. Emily rolled her eyes.

He ushered the girls off the elevator at the top floor and was gone before Andy could cling to his leg and beg him to take her back downstairs. Andy could tell Emily was every bit as freaked out as she was, but her friend seemed determined to appear calm and collected. They paused outside the door for just a moment – the same door each girl had let herself into countless times before – and Emily finally rapped softly.

The door swung open, and Andy took in two things almost immediately: first, that Miranda had redecorated the entire apartment from top to bottom and it was infinitely more gorgeous than she could have even imagined; and second, that the slim young girl who had answered the door and whose back was on display as she walked toward the apartment's sweeping staircase was probably one of the twins. Her guess was confirmed a moment later when Cassidy swiveled on a delicate bare foot, and with her hand on the banister and her half-shaved hair flying behind her, said, 'My mother will be down shortly. Make yourselves comfortable.' Without so much as another glance at Andy or Emily, Cassidy bounded up the stairs like a girl much younger than eighteen, and Andy tried to figure out why she would be home from college in early October.

'What do we do now?' Andy whispered as she took in the rich, pewter-colored carpeting, the chandelier with at least a hundred hanging teardrop bulbs of varying sizes and lengths, the life-size black-and-white photographs of famous models from the fifties and sixties, an assortment of fur throws tossed over Victorian-inspired couches and, most shockingly knowing Miranda's taste (or thinking she did), vibrant purple velvet curtains in a pile so deep Andy wanted to bury her face in them. The room was elegant but light-hearted: it obviously cost more to decorate the foyer and formal living room than the average American family earned in four years, but it still managed to feel accessible, comfortable, and most surprisingly of all, downright funky.

Andy followed Emily into the living room and sat beside

her on a love seat. She crossed and uncrossed her legs, desperately wishing for a glass of water. She surreptitiously glanced around: there was enough uniformed staff flitting about to service Downton Abbey, but no one had offered them a thing to eat or drink. She was considering a trip to the bathroom to adjust her twisted and binding tights when an all-too-familiar voice rang out.

'Welcome, everyone,' Miranda said, clapping her hands together almost girlishly. 'I'm so pleased you could join me.'

Andy and Emily looked at each other for a split second – everyone? – before turning their attention to Miranda, who looked so . . . un-Miranda. For the first time Andy could remember, Miranda wasn't wearing something constructed, buttoned-up, or ultratailored. The vermilion maxi dress fit perfectly and was made of the finest silk with beautiful stitching, but it flowed out around her ankles in a soft, elegant wave. Her arms were bare – again, it was the first time Andy could remember seeing Miranda's shoulders in anything other than black-tie, as even her tennis outfits tended toward conservative – and a knockout pair of diamond chandelier earrings reflected the light in tiny, bright bursts. A handful of Hermès bangles jangled on her left arm, of course, but her only other accessory was a buttery soft leather strip that wrapped two, maybe three, times around her trim waist, overlapping itself in a way that felt artful and casual at the same time. Even her signature bob was somehow less severe; it wasn't mussed, exactly, but it had just a bit of sophisticated bed-head rumple to it. More surprising than the dress and the hair and the jewelry, though, was the single feature one never, ever expected to see on Miranda Priestly: a smile that looked completely human. It almost bordered on warm.

Emily jumped up and beelined for Miranda, where all sorts of air kisses and compliments and admirations were exchanged. If Miranda was faking her pleasure at seeing Emily – and Andy was certain she was – even Andy had to admit she was doing a damn good job. She appeared humble and appreciative as Emily droned on and on about the fabulous curtains and the breathtaking view and the spectacular prints. Just when Andy was thinking things couldn't get any weirder, Miranda motioned toward the dining room and said, 'Shall we dine now?'

Andy looked to Emily, who appeared momentarily stricken. Was no one else coming? Would there really be no cocktails before sitting down to dinner? At this pace, they'd be headed back home in sixty minutes. Andy suspected she was the only one grateful for that particular realization.

They followed Miranda into the dining room. Andy was relieved to see that the expansive table was set for five. Two more people would be joining them! It was hardly a group large enough to hide behind, but it was far preferable to having Miranda focused on the two of them all evening.

Cassidy appeared again just as they were taking their seats. 'Where's Jonas? Won't he be dining with us as well?' Miranda asked, her lips pursed in disapproval. Jonas: clearly not high on Miranda's favorites list.

'No, Mother. And neither will I. The kitchen just told me you're having steak for dinner again? Seriously?' Cassidy plucked a multigrain roll from the reclaimed wooden bowl on the table and began munching it like an apple. Her half-shaved head looked both fierce and trendy.

Miranda looked like she might kill her daughter. 'Sit down, Cassidy,' she said, her voice a growled command, all previous softness evaporated. 'You're being rude to our guests.'

For the first time since they'd arrived, Cassidy turned to look at Andy and Emily. 'Sorry,' she said to no one in particular. Then to Miranda: 'I've been vegetarian for over a year now, and the fact that you refuse to acknowledge it really—'

Miranda's palm flew into the air. 'Fine. I'll have Damien prepare you plates in your room. That's all.'

The girl glared at her mother. She looked like she might shout something back, but instead she grabbed a second roll and bounded out of the room.

They were all alone.

Much to her surprise, however, Miranda recovered and returned to being delightful. During the appetizer course – delicate crystal bowls of tuna ceviche mixed with avocado and grapefruit – Miranda regaled them with anecdotes about fall Fashion Week, with all of its amusing mishaps, faux pas, and all-out disasters.

'So there we were, everyone assembled and twittering with excitement, and all of a sudden the power goes out. Boom. Blackness. I can't even begin to explain what a cabal of models do in the pitch dark. Can you imagine it?' Miranda laughed, and Emily cracked up along with her, while Andy wondered what, exactly, the models did.

As the waiters brought out platters of delicately sliced Wagyu beef, Miranda turned to Andy. 'Do you have any travels planned?' she asked, appearing not only alert but interested.

'Only for the magazine,' Andy said, carefully cutting a piece of meat and then setting it aside, too nervous to attempt eating it while talking. 'I think I'll be heading to Hawaii next month to cover the Miraflores wedding.'

Miranda chewed and swallowed delicately. She sipped her white wine and nodded approvingly. 'Mmm, I've always been curious about the Big Island during the shoulder season,' she said. 'You'll have to let me know what you think.' And then: 'Remind me to give you the name of our driver in Maui, if you're headed there; he really is the best.'

Andy thanked Miranda and glanced at Emily, who immediately shot her a *See?* look. Andy couldn't argue. She never would have thought it possible, but maybe Miranda really had softened over the last decade.

Miranda was recommending a particular villa at Tryall for the girls to visit when there was a noise in the foyer. No one seemed to notice. Miranda went on to describe the villa's beautiful infinity pool and ultramodern bedrooms and breathtaking ocean views. Then she turned her attention to Andy and asked after Clementine.

'What a darling name,' she trilled. 'Do you have any pictures?'

Do you have any pictures? Andy knew better than to whip out her cell phone, but shook her head. 'No, sorry,' she said, 'I didn't bring any photos.' Miranda was behaving like someone . . . normal. She was just about to ask Miranda about Caroline and Cassidy when something near the apartment's front door caught her attention. Both Miranda and Emily followed her gaze, and all three watched as an exhausted-looking Charla tiptoed into the foyer. The poor girl clutched the Book and enough dry-cleaning bags to clothe the entire East Side; she didn't notice their staring until she'd deposited the cleaning in the first closet on her left and the Book – the precious, much-revered Book – on the small console table under an imposing chevron mirror.

'I'm so sorry, Miranda,' Charla whispered.

Andy wanted to spring out of her chair and hug the girl. She hadn't been particularly nice, either in person or on the phone, but Andy understood. And now she looked so terrified.

'Sorry for what, may I ask?' Miranda's eyebrows shot up, but she didn't seem as horrified by the interruption as Andy would have expected.

Charla's eyes darted in the direction of the door.

'Sorry for me!' a voice sang out gleefully. 'She tried to keep me from coming, she really did, but I just had to have an answer tonight.'

Nigel. Who apparently had hitched a ride with weak-willed Charla.

'Charla, that's all!' Miranda called out, her irritation obvious. Charla ducked out into the hallway and closed the door behind her.

'Darling? Where are you? I can never find you in this cavernous dwelling!' Nigel shrieked.

Miranda clasped her hands together. 'Nigel, stop shouting. We're right here at the dinner table.'

To say Nigel appeared in the dining room was an under-statement: dressed in layers of contrasting tartan plaid, right down to his kilt and coordinating knee-high socks, Nigel looked like he'd been beamed down from a Scottish cloud and deposited in the middle of Miranda's apartment. The music seemed louder. The mood felt more electric. Even the room's air, heretofore unscented, took on an odd but pleasant aroma of pine trees and fabric softener. Or was it hair spray? Andy couldn't tell.

Miranda sighed, although Andy could tell she wasn't as annoyed as she was acting. 'To what do we owe this pleasure?'

'So sorry to interrupt, you know I am, but I've been killing myself going back and forth, trying to decide if we should run the spread with the de la Renta gown or the McQueen? They're so different, I know, but I keep changing my mind. I had to have your opinion,' Nigel said, producing two layouts from a snakeskin messenger bag.

If Miranda was surprised that Nigel had hitched a ride with her assistant, barged in on her dinner unannounced, and proceeded to place two layouts directly over her not-quite-empty dinner plate, then she didn't show it. She merely glanced at each spread and pointed a long red finger-nail to the one on the left, a frothy pink confection of a dress that didn't look, at least according to Andy's untrained eye, like it belonged to either designer. 'Clearly this one,' Miranda said, handing the layouts back to Nigel. 'I think the reader will appreciate Oscar stepping out of his comfort zone.'

Nigel nodded. 'That's exactly what I thought.'

As if on cue, a ninja-like staff member removed Miranda's plate and replaced it with a steaming hot latte.

Miranda delicately spooned some sugar into her cup and took a sip. She neither offered Nigel a seat nor implied he should leave. There was a moment of uncomfortable silence before Nigel said, 'Why, look who's here! I almost forgot my manners. The wedding dream team! Hello, Emily. Hello, Andrea. How does it feel to be sitting on this side of the table?'

Really freaking weird, Andy wanted to say, but instead she just smiled. 'Hi, Nigel. Good to see you.'

Nigel studied each of their faces for a few seconds longer than was strictly comfortable before moving on to their jewelry, hair, clothes. He made no effort whatsoever to disguise his evaluation.

'It's wonderful to see you ladies again. So tell me, are we celebrating yet? Or are we still discussing all those boring logistics?'

Andy noticed Miranda glance down at her empty dessert plate with an uncomfortable expression. 'We're enjoying each other's company,' she said primly. And then: 'Marietta, please bring Nigel a plate.'

Apparently Nigel didn't catch her cues. 'Ladies!' he shrieked. 'Aren't we all loving the idea that *The Plunge* will be joining the Elias-Clark family? I know I am!'

When no one said anything, Nigel continued. 'Andy, why don't you tell Miranda your idea for the upcoming cover story?'

Andy must have stared at him blankly because Nigel prompted, 'About moi? And my beloved? Surely you remember.'

'Oh, yes,' Andy murmured, uncertain how to proceed but desperate enough to say almost anything to fill the silence. 'I thought it would be a great idea to feature Nigel and Neil's wedding in *The Plunge*'s April issue.' She turned to Nigel. 'You're getting married over Christmas, am I right? That would be perfect timing for us.'

Nigel beamed.

Emily's head whipped back and forth between Andy, Nigel, and Miranda like she was watching a five-setter U.S. Open match.

Miranda sipped her wine and nodded. 'Yes, Nigel told me your idea, and I actually think it's splendid. Of course, the first-ever story of a same-sex marriage should warrant the June issue. April simply isn't noteworthy enough. But I do love the thought.'

Andy felt her face flush.

Emily jumped in. 'Well, whenever it happens, I know it will be terrific. Andy and I were thinking it could be great to stage a photo shoot of the happy couple applying for their marriage license at City Hall. More of a reportorial feel, something that could really capture this moment in history.'

Miranda's attention zeroed in on Emily with a familiar angry flash. 'City Hall conjures up images of criminals and metal detectors and impossibly dreary people asking for handouts. Nigel and Neil are glamour and style and sophistication. What they are not is City Hall.'

'Agreed, agreed!' Nigel squawked.

'I see your point,' Emily said, and seemed to mean it.

Andy stared at the table and hated herself for not saying anything.

'I certainly support gay marriage, but no one is going to benefit from an article done the wrong way. I know *The Plunge* reader, and while she's perfectly happy gays are permitted to marry, she doesn't want to get mired in some dull political narrative. She wants gorgeous clothes! Beautiful flowers. Expensive jewelry. Romance!' With this, Miranda turned to Andy. 'Don't ever forget: your sole job is to give your readers what they want. And all this talk about gay rights would be a horrible miscalculation.'

'Well said,' Nigel murmured.

Emily looked uncomfortable – she was probably concerned about Andy's response – but she nodded as well. 'That's exactly right, Miranda. Andy and I always try to give the reader what she wants. I couldn't agree more. Don't you think, Andy?' With this, she turned to Andy and gave her a warning look.

It was all right there on the tip of her tongue, but Andy held back. What was there to gain from going head to head with Miranda Priestly? In a way, it was a relief to see the old Miranda back again. Two courses was an extraordinarily long time for someone who lacked all human qualities to fake it, but Miranda had done just that. The charm, the grace, the hospitality were unnerving and unsettling. At least this was familiar ground.

Andy put down her coffee cup. She'd tread as lightly as possible, but she wasn't going to pretend to agree with everyone just for the sake of peace over dinner. Besides, maybe it was good to let Miranda hang herself. Emily would see once and for all that they would be beholden to this woman and all her ideas for a very, very long time.

'I do hear what you're saying, and of course we strive to give our readers terrific, interesting features. From all the feedback we get, *Plunge* readers love getting glimpses into other cultures and traditions – especially when they're really different from their own. Which is why I thought it could be fascinating to have a section on gay marriage all over the world. Things are changing so quickly, and not just in the U.S. There's Europe, of course, but strides are also being made in surprising places in Asia and Latin America. They're not quite there yet, but for the first time there's a lot of optimism. It would make a great front-of-book feature, some-thing that could help set up—'

Miranda laughed. It was a shrill, joyless sound, and once again her thin lips pulled tightly across her teeth. Andy couldn't help but shiver.

'How sweet,' Miranda said, placing her dessert fork across her plate to indicate she was finished. Immediately a team of three descended on the room and removed everyone's plates, despite the fact that two of them were still chewing.

'Sweet?' Andy's voice was a squeak, and she hated herself for it.

'You publish weddings, Ahn-dre-ah. Not a scholarly journal. Not a newsmagazine. Such a feature would be totally inappropriate, and I wouldn't allow it.'

I wouldn't allow it.

Andy's head snapped up as though she'd been slapped, but no one else seemed to notice or care that Miranda had just confirmed beyond any doubt that she planned to approve, edit, delete, permit, forbid, and tweak every word that went into *The Plunge*. Not only that, but she couldn't even pretend before an actual sale took place that it would be any different.

'Yes, but it's our magazine,' Andy said in barely more

than a whisper. She hazarded a glimpse at Miranda, who looked surprised. Once again Emily and Nigel fell silent.

'Your magazine indeed,' Miranda said, leaning back in her chair and crossing her legs, looking as though she were really enjoying herself. 'But need I remind you that you have a long way to go?'

'Of course, there's always room for improvement. Andy and I were just—'

Miranda cut off Emily as though she'd never spoken. 'You can judge any book by its September issue and yours was – how shall I put this – thin. Think of all the companies you'd have positively clamoring to buy ad space once they learn *The Plunge* is associated with *Runway*. With all of the weight and experience and prestige of Elias-Clark behind it. Just think – then you could actually drop my name with credibility.'

Emily looked like she wanted to crawl under the table.

Andy coughed. She could feel her face redden. 'I'm sorry, Miranda,' she said, still surprised Miranda knew the real story. 'We only used the *Runway* name to open doors, but we earned everything else.'

'Oh please, don't have a stroke. Of course you did. You succeeded or we wouldn't be here. But it's time you took it up a notch. Who was that on your most recent cover? Those Greeks?'

Emily told her it was Greece's most famous young couple, the son of the prime minister marrying the heiress daughter of one of the world's richest men. Both were gorgeous Cambridge grads, friends of Prince William and Princess Kate.

'Well, they're forgettable,' Miranda said. 'Enough of the foreigners, unless they're royalty themselves. We want aspirational. And frankly the issue with your own wedding, Ahn-dre-ah, was a big stretch. Maxwell Harrison might come from a storied family line, but he is not compelling enough to drive an entire issue. Who goes to the newsstand to pick up a magazine with a nobody on the cover?'

'We had terrific newsstand sales that month,' Andy managed, although a part of her didn't disagree with Miranda. Still, couldn't there be a kinder way of saying it?

Emily looked ready to jump out of her seat. 'I hear what you're saying, Miranda. I was thinking we should have gone in another direction for the cover, but St Germain was such a coup . . .'

Miranda's laugh sounded like a bark. 'Yes, well, when you work for me, great photographers will be de rigueur. With *Runway* backing you, you'll drive every deal on your own terms.'

'You mean your terms,' Andy said quietly.

'I mean terms that include the best and most famous designers, photographers, stylists, celebrities . . . name them, and they're yours.'

Nigel made a catcalling whistle sound. 'She's the best, ladies! Listen closely: it's not every day you get Miranda Priestly giving you advice like this.'

Andrea and Emily looked at each other.

Miranda wasn't finished. 'And you're going to have to change your staff. I want only the best team. That's why I want you. But the transition will allow us to clean house of some of the hangers-on. Oh, and there will be no more "flexible work schedule" rubbish. No more "working remotely." We banned it at *Runway* and it's made a huge difference.'

Andy's first thought went to Carmella Tindale, her beloved, clog-wearing managing editor who would no doubt get the ax. Even worse than that, though, would be saying good-bye to her own flexible schedule. No more Tuesday or Thursday mornings home with Clem. No more attending her pediatrician appointments. No more determining her own hours and working when it best fit her schedule.

Emily cleared her throat. 'I'm not sure we have a lot of people we could afford to lose.'

Andy shot her a dagger look. 'We have an amazing and dedicated staff who work long hours and sacrifice so much for the sake of the magazine. I wouldn't want to part with any of them.'

Miranda rolled her eyes as if this were all too tiring. 'They work long hours so they can raid the swag closet and talk on the phone with celebrities. At Elias-Clark, they'll have that opportunity tenfold. Which is why they should all be presentable. And trained in the *Runway* manner. I would see to it myself.'

'Yes, I do think—' Emily started, but Miranda cut her off.

'And getting back to Nigel's wedding here,' Miranda said, pausing only a moment to make sure all eyes were on her. 'I would personally guarantee it would be your biggest issue yet. By a large margin.'

'I know I speak on behalf of Emily and myself when I say that we have some clear ideas for how we want that issue to—'

'Friends!' Nigel cried. 'Let us not bicker over details. You all must realize, of course, that when we're talking about the wedding of the century – mine – it is surely I who will make the decisions. Consider me your fearless king, and you all my ladies in waiting.' Nigel pushed his chair back from the table, sprung to his feet, and wrapped his cape around his shoulders.

Emily laughed first and Andy followed. Miranda made a tight, angry smile.

Nigel saluted. 'To wedding unity!' he sang, now on a roll. 'I promise you this: there is enough Nigel fabulousness to go around. Now, what do we say about a toast?'

As though by magic, a waiter appeared from the kitchen with a tray of four champagne flutes and a bottle of Moët. 'No, no, that won't do,' Nigel muttered. He disappeared into the kitchen and emerged with four elegant crystal shot glasses. Upon closer inspection, they looked to be espresso cups, but Nigel didn't seem to mind.

'What's this?' Emily asked, accepting hers daintily between thumb and forefinger.

'Nigel, really,' Miranda said, with what sounded like faux exasperation. Nonetheless, she too accepted a glass.

'To brilliant collaborations among brilliant women!' Nigel called, his own glass raised high. '*The Plunge* is one lucky lady, to have so many who love her.'

'Well put, Nigel,' Emily said, leaning forward to clink his glass. Together, each clinked Andy's and Miranda's before elegantly throwing back the shot.

'Drink!' Nigel shrieked, and Emily laughed.

Andy watched in disbelief as Miranda took a delicate sip and then another. Not wanting to be the only one with a full glass, Andy summoned her college days, took a deep breath, and downed the alcohol in one gulp. It burned her throat and made her eyes water, and she couldn't tell if it was vodka or whiskey or gin or something else entirely.

'This is vile,' Miranda proclaimed, examining the remainder of her shot. 'I'm appalled to think you found this in my home.'

Nigel smiled devilishly. He reached under his shirt and produced a silver and leather flask, monogrammed with a large, flowery N. 'I didn't,' he said with a grin.

The rest of the dessert course passed without incident, but Andy was still reeling from the conversation. Miranda ushered everyone into the foyer, and it was all Andy could do to take her coat slowly and not run from the entire dreadful scene.

'Thank you so much for such an amazing night,' Emily gushed, pecking Miranda once on each cheek as if they were long lost sorority sisters.

'Yes, darling, you really outdid yourself,' Nigel said. Although it wasn't the least bit cold outside, he pulled on a pair of fingerless gloves and wrapped a blanket-size cashmere scarf around his head and neck.

Only Andy seemed to notice Miranda's back go ramrod straight and her mouth clench closed.

'Thank you for inviting us, Miranda. Dinner was lovely,' Andy said quietly as she fiddled with the buttons on her jacket.

'Ahn-dre-ah.' Miranda's voice was quiet too, but there was something steely in it. Something determined.

Andy glanced up and almost lost her balance. Miranda was staring at her with such naked, unabashed hatred that it took her breath away.

Nigel and Emily were chatting about whether it was best to share a cab home or each take their own, so neither noticed when Miranda wrapped her long, lean fingers around Andy's shoulder, pulled her close, and leaned in to whisper in her ear. It was the closest Andy had ever been to Miranda, and it made the hairs on her arms and neck stand up.

'You'll sign those papers this week,' she said, her breath icy on Andy's cheek. 'You'll stop making trouble for everyone.' Then, just as quickly as she claimed Andy, Miranda gave her arm the slightest push. *I'm done with you. Now move along.*

Before Andy could even think of responding, the elevator man appeared in the doorway and good-byes were being exchanged all around. No one noticed when Andy dumbly shuffled onto the elevator without saying another word.

They spilled out onto the street, Nigel and Emily tipsy and laughing, clutching each other's hands.

'Good-bye, darlings,' Nigel called, as he slipped into a taxi without offering the girls a ride, or the chance to take it first. 'Can't wait to get working together again!'

Emily had her arm extended to hail a cab when a Town Car pulled up beside her. A middle-aged man with salt-and-pepper hair and a kind face said, 'You're Ms Priestly's guests? She's asked I see you home, or wherever you need to go.'

Emily gave Andy a triumphant look and flopped happily into the backseat. 'How nice was it for Miranda to have us driven home?' she asked, stretching her legs.

Andy was still in shock. Had Miranda threatened her? Did that really just happen? She couldn't even summon the words to tell Emily.

'What a fabulous dinner! I really love what she did with the apartment, and of course the food was to die for,' Emily prattled on. 'In hindsight, I think it was better Cassidy and her boyfriend didn't join us. It gave Miranda a chance to focus exclusively on us, let us hear her real thoughts for *The Plunge*. I know some of what she said sounded a tad . . . intense. But how incredible that one of the greatest minds in fashion and publishing wants to help us take *The Plunge* to the next level? It's almost unbelievable!'

Why didn't Emily seem more upset? Didn't she see that Miranda admitted she had every intention of treating *The Plunge* as her own private fiefdom? That Miranda would oversee the hiring and firing, dictate every decision from the editorial to the advertising, institute draconian schedules and dress codes? That they would essentially be assistants again, with no real say or influence, mere pawns in Miranda's despotic reign?

'I feel like we weren't at the same dinner,' Andy said.

'I think she's really made a change for the better, Andy. She couldn't have been more gracious tonight.' Emily's smile was beatific, as though she had just emerged from an indulgent full-body massage.

'Emily! Didn't you hear her say, "I wouldn't allow it!" As though it were her magazine? And what about insisting that Nigel and Neil take the June cover? I wasn't going to say anything tonight, but I have a possible lead on Angelina and Brad. Who are we going to give the June cover to? Nigel, flamboyant magazine editor and Priestly muse? Or *Brangelina*? I mean, seriously!'

Emily closed her eyes and exhaled luxuriously. 'Did you not want to die when the assistant walked in?' she asked.

'I know, poor thing. She must have been panicked. Didn't you see? She's still the same Miranda. Treating her assistants like slaves. She barely acknowledged the girl except to dismiss her. I bet Miranda will fire her for letting Nigel follow her.'

'Yes, well what idiot allows anyone – even Nigel – to join her for drop-off? It's positively asinine. We never would have done that. Well, you probably would have, but I'd have shut it down immediately. If Miranda knows what's good for her, she'll fire that girl first thing tomorrow.'

Andy looked out the window at all the gorgeous windows lit up on Fifth Avenue as the car hurtled downtown. So much had changed since she'd left *Runway*. It had taken years and so much hard work and heartache, but Andy finally felt like she had peace in her life: friends with whom she shared things, a loving sister and parents, a career that challenged and fulfilled her, and most of all, a family all her own. A husband. A daughter. It hadn't happened the way she'd expected, but did any of that matter now?

'Wasn't tonight just fab?' Emily sighed. Her eyes were still closed and her cheeks were flushed with pleasure.

Andy said nothing.

'I really think Miranda made a huge overture tonight. And I'm sure it's not just for us. She's definitely changed for the better, don't you think?'

'Em, I—' Andy stopped, too exhausted for the conflict that would surely ensue once she uttered the words she knew she must say. 'Let's have lunch this week and come to a decision on the Elias-Clark offer once and for all, okay? We got sidetracked the last time we were supposed to discuss it. We're clearly coming from different places on this, but we owe it to ourselves and everyone else to make a final decision. Okay?'

Emily opened her eyes. She smiled and poked Andy in the side. 'Fine, lunch it is. And I'm the first to admit that Miranda was a lunatic back in the day and very well may still be a little crazy , but we can totally handle her, Andy. I'm telling you, we make a kick-ass team, and we could accomplish amazing things over at Elias-Clark.'

'Lunch,' Andy said, the now-familiar feeling of dread beginning to settle over her. Tonight had left no room for negotiation, as far as Andy was concerned. It was over, finished, final. She'd worked too long and too hard to get where she was, only to sign her life away again to Miranda Priestly. She would tell Emily that week. There could be no other way.

20

a shipping container of botox

The alarm blared. Disoriented, Andy rolled over to look at her clock and almost fell out of bed: eleven! How was it eleven o'clock?

'Relax,' Max said, placing a warm palm over her exposed arm. 'We're not late. We have plenty of time.'

'Late for what?'

'I just said we're not late.'

'But where are we going? Where's Clementine?'

Max laughed. He was fully dressed in a button-down and jeans, lying on top of the covers, reading on his iPad. 'Clem's napping but she should be up any second. You've been sleeping like a dead person for who knows how many hours. And we are expected for brunch at an as-yet-undisclosed location with your mommy group. Any of this sounding familiar?'

Andy groaned. The previous night's dinner came rushing back to her.

Had Miranda Priestly really hissed at her? The mommy group was great, but getting herself and the baby up and dressed for a brunch across town sounded about as appealing as a trip to the gynecologist right now. 'Unfortunately, yes. The husband brunch. We've spent the last three-plus months divulging the intimate details of all our lives, including yours. Time to meet the subjects of our collective analysis.'

'Sounds terrific. You said it starts at twelve thirty?'

Andy nodded. She was about to tell him about the Miranda dinner when his phone rang.

'I need to take this,' he said, walking out of the room.

Andy peeled off her nightshirt and stretched luxuriously under the covers. Her sheets felt silken and cool against her bare skin, and for a minute or two she was able to stop her mind from returning again and again to Miranda Priestly. As good as her bed felt, her shower was even better, and this gave her a few more minutes of calm. As she did at least once a day, Andy marveled at how their building's combination of unparalleled water pressure and seemingly unlimited hot water made nearly all the other inconveniences of city life – the grime, lack of space, crowds, expense, and all-around general hassle – completely worth it.

She stepped out of the shower and toweled off. Max appeared in the bathroom and embraced her warm, naked body from behind. He buried his face in her neck and inhaled deeply. 'I wanted to wake you up so badly last night,' he said gruffly.

'Then why didn't you?' Andy murmured. She didn't want to admit that she was more relieved than disappointed when she'd come home to discover that Max was still out on his client dinner: she just didn't have the energy to get into it.

'You've had a crazy couple weeks. You needed your sleep.' Max said, rinsing his razor under hot water. 'So how did it go?'

Andy walked toward her closet and grabbed the first few things she saw. She brought them back to the bathroom and began to get dressed. 'It was . . . interesting.'

Max raised his eyebrows at her in the mirror. 'A little more detail?'

'Miranda definitely made a superhuman effort at being charming – it's almost flattering how much she wants *The Plunge* – but then she reverted to her usual inhuman ways.'

'Meaning?'

'Just that she didn't even try to disguise her plan to completely control the magazine and everything that went into it. If anything, I was almost shocked at how brazen she was about it.'

Something about Max's expression irked her. 'What?' she asked.

Max seemed to make it a point not to make eye contact. He studied his cheek stubble intently and gave a little shrug. 'Nothing. I didn't say anything.'

'Yeah, but that look said something. What?' Andy asked.

Max set down his razor and turned to look at her. 'Andy, I know you think I don't really understand how hard it was for you to work for Miranda, and truth be told, I probably don't. No one does. But don't you think you could put it behind you and make the right decision here?'

Andy suddenly felt self-conscious being topless and grabbed for a robe.

'I'm just saying, I don't think Miranda's out to wreck your lives, you know?'

Andy stared at him. 'I know that. That's not at all how

Miranda operates. The life-wrecking is an unintentional consequence, although I'm not sure that makes it any better.'

'You know how to stand up for yourself against bullies, Andy. And when push comes to shove, that's all Miranda really is. Your standard-fare, run-of-the-mill schoolyard bully.'

'Only someone who's never worked for her could make that statement,' she said as lightly as she could manage despite her irritation.

Part of her wanted to avoid any more conversation, but Andy realized that in her effort to erase Miranda from her life over the years, she'd never really adequately described Miranda to Max. He knew she was curt, contrarian, a 'difficult personality.' He was aware of her reputation as a tough and demanding boss. He'd met her enough over the years to see firsthand that she could be brusque and aloof. More than aloof – 'unfriendly' was how he'd described Miranda the first time Barbara had introduced them. But for some reason – or really, because Andy could never bear to talk about it – Max didn't seem to understand the true Miranda. The evil, nasty, even sadistic Miranda who, to this day, haunted his wife.

Andy took a breath and perched on the edge of the tub. 'She's not just a bully, Max. You're right, I could probably deal with that now. It's worse than that. Almost harder to deal with. She is single-mindedly focused on what's best for her, at the exclusion of everything and everyone else. Her assistants, her editors, her so-called friends – because I don't believe she has any real friends, only has acquaintances she needs or wants things from – they're all just bit players in Miranda's real-time video game, where the whole purpose is making sure Miranda wins. At all costs. It doesn't matter if you're a designer or Irv Ravitz or the editor of

Italian *Runway* if you're late for a lunch with Miranda Priestly. She's not going to yell and scream and lecture you on courtesy and consideration. She's merely going to order at the exact moment she's ready, whether you've arrived or not, and then she's going to eat her lunch and leave. Does it matter to her if your kid was sick or your taxi was in an accident? Not in the least. Does it bother her if you're only receiving your soup as she's calling her driver to come pick her up? Not for a moment. Because she doesn't care about you at all – you don't even register on her radar screen as another person with feelings or needs. She doesn't play by the same social rules as you and I. She figured out a long time ago that the quickest means to her end usually includes humiliating, critiquing, belittling, or intimidating other people into doing what she wants. On the rare occasion that doesn't work – like for instance, with us refusing to sell her *The Plunge* – she immediately throws herself into an all-consuming charm offensive: extravagant gifts, solicitous phone calls, coveted invitations. Which is, of course, just another form of manipulating the bit players in her giant game.'

Max set down his razor and patted his face with a hand towel. 'When you describe her like that, she almost sounds like a sociopath,' he said.

Andy shrugged. 'I'm no shrink. But she is truly horrible.'

Max enveloped Andy in a hug. He kissed her cheek and said, 'I hear everything you're saying. She does sound horrible, she really does. And I hate the idea of anyone making you unhappy. But I'd just ask that you think about the bigger picture here, Andy. There's a lot—'

Clementine's wails stopped him midsentence.

'I'll get her,' she said, dropping her robe on the floor and pulling on her bra and sweater. Max didn't seem any closer to understanding. Andy was relieved for an excuse to change the subject.

A half hour later they had miraculously made it to Stacy's apartment on Twelfth Street and Fifth Avenue, and between Miranda the night before and Max's seeming inability to understand her this morning, Andy felt like her head might explode. How was she going to survive being pleasantly social for the next two hours?

'Who are these people again?' Max whispered as they waited for the doorman to clear them.

'Stacy is one of the mommies from my group. Her husband is Mark. I can't remember what he does. Their daughter's name is Sylvie and she's a few weeks younger than Clementine. That's about all I know.'

The uniformed doorman motioned them toward the elevator, which they rode to the penthouse, where an over-weight maid in an apron and orthopedic clogs greeted them at the door, parked Clementine's stroller in the massive foyer, and directed them to the living room. Max and Andy exchanged a look as they followed the woman. They were deposited in a formal dining room with people milling about; Andy noticed nothing, absolutely nothing, but the twenty-foot-high wall of windows that wrapped around three sides of the room and offered the most spectacular south-facing views of Lower Manhattan she'd ever seen. Her new friends were saying hello and introducing their husbands and parking their babies in various swings and bouncy seats, but Andy couldn't focus on anything except the apartment. A sideways glance at Max confirmed he, too, was taking it all in.

The double-height ceilings were interspersed with skylights, which, coupled with the outrageous wall of windows, made the entire room feel like it was floating. A polished stone fireplace the size of a small storefront sat to their left; above the sleek gas fire, an enormous mirrored flat-screen hung on the massive expanse of gray stone, where it caught the reflection of both the fire and the autumn sun and gave the entire room an aura of spectral, almost heavenly white light. The modern, low couches were done in a tasteful mix of gray and ivory, as was the reading nook with the built-in bookshelves. A rough-hewn reclaimed-wood coffee table matched the dining room table off to the side that easily seated sixteen and was flanked by gorgeous ivory leather and chrome high-backed chairs. The only color in the room came from an outrageously luxurious pile rug in abstract loops of cobalt, red, and purple and what appeared to be a hand-blown chandelier that descended nearly an entire story from the ceiling and whose shapes of glass – ovals, squiggles, spirals, and tubes – seemed to explode in a tangle of blue madness. Even the dog, a Cavalier King Charles whose leather collar was stamped with 'Harley,' reclined on a minia-ture midcentury-modern chaise with polished chrome legs and a tightly tufted leather cushion.

'Wow,' Andy murmured, trying not to stare. 'This is not what I was expecting.'

'Pretty outrageous,' Max said, putting an arm around her shoulder. He whispered in her ear. 'A far cry from the old Harrison pad. But amazing. This is the kind of apartment we'll have one day when my wife becomes a media mogul.' He said it as a joke, but it made Andy squirm.

'Andy! Can I get you guys anything? Oh, you must be Max. It's such a pleasure to meet you,' Stacy said, sidling over to them, looking almost *Runway*-esque in her glamorous cash-mere poncho, high heels, sleek blowout, and flawless makeup. Gone were the leggings and hoodies, the bad skin and the unwashed hair Andy had grown accustomed to seeing in meetings every week. It was an epic transformation.

'Hey,' Andy said, trying not to gawk. 'Your apartment is gorgeous. And you look fantastic.'

Stacy waved her off. 'You're too sweet. Can I get you guys something to drink? A mimosa, maybe? Max, I bet you'd rather a Bloody Mary. Our housekeeper makes the most amazing Bloodys.'

Stacy kissed Clem on the forehead and disappeared to put in their drink order. Seeing the other mothers do it, Andy deposited Clem in the circle of babies lying on the designer carpet.

'This is a very bad idea,' she murmured as she placed a burp cloth under the baby's head.

'Tell me about it,' Bethany said. 'Micah already spit up all over it – pureed spinach, no less – and I heard Tucker had a blowout diaper right in the middle of that overlapping color band right there.'

'Doesn't she want to put down a blanket or something?'

Bethany shrugged. 'I don't think it matters. Someone in a uniform just comes rushing over to clean up or clear away or bring more food or drink. There is, no exaggeration, a *fleet* of employees.'

'Did you have any idea?' Andy asked, keeping her voice as low as she could manage. Theo rolled onto his belly and Andy patted him on the back. From the corner of her eye she saw another woman, also in uniform but different from the maid who'd shown them in, hand Max a Bloody Mary so tall, richly red, and mouthwatering as to be magazine-worthy. He accepted it politely, but Andy knew he would find a place to set it down, untouched. She made a mental note to bring him a glass of orange juice.

'Zero. If anything Stacy usually looks more homeless than millionaire. Then again, with our crew, who doesn't?'

Within a few minutes the entire group had assembled,

and everyone was chatting amiably while the babies hung out on the floor. For the most part the husbands were exactly as Andy expected – which is to say, pretty much like her own: in their early to midthirties; dressed in untucked button-downs or hoodies over T-shirts with designer jeans their wives had purchased for them despite protests that their old college Levi's were perfectly fine; sporting close-cropped haircuts, expensive watches, and expressions that clearly stated they would rather have been reading the paper, watching football, at the gym, lying on the couch, anywhere, doing anything rather than milling around a room of strangers while their children howled and their wives passionately debated the right time to introduce purees.

Only a few were really surprising. Stacy's husband, Mark, was a good fifteen years older than everyone else; his salt-and-pepper hair and wire-rimmed glasses made him appear distinguished and more grown-up than the rest of the crew, but the gleeful way he tossed around baby Sylvie and the warm way he greeted each and every person instantly endeared him to Andy. Baby Lola's parents, the two pedia-tricians, made an appearance for the first time, both looking supremely uncomfortable for two people who spent twelve-plus hours a day with children. They wore matching black dress slacks and pressed blue shirts, as though they were seconds away from donning white robes and making rounds. Lola squirmed every time her mother went to pick her up, and the father appeared anxious, disinterested, and even more obsessed with checking his phone than most of the other dads. Both looked desperate to leave this strange get-together where neither knew a soul but where everyone knew their daughter.

Also surprising was Anita's husband, Dean, a rocker type in his twenties with a chain wallet, skater-style high-top sneakers, and a waxed mustache. He was happy and outgoing and didn't seem to feel the least bit self-conscious, which served as such an unexpected counterbalance to his mousy, perpetually shy, and nearly silent wife. Andy was surprised when Dean pulled a guitar from a travel bag, planted himself in the middle of the babies, and began playing rock 'n' roll versions of 'Twinkle, Twinkle, Little Star' and 'The Itsy-Bitsy Spider,' and she almost fainted when Anita offered backup vocals and musical accompaniment by alternating a tambourine, cymbals, and a pair of professional-looking maracas. The babies who could clap in delight did so, and the others squealed or shrieked. At least a dozen parents whipped out iPhones to video the impromptu performance, and a bunch of the mommies started to dance.

'See?' Andy said, giving Max a little poke in the shoulder. 'I only bring you to the best places.'

Max was intently staring at his phone, trying to zoom in on the video he was filming of Clementine shaking a maraca. 'You're not kidding. They should be selling tickets for this.'

The doorbell rang and a maid appeared to tell Stacy that more guests had arrived.

Rachel looked around and made a show of counting. 'But we're all here. Who else is coming?'

'Maybe some of their other friends?' Sandrine offered.

'Ohmigod, you didn't invite Lori, did you?' Bethany screeched. 'She's going to take one look at that guitar and start an immediate friendship circle. I can't handle life coaching on a Saturday.'

Stacy laughed while all the husbands looked first confused and then disinterested. 'No, it's Sophie and Xander.' She turned to the pediatricians for confirmation. 'You said they're stopping by, right?'

The mother nodded. 'She feels so close to everyone, seeing

you all every week and whatnot, so . . . she said she wanted to say hello. I hope that's okay.'

Something about the way the woman said it made Andy feel bad for her. It couldn't have been easy working demanding doctor hours with a new baby, and no matter how important her career was to her, it certainly wouldn't be fun seeing your sister-in-law bond with your daughter, take her to play groups and cuddle her before naps and watch her enjoy all her new jumper toys. Andy promised herself she'd make an effort with the woman, introduce herself and invite her to coffee.

Sophie was, as usual, beautifully turned out. Her long, thick hair shone as she waved hello, her smile lighting up her adorably wind-pinked cheeks.

'I was hoping we'd get to meet the boyfriend,' Rachel whispered under her breath.

Andy nodded. 'Me too. I'm so curious. Although it would've been even better if she brought the new guy. What's his name?'

'Tomás,' someone whispered in an exaggerated accent. 'Sexy, artistic *Tomás.*'

'Where's your boyfriend?' Bethany, never shy, called from her perch on the couch arm.

'Oh, he's just finishing up a call. He'll be right up. He's so excited to meet you all,' Sophie said with a forced-sounding laugh.

Sophie looked worried – the boyfriend must have insisted on tagging along, and she was clearly uncomfortable with everything she'd revealed over the past couple months. The affair with Tomás had intensified to passionate making out although they still hadn't gotten naked or 'really consummated anything,' in Sophie's words, so she was currently trying to convince herself and everyone else that, technically, she hadn't done anything wrong. But it was easy to tell from the faraway look she got in her eyes and the excited way she twisted her fingers that Sophie was falling in love with her cute young photography student, and she was racked with guilt and fear and uncertainty over what to do with the boyfriend. The new-mommies group had become her safe place, a roomful of confidantes so wholly removed from her real life that Sophie felt free to divulge details she wouldn't even have shared with her real friends, and Andy knew she must be near-hysterical at the thought of her two worlds colliding. Andy wanted to reach out and reassure her. *Don't worry, your secret is safe with us. No one is going to breathe a word to your boyfriend . . .*

The energy in the room suddenly shifted, but Andy's attention was diverted momentarily to Clementine, who had begun crying with an immediacy and hysteria that made Andy's heart skip a beat. She scooped her daughter up and scanned her body, her face, her pudgy hands, and her fuzz-topped head, looking for injury or potential cause of pain. Seeing none, she buried her face in Clementine's neck and whisper-sang while she bounced her baby gently on her shoulder. Clem's cries slowly lessened as Andy ran through her mental maternal checklist: hungry, tired, wet, hot, cold, bellyache, teething pain, overstimulated, scared, or lonely. She was just about to ask Stacy if she could take Clem to a quiet room to settle her when she felt Max's breath on her ear.

'Isn't that your Alex?' he asked, clamping his hand over her shoulder.

It took a long twenty or thirty seconds before Andy processed what he was asking. 'Her Alex' could have been none other than Alex Fineman, and although she understood this, she couldn't possibly imagine why Max was bringing him up now.

'My Alex?' she asked, confused.

Max physically turned her in the direction of the foyer, where a man whose back was turned to her was removing his coat and scarf. One instantaneous assessment of the stranger's dark hair, gray New Balance sneakers, and mannerisms as he joked with the maid, and Andy knew beyond any doubt that he was, indeed, her Alex.

In an instant Clementine, Max, Stacy, the entire group of noisy babies and chattering parents evaporated: Andy's field of vision had narrowed to include Alex and only Alex, and yet she was entirely unable to think of a single plausible reason why he was in attendance at her new-mommies brunch.

'Xander!' Sophie screeched in a shockingly un-Sophielike way. 'Come here, love, I want you to meet all my new friends.'

Xander. The word hit her like a truck. In the decade she'd known Alex, no one – not her, their college friends, his mother, his brother, *anyone* – had called him anything but Alex. Not even Alexander. Xander? It was ridiculous just hearing it.

And yet here he was, standing before her, kissing his beautiful younger girlfriend on the lips and flashing that heartbreakingly impish grin to the hosts. He hadn't seen Andy yet, hadn't seen anyone but Sophie, Stacy, and Mark; she sent up a silent message of gratitude for the few seconds she had to compose herself.

'That is Alex, right?' Max asked, scooping a squirming Clementine from Andy's arms. 'You look like you've seen a dead person.'

'I just didn't realize that when Sophie was telling us about her boyfriend, she was talking about him,' Andy whispered, hoping no one else could overhear them. 'Ohmigod.'

'What?'

'Oh. My. God.'

'What's wrong? Are you okay?' Max asked.

Xander. Boyfriend of years. Love him but. Things are different. Seems bored by me. Thinks I'm furniture. Just moved in together. New to New York. Tomás. My student. Much younger. Just innocent flirting. Passionate make-outs. Heavy petting. Think I'm falling for him . . .

She didn't know why it had taken that long to put the pieces together, but once she had, Andy could barely breathe. There was no time to process it, to consider all of the ramifications, to conference-call both Emily and Lily and give them every sordid detail – the next second, Alex was beside her.

'And this is my friend Andy!' Sophie's voice was high-pitched, excited. 'And this is her husband . . . I'm so sorry, I seem to have forgotten—'

'This is my husband, Max.' Andy was relieved to hear that her own voice sounded steady and reassuringly ordinary, despite the fact that she wanted to vomit. It occurred to her fleetingly that this was only the second time Max and Alex were meeting – the first had been years earlier, when they'd all shared that awkward exchange at Whole Foods – but it barely even registered.

'This is Xander, my boyfriend. I told him he'd be bored, but he didn't want to sit home all by himself.'

'Really, man? Because I would've killed to do just that.' Max clapped Alex on the back. 'Good to see you again.'

'You too,' Alex said, looking every bit as shocked as Andy felt.

'You two know each other?' Sophie asked, her brows furrowed in concern.

If only you knew the whole story, Andy thought, *you'd need a shipping container of Botox to eliminate that frown.*

Confident Max would know to lie and make up some story about work or a party a hundred years ago, Andy almost fainted when instead he said, 'We do. Alex here used to date my wife.'

Sophie's mouth dropped open and Andy knew exactly what she was thinking and how she felt. No doubt she was going through the laundry list of explicit details she'd revealed at their last group meeting, not one of which was appropriate for someone who actually knew the boyfriend on whom she was cheating. Andy watched as shock turned to panic.

Sophie's head swiveled between Alex and Andy. 'You two used to *date*?'

Andy and Alex merely nodded, but Max was clearly enjoying himself.

He laughed and held Clementine above his head, bringing her down to kiss her nose and lifting her up again while she giggled. 'Well, *date* is probably not the right word. They were together for six years. Straight through college – can you believe it? Lucky for me, they didn't get married . . .'

'You're Andy? Andy-Andy? Andy from Brown? Andy of girlfriends past? Oh my god . . .' Sophie clapped her hand over her mouth.

'I go by Andrea these days with new friends since it sounds a little more professional.' Andy allowed her voice to trail off. What else was there to say? She didn't know whether to be concerned or delighted that Alex had told Sophie so much about her. What had he said? And in how much detail? She thought back to their breakup, which had been entirely Alex's decision; to his announcement that he was moving to Mississippi without her; to how he was concerned that she would always prioritize work over him; to the fights they'd begun having almost the instant she started working at *Runway*. The bickering, the hurt feelings, the resentment, the neglect, the resulting lack of sex and affection. Had he told her all that?

'I guess you guys didn't put it together that you had a, um . . . that you knew someone in common, huh?' Alex said, looking every bit as uncomfortable as Andy felt.

'No, we most certainly didn't,' Sophie said, all former enthusiasm completely vanished.

'How could we have?' Andy said as lightly as she could manage. 'I only know him as Alex, and although I knew he had a girlfriend, I didn't know her name.'

'And *I* didn't know that the famous Andy had a baby,' Sophie shot back, although Andy hadn't intended her comment as a dig. Sophie turned to Alex and glared at him. 'You never told me Andy so much as got married, never mind had a child.'

'Speaking of said baby' – Alex tugged at his collar, which looked not the least bit constricting, and motioned toward Clementine – 'I haven't had a chance to meet your daughter yet.'

Max flipped Clem around in his arms so she was facing out, and as though on cue, she flashed a wide, toothless smile. 'This is Clementine Rose Harrison. Clem, please meet our friends Sophie and . . . Xander.'

'She's beautiful,' Alex breathed, his sincerity making an impossible situation all the more uncomfortable.

'She is a cutie,' Sophie said, looking around, clearly trying to make an escape. 'I haven't said hello yet to my brother or Lola. Will you all excuse me?'

She was gone before any of them could respond.

'Well, that was awkward,' Max said, the mischief flashing in his eyes. 'I hope I didn't say anything wrong.'

'Of course not,' Andy said, knowing exactly what he was doing.

'I think she was just surprised to make the connection,' Alex offered lamely.

Anita and her rocker husband resumed their baby concert on the carpet, and a maid announced that brunch was being served in the dining room.

'I'll let you two catch up,' Max said, hoisting Clem on his shoulder. 'This one wants to get back to the music, don't you, my love?'

There was a moment of silence after Max left. Alex stared at his feet; Andy nervously twisted her hair. The only words going through her head were *tell him, tell him, tell him*.

'She's beautiful, Andy.'

For a horrible split second, Andy thought he was talking about Sophie. 'Oh, Clem? Thanks. Yeah, we'll keep her.'

Alex laughed and Andy couldn't help but smile back at him. His laugh was so natural, so unself-conscious.

'Weird that you and Soph know each other, huh? She would always tell me about this play group that she took Lola to – I guess it wasn't exactly what she expected – but I never made the connection.'

'Me neither. How could we? There are thousands of new mommies in Manhattan. No reason to think we'd both be in the same group. Especially since Sophie isn't even a mom . . .' She realized that last part sounded aggressive or accusatory or probing, or possibly all three.

'Don't tell her that,' Alex laughed. 'She definitely forgets she's only Lola's aunt. And she talks about babies constantly . . . if she has her way, she'll be a mom soon.'

It was Andy's turn to stare at the floor. She suddenly, desperately, needed to be anywhere but right there.

'I'm sorry,' Alex said, placing his hand on her shoulder. 'Was that weird? Too much information? This is all just so new to me . . .'

Andy waved him off. 'We're grown-ups now. We haven't been involved in years. It's natural we've both moved on.'

The music stopped suddenly and Andy's words rang out loudly, but only Sophie and Max turned to look.

'I think I'm going to get some food,' Andy said.

'Sounds good. I'm going to say good-bye. I just stopped by to meet everyone, but I have, uh, stuff to do.'

They both nodded, accepting his excuse, and kissed primly on the cheek. Andy managed to keep her mouth shut: if they could barely discuss the fact that she had a daughter without extreme discomfort, how on earth could she cavalierly announce that his girlfriend was cheating on him with her photography student?

Andy beelined for the dining room and was momentarily distracted by the awesome display in front of her. 'Brunch' was no less elaborate than an after-wedding party at a Ritz-Carlton, right down to the frog-shaped ice sculpture. Silver platters on gas burners offered heaping piles of scrambled eggs, bacon, home fries, pancakes, and waffles. There were a half dozen types of cereal, complete with glass pitchers of skim, soy, and whole milk, and a fruit bar with slices of watermelon, bunches of grapes, bananas, kiwis, pineapples, grapefruit halves, cherries, cut melon, and berries. Set off to the side was a baby buffet, complete with miniature plates of fruit cut into tiny pieces, containers of YoBaby yogurt in every flavor with coordinating baby spoons, packets of Baby Mum-Mums, and bowl upon bowl of organic Puffs. To the right was a separate table with a bartender mixing mimosas, Bloody Marys, and Bellinis with fresh peach nectar. A woman in uniform handed her a plate and a bundle of silverware; her male counterpart asked if she'd like the chef to make her an omelet or a frittata. Only then did Andy realize the casual meet-the-husbands brunch was a catered affair.

'Wow, this is pretty fantastic,' Max said, sidling up next to her and surveying the food. 'We could probably get used to living like this, don't you think?'

Andy chose to ignore the second part of his comment. 'Worth missing the beginning of the Jets game for?' Andy asked.

'Almost.'

There was no more mention of Alex or Sophie. Andy wasn't sure if Max didn't want to talk about it or truly didn't care, but she wasn't going to bring it up. They took turns holding Clementine and eating, shamelessly stuffing themselves while making halfhearted attempts at conversation with the other parents. When Max gave her the 'I'm ready' look thirty minutes later, Andy didn't argue.

At their apartment, Max kindly offered to put Clementine down for her second nap and stay home to watch the game if Andy wanted to run out for the manicure she'd been trying to fit in for a week. No matter that she'd actually gotten it the day before (men never notice these things); yes, she wanted to head out. In less than ten minutes, she was installed at a table at Café Grumpy and on the phone with Lily.

'It was wrong not to tell him, wasn't it? I should have said something.'

'Of course you shouldn't have said something!' Lily's voice had risen multiple octaves. 'Why would you even think that?'

'I've known Alex since college. He was my first love. I'll probably always love him. I've seen Sophie once a week for a few months now. I don't think she's a terrible person, believe it or not, but I certainly don't feel any loyalty to her.'

'All of that is beside the point. It's just none of your business.'

'What do you mean, it's none of my business?'

Baby Skye howled in the background. Lily asked her to hold on, muted the phone, and came back a minute later.

'Just that whatever is or isn't going on with Alex and his girlfriend doesn't concern you. You're a married woman with your own child, and who's cheating on whom is not your problem.'

Andy sighed. 'Would you want to know if Bodhi was having an affair? You're my friend, and I wouldn't hesitate to tell you.'

'Yes, but the difference is I'm your *friend*. Alex is *not* your friend. He's your ex. And what does or doesn't go on in his bedroom is none of your business.'

'You're a laugh riot, you know that, Lil?'

'Sorry. I'm just telling you the truth.'

Andy asked after Bodhi, Bear, and Skye and hung up as quickly as possible. Emily didn't answer her cell phone, so Andy called Miles's number. Andy knew he'd accompanied Emily to Chicago to meet with a potential advertiser and would be continuing on to L.A. after Emily flew home.

Miles picked up on the first ring.

'Hey, Miles. Sorry to bother you, but I can't find Emily. Do you know where she is?'

'She's right here next to me. She said she's screening you. We're picking up the rental car now.'

'Was the flight that bad?'

'I'm just telling you what she said.'

'Well, tell her Alex's girlfriend is actually in my mommies group and she's sleeping with her student who's barely out of college.'

Andy listened as Miles relayed the message. As she knew she would, Emily took the phone. Their tensions over Elias-Clark aside, Emily would eat this gossip right up.

'Explain, please. You never mentioned Alex has a kid. Which, considering you're still clearly obsessed with him, is surprising information to omit.'

Andy didn't know whether to be more incensed at Emily's accusation or the fact that Miles was sitting there listening to it. 'Can Miles hear you?'

'No, I moved. Now start talking.'

'He doesn't have a kid. His girlfriend's name is Sophie and, incidentally, she's gorgeous. It's her brother and his wife's baby, the cutest little girl named Lola. Anyway, since the sister-in-law works these hideous hours, Sophie brings Lola to the new-mommies group. I think she thought it was going to be more of a play group and less of a new mothers' support group, but she still—'

'I get it. And you know she's fucking her student how?'

'She told me. Hell, she told all of us. Technically, she claims they're not actually sleeping together, but there has definitely been inappropriate—'

'So you're telling me you know this *for a fact*, directly from her mouth, and you didn't say a word to him?'

'Yes.'

'Well, why not?'

'What do you mean, why not?'

'Don't you think it's relevant information for someone to have?'

'Yes. I just wasn't sure it was any of my business.'

Emily yelped. 'Not any of your business? Oh for Christ's sake, Andy, stop being such a good girl and pick up the phone. He'll thank you forever, I promise.'

'I don't know. Do you really think—'

'Yes. I do. I'm hanging up now because I've got to drive two hours after my third flight in a week, and I'm ready to kill someone.'

'Keep me in the loop,' Andy said, but Emily had already hung up.

Andy asked for a glass of ice water and stared into space. Should she call and tell him? What, exactly, would that look like? He'd be shocked, hurt, humiliated. Why should she be the one to deliver such devastating news? Or even worse, what if it wasn't actually news to him? Who was to say he didn't know already, hadn't stumbled upon the sordid affair himself or been on the receiving end of a tearful confession from Sophie? What if, even worse, they had some sort of open relationship agreement, and although Sophie felt guilty acting on it, she wasn't technically doing anything wrong? Then she'd surely be the meddling, creepily overinvolved ex-girlfriend, and any new strides she and Alex had made at getting reacquainted and possibly even learning to be friends again would be solidly, forever over.

It felt absolutely terrible and wrong on every level, but she would keep her mouth shut. She was getting good at that.

21

in your own best interest

Max set a cup of coffee in front of Andy and returned to the pod machine to make one for himself.

Andy pushed it away and groaned.

'Do you want some tea instead?'

'No, nothing. My throat feels like razor blades.'

'I thought this was supposed to be a twenty-four-hour thing? Isn't that what the doctor said?'

Andy nodded. 'Yep. But Clem's lasted three full days and I'm going on my fourth. So I'm not sure I believe him.'

Max kissed the top of her head the way he would a puppy and clucked sympathetically. 'Poor baby, you're burning up. Are you due for Tylenol?'

Andy wiped a bead of sweat from her upper lip. 'Not for another hour,' she croaked. 'I should change the outgoing messages on our home phone and my cell. The voice is sexy, no?'

'You sound like you have the plague,' he said as he shoved some papers into his briefcase. 'Is there anything else I can do before I leave?'

Andy tightened her bathrobe around her and then immediately loosened it again. 'I don't think so. Isla should be here soon.' She swallowed hard and tried not to wince in pain. 'I really should be trying to get to the office today. Emily called three times yesterday, always under the guise of asking how I'm doing, but I know she just wants to talk about Elias-Clark. We're having lunch tomorrow to make a decision, once and for all.'

In the four days since the Miranda dinner, Emily and Andy had both seemed to sense they were never going to see eye to eye on the idea of an Elias-Clark purchase. They were playing chicken now, each waiting for the other to blink . . .

And Andy knew which side her husband was on.

Max stopped what he was doing and turned to her. 'Well, you're certainly not in any shape to go to the office, but I can understand why she wants to talk about it . . .'

Something in his voice made Andy look up. He'd been subtly asking her about it for weeks, expressing more interest than he ever did in her work, and recently it had become not so subtle, with Max constantly inquiring and, since the Miranda dinner, implying that Andy was being an idiot. He never said that, of course, but his favorite word recently was *shortsighted*.

Andy remained quiet. She wanted to ask him how much of his support for selling had to do with Harrison Media, but she knew it wouldn't be a productive conversation.

'It's quite an honor, an offer like that. Not to mention a damn fair price, too.'

'So you've said.' *Like a thousand times already.*

'I just think it's the opportunity of a lifetime,' Max said. He didn't take his eyes off Andy.

She unwrapped a Ricola and popped it in her mouth. 'Hmm, I can't imagine where I've heard that before.'

Her tone must have made it clear that the conversation was over because Max kissed Clementine, told Andy he loved her, and left. Another hot flash came over her, and not wanting to leave the baby alone in the high chair but feeling too lightheaded to move her, Andy slumped on the floor next to her daughter. Andy almost hugged Isla when she arrived a few minutes later and she could finally retreat back to her bedroom, put on clean pajamas, and settle in for a feverish but deep, dreamless sleep. She awoke to the sound of Stanley barking at the front door.

Andy stumbled back to the kitchen, rubbing sleep from her eyes. The nap had helped; she felt better. 'Who was it?' she asked Isla, who was warming a bottle.

'A messenger, I guess. Here, he left this.' Isla handed her a manila envelope that read *Photographs: Do Not Bend!* along both sides.

'Oh, yes. I forgot these were going to be ready today.' She pulled out a sheaf of eight-by-ten glossies from Olive's wedding. The note from Daniel read, *Hope you like them as much as we do. Planned to send to E but she's in Chicago all day. Can you please pass along to her? Let me know your thoughts.*

Andy settled at the kitchen table with a cup of chamomile and spread the dozen photos out in front of her. Her smile grew as she looked from image to image: they were, in a word, spectacular.

She texted Emily. *Just got Olive pics. They're fantastic. Will be a huge hit. Love.*

The reply came back instantly. *Fab! w/Rolex people now. Messenger them to my apt? Need for breakfast meeting tom. Xo*

Andy texted back, *sure thing,* and opened her laptop to begin writing up the Olive nuptials. It was an easier task when she had actually attended the wedding, but Emily's notes were fairly comprehensive. Andy had e-mailed her a three-page list of things to make note of – or, even better, if she got the chance, ask someone – and Emily had done a more than decent job of filling in the blanks.

Isla brought Clem over for a kiss before they headed to Gymboree and a playdate, and after that the apartment was blessedly quiet – perfect for a solid three-hour work session, Andy's first in two days of being sick. By the time Isla and the baby returned, Andy felt nearly cured and, even better, had written three-quarters of the article. She pulled Clem from her stroller and covered her with kisses.

'I'm feeling much better,' she told Isla, who looked at her dubiously.

'Are you sure? Because I can stay later today if you need.'

'No, really, I'm almost okay. I'll put her down for her nap now, and then it'll be dinnertime before you know it. Thanks for everything.'

Clementine slept for an hour and a half, awaking at three thirty with her delicious red cheeks and enormous, toothless grin. It was such a relief to see her healthy again; every time the poor child had vomited or cried, Andy could feel her own insides twisting in pain. She was about to call Agatha to order a messenger, but looking outside at the splendidly sunny October day, Andy decided a stroll to Emily's would make for a nice outing.

'Do you want to come with Mommy on her first trip out

of the apartment in thirty-six hours? Of course you do.'

Andy changed into jeans and a sweater and zipped her daughter into the stroller's lightweight baby burqa. The air felt brisk and refreshing, almost revitalizing, and Andy enjoyed making Clem giggle with silly faces as they walked. She stared at her daughter's smile and knew, more surely than she had known in the many months since they'd first received the offer, that she could not, under any circumstances, spend another year working for Miranda Priestly. It was horrid enough when she was young and single, but there was no way she could tolerate the ever-ringing phone, the relentless demands, the round-the-clock requests that would inevitably take her away from home, from Max, and especially from Clementine. She and Max were just starting to get a handle on life with a baby, and things between them were good – not perfect, but what marriage was? She was happy. They were excellent co-parents and true partners, and he was as attentive and loving a dad as she ever could have hoped for to her daughter. Even career-wise things were going smoothly: nowhere else could she imagine being lucky enough to keep such a flexible schedule, working more when they were slammed or closing an issue and scaling back when the production schedule slowed down. She was her own boss, and her best friend was her partner. And Emily was still her best friend, despite everything. They'd worked too hard and too long to pack it in and head right back to Elias-Clark – not when she was certain they'd be able to sell the magazine to another, saner publisher. It was going to be painful, but Andy knew what she had to say to Emily. It was time. As soon as they sat down to their lunch the following day, she would come right out and say it: the deal was off.

The five steps up from the sidewalk to Emily's front door

made stroller-wrangling difficult. How had she never before noticed those steps? It was crazy how long it had been since Andy had been there – two months? Three? There had been a time, before Clementine and even Max, when Andy practically camped out on Emily's sofa, chowing down on spicy tuna rolls and pounds of edamame, hashing and rehashing their lives in the most specific detail.

Even though Emily was still in Chicago, or perhaps on her way home, and Miles was in L.A. filming his new reality TV show, Andy couldn't bring herself to use her key without knocking. She rapped on the bright red door, which entered almost directly into the living room, and was just about to unlock the dead bolt when she heard something from inside. Laughter? Talking? She couldn't tell who or why, but there were definitely people inside. She knocked again. No response.

where are you? Andy texted Emily.

The response was immediate: *abt to take off from o'hare. Still love the pics?*

where is miles?

la until tomorrow. why? everything ok?

Yes, all fine.

Was it the television? Their cleaning lady camped out while they were away? Friends staying over in their absence? Andy pressed her ear to the door. She couldn't clearly make anything out, and yet she knew – just *knew* – that something wasn't right. And if she had to wager, she'd bet that Miles had lied to Emily about being in L.A. and was shacking up with some girl. Neither Max nor Emily ever directly confirmed Miles was a cheater, but everyone knew it was true.

Without thinking through the ramifications of her decision – most important, without considering what she'd tell Emily when her suspicions were confirmed – Andy inserted her key into the lock and shoved the door open. As soon as she pulled the car seat from the stroller, Clem let out a delighted shriek and began to kick her feet. Andy followed her daughter's gaze to the living room and was not surprised to see Miles draped across the sofa, looking rumpled and possibly hungover in a plaid shirt and ratty cords. It wasn't until Andy stepped farther into the entryway that she saw who sat across from him: Max.

They all spoke at once.

'I'm sorry! I just let myself in, but I was knocking and no one—'

'Hey, Andy. It's been forever. Bring Clem over here to say hello to her uncle—'

'Andy? What are you doing here? Is everything okay with Clem? You know that—'

Then they all stopped at once. Andy spoke first.

'I guess you didn't hear me knocking. I just came over to drop these photos off for Emily. She needs them for a break-fast meeting tomorrow.'

She scooped Clementine from the stroller and walked into the living room. Max scrambled to his feet to kiss them both. Andy surveyed his suit, his briefcase, and the anxious expression on his face and had to force herself not to ask in front of Miles why he'd left the office so early. It had been a particularly rough time at work for him, she knew, and he hadn't been home before eight or nine in weeks. It killed him to miss Clem's bedtime, and yet here he was, stretched out in Miles's living room in the late afternoon, taking small, quick sips from a Snapple and looking as though he'd just been caught with his pants around his ankles.

Clem squealed again as Max reached for her, but something made Andy hug her daughter tighter. She turned to Miles. 'So, what's up?' she asked, trying to sound casual. No one was offering explanations as to why Max wasn't at work and why Miles wasn't in L.A. Why the undeniably guilty expressions?

'Not much,' Miles said, although his tone suggested it was just the opposite. 'Here, let me take those. I'll give them to Em as soon as—'

'Give me what?' Emily's voice rang out a split second before she appeared, holding an armful of file folders and legal pads and a bottle of water. She was wearing sweats and fuzzy socks and glasses, her greasy hair piled unglamorously on her head and not a stitch of makeup on her face. She looked like absolute hell.

So surprised was Andy by Emily's appearance that she almost forgot that her friend had claimed, mere minutes earlier, that she was sitting on the tarmac at O'Hare. Then she saw her own presence register on Emily's face, first as shock and then as panic.

'Andy! What are you doing here?' Emily asked, looking as dumbstruck as Andy felt.

'What am *I* doing here? I'm dropping off photos. What are *you* doing here?'

Silence met her all around. She watched in horror as the three of them exchanged looks.

'What's going on? Something's wrong, isn't it?' She turned to Max. 'Are you sick? Did something happen at work?'

Again silence.

Finally Max said, 'No, Andy, it's uh, it's nothing like that.'

'Well, you're sure not planning a surprise party for my birthday. So why all the secrecy?'

More looks.

'Someone better start talking, because this is getting downright weird.'

'Well then, I guess congratulations are in order,' Miles

said, running a hand through his hair. 'It seems you and Emily are officially successful entrepreneurs. Not to mention you made a pretty penny—'

'Miles!' Emily said sharply, shooting her husband a death look.

'Pardon me?' Andy said. She patted Clem's back as she surveyed the room.

Max began looking around for his coat. 'Andy, why don't we get Clem home – it must be her dinnertime by now – and I'll explain everything then, okay?'

Andy shook her head. 'She's fine. Tell me what's going on. Emily? What does he mean by "officially successful entrepreneurs"?'

No one said anything.

'Emily?' Andy said, her voice growing more hysterical. 'What does he mean?'

Emily motioned for Andy to sit and took a seat herself. 'We signed the contract.'

'You *what?* Who's "we"? What contract?' And then it hit her. 'Elias-Clark? *You sold us?*'

Again, Max was at her side, first trying to hold Clem and, when Andy refused to let her go, nudging Andy toward the door. 'Come on, honey, I'll explain everything on the walk home. Let's get the baby—'

She turned to Max, her eyes blazing. 'Stop trying to shut me up and tell me what the hell is going on. You knew about this? You knew she was just going to sign my name and you *let* her?'

Emily smiled sweetly, patronizingly, in such a way that suggested without a word that she thought Andy was over-reacting in a major way. 'Andy, love, you can't be mad at me for making you a small fortune. It's just what we talked about – you'll have the time and the freedom again to write

377

lauren weisberger

what you want, when you want, and see Clementine more—'

'That is *not* what we talked about,' Andy said, her disbelief growing. 'That's what *you* said and what I disagreed with. More time? What planet are you on? I'll be a hostage! We both will!'

Emily hit the back of the couch with her hand. 'Andy, you're being so small-minded about this whole situation. So shortsighted.' *There was that word again.* 'Everyone agreed it was clearly the right choice, and I made it. I won't apologize for looking out for our best interests.'

She couldn't believe what she was hearing. It was impossible. Nothing was registering or making any sense. Andy could feel angry tears constricting her throat. 'I won't do it, Em. You're going to have to call them up right now and tell them you forged my signature and the agreement is off. Right this very second.'

Andy watched as Emily shot Max a look that seemed to say, *Are you going to tell her or am I?*

Clementine began to cry. Andy tried hard not to join her.

Emily rolled her eyes. 'I didn't *forge* your signature, Andy. Max signed.'

Andy swung her head around to Max, who appeared panicky, just as Clementine wailed, her tiny hands balled into fists, mouth hinged wide open, tongue curled.

'Andy, give me the baby,' Max said in his most soothing voice.

'Get your goddamn hands off her,' Andy hissed, moving away from him. She dug in her jeans pocket and was relieved to find a paci, a bit fuzzy but clean enough. Clem's mouth closed hungrily around it and she quieted.

'Andy,' Max crooned pleadingly. 'Let me explain.'

The revulsion hit her like an electric shock. The words, the pleading tone, the look of contrition – it was all too much.

'How can you possibly explain *forging my signature* on a contract you know I didn't support?'

'Andy, sweetheart, let's not get carried away here. I didn't *forge* your signature. I would never do that.'

Emily nodded. 'Of course not.'

'Then what, exactly, did you do? Because I'm quite certain *I* didn't sign anything.'

'It's nothing so terrible, Andy. My initial investment entitled me to an eighteen percent stake in *The Plunge*, as I'm sure you remember. So really—'

'Oh my god, you didn't,' Andy said, suddenly understanding. The term sheet when they'd incorporated and accepted their investors' seed money had been crystal clear: Andy got a third, Emily a third, and their investors, together as a group, received a third. Of the third the investors received, Max owned eighteen percent of it. Neither Emily nor Andy had been concerned about it at the time, as they had kept complete control of the company – together, their shares could outvote anyone – but Andy had never, ever considered that Max would side with Emily. Agree with her, yes. Try to influence Andy, yes. But actually cut her out of the decision entirely and sign without her knowledge? Not in a million years. Andy did a quick calculation and sure enough, Emily and Max's percentages combined gave them just over fifty-one percent.

'I did it for you,' Max said with a straight face. 'This is an incredible opportunity for you two, and you've both worked so hard. Chances like this don't come around every day. I didn't want you to regret it.' Again, he tried to touch her arm, and again Andy pulled away.

'You tricked me,' she said, the realization hitting her like an avalanche. 'You knew my express wishes about all this and you ignored them. You sided *against* me! You went behind my back.'

Max had the audacity to look offended. 'Tricked you?' he said, sounding appalled. 'I was only looking out for your best interest.'

'*My* best interest?' Andy realized she was shrieking, but she was unable to lower her voice or make it sound any less hysterical. The rage she felt frightened her; more than the shock or the sadness, the tidal wave of anger threatened to overtake her. 'You didn't think for a single second about *my* best interest, or you never would have done this – any of it. You were thinking of yourself and your father's company and your family's name. Nothing more, nothing less.'

Max looked down at his feet and then met her gaze. '*Our* family's company,' he said quietly. 'And *our* family's name. I did this for all of us. I did it for Clementine, too.'

If Andy hadn't been holding her daughter, she may have actually struck Max. As it was, she clutched her daughter close to her and said, 'You're so sick to even think that.'

Emily sighed, as though all of this were just too exhausting. 'Andy, you're overreacting. Nothing's going to change for the next year, maybe even longer. You're still the editor, I'm still the publisher, and I'm sure our entire staff will be happy to come with us. We'll still call all the shots. And we'll probably never even see Miranda. We'll only be one of a dozen magazines in her stable.'

Andy turned to Emily – in her rage for Max, she'd almost forgotten Emily was there. 'You were there, Emily. You saw how she acted. What do you think it's really going to be like? That she'll come to our offices for yoga over her lunch hour, or late-afternoon pedis? We'll drink mimosas and giggle about boys?'

Emily surely understood the sarcasm, but she smiled anyway. 'It's going to be even better than that. I promise.'

'I don't care what you're promising, because I'm out. I

was going to tell you tomorrow at our lunch, but apparently you couldn't wait.'

'Andy—' Max started, but Andy cut him off.

'Don't you say another word,' Andy said in a low, angry voice, her eyes narrowing to slits. 'This is *my* magazine, *my* career, and you prance in here under some bullshit supposedly selfless reason of saving me from myself . . . duping me so you can try to repair the company your family drove into the ground. Well, guess what? It's not going to be on my watch. You can go to hell.'

Emily coughed. For the first time in the whole conversation, she looked worried.

Andy turned to Emily. 'You can tell them I'm out or I will. Apparently I can't undo this deal, but I can sure as hell hand in my resignation, effective immediately.'

Emily met Andy's gaze and the energy in the room seemed to change. Their anger was palpable, but Emily seemed on the verge of saying something truly hideous. Andy watched as Emily opened her mouth to speak and then closed it. Forgetting the stroller and her phone and everything but the baby bundled in her arms, Andy turned and stalked out the front door.

22

details, details

Out of breath from running nearly the entire way home and on the verge of a total nervous breakdown, Andy barely made it through Clementine's nighttime routine: she performed a perfunctory kitchen-sink bath, dressed her daughter in an overnight diaper and footie pajamas, and gave her a bottle, all without crying. It wasn't until Clem was safely in her crib with the lights out and the baby monitor on that Andy let herself lose it. Although she'd only been home an hour, it already felt like a decade, and she wondered how she'd face the long night ahead. Not willing to let Max see her cry, she locked the bathroom door and stood under the shower for twenty minutes, maybe half an hour, the tears mingling with the hot water as her body shook with sobs.

Max still wasn't home when Andy finally stepped out of

the shower and dressed herself in head-to-toe flannel. A quick glance in the mirror confirmed that her face was a horror of crimson streaks, swollen cheeks, and bloodshot eyes. Her nose ran uncontrollably. The word she hadn't allowed herself to consciously think a single time in the year they'd been married kept forcing itself to the forefront of her mind: divorce. This time, there was no way around it. She would refuse to walk one more step.

Remembering that she'd left her cell phone at Emily's, Andy picked up the landline and dialed Jill at home.

'Andy? Can I call you back tomorrow? We're midbaths here. Jared just pooped in the tub, Jake has a fever, Jonah thinks it's hysterically funny to see if he can splash poop water from the bath into the toilet, and Kyle is out tonight at a work dinner.'

Andy forced herself to sound normal. 'Of course, why don't I call you—'

'Great, thanks. Love you!' The line went dead.

She dialed her mother next, but when it rang and rang, Andy remembered that her mother had her book club on Tuesday nights and wouldn't be home until much, much later, tipsy from all the wine, laughing over the fact that another three-hour meeting had elapsed without a single minute of actual book discussion.

Next up was Lily. She hadn't wanted to obligate her friend to what would surely be a long and tearful conversation when Lily undoubtedly had her hands full with Bear and Skye, but Andy had no choice. When Lily picked up on the first ring and said, 'Hey there!' in her usual upbeat way, Andy once again began to cry.

'Andy? Are you okay? Sweetheart? Talk to me!'

'I should never have walked down that aisle!' Andy wailed, vaguely aware she wasn't making any sense but unable to stop herself. Stanley jumped onto the bed and began licking away her tears.

'What aisle? Andy, what's happening?'

Andy told her everything.

Lily was dumbstruck. Finally she said, 'I'm so sorry, Andy. It's such a betrayal.'

'He sided against me,' she said, still unable to believe it. 'He used a legal *technicality* and sold my own company out from under me. Who does that? Seriously, what kind of person?' Her cheeks were wet with tears but her throat felt like cotton. She poured herself some water, drank it all down, and refilled her glass with white wine.

'Oh, Andy. I don't know what to say.'

'I haven't even allowed myself to think about the fact that Emily – supposedly one of my closest friends – conspired against me with my own husband. I can't even process *that* yet.'

From her spot in bed, she heard the front door open. Andy felt her stomach heave. She didn't know how she was going to make it through the next fifteen minutes.

'He's home,' she whispered to Lily.

'I'm here, sweetheart. All night, anytime. Okay? You pick up that phone and call me whenever you need to.'

Andy thanked Lily and hung up just as Max appeared in the doorway. The mere sight of him, looking contrite, holding a bunch of orange tulips in one hand and a Pinkberry shopping bag in the other, caused the tears to start again. Only this time they were accompanied by the sickening realization that he was no longer her husband. She pulled Stanley even closer to her leg and buried her fingers in his fur.

'I swear on Clementine's life that I never wanted to hurt you,' he said plainly, not moving from the doorway. 'On her life, Andy. I swear to you. If you hear nothing else I ever say, please hear that.'

She believed him. Without a doubt in her mind, regardless of how hard it was to trust anything he said, she knew he would never swear on their daughter's life and lie about it. Andy nodded. 'I appreciate that,' she said, wiping away tears. 'But it doesn't change anything.'

Max placed the flowers on the dresser and took a seat at the foot of the bed. His coat and shoes were still on, as though he knew he wouldn't be staying. He pulled a large Pinkberry from the bag, peanut butter and chocolate swirl topped with Oreos, and handed it to her, but Andy just stared straight at him.

'It's your favorite.'

'Forgive me for not being very hungry right now.'

He reached into his coat pocket and handed Andy her cell phone. 'I brought the stroller home, too.'

'Great.'

'Andy, I can't begin to tell you how—'

'Then don't. Save us both even more misery.' She coughed, her throat raw and painful. 'I need you to leave right now,' Andy said, not realizing how much she meant the words until she'd said them.

'Andy, talk to me. We have to work through this. We have Clem to think about. Tell me what—'

Andy's head whipped up and she felt a jolt of rage as her eyes locked with Max's. 'Clem is exactly who I'm thinking about right now. Over my dead body will she grow up watching as her backstabbing father betrays her doormat mother. Not my daughter. So believe me when I tell you that it's in *Clementine's* interest for you to get out of here.'

Max looked at her with tears in his eyes. Andy was surprised she felt nothing. In all the years they'd been together, she'd seen Max cry once, maybe twice, and yet his tears today elicited zero emotion from her. He opened his mouth to say something and stopped.

'I'll go,' he whispered. 'I'll come back tomorrow and we can talk then.'

Andy watched as he quietly shut the bedroom door behind him. A few moments later, she heard the front door close as well. *He didn't take any clothes,* Andy thought. *Not so much as a toothbrush or extra contact lenses. Where will he go? Who will he stay with?* Her mind circled through these concerns automatically; she worried the way she would have over her mother or her friend or anyone in her life she loved and cared about. But as soon as she remembered what he did, she forced herself to stop.

Easier said than done. Although Andy managed to fall asleep around midnight, she woke at one wondering where Max was sleeping, at two figuring out how she would tell her parents and Jill, at three trying to envision what Barbara would say, at four thinking about Emily's betrayal, at five asking herself how she would manage as a single mother, and at six for good, her tears dried up but her head pounding from lack of sleep and her mind racing with worst-case scenarios. Her entire skull ached, from the nape of her neck to the bones around her eye sockets, and her jaw was nearly locked closed with the pressure of grinding her teeth all night. She knew without looking in the mirror that her face and eyes would be splotchy and red, puffed enough to make her look sick or clinically depressed, neither of which was far from reality. Only scooping Clem from her crib and nuzzling her peach-fuzz hair calmed her; the sight of her daughter drinking ravenously from her bottle, the feel of the fleece-encased baby curled up in her arms, and the smell of her silky skin had to be the only things on earth that could have made Andy smile right then. She kissed her daughter, inhaled her delicious neck smell, and kissed her again.

When Andy's phone rang at six thirty, she was perfectly content to ignore it, but she almost jumped out of her skin when the doorbell rang. Her first thought was Max, but she dismissed it immediately: no matter how intense the crisis they were experiencing, it was still his home and his daughter, and he would never, ever ring the doorbell. No one else she knew would even be awake at that hour, never mind showing up at her apartment, and if they were, the doorman would have called. Her heart beat a little faster. Was something wrong? Should she be nervous?

She placed Clementine on her play mat and peered through the peephole. Emily, clad head to toe in designer running wear – sneakers, tights, hot pink fleece, reflective vest, and coordinating headband – was stretching her hamstrings. As Andy watched her, Emily checked her phone, rolled her eyes, and ordered Andy to open the door.

'I know you're there. Max is crashing at my place. I need to talk to you.'

Andy desperately wanted to ignore Emily, or scream at her to go away, or tell her to drop dead, but she knew none of it would matter. Not having the energy or the will to outlast her, Andy opened the door.

'What do you want?'

Emily leaned forward and kissed Andy's cheek, the way she always did, and breezed past her into the apartment, the way she would on a normal day when she hadn't just effectively ended their friendship.

'Please tell me you have some coffee on,' Emily said as she beelined for the kitchen. 'My god, it's brutal getting up this early. How do you do this every day? Do you believe I already ran four miles? Hi, Clemmie! Hi, sweetheart, you look so cute in your PJs!'

At the sound of her name Clem stopped eyeing her mobile for a moment, but she didn't turn around and offer Emily one of her usual heartbreaking grins. Andy sent her daughter a silent thank-you.

'Hmm, no coffee. Do you want one too?' Emily didn't wait for the answer; she grabbed a clean mug from the dishwasher, discarded the old coffee pod, selected and installed a new one, closed the lid, and hit 'start,' all the while delivering an endless stream of chatter about an advertiser who called her at ten the previous night with a silly question.

'Are you really here to tell me about the De Beers people? At six thirty in the morning?'

Emily feigned surprise. 'Is it really *that* early? How uncivilized.' She removed the second mug from the machine, added milk to both of them, and pushed one toward Andy. After taking a long drink, she sat down at Andy's dining room table and motioned for Andy to sit with her. Irritated with herself for taking orders from Emily, Andy nevertheless sat across the table and waited.

'I just want you to know that I feel really badly about how all this went down.'

Once again Emily paused and searched Andy's face. Andy did nothing but stare straight ahead; she was worried she'd murder Emily if she allowed herself to utter so much as a single word.

Emily didn't seem to notice and barreled on. 'As far as this whole contract debacle . . . I admit I probably didn't handle that in the best way possible – I can certainly see that from your perspective – but I just knew in my heart of hearts that once you'd really weighed this incredible opportunity, you'd come to the same conclusion: that we couldn't possibly pass this up. I *knew* it, and I didn't want us to potentially miss out because it took us a little too long to figure it out. Of course, when we found out the Olive issue was in jeopardy, I knew I needed to act immediately.'

Andy said nothing. Emily glanced at her and then became engrossed in the cuticles on her left hand before continuing. 'Just think – with what we made from the sale, you can take some time off to be with Clem, travel, do some freelancing, start another project, write a book – whatever you want! The lawyers couldn't get rid of that year clause, but they were willing to raise their purchase price *significantly*. And that year is going to fly by, Andy! I don't have to tell you how quickly the last couple years have passed, do I? We'll still both have our jobs, doing what we love for the magazine we built together. The only difference is we'll be doing it in far nicer digs. Does that sound so terrible?'

'We won't,' Andy whispered, her voice barely audible.

'Hmm?' Emily looked at her for the first time in minutes, as though just remembering Andy was there.

'I said we won't be doing it in far nicer offices. Or any offices for that matter. I'm done. Finished. I told you yesterday and I meant it. I will announce my formal resignation this afternoon.' The words tumbled out before Andy could think them through, but once she'd said them, she felt no regret.

'Oh, but you can't!' Emily said, the very first notes of panic creeping into her otherwise eerily calm and collected manner.

'Of course I can. I just did. Again.'

'But it's in the sale agreement that our senior editorial team remain in place for one calendar year. If we don't fulfill that end, they have the right to revoke the contract.'

'That really isn't my problem, now, is it?' Andy asked.

'But we signed it, and we committed to the terms. If we renege on that point, all that money could vanish!'

'*We* signed it? Did you really just say that? You have an amazing capacity to rewrite history, Emily. Just incredible. Let me say this once: none of this is my problem, since I no longer work at *The Plunge*. I will take my percentage of the sale price if you can figure out how to work around the editorial clause. If not, you can buy me out according to the terms in our joint employment contract. I don't really care which happens, just as long as I never see you again.'

Andy's voice was shaking, and she was trying not to cry, but she forced herself to continue. 'You can leave now. We're finished.'

'Andy, just listen. If you would—'

'No more listening. That's my decision. Those are my terms and honestly, I think they're pretty generous. Now get out.'

'But I . . .' Emily looked stricken.

For the first time in nearly fifteen hours, Andy felt something resembling calm. It wasn't easy and it wasn't pleasant, but she knew it was the right thing to do.

'Now,' Andy said, the word sounding almost like a growl. Clem looked up at her, and Andy smiled at her daughter to let her know everything was okay.

Emily continued to sit, looking like she couldn't comprehend what had happened, so Andy stood, scooped up Clementine, and walked back toward her bedroom.

'We're going to take a shower now and get dressed. I expect you'll be gone by the time we come out,' she called over her shoulder, and she didn't stop walking until she'd barricaded herself and Clem in the bathroom. A moment later she heard some shuffling as Emily cleaned up her coffee and gathered her things, and then the front door opened and closed. She listened carefully for any other sound and, hearing nothing, exhaled.

It was over. It was over for good.

23

cougar mama to a golden-bronze man-boy

one year later . . .

Andy watched from the dining room as her mother worked her way down the kitchen counter, unwrapping platters of fruit and crudités, cookies and bite-size wrap sandwiches, taking a few moments to rearrange the morsels prettily on each tray. In the last two days, people and platters had streamed through Andy's childhood home in a near-constant flow, and although there were so many others who were willing to do it – friends, cousins, Jill, and of course, Andy – Mrs Sachs insisted on doing all the shiva preparation herself. She claimed it took her mind off her mother, off the last few horrible months of home hospital beds and oxygen tanks and ever-increasing amounts of morphine. They were all relieved the old woman's suffering was over, but Andy could barely believe her feisty, foul-mouthed grandmother was gone.

She was just about to join her mother in the kitchen when she saw Charles walk in, take a look around to make sure they were alone, and wrap her mother in a bear hug from behind. He whispered something in her ear and Andy smiled at the two of them. Her mother was right: Charles was a lovely man – kind, soft-spoken, sensitive, and affectionate – and Andy was thrilled they had found each other. They'd only been dating six months or so, but according to her mother, you didn't need years to get to know someone in your sixties: it either worked or it didn't, and this relationship had been smooth and easy from day one. Already they were talking about selling the Connecticut house and buying an apartment together in the city, and now that Andy's grandmother no longer needed round-the-clock care, Andy imagined they'd move quickly.

'He seems great,' Jill said as she walked in the room and followed Andy's gaze. She grabbed a carrot stick and began to chomp. 'I'm really happy for her.'

'Me too. She's been alone a long time. She deserves it.'

There was a beat of silence as Jill weighed whether or not to say what she was thinking and Andy mentally willed her not to. No such luck.

'You deserve someone too, you know.'

'Mom and Dad got divorced almost a decade ago. I've been . . .' Andy still couldn't say *divorced* in relation to herself; it sounded too strange, too foreign. 'Max and I have only been apart for a year. I have Clem and my work and all of you. I'm not in any rush.'

Jill poured two plastic cups of Diet Coke and handed one to Andy. 'I'm not saying you should rush into anything. Just

lauren weisberger

that it wouldn't kill you to go out on a date. A little fun, nothing more.'

Andy laughed. 'A date?' The word sounded so quaint, a throwback to a different lifetime. 'My world is playdates and ear infections and twos-program applications and ballet-shoe fittings and hiding vegetables in smoothies. I don't know what a date would look like, but I'm guessing it wouldn't include any of those things.'

'No, of course it wouldn't. You might actually have to wear something other than yoga pants, and you'd definitely have to talk about something besides the benefits of Annie's Cheddar Bunnies over conventional Goldfish, but news flash: you can do it. Your daughter spends two nights a week at her father's, you've completely lost all your baby weight, and with a few hours invested in getting a decent haircut and maybe a dress or two, you could be right back out there. For Christ's sake, Andy, you're only thirty-four. Your life is hardly over.'

'Of course my life isn't over. It's just that I'm perfectly happy with the way things are. What's so hard to understand about that?'

Jill sighed. 'You sound just like Mom did all those years before she met Charles.'

Lily walked into the room, holding her frail grandmother's arm and helping her into a seat. Jill handed Ruth a cup of Diet Coke, but her grandmother asked if she could have some decaf instead. Lily agreed, but Jill motioned for her to sit. 'I was just on my way to brew a new pot. Sit and talk some sense into my sister. Andy and I were just discussing that it's high time her nun days were over.'

'Wow,' Lily said, raising her eyebrows at Jill. 'You actually went there.'

'Yeah, I did. If we can't tell her, who can?'

Andy waved her hands as though trying to flag down a cab. 'Hello? Does anyone realize I'm actually sitting right here?'

Jill left for the kitchen.

'Clem's at Max's this weekend?' Lily asked.

Andy nodded. 'I dropped her off uptown on my way out of the city. She ran shrieking, *"Daddy! Daddy! Daddy!"* the second the cab pulled up to the curb and she spotted him. Literally took off and flew into his arms without so much as a glance backward.' Andy shook her head and smiled ruefully. 'They know how to make you feel great.'

'Tell me about it. Yesterday when we took the boys into the city, Bear asked why a man was sleeping on the street. We tried to explain that's why it's important to go to school and study hard, so you can grow up and get a good job. Brainwashing the kid already, right? So Bear asks what Daddy does as a job, and we explain that he owns the yoga studio and teaches classes and teaches other teachers. So what does Bear say? "Well, when I grow up, I want to stay home and wear my pajamas all day, just like Mommy."'

Andy laughed. 'You're lying.'

'I'm not. I have a BA from Brown, a master's from Columbia, and I'm working toward a PhD, and my son thinks I watch Bravo all day long.'

'You'll set him straight. One day.'

'Yeah, in all my free time.'

Andy looked at her friend. 'Meaning?'

Lily diverted her eyes.

'Lily! Spill it.'

'Well, there are sort of two things I think you should know.'

'I'm waiting.'

'One is, I'm pregnant. The second is that Alex—'

'Mommy! Skye is pulling my hair and it hurts! He bit me! And he has a gross booger on his nose!' Bear materialized seemingly out of nowhere, shrieking a litany of complaints about his little brother, and it took all of Andy's energy not to strangle him into silence. Lily was pregnant? That alone was near impossible to fathom, but Alex *what*? Was stopping by to give Andy his condolences? Had been diagnosed with something hideous and terminal? Had moved once and for all to Africa or the Middle East and was planning never to return? And then it hit her. The only obvious answer.

'He finally got married, didn't he?' Andy said, shaking her head. 'Of course, that's it.'

Lily glanced at her, but Bear's cries had escalated, and Skye had toddled in, also in tears.

'Not that I wouldn't be happy for him under normal circumstances – I would – but I can't stand the thought of him married to that lying, cheating bitch. What is it with the two of us? Some sort of weird, shared inexplicable draw to fall in love with people who hurt and betray us. Why is that? Alex and I had our problems, no doubt, but trust wasn't one of them. Or does it really have nothing to do with us – it's just that everyone cheats on everyone these days, it's what the cool kids do, and any expectation otherwise is old-fashioned or unreasonable?' Andy took a deep breath and shook her head. 'How old do I sound?'

'Andy—' Lily said, starting to speak, but Bear threw himself in her lap and almost knocked her off the chair.

'Mommy! *I want to go home!*'

Andy eyed Lily's small but undeniable bump. She had so many questions, and yet her mind kept ricocheting back to Alex.

Bodhi appeared in the dining room and Lily practically threw both boys at him. She gave him the Look, the one with the laser-focused glare and the slightly raised eyebrows and the pinched mouth that said, *You're on kid duty and yet here they are, screaming and snot-covered and yelling for me. Why can't I have a conversation with my friend for ten uninterrupted minutes? Is that really too much to ask?* that every mother perfected within the first week of her firstborn's life.

He gathered them up with promises of Hershey's Kisses and sippy cups of milk, and for just a moment Andy missed Clementine. Being with her alone all week was difficult, and usually Andy loved Tuesday and Friday nights, when Clem was with Max, but seeing Lily's and Jill's boys made her want to hug her daughter close. She had been planning to stay in Connecticut that night and most of the next day, but maybe now she'd head back to the city first thing in the morning . . .

'I can barely believe you're pregnant again! When did this happen? Was it planned?'

Lily laughed. 'We weren't trying, but we weren't *not* trying.'

'Ah, my favorite.' Andy couldn't help but invoke Olive. 'Not not-trying is trying.'

'Well, regardless, we were pretty shocked. Skye and his sister will be eighteen months apart. I'm almost fifteen weeks already, but I was waiting to tell you until we knew the gender. A girl! Can you believe it?'

'I'm sure boys are great too – people swear they are – but there is nothing on earth as wonderful as a daughter. Nothing.'

Lily beamed.

Andy reached across the table and squeezed her friend's hand. 'I'm so happy for you guys. If someone would've looked into a crystal ball that year we lived together in New York and told you that one day you'd be married to a yoga instructor, living in Colorado with three kids who can ski before they walk, would you have ever believed them?' Andy didn't say what else she was thinking: would she have ever believed she'd have founded, grown, and sold a successful magazine, gotten married and divorced, and learned how to be a single mom to an admittedly sweet and easy toddler, all by the time she was thirty-five? It was light years from what she'd expected.

'Alex. He's not married, Andy. It's just the opposite. He broke up with Sophie.' Lily shook her head. 'Or she broke up with him, I'm really not sure how it went down, but they're definitely not together.'

Andy leaned forward. 'How do you know?'

'He called me when he was out west last week.'

'He *called* you?'

'Is that so weird? He had a week off work and was travelling through Denver on his way to ski with friends in Vail. I met him for coffee at a place near the airport.'

'Skiing with *friends*?'

'Andy! I didn't ask for addresses and social security numbers of his entire group, but he made it clear that there wasn't anyone along with whom he was romantically involved. Is that what you wanted to know?'

Andy waved. 'Of course not. I'm just happy to hear, for his sake, that he's not with *her*. How do you know they broke up?'

'He made it a point to tell me. Said he moved out about six months ago and lives in Park Slope now. Claimed he was dating around but wasn't interested in anything serious. He was just very Alex, you know?'

'How'd he look?'

Lily laughed. 'Like himself. Adorable. Sweet as could be. He brought books for the boys. Said we should keep in better touch and to call the next time we're in the city. The usual.'

'Well, I'm relieved for him,' Andy said. 'I'm sure it wasn't easy, but it had to be a lot easier than getting married . . .'

'I didn't tell him anything about you,' Lily said, looking guilty. 'Did you want me to? I wasn't sure.'

Andy had wondered but hadn't wanted to ask. She thought about this for a moment and decided it was better having Alex think she was still happily married and settled into her new life. Not that she would allow herself to consider for a single second that there might still be something between them – that even all these years later, he might still get that same jolt when they bumped into each other or heard her name – because in all likelihood it wasn't reality.

She still couldn't help but ask. 'Did he mention me at all? Ask anything about me?'

Lily looked at her hands. 'No. But I'm sure he wanted to. You're always the big white elephant in the room.'

'Thanks, Lil. You always know just what to say.' Andy forced herself to smile.

Andy glanced up and saw that Lily was staring at her.

'What? Why are you looking at me like that?'

'You still love him, don't you?' Lily asked in a whisper, as though her grandmother, the only other person in the room, would be desperate to hear this juicy conversation.

'I think I'll always love him,' Andy said truthfully. 'He's Alex, you know? But that's all in the past.'

Lily was silent. Andy waited for her friend to say something, but Lily remained quiet.

'And Alex aside, I can't imagine being close to anyone. Not right now. I know it's been a year, but the . . . whole thing still feels so fresh. I'm glad Max and I are finally in a good place, at least for Clem's sake. Barbara's so thrilled that Max is free to date more "appropriate women" that she's practically become a new person. I never thought I'd say it, but she's crazy about Clementine and is on her way to becoming a halfway decent grandmother. All the mayhem of the last year has finally settled down. Quieted. I don't want to date anyone. Maybe one day, but not now.'

Again Lily gave her that look; Andy knew she was lying to her friend – or at least not telling her the whole truth – and Lily knew it, too. Of course she'd begun to wonder if she would ever meet someone, ever get dressed up for a date or look forward to a long weekend away with a man. She wondered if she would ever share the joys and pains of parenting, have someone to confide in, to cook dinner with, and most of all, she wondered if she would ever give Clem a brother or a sister. She knew the chances of all that were good, if she wanted it, although it might look different now: a future boyfriend would probably be divorced himself, and most likely a father. What single guy in this thirties would choose a mother and a toddler when he could start a family of his own with a much younger girl? But that was okay, too. When she was ready, Andy would join a single-parents' group or list herself on Match.com or accept one of the few invitations to coffee she'd received from single dads she'd met at the Writer's Space – the coworking space she'd joined – or on the playground. And hopefully one day she'd hit it off with one of them, and instead of planning a big white wedding or an elaborate Hawaiian honeymoon or decorating their very first shared apartment, they would navigate the introductions and the schedules of their children, their exes, the blending of two completely separate lives. It would be different, but it could be wonderful in its own way. Andy smiled at the thought.

'What are you grinning about?' Lily asked.

'Nothing. Just envisioning myself married one day to a

forty-year-old man with two kids and a receding hairline whose ex-wife hates me almost as much as Max hates him. Words like *custodial* and *weekend visitation* will fill our conversation. We'll figure out how to stepparent together. It'll be beautiful.'

'You'll make a fabulous evil stepmother,' Lily said, standing up to hug her friend. 'And who's to say you won't end up with some hot twenty-two-year-old stud who has a thing for cougars . . .'

'And toddlers . . .'

'He'll love his cougar mama, and you'll love that his biggest worry in life is the state of his tan during the long, cold New York winters.'

Andy laughed. 'I could be a cougar mama to a golden-bronze man-boy any day. For you, Grams, if you're somewhere listening.'

'See?' Lily said, helping her own grandmother stand up and motioning for Andy to walk toward the living room. 'Life is just beginning.'

24

that's all

The word counter on her writing program sent out a silent, blinking alarm: *500 WORDS!* it blared in all caps, a festive purple and green message dancing across her entire screen. Smiling to herself, Andy hit 'save,' removed her noise-cancellation headphones, and headed to the tiny lounge area of the Writer's Space to make herself some coffee. Slumped at one of the two-tops and reading from a Kindle was Nick, a recently transplanted L.A. screenwriter who had penned an outrageously successful pilot for a thirty-minute comedy and was currently working on his first and eagerly anticipated movie screenplay. He and Andy had become casual coffee-room friends a few months earlier when she had joined the space, but Andy had been shocked when he asked her to see an indie film the week before last – so surprised she actually said yes.

Not that it had been graceful.

'You know I have a daughter, right?' Andy blurted the moment he finished describing the Iranian film he was hoping to see.

Nick had cocked his head full of floppy dirty-blond hair, stared at her for just a moment, and then broken into laughter. Merry, sweet-sounding laughter. 'I absolutely did know that. Clementine, right? You remember showing me that picture of her on your phone from her music class? And the one your nanny sent of her with red sauce smeared all over her face? Yes, Andy, I know you have a daughter. She's welcome to join us if you like, but I'm not sure it'll be her kind of film.'

Andy was mortified. She'd asked Lily and Jill a thousand times how she would one day tell a date about Clementine – when was the right time, the right circumstance, and what were the right words to use – and both of them had insisted she would just know in the moment. This was probably not what they had in mind.

'Sorry,' she mumbled, feeling her face turn hot. 'I'm sort of new at this.' *Understatement of the century,* she thought. It had been a year and a half since her divorce, and although the invites hadn't exactly been rolling in, she'd turned down a few out of sheer anxiety and fear. But something about Nick's kind eyes and gentle manner made her feel like it was okay to say yes.

It had been a perfectly lovely evening. She was able to bathe and dress Clementine before explaining to her daughter that she was going out to see a movie with a friend. Not that Clem understood enough to be upset, but Andy always tried to explain everything.

'Daddy?' Clem asked, as she did at least a dozen times a day.

'No, not with Daddy, sweetheart. A different friend.'

'Daddy?'

'Nope. Someone you haven't met. But Isla will read you your stories and tuck you in, and I'll be right here when you wake up in the morning, okay?'

Clem had rested her damp, sweet-smelling head against Andy's chest, snuggled her lovey blanket to her face, and let out a long, relaxed sigh. Andy literally had to force herself out the door.

The date had been perfectly . . . fine. Nick offered to pick her up in a cab, but Andy felt more comfortable meeting him at the theater. He had already purchased their tickets and saved them aisle seats, so Andy bought popcorn and Raisinets and maintained a steady stream of perfectly acceptable small talk in the fifteen minutes before the movie began. Afterward they'd gone for dessert at a coffee shop on Houston and talked about Nick's years in L.A., Andy's new position as a contributing editor for *New York* magazine, and, although she'd pledged not to, Clementine. When he dropped her off, he'd pecked her lightly on the mouth and announced he'd had a great time. He even seemed to mean it. Andy quickly agreed – it had been fun, and way more relaxed than she'd expected – but she forgot about the date, and Nick, the moment she walked in her front door. She remembered long enough the next morning to text him a thank-you, but she stopped responding after a couple back-and-forths and was so totally consumed with Clementine and her most recent assignment and planning an upcoming weekend visit with her mom and Jill that she'd barely even noticed Nick was absent from the Writer's Space the entire next week.

Yet here he was, still totally absorbed with his reading – enough so that Andy could probably slip back to her desk area unnoticed – and Andy felt instantly guilty. For what, she wasn't sure. But for something.

Clearing her throat, she took the seat opposite Nick's and said, 'Hey there. Long time, no see.'

Nick looked up but didn't appear surprised to see her. Instead, his face broke into a wide smile and he flicked off his Kindle. 'Andy! Good to see you. What's going on?'

'Not much. Just taking my five-hundred-word break. I was going to make some coffee. You want some?' She headed toward the coffeemaker on the kitchen counter, relieved to have something to do with her hands.

'I just made a pot. That one there is fresh.'

'Got it.' Andy plucked her mug off the shelf – a photo mug of Clementine blowing out candles on her Elmo first-birthday cake – and filled it with coffee. She fiddled with the milk and Splenda as long as she could, unsure of what to say once she turned around, but Nick didn't seem nervous.

'Andy? Are you around this weekend?' he asked.

He was looking her straight in the eye when she rejoined him at the table.

She hated when people asked that without stating what it was they wanted. Was she available for front-row tickets to see Bruce Springsteen perform at the Garden? Yes, she could probably swing that. Did she have hours of free time to help Nick move from one sixth-floor walk-up to another? No, she was fully booked this upcoming weekend. Frozen and not knowing what to say, Andy stared at him.

'A friend of mine, an illustrator, is having his work shown at the National Arts Club. A private exhibit. A bunch of us are going for dinner afterward to celebrate, and I'd love it if you wanted to come.'

'To the exhibit? Or to dinner?' Andy asked to buy herself more time.

'Either one. Preferably both,' Nick said with an undeniably cute impish grin.

A million excuses ran through her mind, but unable to formulate any of them into speech, Andy smiled and half nodded. 'Sounds good,' she said without the least bit of enthusiasm.

Nick looked at her strangely for a second but must have decided to ignore her halfhearted response. 'Great. I'll swing by and get you around six?'

Andy already knew that none of it would happen – not the swing-by, the inevitable Clem meeting, the date overall – but she felt totally incapable of explaining why. Nick was perfectly sweet, cute, and smart. He seemed into her for whatever reason and was pursuing her in a lovely, low-key, nonthreatening way. Just because she'd felt nothing when he kissed her and almost immediately forgot about him after their date didn't mean they weren't a good match. She could practically hear her sister and Lily: *You're not agreeing to marry him, Andy! It's a second date. You don't have to be madly in love to go on a second date with someone. If nothing else, it'll get you back in the mix, help you remember what it's like to be in the scene again. Go, relax, enjoy. Stop trying to orchestrate every detail. Who cares if it works out or it doesn't? Just try.*

Like it was ever that easy.

'Andy? Is six okay?' Nick's voice snapped her out of her haze.

'Six? Six is great. That totally works.' She smiled widely and felt instantly ridiculous. 'I better be getting back to work!'

'You just sat down.'

'Yes, but this article is due on Friday and I haven't even begun editing it yet!' She sounded flighty and forced to her own ears. How awful must she have sounded to him?

'Will you tell me what it's about?'

'Saturday,' she said, halfway out of the lounge. 'I'll bore you with all the details then.'

Her desk, when she finally reached it, felt like a respite. Andy tried to reassure herself that Nick was a super-nice guy who, if nothing else, would be a fun person to do things with. Why did she need to think beyond that? It was simple: she didn't.

She managed to concentrate for the next hour, putting down another hundred words, and began to feel better about meeting her Friday deadline. Her new editor at *New York* magazine, a *Vogue* transplant named Sawyer, was an absolute pleasure to work for: calm, reasonable, totally professional in every way. He approved – and sometimes assigned – Andy's story ideas, discussed in good detail what he'd most like to see her focus on, and then stood back while she researched and wrote, getting involved again only once she'd submitted copy in order to provide terrific line edits and ask thoughtful, substantive questions. Her current article was, coincidentally, an in-depth feature piece on the ways in which same-sex partners tried to differentiate their weddings from conventional weddings without alienating conservative family members. It would be her largest piece for them yet, and she was pleased with how it was shaping up. It provided her with a decent-enough salary – at least when combined with the interest she made from her cut of *The Plunge*'s sale, since she'd immediately saved and conservatively invested the principal – and the time to work on other projects. Namely, a book. Although she only had a hundred or so pages and hadn't yet shown it to another human being, Andy had a good feeling about that one, too. Who could say for sure if she would ever really publish a roman à clef about Miranda Priestly? All Andy knew was that she loved being back in control of her own life.

An e-mail banner popped up on her cell phone, and Andy reflexively clicked to open it.

Greetings from the City of Angels! the subject line blared. She knew immediately it was from Emily.

Dear friends, family, and adoring fans,
I'm thrilled to announce that Miles and I have finally found a home and are getting all settled in. He's already begun shooting his new series, *Lovers and Losers,* and everyone who's seen the footage swears it's going to be a HUGE HIT (think *Khloe and Lamar* meets *The Real Housewives of Beverly Hills*!!!). My new gig as a stylist to the stars is off and running. I've already signed Sofia Vergara, Stacy Keibler, and Kristen Wiig, and not to drop any names here or anything, but I'm having drinks with Carey Mulligan tonight and will hope to call her an Emily Charlton client by the end of happy hour. We both miss New York, and of course all of you, but life is pretty sweet out here. Do you know it was seventy-eight degrees today and we went to the beach? Doesn't suck. So please please please come visit us soon . . . did I mention we have a pool AND a hot tub? Visit. Seriously. You won't regret it.
Love and kisses,
Em

If Andy had tried to send some sort of message to Emily that they were no longer friends, Emily hadn't received it. Despite Andy throwing Emily out of her apartment the morning after she'd discovered the contract signing, despite her refusing to return any of Emily's calls or e-mails unless they directly concerned the sale of *The Plunge,* and despite her ignoring Emily when they ran into each other socially, Emily wouldn't accept Andy's silence. She continued to text and call and e-mail with random updates or funny bits of gossip, and she always greeted Andy with a big hug and an excited hello when they saw each other. Which is why it was such a relief when Andy got the e-mail from Emily a couple months earlier announcing that she and Miles were moving to Los Angeles. Distance would surely accomplish what Andy could not seem to, and she welcomed the idea of severing ties.

Emily's dismissal from *The Plunge* after a mere ten weeks on the job shouldn't have come as a surprise – this was Miranda, after all – but when Max told Andy, she couldn't help the *I told you so*. A single issue. That was all the time Miranda had granted Emily and her new editor in chief to prove themselves at Elias-Clark before firing the entire editorial team she had so relentlessly insisted on retaining. Although it only added to her PTSD-like symptoms, Andy couldn't stop reading all the different accounts of the firing. A gossip blog had the most comprehensive coverage, probably supplied by Agatha or one of the other assistants who actually witnessed the whole thing, and Andy read it voraciously. Apparently it had been a day like any other, the week after *The Plunge* had published its first issue at Elias-Clark. On the cover were Nigel and his new husband, Neil, who was – at least judging by the photos – surprisingly nebbishy, unfashionable, and older than Nigel by at least two decades. Nigel had gained a bit of pudge, no doubt from prewedding bliss, but combined with Neil's already-challenged appearance, not even St Germain could make them look totally fabulous. Never mind that the first-ever issue of any wedding magazine dedicated to same-sex marriage had gotten tremendously positive feedback from all over the country for its sensitive and insightful coverage of a long-overlooked group – the cover wasn't glam enough, and that was unforgivable. None of it was Emily's fault, but such details didn't concern Miranda.

Andy wasn't sure who leaked it – Emily, Nigel, Charla 3.0 – but all the gossip blogs agreed on the statement that effectively ended Emily's very short reign at Elias-Clark.

'You're dismissed, effective immediately. And take your staff with you.' At this point, Miranda had looked Emily right in the eyes and said, 'We'll opt for a *fresher* team.'

The entry had wrapped up by describing, rather gleefully, how *The Plunge*'s entire staff returned from lunch to discover their key cards no longer permitted them access to the building. Emily had once again been fired unceremoniously by Miranda Priestly, although at least this time there was the generous sale price to console her. Emily e-mailed Andy that all the other staffers had landed on their feet: a few had joined other magazines, a couple had taken the opportunity to go back to school, Daniel had followed his boyfriend to Miami Beach, and Agatha – entitled, aspiring Agatha – was trying her hand as Miranda's new junior assistant. They deserved one another.

Andy's mouse moved to delete Emily's e-mail as she had dozens of others, but something made her pause and hit 'reply.'

Hey, Em,
Congrats on the new gig – sounds like a perfect fit. Congrats too on the house with the pool, etc. Big change from NYC, I imagine. Best of luck with everything.
– Andy

She was just about to start writing again when Nick appeared by her desk. Her entire being willed him to go away, to not interrupt her, and she regretted instantly saying yes to a second date. There was nothing wrong with Nick and nothing wrong with dating, but she should've known better than to mix that world with her new, wonderfully quiet and peaceful writing space. It was her escape from all things loud and overwhelming and kid related, the only place she could be totally alone and still surrounded by people, all of whom were slowly and steadily minding their own business. It was all she could do not to plead with him to leave her be.

'Andy?' he whispered, breaking all the rules. There was zero talking allowed in the quiet work area, where Andy had chosen one of the farthest and most isolated desks.

She turned and raised her eyebrows but didn't speak.

'There's a guy waiting for you in the kitchen.'

'I didn't order any food,' Andy whispered back, confused.

'He doesn't look like a food delivery guy. Someone buzzed him up because he said it was important.'

It was the last thing Andy needed to hear. 'Important' had to mean that it was Max and he was here about Clem. Andy yanked her phone from her bag and scanned it quickly: no texts or messages from Isla, which was comforting, but perhaps the emergency had been so dire she thought Max was more reachable and called him first. Without another whispered word to Nick, Andy flew out of her chair and ran toward the kitchen. Nothing could have prepared her for who was sitting at the same table she and Nick had shared earlier that afternoon.

'Hey,' Alex said, as though it was the most normal thing in the world.

'Hey,' Andy replied, completely incapable of saying anything else.

He raked a hand through his hair and Andy noticed it was shaking. No matter – he looked absolutely adorable in

411

his jeans, navy half-zip fleece, and of course, his signature New Balance sneakers. When he held open his arms and walked toward her to envelop her in a hug, it was all she could do not to cry: the feel of the familiar fleece against her cheek, the weight of his hands on her back, the over-whelming smell of Alexness that literally caused her to choke up. How long had it been since she'd been hugged like this by anyone except her mother? A year? More? It was exciting and calming and soothing all at the same time. It felt like going home.

'What are you doing here?' she asked, still convinced this was all an apparition or, worse, a random coincidence.

'Stalking you,' he said with a laugh.

'No, seriously.'

'I am serious. I ran into your nanny with Clementine today at that cupcake place near you and—'

'You ran into my nanny? And Clementine? What were you doing three blocks from my apartment? Don't you live in Park Slope now?'

Alex smiled. 'Yes, but like I said, I was stalking you. I was sitting in there, eating a cupcake, trying to work up the nerve to show up at your apartment, and in walked Clementine. She's so much bigger than the last time I saw her. She's gorgeous, Andy, and so sweet. I would've recognized her anywhere.'

Andy tried not to get too excited about Alex's admission that he was planning to show up at her apartment, but she could do little more than stare at him.

'So I asked your nanny if you were home. I told her I was an old friend but I think she got nervous about a stranger asking after you, so she said you were 'out writing' some-where. I think those were the words she used.'

'And you just decided to take a chance and see if I was

here, out of the fifty writing spaces in city? Not to mention private offices, libraries, coffee shops, cafés, friends' apartments . . .'

Alex poked her playfully in the arm, and she wanted to grab his finger and kiss it. 'Yeah, or maybe I just noticed a few months ago when you posted on Lily's Facebook wall that you work at a place called the Writer's Space.'

Andy raised her eyebrows.

'I know, I know, I said I'd never join Facebook, but I folded. Now I can stalk exes with the best of them. Anyway, some dude named Nick buzzed me up, and he said he knew you . . .'

'Yeah,' Andy said.

Alex looked at her with a questioning expression, but he dropped it when she didn't volunteer any additional information.

A woman in her midforties walked into the kitchen and began to rummage through the refrigerator. Andy and Alex lapsed into silence as they watched her pull a Tupperware salad from one of the drawers, shake a bottle of vinaigrette, uncap a Pepsi, and, suddenly aware that she was interrupting something, take her lunch to the farthest reaches of the lounge area, where she promptly put in earbuds and began to eat.

'So . . .' Andy looked at Alex and willed him to speak first. There was so much to say, but she didn't know where to begin. Why was he there? What did he want?

'So . . .' Alex coughed nervously and rubbed his eye. 'My contact is driving me crazy, has been all morning.'

'Mmm. I hate when that happens.'

'Me too. I keep thinking about getting the laser surgery and just being done with contacts altogether, but then you hear these stories of people who have all sorts of problems with dry eyes and—'

lauren weisberger

'Alex – it's Alex, right? Not Xander? What's going on?'
Andy blurted out.

He looked sheepish. Anxious. 'It's Alex,' he said. He
twisted his fingers and yanked at the collar of his fleece.
'What do you mean, what going on? Because I wanted to
come say hi? Is that so weird?'

Andy laughed. 'Yes, it's so weird. It's lovely, but it's weird.
When was the last time we saw each other? A year ago? At
that brunch, which may have been the most awkward thing
ever . . .' She was tempted, so tempted, to ask about Sophie,
see what Alex knew after the fact, but she couldn't bring
herself to say anything.

'It's over between Sophie and me,' he said, staring down
at the table. 'Has been for a while now.'

'I'm sorry to hear that.'

'Are you really?' Alex asked with a smile.

'No. Not in the least.'

He smiled. 'I know everything, Andy. All about her student
and the fling and the whole thing. She was so convinced
you'd told me after that brunch that she couldn't help but
admit everything. I still don't think she believes you didn't
say anything.'

'I'm sorry. For everything.' She knew Alex understood
she was apologizing for all of it – knowing but not telling
him, the pain he must have felt when he found out, the
fact that it all had to happen in the first place.

He nodded in understanding. 'Turns out it wasn't really
a fling. They got married almost immediately and she's due
any minute now with their baby.'

Andy wanted to reach across the table and hug him.

'I also know about you and Max . . .' Again, Alex diverted
his eyes.

'Max?' She knew exactly what he meant, but it felt so strange to hear Alex say her ex-husband's name.

'The div— the whole thing that happened between you two.'

Andy stared at him until he met her gaze. 'How do you know about that? Lily told me ten times over that she never said anything to you, that the couple times you guys have talked, neither of you have mentioned me . . .'

'It wasn't Lily. It was Emily.'

'Emily? Since when do you two keep in touch?'

Alex smiled but it was tinged with sadness. 'Since never. But she called me out of the blue a few months ago, talking a mile a minute, thoughts all over the place, almost hysterical. Pretty much exactly how I remember her from the *Runway* days.'

'*She called you?*'

'Yes. Apparently she'd gotten fired by Miranda again, and she and her husband were planning to move to L.A.'

'Yeah, they just did.'

'So she's going on and on about how she screwed up everything, with Elias-Clark and Miranda and *The Plunge* and especially you. She wanted me to know about your, uh, your . . . divorce.'

Although it didn't shock her in the way it used to, hearing the word *divorce* still made Andy squirm. 'Oh my god. She didn't.'

'She said she was finally ready to do something right after screwing up so much, and the one thing that's clearly right . . . that has been right all along . . .' Alex coughed.

Andy was unable to speak. Was this happening? Was Alex really sitting next to her in the dreary kitchen of her writing space insinuating – or, actually, outright stating – that he

thought about her? That they should give it another try?
Despite being a frequently featured scenario in her daydreams,
it still somehow seemed too far-fetched.

She said nothing. He stared first at his feet and then at
the ceiling. The silence probably only lasted twenty or thirty
seconds, but it felt like an eternity.

'What do you say to dinner on Sunday? Early, with
Clementine, maybe around five? We can take her in your
neighborhood, maybe for pizza or burgers? Just something
really casual.'

Andy laughed. 'She loves pizza. How'd you guess?'

'What kid doesn't love pizza?'

Andy looked at Alex and smiled. She got that familiar but
long-forgotten flip-flop feeling in her stomach when he
smiled back. 'That sounds great. Count us in.'

'Excellent! It's a date then.' His phone beeped and he
glanced at it. 'My brother is in the city this weekend visiting
friends in grad school at NYU and I'm on my way to meet
up with him. He's dragging me to a bar crawl. God help me.'

'Oliver? I can't believe he's a real person. I haven't seen
him in, what? Ten years? How is he?'

'He's great. Lives in San Fran, works at Google, has some
insanely sexy girlfriend who calls him day and night. He's
like a full-fledged person. It's the strangest thing.'

'Bring him along on Sunday, I'd love to see him. It's been
so many years . . .'

'I'm not sure that pizza at five o'clock with his brother
and a kid are at the top of his list, but I'll definitely ask him.'

'Tell him I want to see him!'

'I will. I promise. I'm sure he'd love to see you, too. He
always—' Alex's cheeks flushed.

'What?'

'Nothing.'

416

'Alex! He always what?'

'He always thought we would end up together. He's never stopped asking about you.'

'That's probably just because he wasn't a huge fan of Sophie's.'

'No, actually, he was. He thought she was super-hot, and—'

Andy held her hand up. 'I'm good.'

Alex smiled. 'Sorry.'

Andy laughed and watched as Alex stood up and slung his messenger bag across his chest. She wanted so badly to hug him but didn't want to be too forward.

Looking a little shy, perhaps even sheepish, Alex held on tightly to the bag's strap. But he looked at her and said, 'Andy? We'll take it slow, I promise. I don't want to rush into anything, and I know you don't either. We'll be careful.'

'Yes. Careful.'

'You have a daughter to think about, and I totally understand and respect that. And we've both been hurt in our previous relationships, and I'm sure we're both—'

Andy didn't think before she acted. With her mind blissfully free of concerns – about her appearance, his reaction, what either of them would say afterward – Andy reached up on her tiptoes, threw her arms around Alex's neck, and kissed him square on the mouth. It lasted only a couple of seconds, but it was the most natural, wonderful feeling in the world, and when she pulled away again, they grinned at each other.

'*You* can take it as slowly as you like,' she said with a serious expression. '*I* plan to dive headfirst into this with reckless abandon.'

'Oh really? Define *reckless abandon*.' Alex grinned.

And she kissed him again.

acknowledgments

Thank you doesn't begin to adequately express my gratitude to Sloan Harris, my agent, friend, and, when necessary, occasional shrink. There is no panic you can't allay, no problem you can't solve. Thank you for your wisdom, your unerring guidance, and your infinite calm under pressure. It is more appreciated than you'll ever know.

The same goes for Marysue Rucci, who for nearly ten years now (!) has been so much more than an editor: MSR, you've been a cheerleader and a confidante and such a sage and trusted advisor that I barely remember a writing life without you in it. From the earliest brainstorming sessions to the final edited word, you have made this book better in every imaginable way.

To my entire family at Simon & Schuster, thank you for all your brilliant work and creativity. Jon Karp, Jackie Seow,

Richard Rhorer, Andrea DeWerd, Tracey Guest, Jennifer Garza, Jessica Zimmerman, and Felice Javitz: You are the best team an author could hope to have. Special thanks to Aja Pollock for all the ways you bettered the manuscript, and to Emily Graff for everything. Literally everything.

Thanks also to the terrific team at ICM: Maarten Kooij, Kristyn Keene, Josie Freedman, Heather Karpas, and Shira Schindel. I appreciate your savvy advice and terrific ideas (and of course, your group votes). Thanks for so expertly advising me in every conceivable situation.

To the whole amazing crew in London: a tremendous thanks for your boundless enthusiasm and fantastic ideas on everything from this book's inception to publication. We've been working together for over a decade now, and I feel so indebted to (and adoring of) my entire British family. At HarperCollins, thank you to Kate Elton, Lynne Drew, Claire Bord, and Louise Swannell. At Curtis Brown, a million thanks to Vivienne Schuster, Betsy Robbins, Sophie Baker, and Claire Nozicres.

To friends who were so generous with their time and expertise: Wendy Finerman, Hillary Irwin, Matthew Hiltzik, Josh Wolfe, Kyle White, Ludmilla Suvorova, and all my girlfriends, whether here in New York or elsewhere – I'm sending you each a huge hug and a plea to meet for drinks soon. Like, tomorrow.

Words can't express the gratitude I feel for Mallory Stehle and Tracy Larry, without whom this book would literally never have happened. You will be part of our family, always.

Mom, Dad, and Dana: I love you so much. Thanks for keeping me grounded and (semi) sane, and for all the ways you offer help, encouragement, and most important, a good laugh – and always have. Thank you to my whole family, for your constant cheering and understanding and always knowing when not to ask about work: Bernie, Judy, Seth, Sadie, Grandma, Papa, Jackie, Mel, Allison, Dave, Sydney and Emma. The past couple years have been crazy, and we never could have survived it (or enjoyed the wild ride) without each and every one of you.

And most of all, thank you to my husband, Mike, who makes *everything* possible. This book would have never been more than a fleeting fancy without your support, suggestions, ideas, and careful reads at every stage. Thank you isn't enough for all the ways, big and small, you make my life – all our lives – complete. To R and S, thank you for bringing me more joy than I ever could have imagined. It is impossible not to smile when you're near me. I love you three with all my heart.

THE DEVIL WEARS PRADA

THE BOOK THAT INSPIRED THE HIT MOVIE

When Andrea first sets foot in the plush Manhattan offices
of Runway she knows nothing. She's never heard of the world's
most fashionable magazine, or its feared and fawned-over editor,
Miranda Priestly – her new boss.

A year later, she knows altogether too much:

That it's a sacking offence to wear anything lower than
a three-inch heel to work.

That you can charge anything at all to the Runway account, but you
must never, ever, leave your desk, or let Miranda's coffee get cold.

And that at 3 a.m. on a Sunday, when your boyfriend's dumping
you because you're always at work, if Miranda phones, you jump.

But this is her big break – it's going to be worth it in the end.

Isn't it?

EVERYONE
WORTH KNOWING
CAN SHE SURVIVE THE WORLD OF PARTIES, PRADA AND PLAYBOYS?

Bette gets paid to party. And she can hardly believe her luck. Gaining VIP access to Manhattan's hottest spots and meeting 'everyone worth knowing' is a million miles away from her old job. Overnight, New York has become her sexy late-night playground.

But quicker than you can say Chanel, Bette turns up in the gossip columns as girlfriend to a notorious British playboy. It's news that delights her new boss – but her friends want to know what's happened to the girl they love, who always had time for nights filled with 80s music, junk food, trashy rom-coms and her mates.

Can Bette say goodbye to the parties and the Prada and step back into the real world – and find a prince who's got a heart to match his charm?

CHASING
HARRY WINSTON

THREE BEST FRIENDS. TWO RESOLUTIONS.
ONE YEAR TO PULL IT OFF.

Emmy has just split with her boyfriend of five years. A serial monogamist, she suddenly realises how much she's missed the thrill of single life. A new job travelling across the globe could offer her the one thing she is craving, so she vows to find a man on every continent for some pure no-strings-attached fun.

Adriana is stunning and can have any man she desires. Yet all she wants is an eligible bachelor who'll slip a five-carat Harry Winston diamond on her finger.

Leigh has a doting boyfriend that most girls would kill for. But when literary bad boy Jesse Chapman asks to work with her and more, she just can't refuse.

Over cocktails one night, the three friends make a pact – come hell or high water, they must change one thing in their lives by the end of the year…

LAST NIGHT AT CHATEAU MARMONT

HEARTBREAK, HEADLINES AND HERMES...

Brooke and Julian live a happy life in New York – she's the breadwinner working two jobs and he's the struggling musician husband. Then Julian becomes an overnight success – and their life changes forever.

Soon they are moving in exclusive circles, dining at the glitziest restaurants, attending the most outrageous parties in town and jetting off to the trendiest hotspots in LA.

But Julian's new-found fame means that Brooke must face the savage attentions of the ruthless paparazzi. And when a scandalous picture hits the front pages, Brooke's world is turned upside down. Can her marriage survive the events of that fateful night at Chateau Marmont? It's time for Brooke to decide if she's going to sink or swim...